SERVANT AND MASTER

Benedict's lips twitched, drawing my attention to them. "I suggest you rest a minute. You are quite flushed."

As he spoke, I found myself fascinated with the smoothness of his lips and the dip in his chin. My fingers itched to feel the textures filling my vision—rough, silky, smooth, and warm.

I didn't think there was any part of him that wouldn't be warm, very warm. I didn't know whether to be glad I had fainted—for I don't think I would have ever known how heavenly it felt to be held by him otherwise—or to be appalled, a reaction that would have been instinctive two weeks ago.

He reached up and brushed his fingers through the wisps of hair behind my ear.

"Yes," I whispered.

His eyes dilated, his breath rasped, and I bit my lip to keep from whispering again.

"Careful." He brushed his finger over my lip, soothing my bite, and I gasped as a lightning bolt of pleasure struck me deep inside. As he bent his head toward mine, I knew with a shock that he would kiss me. My lips parted. My breath caught. Then his warm, supple lips touched mine. . . .

The MISTRESS of TREVELYAN

JENNIFER ST. GILES

POCKET BOOKS
New York London Toronto Sydney

This book is a work of fiction. Names, characters, places and incidents are products of the author's imagination or are used fictitiously. Any resemblance to actual events or locales or persons, living or dead, is entirely coincidental.

An *Original* Publication of POCKET BOOKS

POCKET BOOKS, a division of Simon & Schuster, Inc.
1230 Avenue of the Americas, New York, NY 10020

Copyright © 2004 by Jenni Leigh Grizzle

All rights reserved, including the right to reproduce this book or portions thereof in any form whatsoever. For information address Pocket Books, 1230 Avenue of the Americas, New York, NY 10020

ISBN: 0-7434-8625-0

First Pocket Books printing August 2004

10 9 8 7 6 5 4 3 2 1

POCKET and colophon are registered trademarks of Simon & Schuster, Inc.

Cover illustration by Franco Accornero

Manufactured in the United States of America

For information regarding special discounts for bulk purchases, please contact Simon & Schuster Special Sales at 1-800-456-6798 or business@simonandschuster.com.

Acknowledgments

To the masterful goddesses who inspired me and paved the way: Daphne du Maurier, Victoria Holt, Mary Stewart, Phyllis A. Whitney, Grace Livingston Hill, Emilie Loring, Charlotte Armstrong, Nora Roberts, Jane Ann Krentz, Karen Robards, Linda Howard, Johanna Lindsey, Kathleen Woodiwiss, Sandra Brown, and Heather Graham Pozzessere.

To my agent, Deidre Knight, thanks for believing in me and for being the best fairy godmother ever. To Micki Nuding, my editor extraordinaire, thanks for seeing the magic. To Maggie Crawford, thanks for believing, too. To Tamberlynn Sorenson, thanks for the polish.

To the women authors whose valued feedback made this book possible: Jacquie D'Alessandro and Wendy Etherington, who are the best buds ever. Karen White, Wendy Wax, Karen Kendall, ladies unrelenting in their support and polish, cheers to the top.

To my wild and wonderful family: My husband, Charles; my daughter, Ashleigh; my sons, Jake and Shane, I thank you all for enabling me to write and for understanding my love for writing. I know it is not easy having a wife and a mother obsessed with her computer screen. To my mom and dad, Diane and Ron Powell, who have always at great cost given their all for their children, and made being at this place in my life possible. To my sister, Tracy Clark, and her zany family, Tye, Shannon, Kacie, and Jeff—believe in your dreams. To my brother, Ron, and Susan; grandparents Maggie and Len Scull; and my aunt Harriet and uncle Carl Powell for their every encouragement. To Grandma Marie for all of her help. To Kelly, Granny Jan, and Marge for helping to keep Pine Ridge and Moonlight Ridge Cottages going. And to the multitudes of the Powells and their offshoots down south that began with Benjamin and Jesse in the early 1900s. Thanks to all of you for the family gatherings that made my life so full for so many years.

To Georgia Romance Writers, the pubbed and unpubbed, for being the wind beneath my wings. Hang in there until your dreams come true.

To Carmen Green, Rita Herron, Anna Adams, Stephanie Bond, Rachelle Wadsworth, Sandra Chastain, Patricia Lewin, Virginia Ellis, Donna Sterling, Deborah Smith, and all the superstars who helped me along my way, many thanks.

To Suzanne Brockmann for making Anne Lovell the Heart of Denver Romance Writers 2001's Unsinkable Heroine.

To the Kiss of Death chapter and the Daphne du Maurier Estate for making the Daphne du Maurier Award that brought *The Mistress of Trevelyan* to the top.

To all the 2002 Golden Heart finalists and fellow winners, your continued support is invaluable. Gold dust is coming your way.

In memory of Eunice Powell, Elmer Powell, and Irene Petty.

And finally in memory of Kathleen Spevacek, may you live on in the hearts of those you loved.

Thank you all for the magic of romance,
Jennifer St. Giles

I dedicate this book of my heart
to all of those who fill my heart to overflowing

1

San Francisco
1873

The house on Trevelyan Hill had always beckoned to me. Its stone turrets, stained glass, and gray spires, often swirled with mists from the bay, rose like a dark manor in the clouds. Even today, an unusually bright San Franciscan day, the mysterious air hovering above the house intensified as I drew near.

Butterflies fluttered over my nerves, making me pause to stare at the house and dab at the perspiration upon my brow. As a child, in the rare moments when my mother and I escaped our laundering, I'd beg to go to Holloway Park. There, I'd sketch the manor's stark beauty and listen to my mother tell of her privileged life in England. She'd always drift off to sleep, dreaming of those days, and I'd make up stories about those who lived on Trevelyan Hill.

Such things as drawing and dreams were foreign to my practical nature, as was my penchant for books, but they were my only luxury. I held on to them as I grew from girl to woman—the art, the books, and the dreams. They eased my soul, and were my only solace during the toiling days of scalding water, lye soap, and scorching irons.

My fantasies of the inhabitants of Trevelyan Hill never matched the rumors about their rich lives. In recent years, tragedy had befallen the Trevelyan family as persistently as the waves of the bay beat against the dark, jagged cliffs visible in the patchy fog behind the manor. The death of their patriarch, rumors of madness, and then the suicide of Benedict Trevelyan's young wife had marked them. Leastwise, suicide was the official ruling concerning Benedict's wife's fall from one of the manor's turreted towers last year. No one had proven Benedict Trevelyan guilty—but there were whispers.

Gathering my courage, I forced myself up the manor's long drive to the perfectly polished mahogany doors. Desperation, or perhaps fate, spurred me. I had decided, and nothing would deter me, least of all rumors. My own life had made me immune to wagging tongues. Closer now, I saw with some surprise that the tall castle-like doors were carved with winged demons chasing after fair, dainty maidens. I'd expected something stately, like a royal emblem, or a proper design. My curiosity about the inhabitants of the manor grew.

My mother had named me Titania after Shakespeare's Queen of the Fairies. I think she'd expected I'd be as beautiful and tiny as she, and not the almost-six-foot plain woman I had become. Somewhere over the years—at my insistence—my name had been shortened to the more suitable form of Ann.

The heat of the afternoon sun must have had a strange effect on me. For as I straightened my dress to walk up the steps of the manor, I suddenly wished to be as attractive as a fairy queen. To be dainty and desirable, even if it meant having to run from demons.

Shaking my head, I put my mind back on my task and smoothed the stolen paper I held in my hand, suffering a twinge of guilt as I read it again. This was the first time I'd ever done anything so unseemly. The moment I'd seen the employment notice in the window of Mr. McGuire's

Bookstore, I had snatched it down, unwilling for anyone else to read it and apply for the position before I could. Benedict Trevelyan was looking for a tutor for his small children, and those interested in the job were to apply in person at his residence.

I bolstered myself with a small prayer and a deep breath, feeling my hopes for a different life than that of a laundress lodge in my stomach as I lifted the gargoyle-like brass knocker.

A butler wearing a suit and black tie answered. At the sight of me, his polite smile immediately drooped and his nose inched higher. "May I help you?"

My attempts to hide the threadbare state of my gray serge dress with extra starch and ironing had apparently failed, and the heat of the day had wilted the crisply efficient air I had striven to achieve. Now that I was here, doubts about the wisdom of what I planned to do assailed me, but I pushed them aside, refusing to turn around and run.

"Yes?" the butler prompted. Though he stood on the step above me, he didn't quite reach my height. Instead of looking me in the eye, he focused at some point below my chin.

I forced my feet to stay planted and continued to hold my head high. "I am here to see Mr. Trevelyan, please."

"Your name?"

"Miss Ann Lovell."

"Regarding?"

"Employment."

The butler finally raised his gaze to mine. That he had to crick his neck a bit to do it clearly displeased him as much as my appearance. His disapproving frown deepened.

"All household cleaning positions have been filled." He stepped back and started to shut the door.

"Please." I held up the bookstore notice. "I am seeking a teaching position."

"I assure you, he is looking for an educated young *man* to fill that position."

"Then the position is still available?" My hopes rose to my throat, nearly choking off my speech.

The sound of heavy-booted feet striding closer preceded a deep, polished voice. "Is there a problem, Dobbs?"

The tone and verve of the unknown man's voice vibrated in the air and ruffled my already quaking insides. The sensation intensified when a towering man appeared at the door behind the butler.

I almost stepped back. The man appeared as tall and as broad as the massive doorway itself. His dark hair gleamed in the sunlight like the rich, deep hues of the polished wood behind him. A distinctive brow and Roman nose topped a freshly shaven jaw that could conquer an empire with its determination. He was dressed in dark trousers and a white shirt. His hair lay damp upon his brow as if he'd just bathed, and he smelled pleasantly of sandalwood. I breathed in, luxuriating in the scent before I could stop myself. The aroma proved most distracting.

Dobbs cleared his throat with a self-righteous flair. "I was just telling the woman that you were looking for a male tutor for Masters Robert and Justin, sir. Not a governess."

Blinking, I attempted to refocus my thoughts. I lifted my gaze. The man had to be Benedict Trevelyan; his gaze, black as a moonless night in its darkest hours, probed mine. This time I had to crane my neck back, an unusual movement for me. I could easily cast him as one of the winged demons carved on the door. His eyes were so dark a woman would never be able to see through to his soul, and I pitied the poor maiden he would chase. No mercy lurked in his measuring gaze.

"And?" Though he spoke to his servant, the enigmatic master of Trevelyan Hill didn't move his gaze from mine.

He pushed the door wider and joined me on the step. I quickly crumpled the notice that I'd ripped from the bookstore's window and tucked my hand in the fold of my dress lest he think my hasty action too presumptuous.

"She found—"

"I found the answer unsatisfactory, Mr. Trevelyan." I spoke with enough force to clearly be heard over Dobbs's disdain. Then I held my breath, forcing myself to stand strong. There were times when the bounds of propriety had to be breached, and this was such a time.

For a brief second, I thought I saw the corners of Benedict Trevelyan's lips twitch, but his eyes remained so dark and unmoved that I told myself I'd imagined it.

"Interesting. Since he is only reiterating my wishes, I am to take it that it is my words you find unsatisfactory, Miss—"

"Lovell," I supplied, offering my right hand in what I knew to be a manly manner. I felt I needed to stand my ground in the face of his challenge. His voice from inside the house had frayed at my confidence; now the pitch of his deep tones reached inside me, shaking unknown feelings to life that made me a bit queasy. I didn't like it.

Benedict Trevelyan hesitated, but only a moment, before he gripped and shook my hand. Though I'd been able to fashion a small hat from odds and ends of materials and netting left over from years past, I did not have the luxury of gloves; nor did he have any on at the moment. I'm not sure what he thought about this impropriety, but the shock of his bare hand upon mine struck me like a lightning bolt. Heat traveled through my veins to unmentionable places and coalesced to a burning in my cheeks.

I quickly promised myself I would buy a pair of gloves should I receive an employment offer. I instinctively knew it would be necessary for my peace of mind. The man was entirely too disturbing, and I had unprecedented trouble centering my thoughts on the conversation.

"Um, they are not necessarily unsatisfactory, Mr. Trevelyan. Unjust would be a more accurate word. A woman can teach as well as a man. What difference does gender make with—"

He tightened his grip and bowed as if greeting the governor's wife. My hands were reddened from years of laundering, not a lady's hands. My voice clogged in my throat, and my thoughts evaporated as his lips, warm and soft, brushed the back of my hand. A fever washed over me, leaving my skin even damper than the humid air had made it.

I forcibly snatched back my hand, and this time there was no mistaking the lifting corners of his mouth, but no matching light reached his shadowed eyes.

"Unjust?" he said softly.

I suddenly realized Benedict Trevelyan knew exactly what he'd done to me. Considering our stations in life— laundress to rich master of the manor—he'd no social obligation to greet me in such a way. A man as practiced as he had to know the effects his charm had on women, and he'd smoothly manipulated me into the traditional womanly role I'd just tried to step away from. I had best tread more carefully with him, I thought.

Gathering my practicality and composure, I narrowed my brows, striving to admonish him. My future depended on it. "Completely unjust. Did you even once consider a woman for the position?"

"No," he said flatly, pulling out his pocket watch. "I have my reasons."

The finality of his tone pricked holes in my confidence, and my hands clenched as the mountain of laundry I saw in the back of my mind grew tenfold, trying to bury me completely. Too many injustices in the world went unaddressed, especially in regards to a woman's capabilities, and I had to speak up.

"Reasons to eliminate candidates without giving just consideration?" I asked softly.

He tensed as I studied him, his stillness similar to that of a predator catching sight of its prey. I made myself meet and hold the intensity of his gaze. I would not let myself feel shame that I hadn't excused myself when told a woman was not wanted.

"Dobbs, please escort Miss Lovell to my study," he finally said.

I managed to snap my mouth shut before Dobbs repaired the surprised crack in his formal mask. Neither of us had expected Benedict Trevelyan would spend another moment upon a closed issue. I had the distinct impression his decisions were always final.

"I will join you there shortly. You'll have exactly ten minutes to state your credentials and explain why you believe a woman would be a better teacher for my sons." He turned on his heel and disappeared into the manor.

Dobbs stood frozen in place, and for a moment, so did I. I had no official credentials beyond my thirst for knowledge, and my mouth went completely dry over the lie I was about to tell.

Regaining his composure, Dobbs stepped aside, motioning me in with an impatient gesture. The look he gave me condemned without a trial. I might as well have been stealing the family silver rather than searching for employment. Even if Benedict Trevelyan laughed in my face, I'd demanded an opportunity to apply for the position, and I had gotten it. Renewed confidence swelled inside me.

I honestly believed in my abilities to teach. Thanks to my mother's determination, I'd had many teachers over the years, and thus, personal experience with what methods of instruction worked well.

A bittersweet wash of memories splashed over my heart. My education had been as important to my mother as food to eat and air to breathe. It was as if she had known I would be alone as she had been.

As I crossed the threshold into the manor, I was surprised to feel small for the first time in my life. Most often I identified with Lewis Carroll's Alice when she grew too big for the room in which she stood. The ceilings, beam after beam of carved wood, arched to an ornate point above the foyer, like I had seen in drawings of European cathedrals. The marbled floor tiles stretched like a black-and-white sea. Heavy, dark wood chests—massive in size—sat between a series of champagne-silk-covered sofas dotted with jewel-like pillows. Gold leaf adorned the fancy wood of the furniture and accented the frames of a multitude of imposing portraits hung on the walls. The faces of the ancestors were stern, as if they judged all who entered and found them lacking. A ramrod suit of armor stood sentry with a sword in his hand, ready to carry out the ancestors' judgments. The room was the epitome of wealth tastefully displayed. Yet all of its richness paled in comparison to the stained glass windows on opposite ends of the hall.

As often as I had studied the house over the years, I'd never seen the window at the back of the hall. It was twice the size of the front and, in my opinion, the saving grace of Trevelyan Manor, countering its darkness. The combined beauty of the windows was indescribable. I stopped in the entryway, admiring the play of multicolored sunlight dancing over me. I could not help myself.

Either I had gotten lost in my astonishment or Dobbs had decided to abandon me in the hall, for the next thing I knew Benedict Trevelyan stood in front of me with a puzzled frown on his face.

"Miss Lovell, my time is limited. Do you wish to speak with me or not?"

"Yes, of course. Please forgive me, but I have never before seen anything so magnificent."

He spun in a circle, his gaze traveling the room. "I suppose the furnishings are impressive. It is not something to which I give much notice."

I shook my head. "No, not the room." I pointed to the stained glass. "The windows. They are like heaven itself." Each of the windows depicted a choir of angels singing to a Christ rising through the clouds. As I held out my hand, I realized little spots of color—reds, blues, purples, and greens—danced over my skin, masking its work-worn redness. "Look, they paint you with their beauty." My hand truly felt beautiful within the colored light.

"So they do." His voice dropped deeper, catching my attention.

I'd forgotten I still held his employment advertisement. He pulled the paper from my fingers. Unable to look him in the eye, I focused on his large hands as he smoothed out the creases. I found myself wondering what strength lay in such powerful hands.

He stood silent too long. I couldn't bear it. I couldn't let a stolen notice rob me of all that I had to offer. I had to say something on my behalf. "Do you not find the facets of light amazing?" I moved my hand through the colored beams filtering into the hall. "The hues hidden within its waves. Its warmth. Its refractivity. Its beauty. Why, one could spend a lifetime discovering more about its miracles. I have often wondered what it would have been like to be Newton or Huygens. To have made some of the discoveries they did in their scientific studies."

"I think you would have found them to be very lonely men, Miss Lovell. The world doesn't take kindly to new theories. Not until long after the discoverer is dead."

I met his gaze then and could not look away. He stared at me intently, his eyes unreadable and as dark as a starless night.

After an uncomfortable moment, he cleared his throat. "I have a pressing appointment, Miss Lovell, and very little time for musings. Your ten minutes are dwindling."

"Of course." I followed him into his office. Deep wood tones dominated the decor—paneled walls, heavy curtained windows, huge shelves of dark leather-bound books, and a massive mahogany desk.

The master of Trevelyan Hill didn't appear to be a lover of light. I found the room as oppressive as a mound of laundry.

My relief that he said nothing of the notice I'd stolen was minimal. The man radiated tension, and I felt it seeping into me. I clenched my jaw and washed my mind with a good dose of practicality. Nerves would not feed me.

He sat behind his desk and, with a curt nod of his head, motioned me to a burgundy leather chair facing him. I thankfully perched upon the seat.

Tossing the advertisement down on the desk amid the neat stacks of paper, he picked up a writing instrument and slid a pad in front of him. "Why don't we start with the name of your schooling institution?"

My stomach quivered. I'd planned to cite my mother's school in England, but now that the moment to lie had arrived, my mouth had gone numb. I bit down on my tongue, hoping to bring feeling back as I sent another prayer toward heaven. I had more to give than the name of an institution, and it was up to me to make him see that. "Sir, if I may. I have several questions first."

He blinked.

Wincing, I pressed on before he could. "If my information is right, your children are young yet?"

He placed the pen back into the inkwell and with deliberate slowness leaned back in his chair, folded his arms, and glared at me. The hard set of his jaw told me I was about to be dismissed.

Perspiration beaded my lip. Throat dry, I swallowed and clenched my hands in my lap, blessing the inner kernel of determination that bolstered me. I had to stay strong—my future depended on it.

"Miss Lovell, I do not have time to—"

"Please," I said, softly but firmly.

"They are five and seven," he finally said after a long pause. Rather than easing, the tension between us increased.

"They are very young and without a mother. Might I inquire as to your reasons for particularly wanting a male tutor during this time as opposed to a governess?"

His lips pressed to a grim line, and I bit my bottom lip hard, already hearing my dismissal. My action drew his attention, and he stared at my mouth. The seconds seemed to grow longer as the tension in the room shifted from impatient antagonism to a physical awareness similar to the moment he kissed my hand. The heat of his regard made me much more aware of everything feminine within me, parts of myself I'd never given the least bit of attention.

I slowly released my lip, then curled my toes, welcoming the pinch of my boots. We both seemed to draw a deep breath at the same time.

Instead of asking me to leave, he slanted his head to one side and lifted his eyebrow, apparently deciding to humor me. "My boys are high-spirited and unruly. I think they need a firm hand."

"A gentle hand can also be firm."

"That has not been the case with their nurse."

"Because one person does not have a certain skill doesn't mean another person is equally lacking."

"True." His response was slow, as if dragged from him.

"Are there more reasons?"

"Dozens. It has been my experience that women have little patience for science and mathematics. They focus on fashion and parties as opposed to academics."

"True of some women," I conceded. "But not true of all, especially of me." To prove my point, I motioned to my starkly plain attire.

"So I see," he said dryly.

Though I had invited the criticism, the remark still burned.

"Miss Lovell, why don't you tell me in as few words as possible what you can offer my children over and above a tutor."

I closed my eyes, determined to state my case. "I hope to teach your children what my many teachers taught me. To love learning. To have a thirst for the next book that will take you to a new land. To have a curiosity and desire to press forward to uncover a new fact or invent a new thing. All the humdrum memorization of lessons can never be as valuable as that."

"Well put, but where does discipline fit into all this enthusiasm?"

"I cannot answer that, for each child is unique. Each child must be studied, encouraged, and if need be, admonished at his own level." I met his gaze steadily. He seemed to mull over my words. The more I gave voice to the feelings and ideas inside me, the stronger I felt.

"Tell me, Miss Lovell. Where did you come by this philosophy of education?"

"I learned what I know from my mother, from the many people of varied knowledge to whom she bartered her services as a laundress so that I would be educated. I learned much the same way as Abraham Lincoln did. Anything I want to know, anywhere I want to go, a book can take me."

"And you think this knowledge you have independently acquired would be more beneficial to my children than a man with the accreditation of a learned institution behind him?"

My heart sank at his incredulous tone. "At this point in your children's development, I most assuredly can offer them something that no institution can give, no matter how learned. It is called heart, Mr. Trevelyan."

He stood.

I stood, knowing that without credentials I had no hope for employment here. Benedict Trevelyan appeared too rigid to consider my unorthodox education. "I thank you for your time, Mr. Trevelyan, and I wish you luck in your search for a *proper* tutor."

"One more question, Miss Lovell. Your parents? How do they feel about you seeking employment here? I am not completely unaware of the whispers behind my back."

"I had a mother only, Mr. Trevelyan. So I am well versed in ignoring whispers. She cannot give her opinion. She recently passed away. Good day."

His voice stopped me at the door. "Be here at eight tomorrow morning, Miss Lovell. I will employ you on a trial basis until you've proven yourself capable. If at any time I find you are not being beneficial to my children's development, I will find another to replace you. Expect me to appear and observe your methods of teaching without warning, for I will be evaluating their progress frequently. Your salary will be in keeping with the current rate for teachers here in San Francisco, payable at the end of each month with Saturdays and half-day Sundays off. Room and board are included with the position, as I think having the teacher available to coordinate my children's development more important than just a few hours a day. I want them to be as well rounded in their education as money can buy. That goes from music to languages as well. If you are not particularly adept at something, then I expect you to hire someone who is, and to participate in that lesson enough to know my child is learning. I have high expectations, Miss Lovell. Have I made myself clear?"

Gratitude flooded my emotions, and I dared not face him. "Perfectly clear, Mr. Trevelyan."

I hurried across the hall, feeling as if I would either laugh or cry at any moment.

Dobbs had a haughty look on his face that was drenched in satisfaction. I held on to my composure long enough to speak to him before I sailed out of the doorway. "See you tomorrow morning, Mr. Dobbs. You will be a joy to work with." My voice rang out loudly.

An amused snort echoed from the office I had just left, and Dobbs paled to the point that I thought he would faint. Smiling, I stepped out into the sunshine, wondering if I would too. I felt light-headed, as if I was floating in the air.

My feet carried me across the street to Holloway Park, to the brightly flowered gardens and sharp scents of marigolds, geraniums, and bluebells. I walked beneath the shady oaks, feeling the soft, springy grass and remembering the past. The birds chirped. The children played. And a light breeze, flavored with the salt and the fish of the bay, trifled with the leaves and then teased the wisps of my hair as it danced by, looking for mischief. The tension wrought so tightly with in me for so long eased.

My mother hadn't given me fancy dresses or a pretty face, but she'd given me something even more valuable. She'd given me her love. I had always known that. But today

I realized that in that love, she'd given me another precious gift—belief in myself, in my worth as a person.

"Thank you," I cried out to the sun, for I knew she watched from heaven, and the warmth of her spirit wrapped around me.

Yesterday, after placing wildflowers on my mother's two-week-old grave, I'd returned to our small shack to finish that day's laundry. Yet once there, I'd found myself unable to clean the mounds of dirty clothes. The bleakness of my future had stared me in the eye. I would have to wash baskets of clothes to feed myself—just as I had helped my mother do since I was four.

The thought of spending another twenty years the way I had spent the last twenty made me shiver with dread, and all of my practicality deserted me. My soul cried for a new book to lose my sorrows in, and I turned right around and went to Mr. McGuire's Bookstore in town.

I never made it into the store. For as I stood outside trying to blink away my tears, Benedict Trevelyan's employment advertisement had come into focus, as had my destiny. I knew at that moment that I would find a way to teach, and I had.

Tomorrow I would return to Trevelyan Hill, to the mysterious manor that had called to me for so long. Soon I'd be able to explore what lay behind its intriguing facade.

I turned to study its turrets and spires from afar, and my thoughts strayed again to the master of the manor. Was he capable of murder?

I rubbed my wrist, remembering the feel of his lips upon my skin, remembering the tenor of his voice and his disturbing size. Deep inside me heat tingled, making a little ache flutter to life.

I knew that once I passed through the demon-carved portal tomorrow, my life would be forever changed, but there was no going back. My thirst to know more was too strong. I could not deny myself this, no matter what dangers lay ahead. I imagine my yearnings were akin to those that had driven explorers to the sea and pioneers to the West.

But, I thought, as I recalled the feel of Benedict Trevelyan's hand within mine and the touch of his lips, I would definitely buy a pair of gloves. Of that there was no doubt.

As the afternoon sun drew closer to the western horizon, painting the sky a swirl of pinks and yellows, I again found myself in front of McGuire's Bookstore. Walking out to Trevelyan Hill and back into town had left a coating of dust upon me, yet the time I spent at Holloway Park had my spirit feeling renewed, like a flower after a spring rain. Not even the impersonal hustle and bustle of people rushing to the shops, banks, and saloons—something that usually made me feel lonely—could dampen my spirit. My life had changed, and I yearned to tell someone of its wondrous new direction.

I stepped through the door to the tinkling of tiny bells and a squawking "How now, Spirit!" from Puck the Parrot as he announced my arrival.

Mr. McGuire was just as I always found him, perched on a high stool at his desk, engrossed in a book. As always, his desk was a precarious pyramid of novels and papers with only a small corner clear on which to rest the current tome he read. I greeted Puck with a soft coo, brushing his red and green plumes with the back of my hand, then cleared my throat twice before I got Mr. McGuire's attention.

His face broke into a wreath of kind wrinkles when he saw me. "Ah, lass, I'm so glad you've come. I've something for ye." He stood, absently pushing his bifocals in place on his pebble nose and tucking his few wisps of silver hair back atop his shiny head.

"Something to read?" The greediness in my voice should

have shamed me, but I fear that when it came to books, I had none.

"I go, I go, look how I go!" Puck, sensing my enthusiasm, answered in kind. The colorful bird quoted Shakespeare, most often the fairy character after which he was named.

Mr. McGuire shook his head as if mystified. "How did you ever guess?"

I smiled at the game we had played before and dutifully replied by rote. "I saw it in my crystal ball?"

"Doubtful."

"A bird whispered it in my ear?"

He moved over to Puck, close to where I stood, and gave the parrot half of a hardened biscuit. After a long moment he spoke. "Possibly."

I blinked in surprise. My mother and I had come when we could to McGuire's Bookstore, using whatever spare monies we had to buy one of the bound treasures from his shelves. And over the years affection had grown between us. Were I able to choose a grandfather, Mr. McGuire, his Scottish burr, and all of his absentminded clutter would be mine. I would never forget the thrill that had gone through my ten-year-old heart the first time he said he had a surprise for me. Always before at this point in our game, when I'd said a bird whispered in my ear, Mr. McGuire would fuss at Puck for giving away secrets. That Mr. McGuire had changed his response now gave me pause. I didn't know what to say next.

Concern deepened his bleary blue eyes. "Your mother's illness and death has sorrowed me greatly. I've lived through losing most of those I hold dear, so I know a good bit of how ye have been feeling. I imagine you've been a mite lonely."

My mother's death had left a huge void in my life, and this dear old man's caring put a comforting arm about me. "You always understand."

He sighed. "Remember me saying a close friend of mine was a professor at the University of Edinburgh? Thomas Stewart Traill, to name him."

I nodded my head.

"He died back in '62 and willed me what he considered his greatest work. He'd had the honor of editing the *Encyclopædia Britannica* and gave a copy of the set to me. I want you to have them."

My soul sang at the possibility of having so much knowledge and learning at my fingertips. I didn't know which had flown open wider, my eyes or my mouth. For Mr. McGuire to give me so great a gift told me that he cared for me as deeply as I secretly cared for him. I could not stop the shower of tears that started to fall.

Looking confused, Mr. McGuire drew his white brows into high arcs above his bifocals. "Now, I meant to cheer ye." He patted my back.

"You have," I cried. "But you give too much. I could not possibly accept something so valuable."

"Humph. That's nothing but nonsense, lass. I'm an old man with none but myself to care for, and I have a mind to see knowledge passed into loving hands before I die."

My breath caught, and I studied his wise features through my tears. I did not see any hint of illness lurking about his age-worn body, but I dabbed at my eyes and looked again. I had to be sure. He appeared as well as ever, and I released my pent breath to argue. "But—"

"I'll not be accepting any buts now. Come and take a wee look at them."

The moment I saw the box of leather-bound wisdom, I knew I was lost. Awe filled me, and tied my tongue as I fingered the gold-leaf lettering upon the spines. These treasures had come straight from Edinburgh, the very birthplace of the first edition of the *Encyclopædia Britannica*.

I could almost feel the information flow into my finger-tips and fever my blood. A plan of instruction slowly formed in my mind. I would teach Benedict Trevelyan's boys everything in these revered pages. Little by little I would read the subjects and bring them to the level that a child might understand. Benedict Trevelyan had high expectations. I would be thorough. I turned to Mr. McGuire and impulsively hugged him hard. "I cannot find the words to even begin to thank you."

A blush rose upon his leathered cheeks, and a merry twinkle lit his watery blue eyes. "Ye can thank me by reading them."

"Oh, I will, I will, a thousand times. I will start this very night, and tomorrow I will stun Mr. Trevelyan with the lessons I have in mind for his sons."

The light of happiness in Mr. McGuire's eyes turned to alarm. "What is this you say?"

"How now mad spirit!" Puck ruffled his feathers upon his perch, disturbed from his biscuit eating by his owner's distressed tone.

"Dear me! I completely forgot to tell you. I applied for the position of governess to Mr. Trevelyan's children today, and I start work first thing tomorrow. Can you believe it?"

"Nay, lass. Surely you jest." He shook his head as if I'd given him grave news.

My excitement dimmed. Mr. McGuire didn't believe in me. Did he not think me capable? "No, truly I am now a governess. Do you fear I am unequal to the task?"

"Never. You are smarter than any lass I've ever known. Any lad, too, now that I think about it. It is Benedict Trevelyan himself who worries me. What if he had a hand in the death of his wife?"

I swallowed the twinge of unease that threatened to rise. Had not I had the same question myself?

Was I being too hasty, too desperate to change my life? I thought of the mound of smelly laundry I'd spent twelve hours cleaning the day before.

No, I decided. Employment to teach Benedict Trevelyan's children would in no way place me in any danger. "His wife jumped from the tower and died last year. Rumor has it that she was mad. Do you know more than that?"

Mr. McGuire sighed. "No, only the rumors. But if ye are going to be up on that hill, I'm going to make it my business to find out. Be careful, lass. Be very careful."

"Lord, what fools these mortals be!" Puck squawked.

Mr. McGuire and I both turned to look at the parrot, who now preened his feathers as if he didn't have a care in the world. It wasn't the first time that I wondered if Puck was more than he seemed.

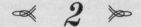

2

I expected the day to dawn bright, to have the warm blessing of sunshine upon the first step of my new life. Instead, heavy layers of thick fog blanketed the morning air.

On my way home from Mr. McGuire's Bookstore the previous evening, I'd spent the money I'd been saving for food and purchased a pair of gray kid gloves to armor myself. I'd also arranged—with some trepidation, for I feared horses—for transportation so that I could bring my books with me. My clothes and personal belongings I could carry in my mother's worn carpetbag. My books were another story—two cartons plus the encyclopedias.

I'd wanted to hire a horse and carriage. In my mind, a

carriage would serve as an adequate barrier from the beasts that pulled it, and I would avoid giving Dobbs any reason to elevate his nose higher. Unfortunately, my few coins had only afforded me a rag-tail horse and a dusty cart, in which I now stiffly rode, seated beside a man who looked and smelled as flavorful as plump red peppers. But I hardly spared him a glance; I irrationally kept my eye on the huge horse, expecting it to do something dreadful.

After stopping at the bookstore to pick up the rest of the encyclopedias, for I'd only taken one volume home with me, we made our way to Trevelyan Hill. The manor house stood eerily in the morning mist, like a specter rising from unknown depths. Its three turrets—two smaller on the end of each wing and one larger in the center—lent a castle-like air to the manor, bringing to mind knights, and ladies, and dragons. Fascination and a sense of excitement gripped me, making me push my fear of horses to the back of my mind. My future lay in the dark house before me.

"Madre de Dios!" my driver cried, drawing a cross over his chest with his finger as he brought the cart to a halt and stared at Trevelyan Hill.

"We must hurry," I said, urging him on. Not only did I pride myself on always being prompt, but I didn't think the master of Trevelyan Hill tolerated tardiness.

Emitting another curse, the driver spurred the horse onward. We clattered up the drive, covering the remaining distance with commendable purpose. The gray mist about us thickened, then swirled like pirouetting ghosts upon the dewy ground. Its damp air bathed me, filled my lungs, and hung heavily about my shoulders—an undeniable presence that encircled us completely. I was unsure if the clinging tendrils of fog welcomed me or were trying to warn me away.

Either way, it mattered not. I'd set a new course for my life, and I would follow it through. The driver came to an abrupt stop. Relieved that I'd soon be far from the horse, I palmed the small coin I'd saved to tip the driver and waited for him to help me down.

I was a good foot or so taller than the driver, and it felt a bit pretentious to await him like a dainty lady. But I did so anyway, firmly reminding myself that I was embarking upon a new life. Once assisted down, I quickly made my way up the steps to the demon door and knocked.

Dobbs answered immediately; the downcurl of his lips only made the upturn of his nose more prominent.

"Good morning." I gave him a sunny smile designed to chaff his dour nature.

He ignored my greeting. Before I could say more, a noise from the driveway drew my attention. Turning, my instructions for the driver to place my bag and my boxes of books inside died upon my lips. For the driver had dumped my things upon the cobblestones and was loudly beseeching the Lord to deliver him from the devil as he clamored back into the driver's seat.

"Wait," I said, holding out the coin. The driver never looked back. He cracked a whip at the horse, which reared up as if Satan himself was hot on his tail, and took off. The cart bounced wildly into the mists, a rickety trap on the verge of splintering.

Dobbs cleared his throat. The disdain on his stiff face was twofold that of yesterday. He eyed my belongings. "I doubt you will be needing that many clothes, Miss Lowit."

"Lovell, if you please," I said, marching back down the steps, refusing to look at him. "But do not apologize. I realize the name is a bit taxing for some minds to recall." I snatched up the bag containing my clothes, my mother's silver brush and comb, and her pistol. She'd learned to shoot straight and taught me to as well, a necessity for a woman alone in the West. "I will take care of my clothes, thank you. Would you please send someone to collect my books?"

When I turned back, Benedict Trevelyan stood next to Dobbs. "I do not find Lovell the least bit taxing. Do you, Dobbs?" His voice was as cool as the morning air, and his dark eyes just as obscure as the blanketing mist. I couldn't tell if he was admonishing Dobbs or if he was amused.

"Not taxing at all, sir," Dobbs answered as he quickly moved down the stairs and took my bag from me. From the red flush staining his face and the antipathy sparking from his eyes, I wondered if he wouldn't burst into flames right then and there despite the hovering moistness.

"Thank you," I said stiffly to Dobbs, determined to be polite. As I walked up the stairs to where Benedict Trevelyan stood, I felt the scrutiny of his dark gaze and suddenly found my attire lacking. I should have worn my brown dress, fixed my hair in another style, done something to alter my appearance from that of the day before. Though my brown dress was of lesser quality than my gray serge, it would have—

My word! When had I ever been overly concerned with my appearance? Until yesterday, no instance came to mind, and I dismissed the unfamiliar and annoying thoughts, bandying about my brain for my usual pragmatism. Benedict Trevelyan interrupted before I found it.

"I am pleased that you are on time, Miss Lovell," he said.

"I am always prompt," I replied, bending my neck back to study his face. His size amazed me anew. Few men made me feel of womanly proportions, and he did so without effort. I tingled in the most disturbing places. My breath quickened, my blood sped, and I could only pray that my cheeks weren't waving my own discomfiture like scarlet flags. I had expected that Benedict Trevelyan's effect on my person would have lessened. It had multiplied.

"Good. Be in my office at half past the hour," he said,

releasing me from the heavy grip of his perusal to look at Dobbs. "Please escort Miss Lovell to the Blue Room and instruct Cook Thomas to add another person for dinner."

"Yes, sir," Dobbs replied.

Benedict Trevelyan nodded succinctly, then turned on his heel and left.

I let my gaze follow him and immediately wished I hadn't. The cut of his shirt and pants were tailored perfectly to his long limbs and stretched taut over his muscles. I had seen many a man's shirt and breeches in my years as a laundress, but had never viewed them with as much interest as I did now.

Truly, I had to have taken leave of my senses. To notice such things was totally unacceptable. I shut my eyes.

"If you will follow me, Miss Lovell."

Opening my eyes, I found Dobbs had joined me at the top of the stairs. If he thought it odd that I was standing with my eyes shut, he didn't comment. I promptly assembled my thoughts with a crisp stiffening of my back. "My books. I can't leave them upon the street unattended."

"They will be fine. I will send someone to get them shortly."

Frowning, I gazed back at my books, especially my new carton of *Encyclopædia Britannica*. I imagined a host of disasters. They could be stolen. A horse could trample over them. I could even see this prune of a butler making sure my things took a tumble down the steps before reaching my room.

I folded my arms and decided to hold my ground. "I will wait here until they are inside, thank you."

"Very well," Dobbs said stiffly. I could tell he wanted to argue with me, and I was sure that only the lingering effects of Benedict Trevelyan's presence prevented it. Dobbs disappeared inside, leaving the door open. I followed him to where I could watch my books and see the stained glass windows. Despite the mists hovering, light pushed through the glass, bringing color to life. Even dulled by the fog, the light's magical beauty touched me much as I imagined the brush of angel wings might feel upon my soul.

Within minutes Dobbs was back with two other men he didn't name. They were less formal than Dobbs in their manner and their dress, one lean as pole and about my height, the other barrel-shaped and shorter. They had salty hair and ruddy complexions, and they both limped as if they had suffered a severe injury in the past; yet they lifted my cartons with little effort. I got the impression the men had spent many years on one of the majestic ships dotting the bay. Their rangy movements reminded me of Captain Balder, a robust sea salt who'd taught me about navigating a ship by the stars and many other wonders of the sea and other lands in his pursuit to marry my mother. He'd said that once a man had sea legs, he kept them for life.

We were an odd procession: stiffly formal Dobbs carrying my bag, I in a dress that seemed so poor compared to the riches about me, and the seamen carrying my books. As we crossed the entry hall, moving up the stairway to the left, my hands felt strangely empty. I had never been on the receiving end of service, and it disconcerted me.

When we reached the second level, the loveliness of the stained glass hall disappeared and the shadows increased. The third floor was darker still, for deep-toned paneling abounded, and only one window at the end lit the passageway. Fashioned from beveled glass, the window started about halfway up from the floor and climbed to a pointed arch. From my childhood drawings, I recalled that all of the windows on the third story followed this cathedral-like theme.

The house smelled of beeswax and lemon, scents that I

generally associated with warmth, yet a chilly draft brushed my face and stole beneath my skirts. I shivered, but not from the cold. Something else besides the morning cool seemed to hover in the air, a presence of ill will. I searched the shadows ahead, saw nothing out of the ordinary, but remembered my driver's fear as he stared at Trevelyan Manor. I'd thought him silly at the time; now I was tempted to draw a cross over my chest as well.

Thick carpets lining the hallway muffled our steps, and no one spoke. Only the sounds of our breathing and the growing sense that someone watched me disturbed the quiet. When I heard the soft click of a hastily shut door, I knew my instincts had been right. Someone had observed our progression and had chosen to remain hidden.

If Dobbs noticed, he didn't comment or hesitate in his determined march. Oddly enough, as he stopped at a doorway, turning to face me, I found his dourness comforting compared to the invisible malevolence behind me.

"Your room adjoins the schoolroom through that door, which connects to the nursery where both Master Robert and Master Justin sleep. Their nurse, Maria, is in the room beyond that." With a stiff gesture that matched his supercilious tone, he motioned me into the room.

I froze on the threshold, flabbergasted at the luxury before me. The room was large, adorned in dainty shades of blue relieved only by white, violet-sprigged wallpaper and the dark lines of rich wood. A massive canopied bed drew my gaze first; its diaphanous silk curtains—the color of a summer sky—hung softly about the bed and were drawn to the side by thick, braided ropes of deep sapphire. The plump mattress begged for one to lie down and made me quite impracticably wonder if I could close the silk curtains and dream the impossible, that such a room was truly mine, that I was a lady to the manor born. I immediately snuffed out such impossibilities. I'd improved my employment situation, but I knew my place. This room would never do. Still I looked about, wanting to absorb it all.

Along the outside wall, offering a mist-shrouded view of San Francisco, were four arched windows with cushioned seats. To my left, a small couch, chair, and table huddled intimately together to make a private sitting area. Then came a closed door that I assumed led to the schoolroom and nursery, as Dobbs had stated. On my right a large armoire, a mirrored washstand, and a desk with chair completed the furnishings.

"Surely there is some mistake," I said to Dobbs.

"This does not meet with your approval, Miss Lovell?"

I swallowed twice before I could speak. "Quite the opposite. This, this is too much. I could not possibly—"

"This is what Mr. Trevelyan requested."

The finality in Dobbs's voice made it very clear that Benedict Trevelyan's requests took precedence over everything and were never bent to the will of others. After having met the man twice, I could very well see why. So why had he hired me?

"Dinner is at eight sharp. Everyone meets in the formal parlor. I will send a maid to help you unpack your things and direct you to Mr. Trevelyan's office."

"Please do not send a maid. That will not be necessary at all. I am certain I can find my way back," I said, stepping aside. The thought of a maid seeing my meager possessions unsettled me as much as the opulence around me. The two seamen set down my books and left.

After another look about, I made up my mind that I wouldn't unpack until I had a room more suitable to my position. I just couldn't see myself living in such grand accommodations. Then Dobbs's other words sank in. "What do you mean, everyone meets in the formal parlor?"

"It is where the family and their guests gather before dinner."

"But won't I be eating with the other household servants?"

"Mr. Trevelyan has requested otherwise."

"Surely there is some mistake."

Dobbs lifted his nose. "Mr. Trevelyan doesn't make mistakes. I assure you, the request for you to dine with the family is most likely due to the fact that his tutor dined with the family, but then Mr. Wainscott was an Englishman of notable ancestry, if impoverished. Is there anything else?"

"No," I said, omitting the *thank you* I might have added. Though he'd left it unsaid, Dobbs clearly implied that I wasn't in the same class as Mr. Wainscott. I wish I could have disabused Dobbs of that, but I couldn't. I was even lower than an ordinary laundress, for I'd been born out of wedlock.

"Very well. And, miss, a word of caution. Please refrain from gossiping about the Trevelyan family with others. I expect you to keep your intrusion into the Trevelyans' private life to a minimum. Unless invited otherwise, stay in your quarters, the schoolroom, the dining room, and the library should you need material for teaching purposes."

Had I really thought his dourness preferable to my silent watcher?

"I will endeavor to be circumspect, Mr. Dobbs. By the same token, I would appreciate it if you could manage not to gawk when you look at me."

His jaw dropped, and purple suffused his face. Before he could say anything else, I busied myself with my bag a moment, then looked at him. "My time is limited. Is there anything else that needs to be said?"

"You have said quite enough already, Miss Lowsit." Turning on his heel, he marched out.

Relieved to be alone, I stood just inside the room for some minutes, trying to grasp my situation, and I must admit that I gawked at the riches surrounding me. It took a muffled click from the door across the way to snap me from my thoughts.

I spun. Sticking my head out the door and glancing down the hall, I saw nothing. No one moved, and all appeared quiet, yet I shivered as a chill raced down my spine. Someone had continued to watch me. Who? Why? The children maybe?

Closing the door with a snap, I noted a large key in the lock and made as much noise as I could as I locked the door. I wanted to send a clear message to my watcher. I wanted that person to know I was aware of his or her presence and I would in no way tolerate the concealed scrutiny.

Then, dismissing the incident, I turned to the room and set my mind upon a more pressing matter. What was I to do about my room? I found myself almost afraid to walk on the thick carpets strewn about the gleaming wood floor. They were so rich it seemed a crime to step upon them. The furniture—fit for a queen—was the finest I'd ever seen, and, I surmised, had to be old as well. Somewhere I remembered hearing that the Benedict Trevelyan's father had spared no expense in building and furnishing the manor, had, in fact, toured all of Europe to find the kingly treasures.

Once I'd spoken to Benedict Trevelyan about the matter, I had no doubt I would be moved to a more suitable room, and I decided to explore the luxury about me with the spare time I had. I dashed to a lofty window to see what it would be like to look out at the world from a position such as this. I sat at the desk and imagined writing in my diary about a day spent as a queen. Then I moved to the cloudy bed, letting my fingertips brush the silks, satins, and velvets ensconced there. But for rare occasions, I'd only known the feel of rough cotton or wool.

The bed was so soft, so airily magical, that I decadently fell back upon the cover and blinked at the diaphanous canopy above me. I wondered if a little girl had ever lain here beneath the misty folds of material and dreamed of a happy life.

From somewhere downstairs, I heard the gong of a grandfather clock tolling the half hour.

My heavens! Where had the minutes gone? For the first time in my life, I had to rush to be prompt. The luxury of the room seemed to have stolen my practical sensibilities. I hurried to the entry hall, thankful to find it empty. I didn't want Dobbs to see me flustered.

Going directly to Benedict Trevelyan's office door, I raised my hand to knock, but never got the opportunity. The door jerked open, and a man wavered at the threshold. I immediately noted that his hair was longer than Benedict Trevelyan's and his stature slightly less imposing. He was about my own height, and he wasn't facing me; he had turned back to the room, shouting. "How can you live with yourself after what you did? She's dead!"

I barely stopped my gasp of surprise. What had Benedict Trevelyan done? Did they speak of his wife, or someone else?

"I do not happen to share your guilt, Stephen. I suggest you go sober yourself up. You are becoming a disgrace to the Trevelyan name." Benedict Trevelyan's voice was calm in the face of the other man's slurred and angry words.

Either Benedict Trevelyan had no hand in the death of the woman they spoke of, or . . . he had no conscience? I remembered the merciless black of his eyes. I knew Benedict Trevelyan had a younger brother who had moved East right after the death of Benedict Trevelyan's wife.

"Pretending none of it ever happened will not make it go away. It will not change what I did, and it will not change what you did either," the man slurred, his words so full of anguish, they seemed as if they had been dragged across shards of glass before being uttered.

"I refuse to discuss this with a drunk."

I started to step back, planning to retreat and return later, but I'd hesitated too long. The man swung on his heel and ran into me. Hard. I cried out, surprised to feel my balance waver. He smelled of whiskey and of trail dust, as if he'd traveled a long road with a big bottle. The man was so sodden with drink that he would have been hard-pressed to stay upright even without the mishap of running into me.

My presence was the apple that tipped the cart. He fell forward, and I fell backward. We landed on the floor with a thud. Or, more accurately, I landed on the marble floor with a thud. The man landed on me with a thump. His face was buried uncomfortably deep into the middle of my stomach, but the most disturbing problem was that after he fell—he didn't move.

"Umm, sir . . . umm, mister!" I squirmed to no avail. The man was dead weight upon my legs. Mortification at my predicament filled me and grew as I heard the suspicious rumble of a snore. About that same moment, my gaze met Benedict Trevelyan's, and I thought I would die with embarrassment. My lord! What a fix!

"Are you hurt?" He stood above me, the stern lines of his face hardened with anger.

I blinked. "I am not quite sure. I have never been knocked down before."

He stared at me a moment, and it wasn't until he spoke that the harshness in his face eased a little. "I daresay there is a first time for everything, Miss Lovell. I must apologize for my brother's rudeness."

Squatting down, he pried his brother off my person, and I went from one uncomfortable situation to another. I immediately wanted the crushing protection of Stephen Trevelyan's body back. For Stephen Trevelyan now lay snoring on the ground beside me, and Benedict Trevelyan knelt over me, deftly examining my shoulders and the back of my head with his large warm hands. My word!

He was too close. I suddenly felt as if I'd been exposed in the middle of my bath, and I wanted to cover myself from his dark gaze. My dazed mind imagined that his eyes heated as he examined me, revealing a fire within the darkness. Imagined or not, the situation was entirely too intimate.

I opened my mouth to order a stop to his examination, but my breath caught in my throat as he threaded his fingers beneath the bun holding my long hair neatly in place. His touch both soothed and seared my skin, filling me with sensations that were unlike anything I'd ever experienced. My blood rushed with dizzying force as warmth suffused my body. I tingled strangely . . . everywhere . . . and had to wiggle my toes to stay sane. For the first time in my life, I wished I were subject to fainting spells.

"I do not feel a goose egg." His voice rumbled over me as pervadingly as his touch.

"A goose's what?" I gasped.

He sat back, releasing my head, and I remembered to breathe. But that was a mistake. His scent—the sandalwood I'd recognized yesterday and something else, a hint of leather and of mint—washed over me, making me hunger for more. It was a scent already too familiar, for I found pleasure in eagerly breathing it in.

"Bump," he said.

"Goose bumps?" I replied, lifting my hand to my neck. I had to look at anything but him, so I stared up at the massive beams arching to the ceiling. Even they reminded me of him, though—large and powerful. Had he given me goose bumps? I didn't doubt it.

He took my hand and placed his fingers over my pulse at my wrist, causing more havoc with my person. I'd never realized how many vulnerable places I had.

"Your heart is racing," he said. "I think Dobbs should send for the doctor."

The sight of my reddened hand in his hit me with a bucket of cold reality. Though I had often rubbed rose oil on my skin after a day's labor, my hands and nails were still those of a laundress. I quickly pulled my disgraced hand from his and pushed myself up from the floor. That, plus the thought of Dobbs seeing me prostrate, settled my sensibilities back into place.

"Absolutely not. No doctor needed. I have a remarkably strong constitution. Mr. Trevelyan, I mean your brother, just surprised me." I'd had my fill of doctors during my mother's illness. In my opinion, they hindered more than they helped.

He hesitated a moment, as if he were about to insist but didn't. "Very well, Miss Lovell. If you change your mind about the doctor, let Dobbs know." After steadying me with a polite hand to my elbow, he stepped back.

I straightened my gown and tried to push my loosened hair back into the confines of a strict bun. When I looked up at him, I found him watching me. His midnight eyes were remote, unreadable, and cold. I knew then I had imagined the heat of last few moments.

"Since my brother has seen fit to return, I think it best if you'd call me Benedict and him Stephen to forgo any confusion. That is, if he sobers up enough to be in polite company. I must apologize again for this incident."

"There is no need to apologize, Mr. Trevelyan. I seem to have been in the wrong place at the wrong time. I did not mean to intrude. . . ." My reeling senses steadied as the normal, comfortable walls of propriety fell back into place. I wasn't about to shake them up by using his Christian name. He didn't insist on the matter, nor did he comment on my accidental eavesdropping.

"No. You were exactly where I asked you to be. The error is on Stephen's part. He should have stayed back East. I am going to have to postpone our meeting until another time. It appears I have a family matter to tend." He frowned at his brother.

I followed his gaze. In sleep, Stephen Trevelyan looked harmless, like a small lad needing a comforting touch from a mother's hand. I wondered what had driven him to drown himself in drink, and to be so angry with his brother. Yet I was in no position to ask questions. I was in the Trevelyan household to teach, and I'd yet to meet my pupils. But first I had to address the matter of my room.

I cleared my throat. "Mr. Trevelyan, I cannot possibly accept the room you have assigned me. It is far too extravagant. Something simpler would be much more in keeping with my position."

He frowned. "Do you not find the room appealing, Miss Lovell?"

"Oh, it is wondrous! Like a sleepy blue cloud on a summer's day." I cleared my throat, discomfited by my outburst.

"Then I don't see where the problem lies. As it connects to the schoolroom and the nursery where Justin and Robert sleep, it is the most practical. It is the governess's quarters, and you are here to teach my children, are you not?"

"Absolutely, but—"

"Then it is settled." He waved his hand as if to swat away a bothersome fly, and I knew it was useless to argue.

He was right. It was the most practical room for me to

occupy as the children's governess. Yet I wondered if I could be comfortable in such luxury. "And about the dining arrangements—"

"Miss Lovell, do you have a problem with that also?" He sounded somewhat irritated.

I swallowed what I'd been about to say. "Uh, no. They are fine." Realizing I'd be unable to sway his decisions at the moment, I moved on to the reason I'd come to Trevelyan Manor. "If I may, I would like to meet Masters Justin and Robert and begin my instruction today."

He quirked a brow. "You are not a woman who wastes time, Miss Lovell."

"I learned the merits of frugality at a young age, Mr. Trevelyan. I waste nothing."

He stared at me for a few moments, seemingly assessing my truthfulness. I met his gaze directly, refusing to give in to the urge to smooth my hair again. An eternity passed before he turned away with a frown and left me wondering what he found displeasing.

"If you will follow me, I will have Dobbs take care of Stephen, and we will locate the children. I believe Maria should have them at breakfast by now. Which reminds me, have you eaten?"

Though I had not, I assured him that I had. My stomach was in so many knots, I didn't think I could swallow a bite this morning. I suddenly wondered if I was equal to the task I had set for myself. Would I be able to teach what was in my heart, or would I fail?

The moment I walked into the kitchen, failure loomed heavily in my mind. The woman I assumed to be Nurse Maria had a broom, which she waved like a flag as she chased a small boy about the room. A thick, white substance lay plastered on the side of her face and hung in her hair. Another, older boy sat at the table, encouraging the smaller boy to run faster. I took a step back, daunted by the reigning pandemonium. "Goodness gracious!"

Benedict Trevelyan lifted a disdainful brow and muttered, "An ineffective response, Miss Lovell. Goodness and gracious have little to do with it. Stop!" he yelled, his voice booming like a cannon. Everyone froze. His ferocious tenor sent a chill through me, and I wondered what madness had urged me to enter the mists shrouding Trevelyan Manor.

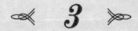

3

"What is the meaning of this? Robert? Justin?" Benedict Trevelyan fired his words like bullets.

Maria spoke first. "The child threw his food. He needs to be punished, just as you said I must do when the children misbehave."

Five-year-old Robert looked fearfully at his father, tears already gathering in his soft chocolate eyes. He had a head full of dark curly hair and rosy cheeks. His small chin trembled as he spoke. "Miss Maria putted milk in my oatmeal. I tolded her not to and she did anyway. When I wouldn't eat it, she tried to force it in my mouth. I do not want milk in my oatmeal! I want Aunt Kaff!"

Benedict Trevelyan was unmoved by his son's tears. "There is no excuse for this kind of behavior. I expect this mess cleaned up immediately, and tonight you will go to bed early with only bread and water. A gentleman does not throw food, do you understand me, son?"

"But—"

"No buts. Do you understand?"

"Yes, sir." Two tears fell from his eyes, and my heart twisted.

"Justin, the same for you. You were not acting in a responsible, helpful manner, were you?"

"No, sir," Justin looked down at his bowl and twiddled with his spoon. I could see a hint of his father's stern nature in the firming of the boy's jaw. Though his hair was a lighter shade, more brown than black, he looked as if he'd be the spitting image of his father someday.

Benedict Trevelyan introduced Maria to me. She only nodded a greeting, and I reciprocated. Then Trevelyan spoke to his children again.

"I want both of you boys to meet Miss Lovell. She is your new governess, and you are to begin lessons as soon as this mess is cleaned up. You are to give her your complete attention and best behavior at all times. Do you have any questions?"

"No, sir." Justin and Robert answered in subdued unison. The air hung heavy with Benedict Trevelyan's displeasure, and I felt my insides churning. His punishment, though not harsh or cruel, unsettled me greatly.

"Where is Cook Thomas?" he demanded.

"At the market," Maria replied. She had a satisfied smile on her face, and I wondered at that moment if the boys weren't in need of a more loving hand rather than the firm hand their father thought necessary. In my mind, I held her responsible for the fiasco. Her black hair was graying at the temples, and she should have known a better way to handle little Robert. I believe the Bible stated that you shouldn't provoke children to wrath, and it seemed to me that she'd done little to avoid the confrontation. I didn't like milk in my oatmeal, either. I much preferred a dollop of honey on those rare occasions we were able to afford the luxury.

"Disaster seems to be the order of the day around here.

Would you like for them to meet you in the schoolroom, Miss Lovell?"

If possible, he was more remote and imposing than before. Maybe he expected me to march out the door. I'm not sure if it was the laundress in me or the fact that he didn't see me as capable of handling his sons, but my hands suddenly itched to clean up the messy situation the Trevelyan household appeared to be in. In my mind, the first thing that needed to be swept out the door was the nurse.

"Not at all. I would like to have time to talk with Master Justin and Master Robert before we get to the schoolroom. Why don't I take charge of this and let Nurse Maria go clean up? I will make sure they are back in her care after their lessons."

He lifted his brow, but I knew not whether he expressed surprise or doubt before he turned away from me to speak to the nurse. "Maria, perhaps your services would be better suited toward tending to my mother this morning."

The censure in his voice eased some of the disquiet in my stomach. He obviously did not hold the woman blameless. Maria's face flushed a deep red. She set the broom forcefully into the corner, then left without speaking.

Her impertinence shocked me, for it was not something I thought Benedict Trevelyan would ever tolerate.

"Maria was my wife's childhood nurse," he said, and I jumped. He must have read my mind, must have been closely observing me without my knowing it. I tingled at the thought, then blinked at the utter ridiculousness of it. A man like Benedict Trevelyan would never look at me as anything but an expendable commodity. In fact, the truth of it was that a man had never—and would never—look at me with anything in mind except how I might be of service. I was not a woman to inspire passion in a man, and I accepted my fate. Therefore I had laundered, turned down the few lukewarm propositions of men interested in a warm body, and now I would teach and do the same.

But the task of teaching appeared more daunting by the moment, for both of the boys were looking at me with mutinous expressions. I held my tongue, biting back the urge to say that old nurses should be put to rest, and focused on the boys. "Well, I daresay our first lesson will be—"

"I don't want lessons." Little Robert burst into a renewed storm of tears. "I want a mother!"

The longing in his cry pulled at my heart.

"Robert!" Benedict Trevelyan bellowed.

I knew from his obvious exasperation that another admonishment on gentleman-like behavior was about to be delivered. A firm hand needed to be tempered by the needs of the child, and my instincts were telling me that little Robert needed a touch of love and understanding. I couldn't imagine what life as a child without a mother would be like, but I knew it had to be terribly hard. For I, though grown, deeply missed my own. Before Benedict Trevelyan or Robert could say anything else, I interjected myself into the situation. "Odd that you should say that, Master Robert, because that's exactly the first thing we're going to study. Mothers. To find a mother, you have to know exactly what you are looking for."

Robert's teary eyes went wide even as he shut his mouth, silencing his next wail. Benedict Trevelyan seemed startled—the grim line of his jaw dropped a bit—but I didn't give any of them time to question.

"Morning is the best time for such a study as that, so we must hurry and get this mess cleaned up, or it will be too late today for that lesson. Master Justin, if you would please fetch me a handful of rags, we will get started. Master Robert, find a stool to make yourself tall enough to reach the sink."

The boys were slow-moving at first, clearly torn between wanting to object and curiosity over what kind of lesson I had in mind. Once they were in motion, I turned my back on them and grabbed the broom Maria had abandoned. Benedict Trevelyan hadn't moved yet. I glanced his way. "Please let me know when you wish to reschedule our appointment. There's no need for you to disrupt your morning schedule a moment more; I am sure the boys and I will deal well with one another."

He blinked, and a mortified flush heated my cheeks. In my nervous haste, I believe I'd just dismissed the master of Trevelyan Hill.

To my relief, he didn't comment, just headed toward the door. "Dobbs will get you anything you need, Miss Lovell."

"Thank you," I said.

"Very well then, Miss Lovell. I will see you at dinner this evening." With that, he left the room, but his departure did nothing to alleviate my chaffed nerves. His presence had a way of lingering long after he had gone.

After the mess was cleared away, in a surprisingly short time, the boys and I stepped outside to the formal gardens that spanned part of the distance between the manor and the craggy cliffs of the bay to my left. To the right lay the stables, and beyond that, a hilly stretch of shady trees thickening to a forest. The sun had managed to chase away the lingering mists of the morn that had greeted me earlier, and a lone gull spun playfully in the blue sky before it called out a good-bye and darted away.

I looked back at the glorious stained window held captive between the two small turrets and crowned by the tallest turret, and drew a deep breath of the invigorating salty breeze coming from the bay. My practical spirit soared with wonder at the change in my life. The colors of the late spring's flowers rivaled those within the stained glass. Bluebells and gladiolas danced behind rows of red, gold, purple, and pink flowers, but were just colorful frames for what would soon be the garden's crowning glory—hundreds of lush green rosebushes laden with a multitude of buds.

A massive white marble fountain graced the center of the garden in the form of a delicate angel. With her protective wings spread wide, she presided joyfully over the surrounding beauty. I promised myself to return with my sketchbook as soon as I could, hoping that before the roses lost their blooms to the fall, I'd be able to afford paints to put this glory upon paper.

The breeze from the bay tugged at wisps of my hair, pulling them from my bun, which had been loosened by Benedict Trevelyan's hand after my fall. I thought it rather unseemly, but I felt too free, too delighted in the morning, to worry with fixing my bun.

"You lieded to me. There's no mothers out here." Robert stamped his foot upon the cobblestone walkway, but there was more disappointment than petulance in his voice.

Returning my attention to the task before me, I turned to the little boy. Rather than chastise him, I wanted to hug him tight, to ease the pain I heard crying from his heart. I had to wrap my fingers into the folds of my skirt to stop myself. Instinctively, I knew that though he wanted love, he wouldn't welcome it from a stranger. I smiled at him instead, which set him off balance, for I think he expected to be reprimanded. "Then you must not be able to see anything at all, Master Robert, because there are dozens of mothers all around us. Why, all of these flowers and plants had to have a mommy sometime." Robert didn't look impressed.

Walking over to a wispy web stretching between the

leaves of two flowering gladiolas, I pointed to a tiny sac cleverly hidden in one corner. "Do you know what is in there?"

"No." Robert scrunched his nose and moved closer to the web. Justin rolled his eyes as if he knew everything there was to know.

"Master Justin, while I tell Robert about the mother spider and her babies, why don't you hunt up another example for us to study."

Justin blinked, much the same way as his father did when confronted with the unexpected. The endearing reaction brought a warm smile to my lips and set off a distant tinkling of what might be warning bells. Surely I couldn't be so impractical as to develop a fondness for anything that Benedict Trevelyan did. I quickly turned to Robert to avoid any excuse Justin might offer, and refused to believe that I was escaping from my own thoughts, too.

When I pointed out the little sac where spider babies hid, Robert beamed with interest.

"How many babies are in there?"

"Quite a few, I should think. Some spider mommies can have hundreds."

"Really? That many in there?"

"They are very tiny."

His dark eyes grew big. Then he frowned and leaned closer to the web, nearly planting his nose in it. "Where is the mommy spider?"

Oh, dear. I'd stumbled onto a problem. Once laying eggs, some spiders moved on or died. What if there was no mommy spider? I examined the web closely, too. "We will have to look for her tomorrow. The spider mommy left all the babies wrapped up in a soft blanket, and inside there she left them food, too."

"How?" Robert asked.

"She worked hard to spin this big web, and then she waited. When a fat juicy insect flew into her trap, she didn't gobble him up for herself. She tied up the bug, put her spider eggs next to it, and made them safe with her own special blanket."

"Miss Lovell."

I looked up to see Justin waving from near the end of the gardens. He stood beneath the full boughs of a sturdy oak with a smile as big as a plum pie. I assumed that he'd found a bird nest.

"Let's go see Master Justin," I said, lightly touching Robert's shoulder.

Justin had found an ant nest. Robert glared at it. "There's no mommies and babies in there. There's only mean ants."

I remembered how formidable I'd thought ants were when I was little. "Ants have a mommy who has thousands of babies. So, yes, there's a mommy in the nest, thousands of babies; and all the ants you see running about are working to feed and protect the mommy ant and her babies."

Expressing his boredom, Justin picked up a stick and started drawing circles in a patch of dirt nearby.

Robert studied the anthill for a moment. "Does the mommy ant leave the babies or stay with them?"

"She stays with them."

"That's nice," Robert said.

Justin came over and stabbed the stick into the anthill. "There," he said. "Now the mommy will leave just like ours."

I stepped back from the angry, scurrying ants, pulling Robert with me.

"You killed the mommy," Robert shouted. Then, slipping from my grasp, he went after Justin with his fists flying.

Justin yelled, and Robert cried. Any minute they'd both topple into the ants.

"Hold it," I shouted, but I might as well have been speaking to a washboard. About that time, I saw Benedict Trevelyan exit the manor. Panic raced up my spine, rendering my bones to water. Please God. I could not have this situation be his first impression of my teaching abilities.

Driven to desperation, I let out a shrill whistle that would have rivaled cannon fire. I daresay they had never heard a lady whistle before, especially not with such volume. I had definitely gotten their attention. Out of the corner of my eye, I saw Benedict Trevelyan quicken his pace in our direction. I stabbed at my hair, stuffing it any way I could to form some semblance of a proper bun.

"Master Justin, put down that stick immediately. Being older means having the intelligence to be kind to those around you. After I speak to your father, you and I will discuss this incident. You will be given the opportunity to explain yourself, and that explanation had better be good.

"Master Robert, dry your tears and straighten your attire to greet your father. The mother ant lives deep in the ground, as do the babies, and they are most likely undisturbed by Master Justin's thoughtless action. You must realize that growing bigger carries the responsibility to carefully consider your actions even in the face of provocation. Twice today, you have created havoc. The first incident has cost you a full dinner. I would hate to see you pay a second price today."

I knew Benedict Trevelyan had to be getting close to us, so I launched into a quick lesson about sound. The diversion would give us all a moment to collect ourselves. Both my new charges carried hurts that would need a great deal of love and understanding to heal, and the task daunted me.

"Now, sirs. I must hear each of you whistle." Robert's attempt was a soundless puff of air. Justin's had more sound, but nothing to brag about.

"You both need a lot of work if you're going to learn how to whistle like a man with salt."

"What's a man with salt?" Robert asked.

I'd learned the expression from Captain Balder, who'd taught me navigation. He'd use it to describe a good ship hand. I knew that Benedict Trevelyan had to be within hearing distance, and failure loomed over me. I hadn't been hired to teach the boys how to whistle and to characterize men as salts. "Why, a man who is, well, uh, a man who is—"

"Worthy?" Benedict Trevelyan inquired from just behind my left shoulder.

He stopped close enough by my side that I felt his body's heat and smelled hints of sandalwood and leather flavoring the air. Sensing the force of his direct scrutiny, my heart wrangled with my mind as to which would function properly.

"Exactly," I concurred as I thanked my mind for winning and chastised my heart for its fluttering ways. "In order to whistle, you must first understand the dynamics of sound. When you whistle, sound is created by how much air you push through how little a space. To accomplish this you must align your lips and tongue just right." I demonstrated another whistle, though not as loud as my last.

The boys tried again, and were encouraged by the slight improvement in their sound-making capabilities. As they practiced, I turned to Benedict Trevelyan.

"We were just about to go in for a lesson in mathematics," I finished lamely. I thought I'd sufficiently braced myself for the strength of his presence, but I found my breath catch in my throat again as I tilted my head up to see him.

Sunlight gleamed off his dark hair and the rich brown of his coat with a vibrancy that matched his eyes. He neither smiled nor frowned, so I did not know what he thought of our activity. His gaze left mine and studied the boys for a moment.

In the full light of the sun, the shadow of his beard darkened his face, and I imagined that the feel of his determined jaw would be as interestingly rough as his coat would be luxuriantly soft. Again I dug my fingers into the folds of my skirts, stilling my urge to touch, then belatedly noticed he'd returned his attention to me. He glanced down at my hands wrapped so tightly in my skirt and quirked his brow, but thankfully made no comment upon my odd behavior. I knew I had to be horribly wrinkling my dress.

"You need to know that the cliffs are forbidden to the children. Near the edge the ground can be unstable, and most any fall would be fatal."

"Thank you. I will make sure the children stay safe." About that moment a gust of wind undid my hasty bun, and my hair blew across my face, blinding me. Before I could reach up, Benedict Trevelyan drew his finger down the side of my face, catching the errant tress in his fingers.

"Yourself, also," he said, taking me by surprise. He didn't release my hair immediately, but slid his thumb across the strands several times, as if relishing the texture of my hair for a moment, before easing the tress behind my ear. I tingled in every place he touched, which made every place forbidden to his touch ache. My curiosity over the mysteries between a man and a woman grew tenfold within a moment's time. It would seem gloves were going to be very little protection from Benedict Trevelyan's touch, for I realized my need was as potent as his appeal.

Perhaps I should have taken offense at his momentary familiarity, but besides my mother and Mr. McGuire, few in this bustling town of ever-increasing strangers had expressed concern for my well-being. Though I held all life sacred, such was not the reality of the West. I had no illusions as to the harshness of life, and his words and gesture touched me inside, easing the loneliness.

He stepped back from me, shaking his head as if to dispel his thoughts, and I drew a deep breath.

"Justin and Robert, do not forget your punishments this evening," he said curtly, then turned and strode purposefully toward the stables.

The boys' whistling efforts immediately fell flat, and the yearning for their father's approval on their faces reminded me of newborn babes crying for help. Benedict Trevelyan had either ignored his sons' needs or had walked away oblivious to them. I felt the kernel of warmth that his concern for my welfare had instilled turn cold, and I wondered if there weren't more hazardous things than crumbling cliffs in a child's life.

This thought tempered my words as I addressed their earlier skirmish. I took care not to delve into Robert's hunger for a mother and Justin's resentment that he didn't have one just yet. I felt those issues—though the root of their problems—would be best discussed when I knew them better. So, after giving Justin the opportunity to explain, during which he remained sullenly silent, I admonished them lightly on gentlemanly conduct, and we wound our way back through the gardens. The boys ran ahead, breaking into a little game of tag. I slowed my pace to afford them more time to play, glad to see a bit of their natural exuberance coming back to life.

As I walked, I looked up, seeking another glimpse of the magnificent stained glass. I froze mid-step, and my blood drained in a rush even as fear twisted inside me. Framed in the tallest turret's window, almost as if she were about to jump, stood a beautiful woman.

❦ 4 ❧

The breeze from the bay ruffled her white gown and black hair in a ghostly sway. I lifted my hand to her, trying to force my voice through the tightness of my throat. "Don't," I cautioned her, wanting to stop her from falling or jumping.

I knew not what she intended. But she did not hear me. I was too far away. Her gaze remained focused upon the horizon, a picture of winsome sadness, of tragedy.

Glancing over my shoulder to see what absorbed her so thoroughly, I realized that she stared toward the bay beyond the dark cliffs, as if looking for a ship from the sea. When I turned back, the woman had disappeared. Fear gripped me as I rushed past the bushes to see the ground beneath the turret's window. Bloodred roses, a large neat grouping of them, lay under the window, mocking my imagination. I shuddered, wondering if I had seen the woman at all.

No, I thought, stiffening my spine as I entered the manor house in search of Justin and Robert. I would not doubt myself. Yet the incident left me shaken and testy. Dobbs stood inside the house, near the doorway, a jackal ready to pounce. "Miss Low—"

"Lovell, but I am willing to make an allowance for your apparent forgetfulness. You may call me Miss L. That shouldn't be difficult. It is spelled M . . . I . . . S . . . S . . . L and pronounced exactly—"

"Miss Lovell!" Dobbs's voice cut through the room, and he flinched, apparently mortified at his loss of composure. I seriously doubted he'd forget my name again. I had the satisfaction of seeing his face mottle to a dark purple before he collected himself and spoke through clenched teeth. "Are you or are you not presently in charge of Masters Justin and Robert?"

"Of course. We are moving from our outside studies to the schoolroom. Do you have a problem, Mr. Dobbs?"

"No, Miss Lovell. You have a problem. They just ran obnoxiously through the house like—"

"Children," I said, preempting whatever colorful analogy he'd been about to utter. "I will speak to them about restraining their enthusiasm for life to outdoor play. But it would behoove you to remember that Masters Justin and Robert are young boys of a tender age and in need of fun and affection."

I turned from him, intending to make my way to the schoolroom, praying I'd find Justin and Robert there and not engaging in further mischief. Three steps away, I recalled the woman in the window. I spoke to Dobbs's back, for he was exiting the room in the opposite direction. "Mr. Dobbs, perhaps you can tell me. I saw a woman in the center turret's window. She had long black hair and wore a white dressing gown as if she were ill. Who is she?"

Dobbs's purple hue blanched white. "Mrs. Trevelyan's death and her ghost are forbidden subjects to the servants in this household. No one is ever permitted in that turret. It has been sealed off from everyone since her death. I suggest you keep your fancifulness to yourself if you value your job. Good day, Miss Lovell."

He couldn't have dealt me a more shocking blow if he

had felled me with his fist. Mrs. Trevelyan, as in the deceased Francesca Trevelyan? Her ghost? Good Lord. She must have jumped from that tower, and the realization cast a shadow over my castle-like image of the manor, that of knights, and ladies, and dragons.

My practicality shouted that I'd seen a flesh-and-blood woman, not a ghostly apparition or even a figment of my imagination, and the incident plagued me throughout the day. I kept Justin and Robert busy. We studied mathematics and science and reviewed the not-too-distant past events that enabled California to qualify for statehood, and then they each chose a game to teach me how to play. They needed to know that I loved to learn, too. That I was willing to listen to them and thought they had something important to say.

Benedict Trevelyan didn't appear again, and I didn't turn Justin and Robert over to their nurse until they were ready for bed after they'd gotten their bread and water—plus a bowl of gravy for dipping purposes, thanks to the cook.

Cook Thomas, I found, was a jovial man who'd spent many years at sea. He had a girth as big as his laugh and a kind nature that reminded me of Captain Balder. I was surprised to learn he'd been Benedict Trevelyan's cook when Benedict Trevelyan had captained a ship by the name of *Freedom*. In fact, according to Cook Thomas, a number of Benedict Trevelyan's crew who'd been injured or too old to find work on another ship worked for him here. This bit of information intrigued me, for it hinted that the master of Trevelyan Hill wasn't as merciless as he appeared. Yet I could very readily picture him at the helm of a large ship, unbending as he headed into a violent storm with an iron-clad determination that gave no quarter for weaknesses. A determination that was as unsinkable as the *Monitor* and *Merrimack* had proved to be during the recent War between the North and the South—an event that hadn't touched our lives in the West as deeply as the building of the railroad or the discovery of gold.

Unlike Dobbs and Maria, Cook Thomas didn't fit with the darkness of the manor house and its master, and the incongruity made me wonder if Benedict Trevelyan was as implacable as he seemed. For the very first thing Cook Thomas did was to ease the severity of Benedict Trevelyan's punishment by giving the boys gravy to go with their bread. His care of Justin and Robert warmed me and won my heart. The children and I lingered in the kitchen, listening to stories of the perils of the sea, for a long time. I didn't return Justin and Robert to their nurse's care until late, leaving myself very little time to prepare for dinner. Entertaining and teaching the children left me as worn as a miner's breeches, but I didn't regret my new path in life. I found the day's work so much more satisfying than a mound of laundry.

Several times during the day, I considered declining Benedict Trevelyan's request to join the family for dinner. It wasn't my place to be a guest at their table, and I was uncomfortable with the completely impractical idea. I also worried it would only give the wrong impression of what I considered my station in life, but I had yet to meet the other members of the household, and my curiosity would give me no peace. Indeed, I fear my curiosity was greater than my sense of practicality—a surprising fact for me to realize. But that was the truth of it. I wanted to see all of the Trevelyans that I knew lived within the manor's dark walls—Benedict Trevelyan's mother, his sister, and his sister-in-law, the late Mrs. Trevelyan's sister. I wanted to know which of the women had been in the turret window this morning. For despite the fact that Dobbs claimed the turret was sealed off, I knew I'd seen someone in it. And I refused to believe in ghosts.

As I stepped into my new room, I immediately detected the scent of roses. It lingered gently in the air as if a bouquet of blooms lay nearby, or a lady with means enough to indulge her senses in such heavenly things had just passed through. Except for the rare occasions when I ventured to Holloway Park and collected the petals of wildflowers for a sachet, I'd known only the acridity of lye soap and the freshness of warm sunshine. The rose scent stopped me in my tracks.

A shiver ran through me as my mind leapt back to this morning. The woman in the turret window, the blood-red roses below, and Dobbs's intimation that I'd seen a ghost . . .

No. Ghosts, if they existed at all, were transparent apparitions bent on instilling fear in the hearts of those unfortunate enough to encounter them. Ghosts did not stand like a flesh-and-blood woman. And ghosts most certainly did not gad about smelling like roses. Besides, I was entirely too practical to believe in such nonsense.

Thus, having garnered my courage, I shut the door and searched my room thoroughly. I felt vindicated when I discovered a few of my belongings disturbed from the place where I had left them on the desk. And I breathed a sigh of relief to find my mother's silver comb, her journals, and her gun all safe in the carpetbag on the top shelf of the armoire. Not that I feared having my things stolen; I just didn't want to ever lose the few mementoes of her. The ewer for the washbasin had been filled and fresh towels placed for my use.

I wrote the incident off as merely a maid's curiosity and ignored the remaining doubt that asked if a maid would smell of roses. Quickly making use of the refreshing water and, to my joy, a small bar of lavender soap, I changed into my brown cotton dress and twisted my hair into a reserved bun. As I did, I remembered Benedict Trevelyan brushing his thumb over its silken texture and threading his fingers through it as he examined me for injury. I found myself studying my reflection in the washstand's beveled mirror, worrying if the Trevelyans—especially Benedict Trevelyan— would find my appearance acceptable.

"For heaven's sakes." I chastised myself for such foolishness and marched to the door. Surely I wasn't a woman given to concerns of that nature.

But before I could force myself to leave, I dashed back to my hat upon the dresser, filched the lace from its brim, and tucked the delicate scrap about the neck of my gown. As I left the room, I blamed exposure to the morning sun for the color fanning my cheeks.

I hurried downstairs, thoroughly convincing myself that my interest in my appearance rested solely upon the fact that I now held a new position in life. It had nothing to do with the look in Benedict Trevelyan's eyes this morning. That was only the wild imaginings of a spinster. In the entryway, I turned a blind eye to the stained glass windows, lest they should tempt me to linger, and I followed the sounds of voices until I discerned the words being spoken. Then I froze, too mortified even to breathe.

"Really, Benedict, this penchant you have of catering to the unfortunate has gone too far this time," a woman said, her voice nasal and cold. "A homely washerwoman is in charge of educating my grandsons? A woman no better than a beggar off the streets? Surely Maria must be mistaken."

"Am I to take it that you'd find a beautiful washerwoman acceptable then, Mother?"

"Botheration. Do not start twisting my words around. What is the truth of the situation?"

"You heard correctly, though I would hardly consider Maria an intelligent source of information," he said, and my stomach cramped and roiled. I knew my station in life, but to hear it put so bluntly was disturbing. *No better than a beggar off the streets.*

I almost missed the rest of what Benedict said, but his deep voice reached through my embarrassment. "The supposed washerwoman is not only cognizant that Newton made scientific studies of the characteristics of light as well as the gravity of an apple, she also seems to be gifted at capturing and holding my sons' attention. And I daresay the woman has a great deal more practical sense than to chase Robert around the kitchen with a broom. So all in all, until I see otherwise, my sons are better off under the tutelage of an intelligent and well-versed washerwoman than under the care of a blundering nurse. Miss Lovell is nowhere near a beggar off the streets. I consider the subject closed."

"He's such a tyrant, don't you agree?" a male voice whispered right next to my ear. I jumped with fright, nearly knocking the man over as my shoulder clipped his jaw.

I'd been caught eavesdropping again. Mortified, I swung around to see a pair of bloodshot blue eyes blinking at me as Stephen Trevelyan rubbed his chin and worked his jaw. He didn't seem to be the least put off about the accident. In fact, he was grinning and looking at me, quite frankly, with interest.

Shocked, I patted my chest. "My word, you gave me a fright, Mr. Trevelyan."

"So sorry. You must be the new governess, Miss Lovell. I am *Stephen* Trevelyan. With Ben at the head of the family, there's only room for one Mr. Trevelyan. So please call me Stephen. May I call you Ann?" He held out his hand, and after hesitating a moment, I shook it, trying to stifle my smile. The man was outrageously familiar, especially in light of his status and mine, yet I liked him.

"I suppose," I replied, a bit disconcerted. He did not

release my hand, and what I noticed most about his touch is that it did not carry the penetrating impact Benedict Trevelyan's did.

"From the blistering old Ben gave me earlier, it seems that I owe you an apology. And now that I have met you, I feel sorely vexed at myself for falling into your arms and not remembering a jot of it."

"I see you two have met," Benedict Trevelyan said. He stared at us from the doorway.

Heat flushed my cheeks, and I pulled my hand from Stephen Trevelyan's. "Yes, just now. Here in the corridor." Though Benedict Trevelyan didn't say anything, the disapproval in the grim set of his lips practically shouted at me. I took another step away from his brother. My feet moved even before my mind registered the implications of such a movement. I had nothing to feel guilty about, but my actions indicated otherwise.

"Are Katherine and Constance down yet?" Stephen Trevelyan asked, his voice several degrees colder than when he'd spoken to me.

"No, but Mother is. She's eager to see you."

"Duty calls, Miss Ann. And please remember to call me Stephen. After all, I hear we became quite close this morning." Winking at me, Stephen Trevelyan moved past and entered the room.

I lifted my hand to my brow, brushing away the perspiration that suddenly beaded my skin. I felt strange, possibly even ill. Stephen Trevelyan's familiarity was a bit disconcerting, but Benedict Trevelyan's scrutiny was completely unnerving. "Perhaps I will go and—"

"Perhaps you would like to accompany me to the garden for a few moments and tell me your impressions of my sons. I know Mother and Stephen will want to spend a few minutes alone. Constance is habitually a quarter of an hour

late, and Katherine . . ." He shrugged. "Well, no one can pre-
dict what she will do. She is shy and may decide to delay
meeting you for a time yet."

Very little news of Benedict Trevelyan's sister, Katherine,
had ever filtered down to my ears, but I'd heard several
things. One was that she had a debilitating illness; the other
was that she was mad, but I had no intention of asking him
about his family. I was practical enough to realize the
boundaries of my station and would adhere to them, no
matter how curious I was.

The fresh air of the garden appealed to me as just what
my nerves needed, even though I suspected that Trevelyan's
presence would immediately nullify any calming effect the
evening breeze and fading light might provide.

I should go back to my bedchamber, I thought. Not to
hide as much as to settle myself back into what I considered
my proper role as a governess. Truly, going from laundress
to walking in the garden and eating dinner with the master
of Trevelyan Hill was more than I felt ready to swallow.
Though it was somewhat comforting that Benedict didn't
consider me to be a beggar off the streets, there was no way
to hide the fact that I did not belong.

Yet complying with his demand that I give him my
impressions of his sons was part of my job, and I could not
deny his request. "The garden is fine," I said.

He motioned for me to precede him across the entryway
and out the rear door to the garden. "This way, then."

As I passed him, the awareness of his presence behind
me penetrated every nuance of my being—his size, his heat,
the surety of his step. Even the power of his gaze upon me
affected me. He was a large man, and never in my life had I
felt more of a woman than I did in his company.

Unfortunately, the garden by day with his sons was not
the same garden by evening with the man himself. The

shadows beyond the angel fountain were darker, the breeze from the bay more invigorating, and the scent of the flowers sweeter.

I slowed my step, not wanting to trespass into the more intimate shadows near the edges of the garden. He adjusted his step to mine; the gentlemanly consideration only made me more aware of him beside me, and I had to force myself to focus on my purpose in being in the garden with him. "What about your sons do you wish to know?"

"As I said. Your impression of them, but first I must mention that Dobbs said—"

My back stiffened. "I apologized to him for that. I will not let it happen again."

He caught my elbow, forcing me to stop and face him. His eyes were too black, as if they held too many secrets to ever lighten with a smile. The sharp angles of his features that I'd taken so close a note of the day before imprinted themselves again into my mind, only deeper and subtly different this time. The Roman nose and conquering chin were the same, but in the dimmer light his lips appeared softer, as did his manner.

A ruffling breeze from the bay played with his raven hair and lent him an air of rakish vulnerability that I didn't want to see, for it made him even more attractive. His fingers upon my arm were warm, so very warm through the fabric of my dress that I knew they'd burn were he to touch my skin directly. A wonderfully pleasurable burn, I thought, remembering the feel of his hands upon my person from this morning. I shut my eyes.

"I'm curious, Miss Lovell. What exactly are you apologizing for?" He released my arm, but the heat of his touch lingered. The urge to touch him, to see if I affected him the way he affected me, washed over me.

My eyes popped open, and I clenched the skirt of my

dress with my hands. What had I been apologizing for? The children. I had to clear my throat to find my voice. "Yes, well, for the children running up to the school room for their lessons. Mr. Dobbs has already called me to the carpet for their boisterous manner."

Benedict Trevelyan's lips twitched, but just as before, the hint of humor never reached his eyes. "As I was about to say, Dobbs informed me that both Justin and Robert were calmer today than they have been in quite some time."

Blinking, I registered that Dobbs had actually uttered something decent about my care of the children. "I am sure the calmness was due to the fact that they had new things to learn and think about today. Both Master Justin and Master Robert are bright children who very much want approval, but I sense they have unresolved hurts that cause them to lash out with their emotions. They need direction, encouragement, understanding, and the sense that they are loved. Once those needs are met, I believe some of their unruliness will subside."

"Only some?" He lifted his brow, emphasizing he'd hoped for more.

I couldn't tell if he spoke in jest or not. "As well as being practical, Mr. Trevelyan, I am also realistic. Master Justin and Master Robert are lively boys. They are children, and a certain amount of enthusiasm and rambunctiousness are inevitable." His gaze focused on my mouth as I spoke, and my throat became dry.

"*Inevitable* has never been a favored word of mine," he said softly, almost as if he spoke only to himself. Then he lifted his gaze to mine, and I tensed as a strange feeling of expectation filled me. "I thought I had more control over circumstances and life for *inevitable* to ever be a part of them. But perhaps I am . . . mistaken."

From the deepness of his voice and the intensity in his

eyes, I thought he spoke of something other than the children, and my breath caught on the notion that the inevitable had something to do with me. I found myself subtly leaning toward him, as if a strong magnet drew me. The thought of being kissed by this man sent my mind and blood racing. He looked at my lips again. Did he want to kiss me?

My lips parted before my sensibilities could stand up and shout their disapproval. When they did, I realized that everything I felt was surely a figment of my imagination, and I was making an utter fool out of myself. I scrambled for something to say as I fought the overwhelming urge to run and hide.

I spoke in a rush. "Cook Thomas mentioned you captained a ship, Mr. Trevelyan. Do you miss it? I have been told there is nothing like seeing the stars with only the ocean on the horizon." Turning abruptly, I looked at the night sky, pretending to study the stars a moment, even though my nervous state made them nothing but a blur.

"Do I hear a note of envy, Miss Lovell?"

"Perhaps," I said, forcing a calming breath to moderate the tone of my voice. "I have wondered many times what the stars are like on the underside of the world."

He stepped closer to me, lifted his hand, and pointed without hesitation, immediately knowing where he stood in the universe. "Instead of the North Star to guide like we have here, they have the Southern Cross. Its five stars would lie in this direction. And over here, Sagittarius aims his arrow at Scorpius's deadly tail, which is marked by a bright red star known as Antares."

Almost seeing the constellations of which he spoke, I leaned his way, and my arm brushed his side. I felt the heat of his hand press against my back, urging me nearer. His voice deepened again, as if he were sharing something very special. "And Centaurus, the half-man half-horse creature of myth, lurks over here, waiting for unsuspecting prey to wander into his arms."

"There you are, Benedict." A woman's sultry voice, flavored with a Spanish accent, startled me, stealing away the vision of stars. I stepped back from Mr. Trevelyan's nearness, turning to see who approached.

A dark-haired woman, dressed in a rich, soft pink gown, approached us. Her walk matched her voice— intriguing and effervescent. She was beautiful in a delicate and exotic way, petite with ivory skin and curly black hair that she'd swept into an elaborate style and held in place by gleaming Spanish combs. She waved her hands as she spoke, and I couldn't help but notice how creamy white and delicate they were. They were beautiful hands. Not like mine. I tucked mine into the folds of my dress. "Stephen suggested you might have ventured into the garden, but I did not believe him. I asked myself, does Benedict ever walk in the garden during the evening? I answer no. He tells me he is always too busy for such a trivial thing. Yet here you are."

"Discussing my sons' unruliness with their new governess," he said slightly forcefully, as if he were rushing to stem the bubbling of the woman's words. He took a step back from me, too.

I didn't think I'd ever met so small a woman, or one who expressed herself in so physical a way.

"Constance, this is the governess, Miss Ann Lovell. Miss Lovell, this is Miss Ortega, my sister-in-law. She has been helping care for Justin and Robert."

"This is a surprise, Benedict. You did not mention you had found someone to teach the children, though Maria and I were managing them well enough. Welcome, Miss Lovell," she said, extending her hand to me.

"Thank you, Miss Ortega," I said, taking her hand. I didn't like the tone she used when she'd spoken of Justin and Robert. She sounded as if they were tiresome pests.

She had a butterfly shake, barely there and barely felt before she turned to Benedict Trevelyan. "Dinner is served, and we must hurry, yes? Cook Thomas is threatening to go back to sea."

"As usual," he said, extending his arm. "Ladies first."

Given no choice, I was forced to walk in front of him again. Only this time, with Miss Ortega at my side, I was acutely aware of my ungainly height next to her petite proportions, and I cringed at the thought that he would be making the same comparison. My brown cotton dress and its borrowed lace, so painfully plain next to Miss Ortega's beautiful muslin gown, had to be an eyesore.

Though I'd resigned myself to my lot in life long ago, I now realized that by escaping the bleak life of a laundress, I'd put myself in a position to continually expose my deficiencies.

Every choice had consequences.

As I entered the dining room, I deducted from the cold stare directed my way that the middle-aged woman was Benedict Trevelyan's mother, and I wondered what other consequences I would face in choosing to pass through the demon-carved doors of Trevelyan Manor. For if looks were capable of killing, I'd be dead upon the spot.

Mrs. Trevelyan sat in a wheelchair pushed up to the table. Her hair was piled in an elaborate style, its darkness a stark contrast to her pale skin. A sprig of white lace about her neck relieved the severity of her black silk gown, but that one bright accessory was overshadowed by her baleful expression and the grim set of her lips. Her husband had died two years before, yet she was still in mourning. Her hands were lily-white, too.

No one seemed to notice that she'd wished me dead with one look. Benedict Trevelyan introduced me to her. She inclined her head my way, but didn't speak. Stephen Trevelyan, a drink in his hand, stood at one end of an ornate mahogany dining table; its curved legs ended in claws that reminded me of the demons and beasts on the manor's front door. The chairs, fashioned with ivy leaves etched in the dark wood, were padded and looked immensely expensive, as did the crystal chandelier centered above us. I marveled at the gas lighting. I had heard of this luxury, but had yet to see it for myself.

"Is Katherine not coming?" Benedict Trevelyan asked.

Miss Ortega threw her hands up, then used them to accent her every word. "She is in one of her impossible moods again. We were absorbed in a fashion article from *Frank Leslie's Illustrated Newspaper*. Did you realize, Benedict, that the elite in New York *do not* wear the same dress twice? When it comes to fashion, we are so appallingly behind here. They recommend a lady travel with no less than sixty dresses. I must order three Swiss muslin evening robes before the weather turns chilly. The climate here is so much cooler than the weather at our hacienda, no? It will be the death of me. But, *madre de Dios,* when Katherine learned Stephen had arrived, she—" Biting her lip, Miss Ortega sent Stephen Trevelyan an apologetic look. "I think your return has upset her."

Sixty dresses! My mind could hardly fathom such an extravagance. Bouncing my gaze to Stephen Trevelyan, I saw an expression of deep pain sweep over his face before he hid it by taking a hefty sip of his drink.

"I will speak to her," Benedict Trevelyan said with almost a sigh, as if the burdens he carried weighed heavily on him.

"I will handle it," Stephen Trevelyan replied, his voice strained.

"Then I take it you are planning to stay sober?" Benedict Trevelyan said, his tone harsh.

Stephen Trevelyan fisted his hands and placed them on the table, his handsome face darkened with anger. For a moment, I thought he'd leap over the table at his brother. "God forbid. I had forgotten how perfect you are."

"That's enough," Mrs. Trevelyan commanded, then picked up the bell resting on the table before her and rang it. "I will have civility at my meals."

Dinner proceeded with an edge of tense politeness between Benedict Trevelyan and his brother. Their mother remained mostly silent unless she spoke to criticize something. Toward the end of the dinner, she excused herself, citing illness. Her departure surprised me a little, since she'd said several times how glad she was that Stephen had returned home.

The moment Mrs. Trevelyan left, Miss Ortega caught Benedict Trevelyan's attention by waving her hand. "I saw the *Commodore* anchored in the bay while I was out shopping today. What cargo did she bring?"

"The last shipment of sugar I will be transporting. I am selling her." Benedict Trevelyan leaned back in his chair and crossed his arms, clearly stating ahead of time that his decision was final. I was surprised he felt the need to make that statement to fashion-minded Miss Ortega.

I thought Miss Ortega paled beneath the brightness of the gas lighting. "But you cannot—"

"Constance, dear, we've been over this a hundred times. You do not need to worry about this. The railroad has changed the shipping industry. There are more profitable business ventures closer to home than having the expense and uncertainty of transporting goods across the oceans."

"What is there besides the railroads?" Stephen Trevelyan

asked. "Which, if you ask me, are overflowing with crooks."

"Steamboats," Benedict answered. "Alan Henderson is selling me his stocks. The company has a monopoly on bay transportation. In return, I am introducing him to several buyers for his cattle in Sacramento. He will be here next week."

"Good. Maybe I can get back the hundred dollars he fleeced from me the last time I saw him. I swear the man cheats at cards, but I have not caught him yet," Stephen said, shaking his head, wry amusement curving his lips. "If I were you"—he nodded to his brother—"I would investigate this stock he's offering thoroughly. Alan and Father had a penchant for bad investments."

"The California Steam Navigation Company has paid increasing dividends for several years. I expect it will only grow as the Bay Area's population continues to expand."

"Perhaps you will take me to see these steamboats that you speak of soon?" Constance spoke to Benedict Trevelyan who in turn nodded to Stephen Trevelyan.

"I presently have not the leisure time to do so. Do you think you will remain sober enough to take her, Stephen?"

Constance interrupted before Stephen Trevelyan unclenched his jaw enough to speak. "Have I mentioned that Swiss muslin robes are all the rage? I will need for you to take me shopping very soon, Stephen. And I must have an authentic paisley scarf. Mrs. Barrow wore one to the governor's tea and looked absolutely divine."

Before Constance finished, she'd added two Saratoga trunks, a white llama jacket, and a ball gown imported from Paris to her list of wants, and all to be done before the next social season.

My head hurt from her chatter. As soon as dinner was over, I excused myself, citing my need to prepare the boys' lessons for the next day. After being exposed to Miss Ortega,

Mrs. Trevelyan, and Nurse Maria, I thought it a miracle that Benedict Trevelyan had hired me at all. Had his wife been anything like Miss Ortega? A woman pampered and catered to? But then, with women so daintily beautiful, what else was a man to do?

It was a good thing that I had such a strong constitution.

Walking back to my room, my mind slowly eased from thoughts of the evening and once again I felt as if I was being watched. The dimly lit hallway seemed longer and the shadows more sinister. Darkness had fallen, and the window at the end of the corridor reflected a shadowy image of myself as I drew closer to my room.

I had never been given to flights of fancy, and I despised myself now for the shiver inching its way down my spine. I closed my eyes to give myself a thorough dressing-down.

Just because I'd managed to change my station in life didn't mean I should lose hold of my practicality. Both my awareness of Benedict Trevelyan as a man and these silly notions that I was being watched had to stop. Thus chastised, I opened my eyes and nearly fell on my face as I missed a step. Behind me, reflected in the window, stood a black-haired woman in a white gown. Crying out, I swung around and thought I saw the fleeing edge of a gown move from sight around the corner. I grabbed up my skirts and dashed toward the disappearing woman, heedless of the noise my thudding steps made.

Turning the corner, I bumped into Dobbs. Unfortunately, the towels he carried like a Leaning Tower of Pisa in front of him went flying. He stood there in the hall, his eyes bulging with outrage and his wispy hair sticking out in tufts.

"Miss Lovell," he said through clenched teeth, "is there a bloody fire?"

"No, just walking briskly. It is good for my constitution," I said, collecting the towels and stacking them again. Stuffing them into his arms, I gave him a sunny smile. "You should watch where you're going."

"Me watch!"

"Yes, you could harm yourself," I said, then left him gasping like a fish out of water.

The scent of roses lingered about me, but I wasn't about to ask Dobbs again about the mysterious woman. I'd yet to meet Katherine Trevelyan, and I wondered why she or anyone else would wish to frighten me.

Were I a woman given to such notions as haunting ghosts, I might have been tempted to flee as my hired driver had fled into the morning mists.

Returning to my room, I firmly shut the door behind me and twisted the key in the lock, determined to put the incident from my mind. Something I had no trouble doing, for I found a shocking display before me.

A small fire had been lit in the hearth, its welcoming warmth chasing away any dampness sweeping in from the bay. The bed had been turned down, the rich coverlets neatly folded back in a queenly invitation to rest, and a reading light had been lit for my pleasure. I stood stunned. My toiling days as a laundress had always been followed by more work to address personal needs—laundry, cleaning, and cooking. During my mother's illness, I'd nursed her as well as tending to our laundry business and our own needs. Her last days were still a blur of exhaustion from which I was only now recovering.

Blinking back emotion brought on by memories and the care Benedict Trevelyan's servants had bestowed upon me, I readied myself for bed. But instead of crawling into the luxury awaiting me, I wandered over to the windows and peered into the night. Before me, in the distance below, lay the twinkling lights of the city as I'd never before seen them. From the heights of Trevelyan Hill, looking down at the city was like looking down upon the stars instead of up. It was a strange sensation and not a comfortable one, so I did not linger. I collected an encyclopedia and settled beneath the covers, intent on planning lessons, but the day's events and revelations took precedent over the blurring words on the page. And one among those incidents called upon my heart—Justin and Robert's resentment and bewilderment over their mother's death.

The thought of children only five and seven and without the gentle, loving touch of their mother hit a painful chord inside me, and I knew I would not sleep unless I went and checked on them. Sliding from the bed and donning my robe and slippers, I quietly went through a connecting door to the schoolroom and entered the nursery.

The moment I stepped into the room, I smelled sandalwood. His scent. My breath caught on the tantalizing aroma. I stopped just inside the door, my gaze searching for Benedict Trevelyan. I only remembered to breathe when I did not see him in the dark shadows. Tiptoeing closer to the small, blanket-covered figures, I found Justin and Robert sound asleep, looking peaceful and much happier than they did during their waking hours.

They must be riding on the wings of angels tonight. That is how my mother always described dreaming—soaring with the angels through the dark of the night, being kept safe until the dawn's warming light.

Satisfied, I stole back to my bed with a vision of Justin and Robert's innocent smiles in my mind and Benedict Trevelyan's scent upon my senses. Just as my eyes grew sleepy, I heard a noise from the empty schoolroom. Bounding up quickly, I rushed to the room but found no one there. Yet the scent of sandalwood was stronger than before, and it lingered in my dreams throughout the restless night. I kept wondering if Benedict Trevelyan had been in the shadows of the children's room after all and had seen me in my nightclothes.

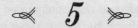

5

"Miss Wovell. Miss Wovell! Justin says we are not going to go at all." Robert pulled on the skirt of my gray dress and jumped with frustration. When excited, he mispronounced his *l*'s as *w*'s. "You promiseded a picnic today! Can we go now?"

In the two weeks I'd been at Trevelyan Hill, Robert and Justin's quirks and problems had become endearingly familiar. I slipped my hand into Robert's to ease him from the habit of grabbing at clothing for attention and tapped him on the nose. "You are certainly correct, Master Robert. We are going on a picnic. But before we take our outing, there are quite a few things we must attend to first. I have heard it said that picnics are best after a morning's work than before."

Robert skewed his face into a frown. "I want to go now."

Considering it was but eight in the morning and Benedict Trevelyan was due back today after a week's absence, I didn't think it prudent for us to go the park without doing our lessons first. Thus far, my time at Trevelyan Manor had passed in much the same manner as my first day, with the exception of seeing Benedict Trevelyan. He was only present at dinner and quickly excused himself each evening to attend to business. Yet since he'd been away, I'd missed even those brief moments of his presence.

I'd had no more sightings of the mysterious dark-haired woman, and no instances of my belongings being disturbed; but the sensation of being watched stayed with me, most often when I was alone and walking through the house.

I'd yet to meet Katherine Trevelyan. She had a respiratory ailment, and from what I gathered through the dinner conversations between Mrs. Trevelyan, Stephen Trevelyan, and Constance Ortega, Katherine was refusing all visitors but for the doctor and her nurse. I'd been surprised to learn that a woman full-grown, for I knew Katherine to be twenty, still had a nurse to care for her on a full-time basis. I wondered anew if there was truth to the rumors of her madness.

Robert tugged on my hand. "Wanna go to the park now, Miss Wovell."

Smiling, I squatted down and brushed an errant lock of dark hair from his forehead, seeing a bit of his father in the set of his chin. He was so young and so eager for love and attention that he'd readily accepted and invited demonstrations of affection. Justin was just the opposite. He kept a granite rock between himself and anyone else.

"If we went to the park this morning, we would not have as much fun as we will if we wait and go at lunch time."

"Why?"

"Because, not doing your work before you play is like putting dark clouds over a bright sunny day. If you get your work done first, you will be responsible, and you will have more fun because you will not be worrying about the work waiting for you."

Robert moved his mouth as he mentally chewed over my advice. "But what if there's always work, like my daddy has? He never gets to pway, and I will not either."

I opened my mouth then shut it as I mentally tripped over his unexpected insight. In scrambling for an answer, I realized something about myself. "I don't think it is because as adults we do not have *time* to play. I think it is because we have *forgotten* how to play."

"Have you forgetted?"

"Forgotten. Yes," I said, standing. "I think I have. You and Justin are going to have to teach me how to play."

"Pwomise?"

"Yes."

"I will go tell Juss." Robert let loose of my hand and started running.

"Remember to walk in the house, not run." My words went unheeded, and I knew I'd receive another remark from Dobbs concerning the boys' behavior. I looked forward to the exchange; besting Dobbs was proving to be most interesting.

The rest of the morning flew by with the work of our lessons. Before long, I was collecting a picnic basket from Cook Thomas with Robert dancing about my skirts and Justin scuffing his shoes across the floor. His face bore a wary look, as if he expected a monster to swoop down and snatch the picnic away. Thanking Thomas and carrying my drawing supplies along with the picnic basket, I led the boys through the house, my spirits matching Robert's excitement. It had been many years since I'd had the pleasure of picnicking in Holloway Park.

Dobbs stood in the foyer and frowned when he saw us. "Miss Lovell, might I inquire as to where you are taking the children? It is barely noon. The boys' lessons could hardly be fin—"

"The lessons are still in progress, Mr. Dobbs, I assure you. We are off to Holloway Park to conduct a botanical exploration, and while there, we are going to study a subject that the adults in Trevelyan Manor have completely forgotten." I saluted the suit of armor, paying homage to the metal rather than to Dobbs, who was doing his best to project a godlike image.

He lifted a skeptical brow, indicating that there was nothing he forgot.

Opening the demon-carved doors—their gleaming darkness never failed to remind me of Benedict Trevelyan—I motioned the boys out and sent Dobbs a sunny smile. "We are off to study fun." I shut the door on his frown and turned to face the bright sun. Instead, I met Stephen Trevelyan's grin.

"Uncle Steph, we are going to learn fun. Wanna come with us?" Robert pulled on Stephen Trevelyan's coat. I noticed Justin kept walking down the stairs then waited at the bottom, putting himself on the fringes to watch rather than to participate—something he did often.

The boys' uncle bent down, lifted Robert into his arms, and affectionately tickled him. "Since you are the fun expert, you must be teaching the class today."

Robert blinked. "That's what Miss Wovell said. You come teach her fun, too? You are lots of fun."

Seeing Stephen Trevelyan tease Robert was the first real affection I'd seen any of the adults in Trevelyan Manor show; it warmed me. I didn't want to deprive the children of an opportunity to have fun with their uncle, but having Stephen Trevelyan join us in the park seemed a bit too familiar. My shoulders tensed.

Stephen ruffled Robert's hair. "Maybe later. I promised Aunt Constance that I would take her shopping."

Robert poked out his bottom lip. "Aunt Constant is mean. She doesn't ever like to play anything. She's not like Aunt Kaff. Aunt Kaff is fun when she's not painting, even if she does not like talking."

Stephen Trevelyan set Robert down and chuckled. "Aunt Kaff loves talking, you just have to know how to listen, and

Aunt Constance only likes to play shopping. That does not make her mean, only expensive. I will bring you and Justin a treat from Winkle's Confection Shop."

Robert grinned wide. "A candy stick?"

"If you like. Or would you rather have gumdrops?"

"No. A candy stick is better."

Stephen Trevelyan turned to Justin, studying him a moment. "And what can I bring you?"

Justin shrugged, looking down.

"If I remember correctly, gumdrops were your favorite."

"That was before you left," Justin said, keeping his gaze on his feet. "I do not want anything now."

My stomach clenched as I realized his mother wasn't the only person Justin felt that he had lost.

"Gumdrops it is, then," Stephen Trevelyan said. When he looked at me, his smile was forced, and dark shadows had crept into his eyes. "I will try and make it over to the park. If not, then I will join them in a special game later."

"We will see you then," I said, taking Robert's hand and moving down the steps.

"What would you like, Ann?"

Stephen Trevelyan's question nearly had me stumbling down the stairs. I looked back at him, blinking with surprise, though it wasn't the first time he'd referred to me by my first name. "Nothing. I am quite all right, thank you."

He nodded his head and turned away. I held Robert's hand tighter as we left, thankful that his excited chatter filled the quiet void.

Justin walked beside us, scuffing the ground with his shoes. I worried about him, and wondered what I could do to help ease the hurt I knew he held locked inside him, but at the moment I was more worried about Stephen Trevelyan's friendliness toward me.

Was he only being polite? I had no experience amid the Trevelyan's social realm and wondered if Stephen Trevelyan's overtures skirted on the edge of a familiarity I shouldn't allow.

In truth, I had never thought I'd ever be confronted with such a dilemma. During dinner every night, Stephen Trevelyan spoke to and treated me much the same way as he did the effervescent Constance and his morose mother. He didn't seek me out apart from the meals; but on occasion, just as when he asked if he could bring me a confection, I felt more than a stranger in his regard. I'd expected there to be a greater distance in my relations with the Trevelyans, a difference as great as there was between my hands and Miss Ortega's.

By the time we reached the park, I had to push the question away unanswered, as the outing quickly spiraled into disaster. With Justin and Robert pandemonium struck like lighting from a clear blue sky. It was quite disconcerting. Though I knew I'd never be chasing Robert around with a broom, I could easily see how their nurse had ended up with oatmeal in her hair. Especially if she'd not been adept at avoiding the boys' sudden dives into the emotions churning inside of them.

"Let's play Cowboys and Indians!" Robert ran up a hill, using his finger as a pistol.

"I shot you," Justin said, doing the same. "You are dead. Just like our mother."

"No, I am not. You can't shoot me dead," Robert shouted, running at Justin, fists raised to do damage. I dropped the picnic basket, ignored its end-over-end descent down the hill, and snatched Robert up before he and Justin could come to blows.

"Master Justin, please retrieve our lunch basket. Hopefully, we will not have to throw all of Cook Thomas's goodies away." I set Robert on his feet and looked him sternly in the eye. "If you start a game, and especially if you start shooting first, then you cannot complain if someone shoots back. You may be playing now, but when you grow up and own a gun, you have to face the reality that shooting kills."

Justin came back with the basket, and I turned my stern gaze on him. "A man's words are just as damaging as a weapon. Your brother is as hurt as you are that your mother died. Is it your intent to keep sticking a hot poker into his pain? Would you want someone to do that to you?"

A welling of tears filled Justin's brown eyes, and I saw him take a deep breath. Emotion clogged my throat. I wanted to pull him into my arms, but as rigid as he held himself, I knew Justin was far too hurt to accept comfort yet. I gentled my voice. "Did you know that all over this huge land we live in, even all over the world, there are girls and boys just like you? There are many girls and boys who have lost their mother. I lost my mother, too. But you two are lucky. You have a father and a family left. Some girls and boys don't. I did not. Have you ever heard the story of Cynthia Parker and the Indians?"

Justin and Robert shook their heads; I could see my words had reached them. It was a start to a long journey. "Let's set up our picnic, and I will tell you little Cynthia Parker's story."

We sat on the blanket, Robert and Justin wide-eyed about hearing a real Indian story. "I have to tell you that my story starts sad and ends sad. There are heartaches in life, painful things that happen and disappointments that steal away dreams. But we have to let those hurting things fall from our hands so that when we find special moments of happiness, we can hold on to them. The heartaches are like the thorny stems of roses, while happiness and love are the soft, beautiful flowers themselves. If your hands are full of the thorns, how can you hold the roses?"

I let that question linger a short time; then I began the story. "About forty years ago in Texas, near the Navasota River there lived several families. The Parkers were one of those families. For many years we have been fighting Indians, and for many years they have been angry with us because they lived here first. This was their land, and now we call it our land. In Texas, the Comanche and Kiowa warriors were very angry over this. They attacked the village where the Parkers lived. Cynthia was nine years old, and her brother was six. The Indians did awful things to Cynthia's family, killed most of them, and stole her and her brother.

"Her brother went to one Indian tribe, she to another. Her whole life changed, but she did not hold on to the thorns of her pain. She lived with the Comanche Indians where a family adopted her. She learned the ways of the Indians. She understood that they were people, too. They had families and rules; they had hearts and knew pain. She also learned that many of the Indians suffered awful things from white people. Cynthia grew up among the Indians and learned to love their ways.

"Then one day she fell in love with a young chief and married him. There were many roses in her life over the next fifteen years. She loved her husband deeply, and she loved her children, too. Then, fifteen years after she married, soldiers attacked her Indian village, killing many. Her husband, Chief Nocona, was killed. Her two sons escaped, but Cynthia and her baby daughter were taken captive. She tried several times to run back to her Indian family, but she was forced to live apart from them until she died. To this day, her first son, Quanah, is holding on to the thorns of losing his father and his mother. He is attacking and hurting people because of his anger and pain. I hope that someday he will let go of the thorns and find the roses. That is a very important lesson to learn in life. Now, we had better get to our science exploration before we run out of time for our picnic. How many different trees can you find?"

Robert eagerly began picking out trees. Justin did so more slowly, staying distant; but the more we explored, the more Justin's aloofness faded. He had a remarkable aptitude for remembering anything I told him and could quickly differentiate between the deciduous and evergreen trees. He soon could name oaks, maples, poplars, and birches based on the shapes of their leaves.

"The next thing is to take our leaf collection and begin our science notebooks."

"My own science book?" Justin asked, interest sparking in his eyes.

"Most definitely. Information isn't any good unless it's ordered." Back at our picnic blanket, I handed Justin and Robert each a piece of my precious drawing paper and a sharpened pencil. Then placing an oak leaf before us, I showed them how to make a sketch of the leaf. Next to that, I drew a miniature oak tree, pointing out the differences in the crowns of oak trees and maples and birches.

Justin came alive with a pencil in his hand, meticulously applying himself to the task. As the boys worked, I once again turned my hand to sketching the house on Trevelyan Hill. My skill as an artist had improved greatly over the years, and the drawing took on life as my pencil flew.

But this time, unlike my childhood renderings, the house was darker, with a more sinister appeal. I even grew fanciful and drew a dragon hovering amid the dark clouds over the mansion. Thank goodness Robert, having grown tired of drawing leaves, interrupted my musing. I kept picturing the mysterious woman standing in the turret's window and had almost drawn her there.

I set my drawing tablet aside, and while Justin continued, absorbed in creating his science notebook, Robert and I lay on our backs looking for animals in the fluffy clouds dotting the blue summer sky. The warmth of the sun mixed with the breeze of the bay to provide a soft, cozy cocoon around us. Having spent so many days of my life laboring indoors, I reveled in the freedom of basking in the park, teaching about nature. Robert found three sheep. I saw a kangaroo and a whale.

"Do you see a tiger anywhere?" I asked, trying to get him to imagine more than just sheep.

"This is fun, Miss Wovell. There's another sheep."

Laughing, I reached over, tickling him. "Surely, there's more than just sheep up there. Let your imagination fly like a bird."

"What's magination, Miss Wovell?"

"To think something is more than it is, Robert," came Benedict Trevelyan's voice. His reply seemed almost admonishing.

My heart leapt to a gallop. I sat up so fast the horizon wavered before righting itself. "Mr. Trevelyan. You are home," I said inanely as I straightened my rumpled clothes. To my dismay, I saw the hem of my dress and petticoat had caught beneath me, exposing my legs to an inch above my button boots. I hastily snatched it down.

I couldn't see his expression. The sun behind him was too bright, but he didn't sound as if imagination was high on his list of approved academics.

"Yes, it would appear that I am indeed home. Are you by chance studying the weather, Miss Lovell?"

"Not exactly."

"We are having a picnic," said Robert. I winced at how trivial it sounded.

"We are making science books," said Justin.

"I drawed leaves," said Robert. "Wanta see?"

For some reason, I found myself tensing, wondering if Benedict Trevelyan would see the value in our work today.

"I believe I will take a look at your pictures."

Robert scrambled up. I leaned to my side, intending to rise, but with the sun blinding me, I hadn't realized Benedict Trevelyan's intention to sit. He came down as I moved upward, and his shoulder brushed intimately across my breasts.

"Oh, my," I gasped. Heated, unbelievably pleasurable sensations tingled through me, setting fire to my cheeks. His scent, made headier by the warmth of the day, washed over me. I shamefully drew a deep breath, fearfully realizing how much I'd missed the secret excitement his presence stirred to life inside me. How much I'd missed his smell and his dark appeal.

I remained on my knees, completely overtaken with what had happened, as if I'd been frozen in place. My gaze fixed itself to the manly curve of his chin, the slight indentation dividing it, and the hint of supple softness where his blood pulsed on his neck.

He lifted his hand and reached out for me, but a breath away from the curve of my neck, he stopped. He was so close that I could feel the heat of his palm warm my skin.

"Miss Lovell—" His voice was barely a whisper. "Unless you are inviting certain attentions, I suggest you either stand up or sit back down."

Blinking, I shot my gaze to his and found his dark eyes gleaming, as rich and deep as the demon door glistening in the sun. His hand fisted as if fighting the urge to touch me . . . or kiss me? My knees wobbled.

I quickly sank back to the blanket before I fell. Standing was completely out of the question, but my mortification was so great that even sitting upon the blanket seemed intolerable. I focused my gaze upon the hilly horizon of Holloway Park and forced myself to breathe, oddly praying for a band of Indians to attack and drag me away, thus saving me from facing my unseemly behavior.

"See," Robert said, rushing up with his pictures and his leaf collection. I then realized that what had passed between me and Benedict Trevelyan had only taken a moment. But that moment had stretched in time and had gone to thoughts and things I had best forget ever existed. For I had no doubt that the intensity I read in his gaze had been desire. Desire I'd never seen before, nor felt, but had read about.

Books had taken me places where I never thought I would go. Perhaps, given my reaction to Benedict Trevelyan's nearness, it would have been better if I had remained illiterate.

"We learnded oaks, maples, poppars, and urches. Right, Miss Wovell?" Robert said, forcing me to collect my wits.

"Poplars and birches," I corrected. Only then did I notice that Justin had yet to greet his father. Still working on his drawing, he sat on the far corner of the blanket.

Benedict Trevelyan's gaze rested on Justin's head briefly, and I thought I saw pain slash through his eyes before he examined Robert's pictures. "Miss Lovell has kept you very busy."

I bit my tongue to keep from telling Benedict Trevelyan that Robert had worked hard. "Master Justin, would you like to show your father how well your science book is developing?"

Justin looked up then, and I thought he was about to say no when his father said, "Yes, Justin, let me see what has you so involved that you have rudely neglected to greet me."

Wincing, I felt my heart squeeze as I looked into Justin's shadowed eyes. His father had been right to address Justin's attitude, which surprised me because I'd sensed respect and fear of his father before, but not resentment. I wondered what was amiss.

Justin slowly rose and held his pictures out to his father, who took them and, with a lifted brow, studied them.

"You have a talent, it seems. Your aunt Katherine would be proud." Benedict Trevelyan set the drawings on his knee and looked at Justin. "So, son, why the silence?"

Justin scuffed his feet.

"I will have an answer, or you will have a consequence," he added quietly.

"You went away," Justin said under his breath. "Someday you will go away and not come back."

Benedict Trevelyan sighed and handed Justin back his pictures. "We have had this discussion before. I have a business to run, and being away sometimes is unavoidable. You need to stop imagining that I will not be coming back. It is senseless. Do you understand?"

"Yes, sir." Justin kept his gaze on his shoes.

I dug my teeth into my tongue. Couldn't Benedict Trevelyan see how badly his son was hurting? How badly Justin needed reassurance, not a dressing-down?

Benedict Trevelyan stood, surprising me with the suddenness of his movements. "Miss Lovell, after you've finished with this outing, please meet me in my study."

Standing also, I met his gaze. "I will be there," I said tightly.

"I have no doubt of that, Miss Lovell."

Robert came up to his father and pulled on his coat. In Robert's hand was my sketch of Trevelyan Manor and its hovering dragon. I suddenly found myself praying for a miracle. "Miss Wovell says you forgotted how to have fun."

"Indeed?" Benedict Trevelyan's brows lifted. He didn't sound pleased.

"Will you stay and learn to have fun with us?"

My word! Could this get any worse? I refused to stand there like a ninny while my life went up in flames. Maybe if I didn't draw attention to my sketchbook, it would go unnoticed. I had to force myself not to snatch it away from Robert and to turn my attention to our picnic.

Unpacking the basket, I placed the cheese, meat pies, and apples upon the blanket, spying a large chunk of chocolate cake, which I left in the basket until later. Everything smelled and looked heavenly. At least my last meal would be a tasty one. I'd have to thank Cook Thomas.

"It would seem you have an amazing talent for art as well, Miss Lovell," Benedict Trevelyan said.

I looked up to see him studying my sketch. My life seemed to be developing a penchant for marching from one disaster right into another.

"And an amazing imagination as well," he added, handing the sketch out to me.

I grasped my tablet between my numb fingers. "Thank you," I murmured, focusing my eyes on the middle of his chest. He wore a dark suit with a matching vest over a white ruffled shirt and a neatly knotted ascot. The cut and quality of his clothes had a distinct European richness to them without being flamboyant.

I'd seen all manner of men upon the streets of San Francisco, from the pretentious frills of a dandy to the deadly roughness of a gunslinger. Benedict towered above them all in his elegant simplicity. There wasn't a doubt in my mind that he was more dangerous than any gunfighter whose spurs marked the West.

He left then, but his presence lingered, dimming the brightness of the day as a cloud dims the sun. I looked to

Justin, remembering his reluctance to take pleasure in the day as if fearful it would be stolen away, and thought he'd been right after all.

I didn't look forward to my meeting with Benedict Trevelyan for I feared I'd not be able to hold my tongue. Actually, I knew I wouldn't, and that didn't portend well for my employment. So I set about making the picnic as much fun as I could muster, even as my stomach churned. My heart had wrapped around little Robert and Justin. I felt that more than just my future was now at stake.

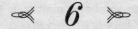

Though I approached Benedict Trevelyan's study armed with the two weeks worth of work that Justin and Robert had penned, I didn't expect it would sway the tide of his disapproval of my teaching methods. I found myself wishing that it was today Stephen Trevelyan had appeared in a drunken stupor and argued with his brother. Even being embarrassingly pinned beneath Stephen Trevelyan seemed preferable to the rocks churning around in my stomach.

I feared that part of my nervousness had nothing to do with my concerns for Justin and Robert or the status of my own employment. It stemmed from that heated moment of desire between the master of Trevelyan Hill and myself.

The notion that a man such as Benedict Trevelyan had, even for a brief beat of time, found me desirable intrigued me. Perhaps being christened Titania after the Queen of the Fairies had some effect upon me after all, because I in no way had the least inclination to run like the fair maidens fleeing from the demons upon the carved entry doors to the manor. Though fleeing would have been a response in keeping with the propriety I thought essential to my well-being, I found myself intensely curious, wishing to study this new revelation of attraction to a man as I would delve into a book about science. A magical queen wouldn't flee, would she?

Through the open door, Benedict Trevelyan's study looked just as gloomy and oppressive as it had before. Were I to choose a place within Trevelyan Manor for myself, it would be in the foyer, where the myriad rays of colored light from the stained glass windows would dance throughout the day, coloring every shadow with beauty.

Finding myself alone and unable to resist, I paused a moment in the entry hall and drank in the window's glorious display. I held my reddened, wash-worn hands out and spun around, watching the colors paint them and the boys' study papers I held with a beauty no woman would be ashamed to show. When I came to a stop, Benedict Trevelyan stood before me.

"Might these be for me, Miss Lovell?" He lifted an eyebrow. The movement sent a shiver through me that had nothing to do with cool temperatures. Nevertheless, I drew a steadying breath, straightened my shoulders, and set my mind upon the purpose of our meeting.

"Yes," I said, extending my hand to him. Within the intimacy of the colored light, the distance between us seemed to shrink to mere inches, and the dancing colors covered his broad chest. He'd removed his coat, ascot and vest, leaving only his white ruffled shirt to cling to the contours of his imposing frame.

My word, I thought I'd never be tempted to launder another man's clothes in my life, but somehow my fingers itched to touch what had lain against him, even if it were under the guise of laundering.

As he took the papers, his fingers brushed mine. I lifted my gaze to his. Within his dark eyes, I saw a spark of the look we'd exchanged in the park. That moment would most likely burn forever in my mind, but his presence now fanned the memory of it to a scorching flame of such heat that it shocked me back to reality. Fairy queen indeed! I had to have completely taken leave of my senses.

It suddenly seemed of great import that I reach the oppressiveness of his study. I jerked my gaze from his and marched that way. "We have much to discuss since you last asked me my impressions of Masters Justin and Robert. I have been able to formulate a deeper assessment of their needs since then."

"Why am I not surprised?" he said, his voice not far behind me.

Once inside his study, a sense of balance settled over my nerves. I sat in the chair before his massive desk, purposely avoided looking at him, and hurried on with what I felt was necessary to say. If he intended to dismiss me, then I'd at least have the comfort of speaking my mind. "I realize that a picnic in the park may not fit any conventional methods of teaching academics, but there are things in a child's development that are just as important as learning facts."

"I assume you are about to inform me of those things." He tossed the boys' papers on his desk. Disturbingly enough, he didn't sit down, and I was forced to twist around to see where he went.

Moving behind me, he walked to the curtained window and slid back the heavy green velvet drape to peer outside. My planned speech flew from my mind as a shaft of summer-bright sun pierced the gloom. The dark wood tones around me suddenly gleamed with light and warmth, mirroring what the heat of desire did to his dark eyes. Would the rest of Trevelyan Manor come to such life under the brightness of sunshine?

Thankfully, he dropped the curtain closed, and I dismissed my fancifulness.

"You were saying, Miss Lovell?"

I cleared my throat. "Yes, about Masters Justin and Robert. They are quite frankly starving for certain things." Unable to continue to sit and twist around to look him, I stood.

My words had brought a deep frown of displeasure to his brow. I plunged ahead before he could respond, pacing as I spoke. "Like the tiny acorns of the towering oaks, they need the warmth of sunshine and the richness of the earth to grow strong and tall. Master Robert is so young and eager to be loved. He needs some of the sunshine of life—fun and laughter, encouraging words and tender touches to free his mind from worry. How can he concentrate on learning if he sees nothing but heavy clouds on his horizon? And Master Justin doesn't believe there is any sunshine to be had. I think that—"

"Miss Lovell," he said sharply, cutting through my speech. I stopped pacing and stared at him. "My sons are not plants, nor are they poetry in need of flowery descriptions. What is the practical point to your"—he waved his hand as if swatting away an irritating bug—"allegorical lecture?"

I opened my mouth, shut it, then opened it again. "My point?"

"Exactly."

Squaring my shoulders, I drew a bolstering breath. He'd invited my directness and, in a roundabout way, my opinion when he asked for my assessment of the boys two weeks ago. Justin and Robert coveted their father's approval, and in my opinion, his relationship with them went right to the heart of the matter. "You may dismiss me for my impertinence and my honesty, but you give your sons stern discipline. Might I suggest you offer an encouraging word to temper that discipline?"

I expected to hear the sharp edge of his tongue rebuking me for even thinking of questioning him. Instead, he stared at me, fisting his hands. A dark emotion flooded the room as his eyes became blacker. I knew not if it was mere anger rushing through him or something more frighteningly elemental than that.

I took a step back from him. When I did, surprise flitted across his face before I thought I saw something akin to despair in his eyes. But he turned quickly away from me, and I wondered if I hadn't imagined the look—imagined it because of my own yearning for a crack in his harshness.

He kept his back to me as he poured himself a drink from a decanter on a small table not far from a hearth so clean and devoid of wood or utensils that I didn't think a fire had ever been lit there.

"On my desk you will find two weeks' wages."

Nausea and a wrenching pain inside me almost brought me to my knees. It wasn't as if I hadn't expected such an outcome, but the reality of it was more brutal than I had imagined. Turning so he wouldn't see the tears gathering in my eyes, I walked toward his desk. My knees trembled greatly, my heart more so.

Most of me wanted to leave without the money upon the desk; but I'd known too much of hunger in my life to let pride rule me. I would need funds to survive until I secured another respectable position—a daunting task for a woman alone in the West. The money felt crisply cold in my palm, and I found I could not leave without saying one more thing. "Please, in securing a tutor for Masters Justin and

Robert, look for a teacher who knows kindness as well as academics."

"Miss Lovell! Are you leaving my employment?"

The sharpness in his voice forced me to face him. I blinked away the tears in my eyes to bring his face into focus. Perhaps I had been mistaken in what I thought to be anger in him before, because the room crackled with the force of it now.

I gulped in air before I could speak. "Is that not what this meeting is about? Did you not just dismiss me?"

"I see my estimation of your amazing imagination earlier was an understatement. If I no longer have use for your services, I assure you, Miss Lovell, that you will hear those words directly from my lips. I merely thought that, given your circumstances, rather than waiting for the month's end, you would have use for an allotment of your wages."

I blinked. "My circumstances?"

"To be blunt, I have noticed you've only two dresses and thought maybe . . ."

I blinked again. "Are you instructing me to purchase a dress?"

"Ironically enough, that would seem to be the situation. If you are going to be escorting my sons about, it is within keeping of the Trevelyan image that a certain manner of dress be adhered to. I have spoken with Mrs. Talbot, the owner of Talbot's Fashion Emporium, a dressmaker shop off Hyde Street. She has had the misfortune of being left with several dresses she made for a schoolteacher who ran back East after only a month in the West. I will, of course, cover the expense of the dresses, but thought there might be other things you would wish to purchase."

I was speechless for a few moments as we stared at each other. I knew not what mortified me more—that Benedict

Trevelyan found me lacking, or that he'd spoken of my need to another. "I couldn't possibly accept—"

"I provide uniforms for all of the household staff. I consider this to be the same. And I suggest you select clothing in sunnier colors than gray or brown. I am sure Justin and Robert will appreciate that." He lifted his brows and inclined his head, giving added meaning to his words as he used my own reasoning to further his point.

The flood of my embarrassment ebbed a little. He'd only given me as honest an opinion of a situation as I'd given him. I lifted my chin, determined to say more about his dealings with Justin and Robert. "Might I also offer a suggestion?"

His lips curved to a wry angle. "I doubt you will comment upon your dress, so I assume this is in regard to my sons?" He waved his arm. "Please, do not feel the need to hold your tongue at this point, Miss Lovell."

"I will be instructing Master Justin in the game of chess. It's my opinion that maneuvering the pieces and learning the strategy of the game will give him a sense of control over at least some things, so he does not feel completely at the mercy of life's whims. If you were to play with him on occasion, encourage him, the insecurity he feels may lessen. As for Master Robert, I think both he and Master Justin will benefit from weekly outings. There are a great many things to learn in our city. Should you be available on occasion, accompanying us might afford you the opportunity to have a few moments of fun with them. If you disapprove of this as part of their instruction, I will be glad to schedule these outings on Saturday."

"You do recall that Saturday is your day off."

"I am aware of that."

"Yet last Saturday I am told you spent the day with Justin and Robert, nor did you leave the house on Sunday."

"We were unable to finish our planting project Friday, and I felt it necessary to complete the task on Saturday." I'd decided to stay here and work on lessons after that, for I'd not the funds to do anything in town. Suddenly the money in my hand gained even more significance, and I met Benedict Trevelyan's gaze across the room, my eyes widening with understanding.

He cleared his throat and turned from me. "Outings on Saturday will not be necessary. You may inform me of your plans, and we shall see about them and my involvement. Is there anything else, Miss Lovell?"

Though I could think of several other things, I'd said more than enough for now. "No."

"Amazing." He glanced back at me. "I expect I shall see you at dinner tonight, then. And one more thing—don't let your projects carry over to your days off other than occasionally. I expect you to manage your time more efficiently." This time he turned with a dismissing finality, and I left his study, feeling the need to tread quickly through the dancing lights in the entry hall, lest he find me lingering there again, mismanaging my time.

Humph. The man seemed impossible to please.

I arrived for dinner early, wearing my brown dress, but this time I didn't bother to adorn it with the black lace, having realized that my efforts had only drawn attention to the meagerness of my belongings. Or perhaps after two weeks I had less of a need for pretense than before. Walking into the parlor, I came to a sudden stop. Upon the brocade settee sat a young lady dressed in white. She could very well be the mysterious woman who'd made those ghostly appearances. Her skin was incredibly fair, almost as white as the china that graced the table. Her hair, as dark as a moonless night, was pulled into a severe bun, so tightly wound it was diffi-

cult to discern its length. Her hands were as white and delicate as a dove's wing, and flowed just as gracefully as she
sewed.

Now that I was pressed to recall specifics, I realized that
both times I'd seen my mysterious ghost woman at a distance, and her features had been less than clear. It was disturbing to realize that I might be in need of spectacles. I
cleared my throat, hoping to draw her attention away from
the embroidery she intently worked upon. She didn't stop,
didn't look up, and didn't offer any greeting.

Before I could decide what to do in the face of her seeming rudeness, Stephen Trevelyan breezed into the room. He
came to an abrupt stop when he saw the woman. Emotion
so intense that I'd have been hard-pressed to give it any
other name but pain settled on his face.

"Excuse me for a minute, Miss Ann," he said, handing
me an elaborately wrapped package. To my surprise, he
crossed the room and knelt at the woman's feet. She
stopped sewing then and looked up. Deep trouble marred
the perfection of a face that took my breath away. Her eyes
were the color of antique gold, and the delicacy of her features made me think that any disturbance would shatter
them. It was as if she were the finest life-size porcelain
doll.

Stephen Trevelyan didn't say a word. All he did was bow
his head, placing his forehead upon her lap. Moved, the
woman started to touch him, hesitated, and then placed her
hand lovingly upon his head.

His shoulders relaxed at her touch, as if he'd been holding his breath and had finally exhaled.

"Touching, is it not? The act of absolution. It would
seem my sister has forgiven her fallen knight," Benedict
Trevelyan whispered in my ear, sending such a shock of
pleasure to my toes that I had to strain to hear the rest of his

words over the roaring of blood that made me light-headed. The man had a strange effect upon my senses.

Forgiveness? For what? "Absolution" seemed a strong word for him to have chosen for a mere estrangement between siblings. Seeing Katherine Trevelyan, of whom many dark things were whispered, was as disconcerting as meeting Benedict Trevelyan himself.

I turned abruptly to find him but inches away. My breath caught, and our gazes met. He searched my face for answers that I did not know the questions to. Perhaps he was remembering our encounter in the park. I sensed a change between us. The words we'd exchanged in his study, rather than creating distance, had formed an odd bond.

His gaze dropped to my lips, and I swallowed, wondering how, with so little a movement, he could change the world about me, the direction of my thoughts, and the very beat of my heart.

He must have heard a noise that I didn't, because before I could blink, he stepped away and whipped around to greet Constance Ortega. She flitted into the room wearing a sapphire blue gown that shimmered with stars and matched the huge blue jewels encircling her neck and dangling from her ears. I wondered if important company was expected and felt an unaccustomed flutter of panic in my breast at the notion.

I'd resigned myself to being a guest at the Trevelyans' table despite my station as an employee. The West was wont to flout Eastern protocols, though it coveted its luxuries, and finding a personage of learning but of meager means as a guest at the table of the rich was not beyond belief. But I had no wish to meet the Trevelyans' equals and put that supposition to the test publicly.

Meeting the disapproving gaze of Benedict Trevelyan's mother was difficult enough. I'd attempted several times during Benedict Trevelayn's absence this past week to dine in my room, but both Dobbs and Stephen Trevelyan had insisted otherwise.

"You are looking especially turned out tonight, Constance. The Ortega sapphires are as opulent as ever," Benedict Trevelyan said. "Is this a special occasion?"

Constance Ortega gave him a broad smile. "This dress arrived from New York today. I just simply had to wear it. Is it not divine?" She pirouetted daintily.

"Quite nice," he added. "Alan will think you have dressed so elegantly just for him."

Alan? I wondered. Was company expected? Then I remembered Benedict mentioning his business partner before.

Constance scoffed, "That man. He thinks everything is just for him. He will be joining us for dinner, yes? And did you sell the *Commodore*?"

"Yes, I sold the *Commodore*. Business is fine, so there's no need for you to worry. I believe Alan will be staying tonight, at least. Though I do not know if he will be returning directly back to Kansas City or not."

"Splendid." Constance Ortega said. "He can tell me all the latest news."

"Which you will undoubtedly wrangle toward fashion, costing Benedict more money. It is a wonder he allows me to visit." We all turned to the expensively dressed speaker standing in the doorway. He was a handsome man, slight of frame, much older and much shorter than I expected. The top of his head reached the bridge of my nose. Still, when he walked into the room, he filled it with an Old World gentlemanly flair that made him appear much bigger. "Might I say you ladies look beautiful tonight."

Constance raised her eyebrows, giving my dress a dismissive glance before she smiled and held out her hand to the man. "You may, but only if you will sit next to me at dinner."

"It will be my pleasure," he replied, bowing and kissing her hand as if she were a queen. He stood, then looked my way and cleared his throat.

Benedict stepped up. "I apologize, Alan. Let me introduce you to Miss Lovell, Justin and Robert's new governess. Miss Lovell, Mr. Henderson, a family friend and business partner of my father's until he sold out, moved to Kansas City, and struck gold in cattle."

"The governess?" Mr. Henderson's brows shot up in what I thought to be disapproving surprise, then he made an attempt to hide his hesitation. "Ah, yes, the governess. A pleasure, Miss Lovell." Mr. Henderson held out his hand, and I again had no choice but to place mine in his. He bowed before me just as he had before Constance, but his gesture made me feel more uncomfortable rather than more accepted.

"Thank you, Mr. Henderson. It is a pleasure to meet you as well."

Mr. Henderson released my hand. Then he directed an admonishing gaze toward Benedict Trevelyan. " 'Efficient' and 'practical' nowhere near describes Miss Lovell's queenly stature. Not what I would expect in a governess."

My cheeks flushed. I didn't know if I was more embarrassed by Benedict's description of me—though it was how I saw myself—or by Mr. Henderson's prevarication. Queenly stature indeed. Before I could decide how to respond, Constance Ortega interrupted.

"Why, Miss Lovell, what is that absolutely divine package you have?"

I glanced down, seeing that I still held the box Stephen had given me. I'd forgotten it in my embarrassment. "It is Mr. Trevelyan's," I said.

Benedict Trevelyan frowned.

"I mean Mr. Stephen Trevelyan's."

"Actually," Stephen Trevelyan said, walking up with Katherine Trevelyan, her arm tucked in the crook of his, "it is a gift for you, Miss Ann."

"Still wooing the ladies, Stephen?" Mr. Henderson said. The room seemed to fall quiet at his remark. As a governess I shouldn't have been addressed as a lady of the family, and to speak so openly of wooing . . . well, that was rather improper.

"One can only hope," Stephen Trevelyan replied, cheerfully filling the void. "Open the box, Miss Ann, and let me know if I have succeeded."

I held out the gift. "I really cannot accept this, Mr. Trevelyan—"

"I insist," Stephen Trevelyan said, refusing to take the gift back. "Open it."

I had no choice without seeming rude. My hands shook a little as I slipped off the ribbon and loosened the golden paper. The smell of rich chocolate immediately enveloped my senses as the elegant scroll of Ghirardelli met my eyes. His thoughtfulness touched me. "Thank you, Mr. Trevelyan, but you should not have bought me anything."

Stephen Trevelyan shrugged. "I could not get Justin and Robert a treat without rewarding their diligent teacher. And I must say, this 'Mr. Trevelyan' situation is most annoying. If I cannot induce you to call me Stephen, I insist that you at least call me Mr. Stephen."

Another barrier between the Trevelyans and myself fell away, like sand between my fingers. I couldn't seem to hold onto my distance. I tucked the box of chocolates into my hand. "Then you must call me Ann," I said, wondering where this path would end. To refer to myself as Miss Ann seemed pretentious.

Constance Ortega laughed. "My, I had not made the connection before, but Anns have had ill luck among royalty. Why, did not Henry the Eighth behead an Ann for—"

"Connie, you pick the most morbid facts of history to dwell upon," Stephen Trevelyan said, interrupting.

"Not to worry," I said. "My actual name is Titania." The moment my name left my mouth, I pressed my fingers to my lips in shock. Never in my entire life had I told anyone the name I'd been christened with.

"Aha," Mr. Henderson said. "I was right. Definitely a queenly beauty."

"My word," Stephen Trevelyan said, untangling himself from his sister and extending a courtly bow to my feet. "I had no idea we were being graced by the presence of a queen. Please forgive our slight."

Burning heat fanned my cheeks. What had possessed me to expose myself so? I didn't know what to make of this whole exchange. Stephen didn't seem to be mocking me, but I still felt the sting of embarrassment.

Benedict Trevelyan frowned. "Stephen, if you are truly paying homage, then why not offer Miss Lovell a sherry instead of mocking her with archaic foolery?"

"She said to call her Ann," Stephen Trevelyan said. "Or, more beautifully, Titania. But you are quite right, Benedict. I will fix everyone a drink. After all, that's what I do best, is it not?" The tension between the Trevelyan brothers always lurked beneath the surface, rearing its head at unexpected moments. I noted that Mr. Henderson kept glancing at the two brothers.

"And what country was Titania queen of?" Constance Ortega asked. "I do not recall—"

"In Shakespeare's *A Midsummer Night's Dream,* Titania is Queen of the Fairies," Benedict Trevelyan said.

"She falls in love with a mere mortal," Stephen Trevelyan added from across the room.

"Actually, it was an ass," Mrs. Trevelyan said, rolling into the room in her wheelchair like a dour cloud.

Mr. Henderson laughed. "I see you're as sharp as ever, Rosalind. Illness has not dulled your wit. Titania did indeed become enamored of an ass."

I might have found the moment mortifying were it not for Stephen Trevelyan. He crossed the room and handed a glass of sherry to Constance, his mother, and me. "Then I will hold out hope for myself," he said, moving over to a decanter of amber liquid. "I do believe the mortal was only made to look like an ass by a mischievous spell, Mother, Alan." He poured three more drinks, giving Alan one, and carrying one to his brother. "Here's a toast to being"—he glanced at everyone in the room—"an enamored ass."

"On that note of intellectual insight, I think we will adjourn to the dining room," Benedict Trevelyan said dryly.

Mr. Henderson extended his arm to Constance Ortega. She nodded like royalty receiving her due as she passed by me. It was only as Katherine Trevelyan glided by with her dress flowing about her like a cloud that I realized she hadn't said a word at all. Hadn't participated in the conversation. It was as if she wasn't there, and I shivered as I caught the scent of roses wafting from her.

The same aroma of roses, only thicker, more sweetly overpowering, assaulted me when Stephen Trevelyan rolled his mother into the room. I remembered that the same scent had been lingering in my room when my belongings were disturbed.

Before I entered the dining room, Benedict Trevelyan put his hand upon my arm, drawing my attention as he spoke softly. "Miss Lovell. I have neglected to tell you something important. My sister, Katherine, she is deaf and does not speak. You will have to make allowances for her—"

"Please," I said, placing my hand on his, feeling the

vibrant warmth of his skin. "There's no need to say any more. I understand." My heart went out to Katherine Trevelyan. What must it be like to be locked in a world of silence? I then remembered Robert saying "Aunt Kaff" didn't like to talk. She couldn't. "Does she know sign language?"

"Yes—she's very eloquent with her hands, you might say." He looked at my reddened hand upon his, and I moved to pull mine away, but he flipped his over and caught my fingers. "I captained my ship for many years. My hands became callused and roughened, for I joined my crew with the work, never believing I should ask a man to do what I was not willing to do. I make no apologies for the honest work I did or the calluses I garnered. You should not either."

He released my fingers, but my skin continued to burn from his touch. Never was I more thankful that he continued to call me Miss Lovell. To relinquish that barrier of formality between us would make things entirely too uncomfortable. I entered the dining room in a daze, somehow finding the presence of mind to seat myself.

It wasn't until well after the first course that the echo of Benedict Trevelyan's words and the heat of his touch settled to a steady throb in my mind. Only then was I able to reflect on the events of the day. Many things had been brought to my awareness. They swirled like a storm through my thoughts.

I'd gained a sure footing in my teaching methods. So far Benedict Trevelyan had no complaints concerning my role as governess. I also decided that the boys and I would take sign-language lessons. I was very curious to know more about Katherine Trevelyan. She wasn't what I expected at all. And Benedict Trevelyan . . . he was more than I expected. So much more that I stood on ground that shook with every glance he directed my way.

During my time here, I'd become less of a stranger within the Trevelyan home, yet it wasn't a safe harbor. The sensation I had was one of slowly moving into a dark storm. Or, even more accurately, I was Alice in *Through the Looking Glass*, with the room, the house, and the world about me suddenly growing smaller, trapping me inside as the Queen of Hearts called for my head.

I flicked my gaze at the others, finding both Mrs. Trevelyan and Katherine Trevelyan staring at me. At that moment I knew what poor Anne Boleyn must have felt as she was condemned and beheaded for crimes with no true judge or jury on her side.

Shuddering, I glanced through my lashes at Constance Ortega. She was in the midst of listening to Mr. Henderson recount how he witnessed the infamous Jesse James and his band of outlaws robbing the box office of the Kansas City Fair last year.

"From the articles in the *Kansas City Times*, you'd think Jesse James is Robin Hood or a noble knight. It is disgusting. The man's a common thief and should be hanged." Mr. Henderson said.

"I hear there is more to the story," Stephen Trevelyan said.

Mr. Henderson raised his brows. "Are you condoning crime?"

"No," Stephen said. "But I do think extenuating circumstances play into situations. When Jesse was younger, Federal soldiers terrorized his family. They flogged Jesse and dangled his father repeatedly from a tree with a noose around his neck, leaving him so damaged that they might as well have murdered him. If the South had won, Jesse James most likely would not be an outlaw now. He would be some war hero fighting for independence. I say, circumstances can drive any man over the edge."

The glance he sent Benedict Trevelyan made me remember Stephen's drunken accusations on my first day in the Trevelyan home. *How can you live with yourself after what you did? She's dead! Pretending none of it ever happened won't make it go away. It won't change what I did, and it won't change what you did either.*

"I agree with Stephen," Constance said. "Circumstances change everything."

I shook my head. "Justify crime by circumstances, and you will throw away justice. There would be no point in laws or punishment for those guilty of breaking the law."

"Justice has a way of serving herself in life. The guilty always suffer—don't you think so, Benedict?" Stephen Trevelyan asked.

Benedict Trevelyan ignored the question and changed the subject after giving his brother a cold look. I shivered.

Throughout the meal, I wondered what personal experience drove Stephen Trevelyan to defend an outlaw. And I wondered even more what had kept Benedict Trevelyan silent during the discussion. He was such a rigid man; I had expected him to argue against his brother. That he didn't spoke volumes to me.

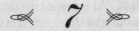

I'm not sure what devil possessed my dreams, but I found myself once again upon my knees on a picnic blanket in Holloway Park with Benedict Trevelyan sitting a mere foot before me. Only this time, when my gaze collided with his and desire flared between us, he grabbed my shoulders.

Then those lips that were so stern fell upon mine with unbelievable softness. I leaned his way, and his arms encircled me, brought me close to his warmth, melting me into him. I floated within the pleasantness of his embrace, like a cloud on a summer's day being caressed by the sun.

Slowly, a darker presence penetrated my haze. The sensation that someone stood watching me renewed itself, racing up my spine, shocking me awake. My heart leapt to my throat as I spied a black form hovering at the end of my bed within the room's midnight shadows. I tried to scream, but fear swelled so quickly within my breast that my cry for help turned to a croak.

The sound alerted my intruder, for the black form stepped back from my bed and disappeared into the darkness. The click of a door shutting spurred me to action. I scrambled to my feet, anger bursting inside me. How dare someone enter my room and frighten me so!

I didn't know which way the intruder had left, but I automatically rushed to the door leading out into the hall, since that is where I most often felt as if someone watched me.

Jerking upon the handle, I jarred my clenched teeth when I met with resistance. The door was locked, just as I'd left it before retiring to bed. I swung around, hurrying to the schoolroom and nursery. I never locked that door, in case Justin and Robert should ever need me during the night.

I didn't see anything lurking in the dim moonlight of the schoolroom, but I decided to take no chances. I returned to my room to light an oil lamp and retraced my steps. Nothing in the schoolroom appeared disturbed. Rather than thoroughly searching the closets and under the desks, I followed my need to check on Justin and Robert. Once I saw they were asleep and safe, then I'd come back and examine the room more closely.

As I passed through the schoolroom, the faint wisp of Benedict Trevelyan's scent brushed across my senses, equally disturbing and comforting in its presence. I couldn't fathom that the master of Trevelyan Hill would enter my room at any time, and certainly not in the middle of the night. Such a breach of propriety didn't seem in keeping with his nature. Yet did I really know him?

The rumors of his wife's death crawled through my mind like scurrying spiders, and I hastened to the nursery, pushing on the door as if my life depended on getting there to escape my thoughts. The door flew open and banged against the wall.

Justin and Robert continued to sleep, safely tucked beneath their covers, but my sigh of relief became a small scream as a man abruptly rose from the rocking chair in the shadowed corner.

In my haste, I tripped, falling back against the doorjamb. Unbalanced, I fought to keep my hold upon the oil lamp as I struggled to stay upright.

Benedict Trevelyan appeared from the dark shadows. He rushed at me, grabbing the lamp from me and catching me about the waist. We both might have fallen had he not pulled me tightly against him and I braced myself in his arms.

"Damnation, Miss Lovell. Would you kill us all in a fire? What are you doing here?"

"The boys . . . I was worried . . . my word! You have frightened me out of my mind."

And truly I must have taken leave of my senses, because my hands were splayed upon his chest as if fastened by an unknown force to his heat and bolstering strength. I was consumed with the feel of him beneath my fingertips and the penetrating effects his body had upon mine. The hard muscles of his thighs and loins, buffered by the molded wool of his trousers, pressed into my softness, leaving me with no illusions to his power or his maleness. He was a man of large proportions.

His white shirt lay unbuttoned, exposing a fluidity of smoothly sculpted muscles corded with power that drew my gaze to the contours beneath my fingers and beyond. Black hair, soft and curly, smattered his chest then funneled into a straight line that disappeared where my hips met his . . . I snatched my gaze back upward and lifted my hands from him as if burned. "Oh, my . . . I . . ."

He blinked at me, and a look of interested surprise overtook his irritation. Any doubts that I had about his character just moments ago flew from my mind.

"Miss Lovell?" he questioned, pulling me even closer.

"Mr. Trevelyan," I gasped, my hands falling to his shoulders as the pressure of his chest upon my breasts lit a fire in my blood. Heat flushed my cheeks and pooled in unmentionable places that ached to feel more of this man. I moaned, needing to breathe, needing something more than—

He groaned, a deep, harsh sound of turmoil. I shot my gaze to his face. His mouth lay in a grim line above his clenched jaw, and his dark eyes burned as hotly as the flame of the lamp reflecting in them. He slid his hand down my back, halting at the curve of my hip, and pulled me tighter to him. Every womanly nerve within me clamored for his attention while every practical part of me screamed in alarm at the insistent press of his maleness against me.

His gravelly voice raked over my sensibilities. "I am not a man given to cautioning others of their folly, but you again tread upon dangerous ground. I suggest you return to your room quickly, or—"

He didn't have to tell me what the "or else" would be.

"Yes," I said, backing away as he released me slowly, almost reluctantly.

He stared at me intently as I did, and I realized that my threadbare nightgown was practically transparent in the lamplight. But it could have been as thick as newly sheared lamb's wool, and it wouldn't have mattered. Not at this moment.

Holding the lamp higher, he stepped forward as I stepped back and I began to babble. "I did not mean to disturb you . . . an intruder was in my room . . . I wanted to assure myself that Justin and Robert were safe . . . I am sor—"

"What?" The power of his voice slashed through mine. He grabbed my arm, wrenching me to a protective place behind him. "An intruder in your room?"

"Yes. Standing at the foot of my bed. I awakened to see—"

"Why did you not tell me immediately?" He didn't wait to hear another word. He marched to the open doorway of my room, lamp raised to dispel the shadows. Compelled, I followed, and gasped as I stepped into my room, nearly bumping into him. A window was opened wide to a marauding breeze; it billowed out the heavy drapes and stirred the bed curtains, making them sway like ghosts about my bed.

"I did not have that open," I whispered, shuddering.

Unable to speak, I watched him cross to the window, peer out into the night, then shut and lock it. When he found the door to my room locked, he didn't comment on it, but proceeded to search the entire room—under the bed, behind the drapes, in the armoire, and even within the cedar chest at the bottom of my bed.

It wasn't until he displaced my robe from the bottom of my bed that I again gave thought to the state of my undress. Hoping to escape his notice, I quietly gathered my robe, and as I slid it on, I glanced his way.

He had stopped his search and stood about three feet away. I had one arm in my robe and my other arm back behind me, searching blindly for my sleeve.

"Is it your wish to see me burn alive?" he asked, seemingly frozen in place. His gaze had centered itself below my chin. The look in his eyes surpassed the gleam of the demon door or even the blaze of a roaring fire. It equally thrilled me and frightened me. When I looked down I saw that my gown was stretched tightly across my chest, leaving the coral tips of my breasts clearly visible.

I groaned in embarrassment, turning from him and struggling harder to find my errant sleeve. I didn't think I'd ever be able to face the man again.

Suddenly I felt the neck of my robe lift, and his firm hand guided my arm into my sleeve. Then he settled the robe on my shoulders.

"Forgive me," I said. "I had not realized—"

"It is entirely my fault. We shall leave it at that and not speak another word of the matter. I see no sign of an intruder. Is it possible that you're mistaken about not having the window open and only saw the bed curtains move in the darkness?"

Though I knew this to be completely impossible, I swallowed my pride and latched onto this excuse, instinctively knowing that this torturous encounter would end sooner if I did. "I may have. But would you search the schoolroom and the nursery also?"

I kept my back to him, still unable to face the rawness of what had sprung between us. For in his eyes, in his voice, I'd witnessed a hunger that went deeper than desire, an emotion of need darker and more desperate than I'd have ever thought possible. That need frightened me more than any intruder could, because that need was within me as well.

"I had planned to search both rooms. In fact I am going to rouse Dobbs and have the entire house checked."

"No," I said, biting my lip, turning to him. I focused on his neck. He'd buttoned his shirt and rolled down his sleeves, but it didn't help. I could clearly recall what lay beneath. "I had been sleeping, and I might have imagined it. There is no need to awaken everyone." It would be too embarrassing for the entire household to be a party to this mess.

If I truly believed my life had been threatened and that threat had come from someone outside of the Trevelyan household, I would have run through the house awakening everyone myself. But I strongly felt that whoever had come into my room had already gone and would deny being there.

I ruled out Benedict Trevelyan as my intruder, for I realized I would have seen the white of his shirt in the darkness or detected his scent. Besides, his concern had been too real, and at some point tonight, after I'd collided with the heat of his gaze, I knew if he'd been standing over me, I would have known it was him. His presence loomed even larger than his size.

In fact, I felt his searching regard now, but refused to meet it. He didn't press me.

"Very well. I will knock after I have finished checking the nursery and the schoolroom."

I didn't breathe or move until I heard the door to the schoolroom shut. He took the lamp with him, and I welcomed the darkness. I didn't want to see my face in the mirror, didn't want to face what I knew had to be in my eyes— an awareness of a desperate need deep inside of me that was stronger than any rule of propriety I'd ever learned.

My father, though born a gentleman in England, had played slave to his base nature. Besides a fever for gold, he'd had a flair for seduction, which he plied without con-science. He'd eloped with my mother, supposedly saving her from the religious fervor of my fire-and-brimstone grand-father, then abandoned her a week later when gold was dis-covered at Sutter's Mill. The marriage license proved to be false. I hated to think that I'd inherited his wantonness.

Not more than five minutes passed before I heard Benedict Trevelyan's knock from the schoolroom. Walking over to the door, I barely cracked it open. "Yes," I said, hold-ing my breath.

"I did not find anything amiss. Justin and Robert are still asleep, and their nurse's door is locked."

"Thank you." I shut my eyes and leaned my head against the cool wood of the door, thankful that he didn't ask me to open it wider.

"Miss Lovell?"

"Yes?"

"Might I ask why you went immediately to Justin and Robert's room instead of screaming into the hall when you thought there was an intruder?"

I blinked and didn't know what to say. "I am not sure. With my door to the hall locked, all I could think about was seeing that they were unharmed."

"Has anything led you to believe that my sons are in dan-ger?"

I pulled the door open then, unable not to look into his eyes. "No. I assure you. If I ever thought anything of that nature, I would tell you immediately. You can trust me."

His gaze searched mine before he handed me the lamp.

"On certain things, Miss Lovell, I am not a man to be trusted. Do not make that mistake," he said softly and then turned, walking into the shadows.

Shutting the door, I leaned against it, clinging to the cool wood. What could I not trust Benedict Trevelyan in? I automatically pressed my fingers to my lips and thought that I knew.

Sleep was out of the question after he left. I spent the rest of the night trying to immerse my mind in a volume of the *Encyclopædia Britannica*.

It wasn't until I happened upon articles concerning the phenomena of electricity that I was able to remotely distract myself. Even then, my thoughts were still centered on Benedict Trevelyan. As I read suppositions on the properties of electricity from scientists connected to the Royal Institution and the Royal Society, I wondered if Benedict Trevelyan and I were afflicted with such a thing. The observations made when one received an electrical shock perfectly described what I experienced when Benedict Trevelyan touched me or even looked at me. But as the night waned to the morning, I knew that even if there was a certain awareness, a kindling of desire, between Benedict Trevelyan and me, I had to firmly put it behind me. I was a practical woman and knew without a doubt that nothing could come of such feelings. He was a man of riches and prestige. I was a woman of little means who couldn't even call legitimacy my own. I'd never belong in his world, and I'd never trespass into the shadowy realm where a woman knew a man without the protection of marriage.

Despite my lack of sleep and last night's odd events, I left the manor with cheerful alacrity the next morning. The dew, still fresh upon the ground, cut the dust and washed the grass and trees to a bright sparkle. A chorus of birds sang, inviting my heart to sing with them.

Saturday had dawned—my first official day off since beginning my employment—and an excitement bubbled inside me that nothing could dampen. Not a finger of fog reached inland from the bay to cloud the day, and a brisk northeasterly breeze joined the bright summer sun to dispel any early-morning shadows.

I had many things I wished to accomplish on what I considered to be my first day of real freedom, ever, and I knew who I would share my excitement with first.

I went to Holloway Park to gather a handful of bright yellow wildflowers for my mother's grave. But just as I left the cover of a copse of shade trees, I saw Miss Ortega and Mr. Henderson. Both held the reins of their horses as they stood, clearly arguing about something, but they were too far away to hear. I was about to call out to them when I saw Miss Ortega slap Mr. Henderson's face and mount her horse. Her reckless pace brought her my way so quickly that I didn't have time to step back into the shadows. She glared at me as she passed, not bothering to stop and greet me. This suited me just fine. I didn't have to get near the beast she rode.

But I had counted my blessings too soon. Mr. Henderson headed my way, riding an even bigger horse. I backed up until a tree halted my retreat. Thankfully, when he dismounted, his horse found a patch of clover to eat, and Mr. Henderson left his horse grazing as he came to where I stood.

"Good morning, Miss Lovell. I hope you had a good night's rest."

"Well enough," I replied, though I hadn't slept much at all after the intruder and my encounter with Benedict Trevelyan. Mr. Henderson's cheek was marked with a bright red handprint, and I wondered what he'd said to provoke Miss Ortega's apparently formidable wrath. We both ignored the incident, though it stood there with us, begging for attention. Glancing at his horse to make sure it was keeping its distance, I noted full saddlebags strapped on. "Mr. Trevelyan mentioned you would be leaving to-day."

"For a short time. I am riding north on business, then I will stop back by here on my return to Kansas City."

"I have heard a great deal about Missouri. How long have you lived there?"

"About a year. I won a deed to a cattle ranch in a card game and found the gold I had been looking twenty-five years for in cattle."

"You were a miner then?"

"Benedict's father and I met here in '49. He was already a prosperous businessman in shipping, but when the gold fever hit, he made a fortune transporting people to California."

It was on the tip of my tongue to ask him if he knew of my father, but I didn't. I didn't want to know what had become of the man who'd abandoned my mother. *Justice has a way of serving herself in life. The guilty always suffer.* Stephen Trevelyan's words from dinner last night ran through my mind. My hands clenched. I hoped so, I thought. For I knew without a doubt that the innocent always suffered. My mother had. Justin and Robert were.

I looked up to see Mr. Henderson studying me intently. He smiled. "Do you often walk alone in the park during the morning?"

"No. This morning I'm after a handful of those flowers over there." I pointed to a bright patch just ahead. "I am taking them to my mother's grave."

"My condolences then. Grief has a way of touching us all, don't you think, Miss Lovell?"

"I suppose. Have you recently suffered a loss?"

Mr. Henderson hesitated, and the ease on his face turned to grim lines. "No, not recently." He cleared his throat.

"Well. No doubt I will see you upon my return. It was a pleasure to meet you, Miss Lovell."

"And you as well, Mr. Henderson." He left then, and I went back to gathering flowers, wondering what Miss Ortega and Mr. Henderson had been arguing about. When I reached the cemetery and found the small wooden cross marking my mother's grave, I put thoughts of those at Trevelyan Manor aside. One day soon I'd replace the cross with the permanency of stone; no matter how quietly my mother had lived her life, she deserved to be known even long after I was gone from this earth. I'd given a lot of thought as to what I'd have engraved on her headstone and settled for a verse of simple beauty.

Her life was as finite as the earth,
but her love reaches beyond the stars.

I meant to save going to Talbot's Fashion Emporium as my last errand for the day, but I found myself standing before the shop door, peering inside like a child before a confectioner's. I'd no sooner pressed my nose to the window, looking at a beautiful lace shawl draped elegantly over a tasteful chair, when the front door popped open. A gray-haired woman whose smile and eyes twinkled as brightly as stars introduced herself as Mrs. Talbot and invited me inside. I nearly had to shield my eyes from the peacock blue of her dress. The color was so bright that I at first wondered how anyone could wear it and not feel out of place; but within seconds of following Mrs. Talbot into the shop, I knew the vibrant color suited her perfectly.

She'd yet to even know my name or purpose but had welcomed me as if I were a lady of means.

"Now, dear, I must tell you that gray is definitely not

your color," she said, clucking at my dress. "You have come to the right place. I have this absolutely divine blue fabric just in from New York this week."

"Mrs. Talbot, I am afraid I'm not here to order a new dress. I am newly in Mr. Benedict Trevelyan's employ, and he referred me to you. I believe you have several dresses already—"

"Why, my dear! You are perfect for them. Please, come with me."

She led me to a fitting room and then began bringing in armfuls of things. I tried to stop her several times, but she wouldn't hear of it. She kept saying, Just a little more and she'd have it all.

"There," she said at last. "This is the lot of it."

"But surely there is some mistake. This is too much, Mrs. Talbot. I truly could not take all of this." I couldn't fathom the bounty she'd spread about the fitting room. Besides five dresses, there were undergarments, hats, gloves, parasols, handbags, nightgowns, robe, and slippers. My word, if I were to actually wear it all, I'd need my own laundress.

"You cannot?" Mrs. Talbot's face crumbled. "Do you not like the style of the dresses? I can possibly change them."

"No, please. They are beautiful. It is just that there is so much, I could not possibly allow Mr. Trevelyan to pay for all of this. Two dresses and one pair of shoes should do."

"Oh, dear. This leaves me in quite a quandary," Mrs. Talbot said, sending the wrinkles between her graying brows into a deep frown. "You see, I ordered and tailored all of these things for a woman who moved back east. She left me without payment and with no forwarding address. I have not told Mr. Talbot about the situation either." She lowered her voice. "He owns the dry goods store next to me and keeps saying that I have no business sense whatsoever. Why, if my fashion emporium does not make as much as his store this year, then he says he will close the doors to my shop!"

My back went ramrod-stiff. "That is awful!" I said, gasping with indignation.

Mrs. Talbot sighed. "I see you are but a chick from the egg yet, Miss Lovell. This is a man's world, and the West is even more unbalanced than the East. I daresay it will take something on a scale as big as the war between the North and the South to set things right for women."

I immediately felt a kinship with her dilemma, for all too often my mother and I had suffered from this unbalance. But the only way I could consider accepting such a wealth of clothing would be to pay Benedict Trevelyan back for all of it but the two dresses and one pair of shoes I deemed necessary for my employment. I explained this to Mrs. Talbot, then asked for a detailed account of the costs.

"Bless you, dear. In fact, I am going to give you a special price for the items. We women must help each other."

Nodding, I agreed with her. She promised not to mention my intentions to Benedict Trevelyan. He was not a man who liked to have his wishes altered.

After Mrs. Talbot's, I stopped at the Music Academy, making arrangements for several personable pianists to come to Trevelyan Hill and audition for the position of Justin and Robert's music teacher once I confirmed a date and time with Benedict Trevelyan.

Music would improve the dreary tone within the Trevelyan home. I also visited the Institute for the Deaf and Blind. I knew nothing of communicating with someone locked into a world of silence and thought that the boys and I would benefit from having a teacher come to us. I didn't know what education Katherine Trevelyan had

had, but I assumed it would have been nothing but the best.

I walked into Mr. McGuire's Bookstore a woman who'd moved into a different world in two short weeks, a world that was just as frightening as it was exciting. I found comfort in seeing that Mr. McGuire hadn't changed in the least. As always, he was engrossed in a book and nearly buried by the mounds of tomes around him.

"Something is rotten in the state—"

"Why the gloom, Puck?" I said, running a finger along his tail to ruffle him. "Do you not know the sun is the master of the sky today?"

"Squawk." Puck inched himself away from my touch, moving to the opposite end of his wooden perch.

"I see you are fickle with your affections as usual."

"Perhaps he is but trying to warn ye, lass." Mr. McGuire's voice rolled with gloom.

I turned to him, concerned. "What is amiss?"

Oddly, before answering, he glanced about the shop as if ensuring we were alone. Then when satisfied, he set the Closed sign in the window and locked the door. By the time he finished, I'd surpassed concern and moved into the dangerous ground of real fear. In all the years I'd known him, he'd only closed the shop during the day for a funeral. That had been my mother's. "What is it? Are you ill?"

"I have something to tell ye, lass. And I want no other ears aboot."

"Has harm befallen someone?"

"Aye, but that harm happened about a year ago." He pushed his spectacles higher, staring directly into my eyes. "I spoke to the man who used to be Francesca Trevelyan's doctor. He swears she didn't commit suicide, not by throwing herself from the turret window. He says he has proof that she was murdered."

8

My breath caught in my throat. Since my life had been fraught with rumors, I was accustomed to easily dismissing them. But proof of murder was an entirely different matter. "What proof? Why has he not notified the authorities of this and an arrest been made?"

Mr. McGuire shook his head, tumbling wisps of gray hair over his forehead and knocking his bifocals to the end of his nose. "Ah, lass, there's a different set of rules when it comes to the rich. Ye've seen enough of the West to know that. The doctor gave his expert opinion on several occasions at official inquiries, and each time his theory didn't hold sway against Benedict Trevelyan's influence and desire to have the death declared a suicide."

My heart and stomach collided, making me suddenly ill.

"O, let me not be mad, not mad," squawked Puck.

I blessed Puck for the interruption, then prayed my legs would hold me upright as I moved toward a chair. My mouth felt dry, and a dizzy sensation tilted the room before me. I managed to sit rather than fall, but I had to swallow three times before I could speak. "Mr. Trevelyan has deliberately thwarted efforts to find his wife's murderer?"

Never was I more thankful that Mr. McGuire's eyesight was poor at a distance. For he surely would have noted my shock, and I would have been hard-pressed to explain how deeply my emotions had already been ensnared by the Trevelyan family after only two weeks of employment.

Mr. McGuire shrugged, his watery eyes gravely concerned. "Seems to be so, lass. Ye must take care."

I nodded my head, still trying to grasp what Mr. McGuire meant. "You must tell me. What exactly did the doctor say? Why is he so sure Francesca Trevelyan was murdered?"

"It's a good thing ye are sitting down, because the truth of it isn't pretty. Seems that Francesca Trevelyan was a wee lass, given to vapors, and oft' took laudanum for severe headaches. Dr. Levinworth began seeing her when she married Benedict Trevelyan and swears the lass ne'er would have chosen such a painful death. Ye ken what I mean?"

I forced myself to breathe before I fell unconscious. "She would not have jumped from the mansion's tower."

"Aye. Dr. Levinworth says she'd have overdosed on laudanum and died in her soft bed were she of the mind to do herself in." He paused and pushed his bifocals back to the bridge of his nose then lowered his voice. "There's more. The lass smelled heavily of laudanum at the time of her death, and her injuries indicate she fell headfirst from the tower instead of feetfirst, as you'd expect."

I shivered, seeing in my mind the gruesome image of a drugged Francesca being thrown from the tower window, unable to stop her brutal death. I was familiar with laudanum. My mother had needed it the last few days of her life, and I knew the drug to be powerful enough to have rendered any man or woman helpless. My stomach heaved at the wickedness of such an act, and my heart immediately denied that Benedict Trevelyan could be so cruel.

"I fear there's yet more." Mr. McGuire cleared his throat, a blush creeping across his wrinkled, spotted cheeks. " 'Tis a bit unseemly for me to mention such a thing, but ye must know. She was with child when she died, she was."

"Oh, no!" I cried, my heart hurting for what Benedict Trevelyan must have felt in losing not only his wife but an unborn child as well.

"Frailty, thy name is woman," Puck squawked. I glared at the infernal bird, wondering what imp inhabited his feathered spine. His quips were too uncanny to ignore; nevertheless, ignore them I did. "That's so tragic."

"Aye, the lass was three months along, according to Dr. Levinworth. It was this fact Benedict Trevelyan paid the officials to hide."

"But why? I don't understand what—"

"Benedict Trevelyan had only returned home a week before she died. He'd been gone six months."

McGuire's words rang like a death knell in my mind as I hurried back to Trevelyan Hill. All the brightness of my day of freedom had been stolen. Even the prospect of wearing one of my new dresses to dinner held no joy.

The air was heavy in my lungs, almost too thick to breathe, forcing me to gasp for air as I rushed up the hill to the manor at a painful pace. Whether I was fleeing from what I'd learned or hurrying to find proof that Mr. McGuire's implications were false, I knew not. I just wanted to get to Trevelyan Manor as quickly as possible.

Dark emotions ran deep within Benedict Trevelyan. I'd already seen glimpses of them, had already felt them rearing to the surface at unexpected moments, though I'd only known him a short time. He was a man capable of passion. He was a large man, a man of great strength, and more damning than anything else, he was a man of stern rigidity. What would such a man do when faced with an unfaithful wife who carried another man's child?

I drew closer to the house on Trevelyan Hill, not in the least surprised to see billowing clouds of fog cover its towers, roof, and upper windows, obscuring its stained glass windows as if to wipe any redeeming quality from its facade. I stopped in the street, thinking to catch my breath, but I believe it was more to give myself time before I faced the demon door and those who lived within the manor.

I heard the pounding hooves of a horse only moments before a dark specter charged from the mists, sending the fog in an uproar. Fingers of it whirled around me, brushing over my skin and making me shiver. Though a handful of feet separated me from the horse on the street, I still jumped back and cried out with fright. I again cursed my fear of horses, a completely impractical fear for a woman living in the West. Especially big, dark, hulking horses like the one Benedict Trevelyan rode so effortlessly, a man with iron hands who wore velvet gloves. He was in complete command and yet so gentle.

He must have seen me or heard me cry out, because he brought the horse to an abrupt, pawing stop and dismounted. I didn't take my gaze off of the beast as I stood there, frozen in place, paralyzed.

"Miss Lovell, I was just going to look for—"

The horse pranced to the side, nearing me, and the scream that was locked within my throat loosened with a fervor.

Benedict Trevelyan grabbed my arm. "Good God, woman! What in the devil is wrong with you?"

"The horse," I managed to gasp.

"What is wrong with it?" He glanced at the beast. "Damnation, Miss Lovell, if you see something bloody amiss with my horse, speak up."

I swallowed and finally could move enough to step back. "It is big." Pulling my gaze from the threat of the beast, I looked at Benedict Trevelyan, and for an unguarded moment, I saw what I could only describe as pain slash across his face, as if I'd taken a sword and struck him. Then what I'd seen disappeared so quickly behind a cold mask, I wondered if I had imagined it.

"Some things God made large. I thought you of all people would understand that." His reference to my height was unmistakable, and I wondered why he'd taken offense. It was as if I'd spoken of him, not his horse. The measuring stare he leveled on me clearly said that I'd shrunk considerably in his eyes. Apparently fear had no place in his life. His finding me lacking bothered me greatly. I wanted him to understand.

He turned away, adjusting the horse's reins, and I thought he was about to remount. Without thinking of how forward it would be, I placed my hand on his arm. Even through the material of my glove and his clothes, I could feel the heat of his body, feel the supple movement and strength of his muscles as he moved. I gasped, but didn't let go.

He froze, slowly focusing his gaze on my hand touching him, then met my gaze directly. Disdain no longer lurked in his dark eyes. A hunger had replaced it. Suddenly, I was thrust back to last night and the stark moment we had stared at each other in my bedroom.

I snatched my hand back. Fire flooded my cheeks as embarrassment and desire ran rampant inside me. I hurried to explain, glancing warily at the horse. "It's so powerful. When I was little, waiting for my mother at the doorway of the baker's, I saw a boy kicked and trampled by a horse. He died. It was awful."

Embarrassing me more, tears welled in my eyes. I looked away, my gaze settling on Trevelyan Manor; but instead of seeing in my mind's eye the dying boy, I saw Francesca

Trevelyan, a broken and lifeless sacrifice at the house's foundation.

I fisted my hand, remembering the warm, strong feel of Benedict Trevelyan. I in no way felt as if I'd touched a murderer. Yet how could I know for sure? What darkness lurked within the shadows of his eyes?

"The only way to conquer your fears are to face them," he said softly, drawing my attention. He held out the horse's reins to me.

I shook my head, backing up. The image of Francesca turned to an image of myself beneath a horse's hooves. "No. I could not possibly ride that beast."

His laugh was strained, but I was thankful to find his manner a great deal less condemning than before. "I am not suggesting you ride Fjorgyn, only that you walk her a step or two."

"Fjorgyn?" I remarked. Desperately looking for a way to stall the inevitable, I searched my mind for where I'd heard the unusual name before, rolling the horse's name off my tongue again, until it came to me. "The mother of Thor, the god of thunder. According to Norse legend, Fjorgyn, the goddess of the earth, was one of Odin's wives."

He raised his brows. "This time, Miss Lovell, you must tell me how you happened upon so obscure a fact. Most hear of Thor, or Odin, or Loki, and some know of Odin's wife Frigg because she is the namesake for Friday, but Fjorgyn?"

"I owe my knowledge of Odin and his wives to cursed stubbornness."

Amusement curved his lips. "Well, you cannot leave the story there. You will have to tell me more while I escort you up the drive." He gestured me forward and then fell into step beside me. He didn't comment on the wide berth I'd given his horse to step by him, and I was glad to see that he let the reins completely out, allowing the horse to follow at a distance.

Walking in the mists, I was more aware of him beside me than of the horse behind me. It was as if I was in a dream. The disturbing things I'd learned from Mr. McGuire didn't seem real. Death and murder weren't a part of this moment or even remotely connected to the man half-smiling at me. His riding coat was a deep, rich brown and topped a ruffled shirt, fawn breeches, and black boots. A lock of his dark hair had fallen to his forehead, adding to his rakish appeal, making him look younger and freer. Something inside me ached to know this man.

I found myself pretending. I was someone different—a woman who inspired passion. He wasn't my employer, but a man taken by me. And we were somewhere else, a place where he held my hand, and we strolled through the park with no more care upon our shoulders than observing the weather.

He had an effect on me that made other things fall into insignificance. I hardly noticed the fog closing in or the damp chill in the air. And I in no way connected him to murder.

"Miss Lovell, your story?"

Prompted, I snatched myself back to reality. "There is not much to the story. I may have mentioned Captain Balder to you. Whenever he was in port, he would come to have his clothes laundered, and my mother bartered lessons for me with her labor. He got clean clothes, and I learned about navigating by the stars, foreign lands, and how to swim."

"So he taught you about the gods of the Vikings?"

"Not directly. You see, every time he came to see us, he asked my mother to marry him. She would refuse, and then he would tell her she was cursed with stubbornness."

"I do not understand how that corresponds to Norse legends," he said, his brow furrowing.

I couldn't help but grin at the memory washing over me. "Captain Balder, also named after another son of Odin, had a wife in every port. What was good enough for his Norse ancestors was good enough for him. If Odin could have five wives or more, so could he. I learned about the Viking gods by listening to him give examples of what great sons polygamy produced. I do not think Captain Balder ever realized that he sunk his own ship by doing so. My mother went to the bookstore, read about the Norse gods, and decided the whole lot of them were immoral barbarians that she was better off without."

His laugh started low at first, then rumbled out loud and deep, surprising me, for I didn't think I'd said anything particularly funny. Still I joined him, embracing the memory. It surprised me to hear him laugh. I'd not expected moments of lightness from him. Here in the mists, it was almost as if he was a different person than the master of Trevelyan Hill in his dark study.

We laughed briefly, and the humor touched me, easing some of the burden that had settled on my heart at Mr. McGuire's. I wondered if I would ever have the courage to ask Benedict Trevelyan about his wife. For I didn't want to know the truth of things as we walked through the fog; I wanted to hide within it and pretend that the very manor before us didn't exist, that the tragic death of its mistress had never happened.

As we neared the steps, he stopped. "Tomorrow, Miss Lovell," he said, "meet me in the stables at six-thirty in the morning, and I will introduce you to another of Odin's wives."

I swallowed and may have nodded, but whatever I did must have indicated that I would meet him.

"Good," he said, mounting his horse. "And one more thing, Miss Lovell. I would not mention the intruder incident last night to anyone else. It is only something that will upset my mother and my sister. And you did say that it was possible you dreamed the problem, correct?"

This time, I did nod. Satisfied, he cantered off into the mist, and I wondered what my association with him was going to cost me.

"Miss Lovell, you have caused quite a disturbance," Dobbs said the moment I stepped inside.

"I have?" I replied, snapping off my gloves as if I'd done so all of my life. That one act seemed to symbolize how drastically my life had changed, and I loved it. If Dobbs hadn't stood there glowering at me, I would have put them on and snapped them off again. Satisfaction and a sense of achievement flooded through me as I laid my gloves over my arm and gave Dobbs my attention. "Please explain."

"Mr. Trevelyan has been in a quandary ever since the heavy fog began moving in. You left this morning without speaking to anyone. None knew where to even begin looking for you. This left me in an intolerable position. The master has raced off to search for you. And now I will be put to the task of sending a footman after him. This kind of behavior is most unseemly, and I will not tol—"

"I have already spoken to Mr. Trevelyan, Mr. Dobbs. He is quite aware of my return. Is there anything else?"

Dobbs blinked. His mouth fell open, then clenched shut.

I turned to leave, determined to avoid his dour lecture. I didn't want anything to dispel the lingering mists from my mind—mists that I knew cloaked what I should be thinking, given what I'd learned today.

"There is the matter of Mrs. Trevelyan."

I froze mid-step, my nerves jangling. Why would Dobbs

speak to me of Francesca Trevelyan? Had Mr. McGuire spoken my name to Dr. Levinworth, and he in turn mentioned my name . . . That didn't make sense. I shook my head, almost stumbling over my own feet as I turned his way. "What do you mean?"

"Mrs. Trevelyan has been demanding to see you since this morning. I will notify Nurse Maria of your arrival, and she can escort you to her."

Of course. Dobbs spoke of Benedict Trevelyan's mother, not his deceased wife. I nearly shuddered with relief and chastised myself for jumping to that conclusion.

"Tell Nurse Maria that I will be in my room." Turning, I hurried up the stairs. I wanted time to freshen up before facing Mrs. Trevelyan. Instinct told me that I'd need every ounce of my confidence to visit with a woman who only spoke to me when politeness demanded it of her.

In my room, piled like a mountain of blessings, were the packages from Mrs. Talbot's store. I set myself into a whirlwind of activity, and by the time I heard Maria's knock on the door, I'd managed a refreshing scrub and slipped into one of the simplest of my new dresses. Remembering Mrs. Talbot's remark that the lavender pinstripe suited my coloring well, I put it on. I did so, not because I imagined Mrs. Trevelyan might say anything positive about my appearance, but because I'd shortly be seeing Benedict Trevelyan across the dinner table. Not even the thought of Constance's chatter could dampen the confident excitement my new dress inspired.

It didn't escape my notice that Benedict's mother had waited until my day off to call for me. I also resented that I couldn't stay in my room and drown myself in my new things—an indulgence I'd never been able to luxuriate in.

Maria led the way, acting as if I was a heretic about to meet the Inquisition. And perhaps I was; the glaring looks

Mrs. Trevelyan had sent my way since the beginning of my employment had all but burned me at the stake.

Mrs. Trevelyan's room was on the first floor, situated in the opposite wing from mine and impossibly more oppressive than Benedict Trevelyan's study. The moment I stepped into her rooms, I felt as if I couldn't breathe. The temperature had to rival that of a desert at high noon. I immediately broke into a sweat.

Covering the windows hung red velvet curtains, so tightly drawn that not even a sliver of sunlight stole into the room. The furniture, hulking masses of black wood, filled the outer rim of the room. The softness of the carpet beneath my feet might have dispelled some of the gloom, but its dark red hues offered no relief from the depressing tones.

I'd always been a lover of scents, with roses being one of my favorites. But the cloying aroma here was too sweet, sickly sweet, and caused my head to ache. In the center of the room stood a single red and gold brocade wing chair, which Maria motioned me to before leaving. As I sat, I noted an altar with dozens of burning candles, set up to the right of a hearth. The blazing fire offered no comfort.

My Inquisition notion didn't seem too fanciful. A minute or so passed before Marie wheeled Mrs. Trevelyan in, dressed as usual in black, with her customarily dour expression in place. She had her wheelchair parked directly in front of me.

Rather than greeting me in any way, she continued to work on an embroidered tapestry for several minutes, her fingers adeptly weaving a threaded gold needle through the cloth. I'd never seen a gold needle before, and I wondered if she had them custom-made. My mother had taught me how to embroider, but I'd never spent my spare time doing so. Any time I could avoid having material in my hands, I did so.

She glowered at my lavender dress and cream-colored boots. "Well, I see you have finagled new clothes out of my son already."

The cordial greeting sitting on the tip of my tongue jumped back down my throat. I had to swallow before speaking. "Your son was generous enough to insist I be properly attired to escort his sons about town. However, whatever monies were spent on my behalf I consider to be a loan only, which will be paid back over the course of my employment."

She leaned forward in her chair and lowered her voice. "You will not be here that long. I have already seen one woman nearly destroy my family, and I am not about to let an upstart laundress come in and do the same."

Her frankness and antipathy I had expected, but it was the pure hate emanating from her that slapped me in the face. "I assure you, my intent is to see to Master Justin and Master Robert's education and well-being. I have a job to perform in this household, and that is my sole purpose here." Anything else was completely preposterous, only mad musings for the darkness at midnight—not a topic for a chat over tea.

"Heed my words, Miss Lovell. You have already sown the seeds that could destroy what little remains of my family. I will see you burn in hell beside his first wife if those seeds begin to sprout. Now tell me, what exactly are you teaching my grandsons?"

I blinked. The woman had just threatened to terminate my employment, threatened to see me in hell, and now wanted to discuss her grandsons? Even though I realized she fiercely loved her family, it did not excuse her rudeness. I'd heard she'd been in declining health since the loss of her husband, the family's patriarch, two years ago. Yet I could conjure up very little sympathy for her plight, nowhere near enough to excuse her actions. In my opinion, the woman was making herself ill, the way she sequestered herself in this inferno-like dungeon of a room.

Gripping the arms of the chair, I considered marching angrily from her rooms and telling Benedict Trevelyan that his mother was a lunatic. To sit here and meekly let her bully me about was intolerable.

I rose, deciding I wasn't going to carry any tales, but I'd stand my ground when it came to respect. "If you have an interest in what your grandsons are learning, I suggest you join our lessons or spend a little time with them directly. I do not take kindly to being threatened. So should you wish to have a cordial conversation with me in the future, I suggest you keep that in mind. Good day to you." I marched from the room, thinking that if Benedict's mother wasn't wheelchair bound, she could very well have murdered Francesca. I was shaking from the encounter, but I felt as if I'd made another step in establishing a life for myself beyond the lot of a laundress.

In the third-floor hallway, I passed Maria, who looked at me in utter surprise. I assumed it was because she'd expected my meeting with Mrs. Trevelyan to have lasted longer. That was until I reached my room and found the new things from Mrs. Talbot's dumped in a nasty pile on the floor. Nothing looked as if it had been destroyed, just thrown down as if it all were of little worth. This time I had no doubt as to whom had been in my room and why.

Apparently Mrs. Trevelyan didn't need to be able to walk. Not when she had servants to carry out her ill will.

I stood there with my hands clenched as I fought back tears. The jumbled mess was only clothes, and not even dirty ones at that. I'd been cleaning up worse piles most of my life, and I shouldn't view this one as being any different. But I did. These were my new things. I found I wasn't as practical as I thought myself to be, for I barely restrained myself from going to Maria's room and returning the favor.

9

During the night, I hoped for rain. None appeared, no matter how many times I peered out of the window. I cursed my unfailing good constitution, for I failed to develop an ailment, no matter how hard I prayed for one. I searched my mind for any legitimate excuse to keep me from the stables but found none worthy enough. I then resorted to wishing lightning would strike.

It didn't.

Sunday morning dawned brightly, promising a healthy dose of sunshine. I didn't even have the luxury of using my lessons with Justin and Robert as an excuse to avoid the stables, for I had half of the day free. Still, I dallied, spending an inordinate amount of time deciding what to wear before finally settling on a gown of deep blue with tiny black pinstripes. I thought the color complemented my gray eyes and brown hair. I fussed with my hair. I dusted my room, twice. Then I sat back down and waited for something, anything, to happen until my conscience wouldn't allow me to delay any longer.

Much to my consternation, no accidents befell me as I walked to the stables. And worse yet, any reason I could think of to avoid the horses did nothing but draw another condemning look from Benedict Trevelyan in my mind's eye. It daunted me that even when he wasn't about, I could shut my eyes and see him all too clearly.

As I neared the entrance to the stables, he seemed so real in my mind that I could hear his deep voice speaking as if wooing a lover.

"You are greedy for affection this morning, aren't you? You love being stroked, love the feel of my hand upon your neck." I closed my eyes. My hand instantly went to my throat and touched the spot where I imagined I could feel him.

"There. Hold right there. Doesn't that feel good?"

The sound of an answering whinny brought my eyes wide open. I stepped into the shadowed recesses of the stable, where I found Benedict Trevelyan in front of a stall, caressing a horse bigger and blacker than the one he'd ridden yesterday.

A layer of fresh hay covered the floor. I could smell the sunshine sweetness of it among the strong odors of animal and leather. Dust motes danced in the streams of light threading their way through the stable, giving an overall ambience of warmth—definitely not the dank lair of a beast. Above each or the stalls were names branded into the wood—Odin, Frigg, Fjorgyn, Balder, Hodr, Rind, Indu, Bragi, Loki, Vali, Freyja, Sigyn, Narvi, and more, all from Viking legend—and I found myself rather interested. It would seem the master of Trevelyan Hill had a penchant for the unusual, something the oppressive staidness of his study didn't reveal.

"Good morning, Miss Lovell. I see your punctuality does not apply to appointments with horses."

My eyes adjusted to the dimmer light, and I saw that he—dressed more simply than the day before in riding pants and a shirt—regarded me with dry amusement.

Considering the effect his casual dress and relaxed air had upon my sensibilities, it was a wonder I could speak. "I, um, mistakenly thought it would rain. Did you not hear the thunder?" Surely he had to hear it. My heart was roaring.

He only lifted an eyebrow in the face of my blatant lie. "Indeed. Thunder? Perhaps you heard Thor being set free in the pasture. He tends to make a lot of noise. But there's no harm done. I have plenty of time this morning, and Gunnlod is a patient girl." He brushed the horse's mane.

I blinked with disbelief when the horse seemingly nodded its head up and down as if she'd understood what he'd said. I had to have imagined it. "She is named for another wife of Odin's? The giantess?"

"Correct. She's big, but she's gentle. When you are ready to ride, she will be perfect for you."

Shaking my head, I stepped back. "I do not think that I will be ready for that for at least"—I looked at the horse—"ten years."

He laughed. "I will give you ten days, but let's not borrow tomorrow's trouble. Come say hello to Gunnlod, and then I will take you to see her colt."

Reluctantly, I took two steps closer, stopping a few feet away.

"Bragi would be the colt?" I asked, following Odin's family tree, hoping that Benedict Trevelyan would forget about introducing me to the horse if I kept him talking.

"Right again," he said, then surprised me by reaching out and taking my hand, pulling me beside him. "Come along, Miss Lovell. Gunnlod does bite, but only apples and at Odin when he's in her way." To prove his point, he held out an apple.

I had no time to think about the warmth of his skin against mine or the comfort his touch imbued on my nerves, for Gunnlod's giant head pushed farther from her stall to merely inches from where I stood. To my surprise, she gently extracted the apple from Benedict Trevelyan's hand, leaving all of his fingers intact. I laughed as she crunched, eating the whole fruit in seconds. She seemed— harmless? No, just less of an ogre than I imagined.

"Your turn," he said holding out an apple to me.

"No, Mr. Trevelyan. I must say, you do that so well, I would just as soon watch you—"

He plopped the apple in my hand. "Miss Lovell, surely a woman who had the wherewithal to apply for a teaching position with no credentials can muster up the courage to feed a gentle horse an apple."

I looked at the apple, then at him. I blinked several times, searching for anything to distract him. "Mr. Trevelyan, if you have any complaints about the proficiency or methodology of my performance as a teacher, please do tell—"

"Miss Lovell, as of this moment I have none. Unfortunately, I am not as patient as Gunnlod and would greatly appreciate it if you would cease delaying."

He knew what I was up to. I drew a righteous breath, set to deny his charge. Then I met his amused gaze and exhaled in defeat. "Very well. If you have no wish to discuss—"

"Miss Lovell."

I sighed. Holding my hand flat, with the apple on my palm, I extended my arm as far as I could. I thought my heart would leap from my chest as the horse swung her head my way. She parted her lips, revealing her huge teeth as she opened her mouth. My hand shook, my body shivered, and my breath caught in my throat, nearly strangling me.

Then suddenly I felt myself encased in steady warmth as Benedict Trevelyan stepped in behind me and slid his hand beneath mine. "Easy now. If you jerk your hand away, you will frighten her."

Frighten her! What about me? I barely felt the horse nab

the apple from my hand as my fear fell beneath the onslaught of new sensations Benedict Trevelyan brought. Just inches from my ear, the deepness of his voice and the heat of his breath reached inside me and set me afire. It was as if my body were a hearth and my unmentionables the dry kindling waiting for his spark. I was aware of every brush of his body through the fabric of my dress. I was aware of every breath he took and of every breath I couldn't seem to draw. And everything that happened the other night flooded my mind. I remembered in every detail the contours of his chest beneath my fingertips, the heat of his maleness pressed to my softness, and the intensity of his gaze as he had stared at me in my nightgown.

I grew light-headed. I'd been too nervous to eat this morning, had only picked at my food last night, and now the flood of sensations sweeping over me seemed to be carrying me away with them. Spots wavered before my eyes. My arms and legs became heavy with a tingling sensation. My blood rushed faster and roared a warning in my ears. "Mr. Trevelyan, I do believe that I am going to fai—"

The last sensation I had before a dark fog filled my mind was that of strong arms wrapping around me, picking me up before I fell.

I quickly recovered my senses and found myself ensconced in Benedict Trevelyan's arms, my heart still thundering, my mind dazed. Heavens, the man had the most unprecedented effect upon me.

He'd carried me to a bench inside the stables. The wall above us had various metal bits and leather reins neatly hanging from shiny hooks. Wooden structures draped with colorful blankets supported expensively carved saddles. I could smell lemon oil, hay, animal sweat, and earth. But stronger than any other scent around me was his scent. He stared at me, a deep frown furrowing his brow. I stared at him, taking in the shadow of his granite jaw, the curving softness of his lips, and the heated interest in his eyes.

"Forgive me, Miss Lovell. I had no idea how deep-seated your fear was. Are you all right? Do I need to call the doctor?"

Never in my life would I tell him that it wasn't my fear of horses that had overwhelmed me. "No. No doctors. I am of the opinion that unless I am upon my deathbed, they are more apt to hinder than help. A cup of tea most often does more good."

His lips twitched, drawing my attention to them. "I see we are of the same opinion, then, but I swear by a properly aged brandy rather than tea. Since we have neither here, I suggest you rest a minute. You are quite flushed."

As he spoke, I found myself fascinated by the smoothness of his lips and the dip that split his chin. My fingers itched to feel the textures filling my vision—rough, silky, smooth, and warm.

I didn't think there was any part of him that wouldn't be warm, very warm. No wonder I was flushed, and in a quandary, too. I didn't know whether to embrace the fact that I had fainted—for otherwise I don't think I would have ever known how heavenly it felt to be held by him—or to be appalled, a reaction that would have been instinctive two weeks ago. A few short weeks ago, I would have found the notion that a man could make me faint laughable.

"Somehow, Miss Lovell, you have managed to attract a piece of hay." He reached up and brushed his fingers through the wisps of hair just behind my ear. His action brought to mind the words he spoke to Gunnlod as I stood outside the stable. *You are greedy for affection this morning, aren't you? You love being stroked, love the feel of my hand upon your neck.*

"Yes," I whispered to the voice in my mind.

His eyes dilated, his breath rasped, and I bit my lip to keep myself from whispering yes again.

"Careful," he said. "You will hurt yourself, you . . . should not . . . do that." He brushed his finger over my lip, soothing my bite. I gasped as a lightninglike bolt of pleasure struck me deep inside. I freed my lip, and he bent his head toward mine. I knew with a shock that he would kiss me. My lips parted. My breath caught. Then his warm, supple lips touched mine, briefly, fleetingly, as if it were something not quite real. Indeed, were it not for the strength of his hands digging into my arm and leg where he gripped me, I would have thought I had imagined it.

He stared at me, his face but inches from mine, his eyes so intense and black that I was but seconds from drowning within them. He appeared flushed and quite shocked as well.

I could not possibly allow myself to faint again. Yet that dizzy sensation seemed determined to render me senseless again. Practicality saved me, or ruined me—I was not sure which—for when I tried to sit up, he helped me do so, then quickly moved away from me. I immediately felt the loss of his body next to mine. He looked at me, then began to pace as stiffly as the granite his eyes and fisted hands had become.

Had I thought everything about him warm? He seemed cold now, as if winter had suddenly rushed in and covered him with frost.

"Miss Lovell, I fear I have taken horrible advantage of your weakened state. I understand if you wish to leave my employ."

His words sparked my anger. I jumped up from the bench, steadying myself. "Are you terminating my employment, Mr. Trevelyan?"

"No, but I understand should you wish to. I should not have kissed you—"

"Let me be perfectly clear about this matter. If and when I have no use for you as an employer, you shall hear those words directly from me."

His eyes widened as he realized that I'd used—almost exactly—the words he had said to me in his office Friday afternoon.

Some people are given to misinterpreting the actions of others, led astray by the intricacy of their thoughts. Apparently, Benedict Trevelyan and I were two such people. Just so he would have no doubt that as an employer and as a man he had in no way taken advantage of me, I let him know exactly what I thought about the situation.

"I am insulted that you think me such a ninny. I assure you, Mr. Trevelyan, that had I found your kiss repulsive, I am intelligent enough to say no. Why, I am even capable of protecting myself in certain situations. I can shoot straight and know all men are vulnerable if you know where to strike. Besides, I cannot say that you really did kiss me. I hardly felt your lips upon mine."

Turning on my heel, I marched from the stable, barely restraining myself from kicking at the hay. I had always known I wasn't a woman who incited passion; but I suppose in my secret dreams, I hoped that should I ever be kissed, the man would have felt something more than guilt. I expected that when the grand event happened, there'd be no question in my mind that I had been kissed either. Shouldn't it have been like I felt before swooning, instead of a frustrating feather of a promise?

When I reached my room, I determined I wasn't fit company for anyone and spent the rest of my leisure time with my sketchbook. I could not decide if I wanted Benedict Trevelyan to kiss me again or not. Sitting on the cushioned seat beneath the window, I drew until the lowering of the afternoon sun and the tolling of the grandfather clock told me that my first day and a half of freedom had ended. The picture I had drawn of Benedict was the best I had ever done. I drew him at the helm of a ship amid a raging storm, his hair wildly blowing, his dark eyes daring and determined, his muscled limbs and torso bursting with energy. Every stroke I had drawn held a sensual longing that was made readily apparent in the miniature picture I had sketched in an upper corner—that of Benedict kissing me as if I were the only woman in the world for him.

Heat fanned my cheeks, and I nearly ripped the picture from my pad, but I couldn't. So I gathered a good dose of my practicality and ignored the portrait and my spinsterish musings. Though I might entertain in my dreams a kiss from a man such as Benedict, such things had no business in reality. His kiss in the stables was but a brief incident of intimacy brought on by my foolish behavior. Fainting, indeed. Why, I was shamed on behalf of my stout constitution and issued myself a stern lecture. After that, I busied myself planning the lessons for the next day over several cups of bolstering tea before changing for dinner.

Last night it had only been Benedict Trevelyan, Stephen Trevelyan, and Constance Ortega at dinner. Both Mrs. Trevelyan and Katherine Trevelyan had sent their excuses, something I had almost done after finding my new belongings tossed to the floor, but then I decided to present a calm, unruffled facade to Mrs. Trevelyan's chicanery.

And tonight I would do the same, only this time it was because of Benedict Trevelyan. He'd mentioned at dinner last night that he would be traveling frequently over the next few weeks, and fool that I was, I didn't want to miss seeing him.

As I left my room, I again felt as if I was being watched. It was a most exasperating situation. Though no one stood in the hall and all doors appeared shut, I decided to confront whoever was spying on me.

I turned in a pirouette, holding my dress out prettily. "Don't you like this? It is so comforting to know that you are watching over me. I give you my thanks." Then I curtsied and started walking primly down the corridor, but then decided to go one step further. I swung back around and began opening every door all the way down the hall. There were nine other rooms besides the schoolroom, the nursery, and mine, and only one of them was locked— the door to Nurse Maria's. The rest of the rooms were neatly turned out and apparently unoccupied. I decided that I had a good idea who my watcher was. Having settled that matter, I headed downstairs, feeling rather triumphant.

Entering into the parlor adjoining the dining room, I met Benedict Trevelyan's gaze first. He stood across the room, one elbow on the mantel and an uncustomary drink in his hand. It looked suspiciously like brandy. He gave the appearance of being relaxed, but I felt an undercurrent of wariness from him.

My lips twitched as I recalled that he'd substitute a brandy for a doctor. It would seem he was in the need of bolstering, too. Our gazes held for a moment longer than usual, but his manner toward me didn't change. "You look lovely tonight, Miss Lovell."

"Thank you, Mr. Trevelyan," I said, slipping farther into the room, feeling confident in a cornflower muslin gown with sprigs of white lace adorning its modest neckline and sleeves. "I find this shade of blue perfect for a summer evening."

He visibly relaxed. Apparently my response eased him from the eggshell on which he'd perched. "It suits you," he said. "Would you care for sherry?"

I glanced at his brandy. "No, thank you. I had tea earlier. Several cups of it."

His lips twitched, and I felt relieved to find humor had found its way into the situation.

Stephen Trevelyan sat near his mother in the midst of a hushed conversation. Katherine, alone on the settee, was engrossed in her embroidery. Constance always waited until a quarter after the dinner hour to make her grand appearance.

Crossing the room, I sat next to Katherine. She glanced shyly up at me, smiled, then turned back to her work. I saw that the tapestry she worked was a hunting scene done in deep colors and accented with gold. She used a gold needle, just as her mother did.

"How do I tell her the tapestry is beautiful?" I asked, looking up at Benedict Trevelyan. His eyebrows lifted in surprise. He moved to the edge of the settee and touched Katherine's shoulder. When she lifted her gaze, he motioned with his hands, ending with a finger pointing my way.

Katherine turned, motioning with her hands. The gesture was so simple, and I knew immediately she'd thanked me. "You are welcome," I said. She nodded and I smiled.

Speaking to her reminded me of the arrangements I had made the day before. I looked back at Benedict Trevelyan. "Yesterday I arranged for Justin and Robert to begin music lessons. We will start learning the rudiments of music on the piano and then decide if they have an aptitude for another instrument. I know several teachers whom I have heard play and I think are good candidates to instruct the children. If you can give me a convenient time for them to come and audition for you this week, I will set up the appointment."

He blinked.

"Is that not to your liking, Mr. Trevelyan?"

"Not at all, Miss Lovell. You have taken me by surprise. I do not expect you to spend your day off arranging lessons for my children."

"It was an errand I thoroughly enjoyed. I have also arranged for the children and me to receive sign language instruction, beginning this Thursday. A Mr. Anthony Simons will be arriving at ten-thirty in the morning."

In the middle of drinking a sip of brandy, Benedict Trevelyan choked. I jumped up, concerned, but didn't move his way after he held up a staying hand. When he regained his breath, I noticed the room had gone completely silent. Mrs. Trevelyan was staring at me in horror, and Stephen Trevelyan looked rather amused. Katherine continued to sew, unaware.

"Whoever thought man was the architect of his own fate had yet to encounter a woman," Stephen Trevelyan said, then laughed. I thought I heard very little humor in his voice.

"What is wrong?" I looked to Benedict Trevelyan for an answer.

"Anthony Simons and my sister were engaged to be married last year."

My hand flew to my heart. Mr. Simons had been quite handsome in a golden-haired-poet sort of way, with eyes so kind I had wondered if I had met a saint. I could clearly picture her with him, the angel and the saint. "What happened?"

"No one knows," Stephen Trevelyan said. "Neither Katherine nor Anthony will say." He shrugged. "Their engagement was marred by the death of my father, then by"—he shot a dark look at his brother—"Francesca's death. Maybe it was all too much for Katherine to bear. She was close to both of them. She shut herself off from everybody after their deaths."

"That's enough said," Benedict Trevelyan interjected.

"I will cancel the lessons," I said, even as I wondered if I should. Why had Katherine secluded herself from the world? Unless . . . my eyes widened at the awful thought. Surely I was letting my imagination run far too free. Just because Katherine broke her engagement didn't mean that Francesca had come between Katherine and Anthony. But then what if . . .

"No," Benedict Trevelyan said, and I jumped, thinking he'd read my mind. "I will tell Katherine that Anthony is coming later. She can decide whether she will see him this time."

"Who can decide to see whom?" Constance asked, floating into the room in a white and silver gown as light and delicate as a cloud. She wore her hair in an intricately woven upsweep with fat pearls upon her hair combs, at her neck, and dangling from her ears. She fluttered her perfect white hands. I clenched mine.

"If you wish to hear all the news, Constance, you should make the effort to be on time," Benedict Trevelyan admonished. "For now I am starving and have no wish to delay dinner any longer." He motioned to Katherine, who rose and went to the dining room.

Constance pouted.

"Pay him no mind. He's been worse than a barrel of sour apples ever since he left the stables today. You look absolutely divine and well worth the wait, Connie, dear." Stephen Trevelyan offered Constance his arm. "Come with me, and I will give you the latest news."

I followed behind Benedict Trevelyan as he wheeled his mother toward the dining room. My heart tripped over Stephen Trevelyan's words. Perhaps there'd been more behind Benedict Trevelyan's kiss than I thought; why else would he be upset? He was most likely worried that I'd see the incident as meaning more than it should. My practicality would never allow that.

I had expected that this evening would end just as every other evening had. Benedict Trevelyan would excuse himself to work in his study. Stephen Trevelyan would have an engagement to attend in town. Mrs. Trevelyan, Katherine, and Constance would disappear to their rooms.

But tonight was different. Stephen Trevelyan offered to play the piano if Constance would sing, and we all, including Katherine, retired to the music room. Stephen Trevelyan played the piano with such a lively hand that I couldn't help but relax and tap my foot to the beat. Hearing Constance sing was a blessing to my soul and the first thing about her that I could say I honestly liked. She was utterly awful, knew it, but sang anyway with a sultry poise that I had to admire.

When they'd finished, Katherine surprised me by getting up and pulling Benedict Trevelyan to the piano, gesturing for him to play. Sighing, he sat down at the keys. Then Katherine knelt on the ground beside the piano and placed her cheek against the sleek wood as he began to play. His large hands gently slid over the keys in a graceful dance of movement and feeling. My heart felt as if he were playing the melody upon my soul. Each touch, each fluid movement of his strong fingers, stroked my emotions. I stared, mesmerized by the magic he wove, and knew I'd never tire of watching him.

I'd little opportunity to educate myself with a vast knowledge of great composers; yet I thought I'd heard the haunting melody he played before. Only its deep bass notes seemed unfamiliar. I must have been frowning, my puzzlement apparent, because Stephen Trevelyan leaned my way and whispered, "It is Beethoven's *Moonlight Sonata* played an octave lower so that Katherine can feel the vibrations of the notes more easily. She idolizes the composer, and this is her favorite composition to feel."

I glanced at Katherine, my heart wrenching over the tear I saw fall down her cheek. "I understand why she loves his work. Not only is it beautiful, but he too became deaf. Yet even after he could not hear anymore, he still wrote music we will never forget."

"I think the smartest thing my brother has ever done was to engage you to teach Justin and Robert. I only hope it is not too late."

All humor had drained from Stephen Trevelyan's face, and his eyes were filled with stark pain. Too late for what? I wanted to cry out to him, but he moved away. Looking up, I found Constance, Mrs. Trevelyan, and Benedict Trevelyan all staring at me as if I'd committed a heinous crime by whispering with Stephen Trevelyan. I had to remind myself again; I might have changed the direction of my life, but I'd in no way found a safe harbor.

Nothing made that more apparent to me than when I returned to my room. Upon my pillow lay a note. Written in an elongated flowery style were five words: *Remain at your own peril*. The signature beneath was comprised of one letter. The letter *F*.

❦ *10* ❧

The day was too sunny, too serene, for me to have a threatening note in my pocket. I hadn't decided yet whether to tell Benedict Trevelyan about it or keep it to myself. Mrs. Trevelyan seemed to be determined to make me leave. At least it was she to whom I attributed the note.

But more disturbing than the warning was Stephen's

comment during the music last night. *I only hope it isn't too late.* Too late for what?

This morning I'd asked Dobbs if he'd let Stephen Trevelyan know that I wished to speak to him. Dobbs only raised his nose disapprovingly and didn't respond. Since I hadn't heard from Stephen Trevelyan all day, I assumed Dobbs hadn't relayed my message.

"Miss Wovell, we have ten baby plants now." Robert came to a smiling stop before me, rosy cheeks framing his bright eyes.

"That is because you have taken very good care of them. And the grown-up word for baby plants is sprouts. We have ten sprouts in the herb garden."

After our first lesson looking for mommies in the garden, I thought it would be good for Robert and Justin to have something to care for, so we'd planted dill, sweet marjoram, parsley, and ginger mint—herbs that Cook Thomas said he would purchase from Justin and Robert rather than from the market. Justin reluctantly did what he had to do to care for his side of the garden. Robert tended to his with enthusiasm and considered himself the proud father of "baby plants." I was not sure how he was going to react when it came time to harvest the herbs—but I wasn't going to borrow tomorrow's trouble.

I sighed, never realizing how complicated life could be. It had always seemed so simple before.

"I am ready to do numbers now," Robert said. "But I cannot 'member how many rocks I am supposed to find." His nose scrunched as he thought hard.

"Mathematics is the proper word." Smiling, I closed and set aside my drawing pad. "Do you remember what I told you to do so you could easily count how many rocks you needed?"

Robert wiggled his fingers. "I am supposed to count these."

"Right. You need to have two rocks for each finger. When you have collected that, I will teach you a secret about mathematics."

Robert looked at his brother. "Will I be as smart as Justin?"

"You are already smart. And someday when you are older, there will be things that you will be very smart in. And there will be some things that Justin will be very smart in. That is the beauty of the people in the world. Nobody is the same. Everybody is different. There is only one you in the whole, big world, and that makes you very, very special indeed."

His eyes widened. "There is only one me. That means when my daddy goes away on bizzess trips, he won't find another me who is better and love him best, will he?"

"No, dear. He loves you and wants you to be the very best you can. Now collect the rocks you need from the edge of our garden, and we will work on your lesson." Robert went over to the pebbles encircling the garden and meticulously set to work.

We were on a blanket at the back of the formal gardens, close enough to hear the waves of the bay slap against the rocks and feel a steady breeze crest over the cliffs. The beds of roses I'd been attempting to sketch stretched like a red-and-pink stained glass sea across the cultured hedges. An entire world of insects buzzed about the sweetly fragrant air, each fluttering or bumbling along, feasting on nectar as if tomorrow would never dawn. Justin stood with his sketchpad, busily drawing. He had his nose nearly planted in the center of a huge magenta-colored rose. I hoped it wasn't a bee he was examining.

During our morning lessons we read about John Muir and James Audubon. Their contributions to our knowledge of the natural world interested Justin, and he decided afterward that he wanted to add to his scientific notebook today. Since our time at Holloway Park, when he'd categorized the trees, he'd remained withdrawn, doing his lessons without any excitement unless it involved drawing, like now, or when we played chess. He loved the game, had taken to it better than I could have hoped, but then I knew the control and solitude of the sport would appeal to him. Unlike Robert, who had to have things busy to keep his interest.

I believed it wouldn't be too much longer before Justin would be ready to play a game of chess with his father.

I had fewer problems with the boys suddenly erupting into a fight. But I didn't pride myself in thinking it was because I'd made great strides in healing their hurts. It was most likely because I kept them quite busy.

Hearing the thunder of hooves and the sharp sound of a whinny, I jumped to my feet, trying to swallow my sudden fear, determined to conquer my weakness. Rambling in from the trees near the cliffs appeared Benedict Trevelyan, a picture of windblown elegance and strength despite the mud splattering him. He'd been heading for the stables, but when he saw us, he changed his direction to come our way.

I gasped in dismay and started backing up. If I had had the notion that Gunnlod was as big as a horse could get, then I'd have been proven wrong. The horse he rode now was massive. Black and wild. Huge and dangerous.

When he reached the last tree, he pulled the horse to a dancing stop and dismounted, thankfully tethering the beast to the tree before nearing us. I looked around to find that Robert and Justin had joined me near the blanket, both staring at their father with hungry eyes.

I decided on the spot that Friday, we'd make an excursion into town. My mind scrambled for a plan of activity sure to meet with Benedict Trevelyan's approval—the bank.

What parent doesn't wish for his child to have an under-standing of finances?

"Ah, Justin, Robert, Miss Lovell, just the persons I wished to see," Benedict Trevelyan said, striding towards us.

I saw Robert and Justin's mouths pop open. I believe mine did, too, before I recovered my wits. Something about Benedict Trevelyan's manner seemed so much less removed than usual. "And how may we help you today, Mr. Trevelyan?"

"It occurred to me as I was out riding that Justin and Robert are of an age to begin learning to ride."

I felt both the boys press in upon my skirts. This new idea of their father's wasn't exactly their idea of fun. Mine either. "On that, that . . ." I stammered incredulously.

"Horse," Benedict Trevelyan supplied, not sounding the least bit happy with my response. The words had flown from my mouth before I could stop them, in my panic. I felt Justin and Robert press even closer to my side, and I knew this entire situation was spiraling toward a disaster I had to stop.

I'd hoped for some activity to bind father and sons together, but why had it cursedly come down to horses? The boys needed their father's approval, and I wasn't about to let them face the beasts in the stables alone. We would learn to ride, it seemed. Oh, Lord, I thought, remembering to finally breathe.

I blinked, then shook my head as I realized the master of Trevelyan Hill had been speaking to me. "I am sorry. Could you repeat yourself? I did not quite hear what—"

"I said, Miss Lovell, that I am not an idiot. Justin and Robert could not ride Odin even if they were begging to do so. The stallion is high-strung and tests even my skill."

"So that is Odin," I murmured, tipping up on my toes so that I could see the horse over Benedict Trevelyan's shoulder. Odin pranced as if he ruled the world and nobody had better get in his way. "No wonder Gunnlod bites him."

"What?" Benedict Trevelyan followed my gaze, his frown of outrage turning to puzzlement. "Why would you say that, Miss Lovell?"

I shrugged, not quite sure how to express my opinion. "He looks as if he needs to be bitten every now and then to remind him he is not a god. Were I of the nature to believe in such things, that horse appears to be a reincarnation of his namesake."

"I thought the same thing the moment I saw him. That is why I bought him and named him." Benedict Trevelyan returned his gaze to mine. "Now, I believe we were discussing riding lessons."

"Yes. When do you want the children and me to meet you at the stables?"

"Tomorrow at two." Benedict Trevelyan squatted down to Justin and Robert's level. "There is a surprise for you two in the stables."

"Can we come see?" Robert jumped up and down. Justin stayed back.

Benedict Trevelyan's gaze lingered on Justin for a moment before he smiled at Robert and ruffled the boy's hair. "I will show you tomorrow."

"We will be there. You haven't forgotten that the music teachers are auditioning in the morning?"

He stood, and it seemed he was a good deal closer to me than before. "No. I do not believe I have forgotten anything you have said to me." His gaze focused on my lips.

My eyes widened. The intensity of his gaze brought our encounter in the stables to mind. Had I really told him that I'd barely felt his lips upon mine?

My, but the memory of them now was like an earthquake. The sensations he evoked shook me to my core, and

I must have wavered on my feet, for he grasped my shoulder. "Miss Lovell?"

"Ah, there she is!" Stephen Trevelyan yelled, as if he'd struck gold.

Startled, I looked up to see Stephen Trevelyan escorting Constance on one arm and Katherine on the other. Both women were beautiful in pastel muslin day dresses. Since we'd come to work on the garden, I'd worn my old brown dress. I wished I hadn't.

"Is something wrong?" Stephen Trevelyan asked as he approached. He looked back and forth between his brother and me, making me realize that Benedict still held my arm.

"No. I was dizzy for a moment." I stepped back from Benedict Trevelyan, feeling as if I stood at center stage of a show when I hadn't even auditioned to be in it. He didn't release my arm, only frowned. Everyone seemed frozen. I didn't know what to do next. Stephen Trevelyan and Constance looked uncomfortable, as if they'd found us being improper. Katherine appeared concerned, but when her gaze connected with mine, she quickly averted hers.

Thank God for Robert. He leapt into action. "Uncle Steph, Aunt Kaff. Come see the babies." Running over to pull on his uncle's sleeve and aunt's skirts, Robert freed everyone from the ice that held them.

"Babies?" Stephen and Benedict Trevelyan said simultaneously.

"Of sorts," I said, motioning to our herb garden. "More accurately called sprouts. It is a business venture we have embarked on. Cook Thomas has put in an order to buy our herbs once they have matured."

The proper rationale for an outing Friday fell suddenly into place. Besides, if I kept Benedict Trevelyan engaged in other activities, we'd spend less time in the stables. "In fact, I meant to speak to you, Mr. Trevelyan, about taking the boys to the bank this Friday. We need to investigate what they may want to do with the money they will earn."

"I will save mine," Justin said, surprising me by speaking with a crowd about.

"Buy candy," Robert said, being as solemn as any five-year-old could.

"We will see," Benedict Trevelyan added. He nodded toward the plants. "You and Justin have been busy. Who takes care of the plants?"

"I do mostly." Robert shot his gaze toward Justin. "Jus helps some, too, but he doesn't like the dirt as much as Miss Wovell and I do. He likes to drawded."

"Draw," I corrected.

"Is this yours, Justin?" Stephen Trevelyan bent down and picked up my sketchpad.

"No, um, that is mine," I said, but Stephen had already started flipping through the pages. Thankfully he held up the sketch of Trevelyan Manor with the dragon hovering over it. I didn't want anyone to see the portrait of Benedict Trevelyan I'd drawn.

Katherine halted my flood of embarrassment. She walked over and ran her fingers over the sketch. Then, turning my way, she made the same gesture with her fingers that Benedict Trevelyan had when he told her for me that her tapestry was beautiful.

"How do I tell her thank you?" I couldn't remember.

Benedict Trevelyan showed me the movement, and I thanked Katherine. Reaching behind Justin, I pulled out his sketchbook from where he'd hidden it beneath his shirt. I handed it to him. "You are very talented. I am sure Uncle Stephen and Aunt Katherine would say so too."

Justin didn't say anything. He didn't look up. He just held his sketchbook out to his uncle.

Stephen squatted down and looked up into Justin's face.

He took the sketchbook from Justin, but didn't open it. "If you would rather not share right now, I can wait."

Justin shook his head, a world of anger in his voice. "You will just go away again."

"Justin," his father said sharply.

"It is true," Justin cried. "Everybody went away when my mother died. Even if they stayed here, they did not love us anymore. We are only in the way." He looked resentfully at Constance, Katherine, and Stephen. "I do not want anybody to love me ever!" He turned and ran toward the house.

"Justin," his father shouted.

"Wait," I said. But before I could set my hand on Benedict Trevelyan's arm, Katherine stepped up and did so, shaking her head. Her troubled gaze followed Justin, then she looked at all of us, as if she couldn't fathom what had happened. Tears filled her eyes, and I could clearly see her frustration. What would it be like to be locked into a world of silence, completely dependent on others to tell me everything?

She signed something to Benedict.

Benedict shook his head and signed back, saying at the same time, "He cannot allow his emotions to rule his actions."

Katherine shook her head, disagreeing with Benedict. Then she shook her head at everyone and ran for the house.

"I will speak to Justin later," I said, my heart burdened for the child. He didn't need a dressing-down for his outburst just yet. Not when his emotions were so raw.

Benedict Trevelyan fisted his hands. I could see the turmoil wrenching his jaw taut and felt his frustration. I could see that he wanted to reach his son but didn't know how. I wasn't sure if anyone could reach Justin. Not yet—he didn't want to be touched.

Stephen Trevelyan stood and handed me Justin's sketchbook. "I will look at it when he is ready." He turned to his brother. "He's right, you know. How can you punish him for speaking the truth?" He smacked himself. "How remiss of me to forget. It's the truths you do not want to hear that you punish others for speaking."

"You are showing even worse manners than my son. I suggest you see me in private to finish this discussion." Benedict Trevelyan's voice sliced with barely restrained violence. I thought for a moment that the brothers would come to blows.

Constance intervened. "Stephen, be a dear. If you are not going to ask Miss Lovell why she requested Dobbs to send you to her, then please go pick me some of those fat roses over there. I think I will wear them in my hair tonight."

Stephen Trevelyan turned from his brother, shaking his head. "Since Connie was nice enough to remind me, please tell me what I can do for you, Miss Ann."

"I . . . what I needed was, uh, to see if you would play a chess game with Justin. He's just learning, and I thought a patient opponent would—"

"Since I am not needed here, I will get Odin back to the stable." Benedict Trevelyan whipped around on his heel to leave, and I realized how badly what I had said sounded. Truth was, I'd wanted to ask Stephen Trevelyan what his comment last night meant. My lying skills were dismal.

"Mr. Trevelyan," I called out.

He turned back.

"Justin wanted to hone his skills at chess so that you would be impressed with them. What I am trying to say is that you are needed."

He didn't say anything in return. He glanced at Constance, who was smelling one of the large, deep magenta roses. "Constance, if you pick my mother's Great Westerns, she will most likely faint. They were my father's favorites. He brought the hybrid back on their last trip to France."

Constance shook her head. "She never tends them anymore. They just waste away in this garden." Benedict Trevelyan lifted an admonishing brow. She pouted. "I will order roses from the florist for my hair, then. Does that make you happy?"

Benedict Trevelyan shrugged and walked away.

Stephen Trevelyan held out his arm to Constance. "I will be glad to play with Justin at any time, except today. Connie and I are going to the bay. She wants to see the steamboats. What other time would be best?

"Tomorrow afternoon after the riding lesson."

"I will be there." He escorted Constance back toward the house.

It was then that I felt a tug on my skirt and remembered that Robert still stood next to me. His eyes were huge, and he looked very scared. He'd gotten lost in the adult shuffle of treacherous undercurrents. I couldn't even blame the other adults for it, either. The boys were in my charge, and I was as guilty as everyone else. I knelt down and hugged him. "You were a very good boy to be so quiet while the others talked."

He hugged me back. "Miss Wovell. Is everything going to be awright?"

"All right," I corrected. "And yes, it will be. Did you get all of your rocks together?"

"Yes. Two for each finger."

We sat on the blanket adding and subtracting rocks until he had a clear understanding of both concepts and couldn't sit still any longer. I could see he was still worried. "Do you think Jus is alwight?"

"I am sure he is, but lets go find him, and I will read you both more of *Through the Looking Glass*." The worry fell from Robert's eyes, and he jumped up with excitement. "Tell me more about the cat that smiles."

"I will as soon as we gather our things." He quickly went to work, and I sighed, relieved that at least he was back on steady ground. Now I had to see about Justin.

I found Justin asleep in his room, sprawled on his bed with traces of tears upon his cheeks. Covering him, I placed a feathery kiss on his head and turned back to Robert, blinking tears from my own eyes. Somehow, I vowed I would reach Justin. And in the meantime, I would safeguard Robert's heart. "Let's go to my room to read."

Soon we were cuddled on the settee in my sitting area, reading about Alice and the Cheshire cat. I'd read not more than half a page when I saw that Robert had fallen asleep. I was just placing my robe over him when I saw the door to the schoolroom move a tiny bit. Someone was in the schoolroom. "Justin?"

Walking swiftly toward the door, I pulled it open. The room was empty. Or at least I thought it was empty until I saw the light pink hem of a dress disappearing into the wall beside the hearth.

A secret passage! My mind raced. I couldn't believe it. Katherine had had on a pink dress. I dashed across the room, my fingers digging at the paneling until I found the hidden door that hadn't quite closed behind Katherine. Stairs led both up and down. A spider scurried across the floor. In my mind, it was large for a spider, and I hesitated.

Spiders weren't as bad as horses, but that didn't mean I wanted to make their acquaintance either. The glow of a light from below indicated the direction Katherine had taken. Wincing and drawing a deep breath, I quickly followed, knowing that I'd found the answer to how the intruder had disappeared so quickly that night. Why hadn't Benedict Trevelyan said anything about the secret passage then? Surely he had to have known.

I made it to the next landing, heard the swish and the click of a panel shutting, and found myself plunged into total darkness.

Fool. Shuddering, I wrapped my arms around myself, disbelieving how stupid I'd been. My only thought had been to catch Katherine with no consideration to my own safety. I'd no light with me. Reaching out, I grasped the rail of the stair, deciding to follow the steps down. There had to be a door at the end. I just had to find it.

One step brought my face into a spiderweb. I screamed in surprise, then shamefully panicked when I felt something crawling on my neck. Brushing frantically at my skin, I quickly backed away and ran into a wall. At least, I thought it was a wall, but it gave away beneath my weight, and I landed with a painful thump on the floor of a room filled with light. I'd found another secret door. Instead of leaping to my feet, I continued to swat at myself, desperately assuring myself no spiders were on me—

"Good God, Miss Lovell! What in damnation are you doing?"

I rolled to my knees at the sound of Benedict Trevelyan's voice. Looking up, I found him standing naked in a tub of steamy water not more than four feet away. He wasn't the least bit self-conscious about being found naked. I decided at that second that I didn't need spectacles after all. I could see quite well. Every hair, every droplet of water, every muscle, every nuance of Benedict Trevelyan's large male body, imprinted itself upon my mind. He was huge . . . everywhere . . . and I found myself looking especially there, too fascinated and shocked to do anything else.

Then, right before my eyes, that huge thing that made him male became immediately bigger, immensely bigger.

"My God," I gasped.

"Though some men wished to be worshiped, I am not one of them, Miss Lovell. But I thank you for the compliment." Benedict Trevelyan sounded dryly amused. He stepped from the tub and turned his back to me, reaching for a towel.

Only then did I gather my wits enough to absorb what had just happened, what I'd just seen, and where I was. I'd landed myself in the master of Trevelyan Hill's bedroom. Shaken, I turned my back to him and sat on the floor. Standing would have been beyond my capabilities. I shut my eyes, too. Otherwise I would have been too tempted to peek.

"My word, Mr. Trevelyan, I must profusely apologize. I was reading to Robert about the Cheshire cat, you know, the one who talks to Alice after she has fallen through the looking glass, and I looked up to see the schoolroom door move, and I thought it was Justin, he'd fallen asleep on his bed, there were tears on his cheeks, so I went after him, but it wasn't Justin, for I saw the hem of Katherine's pink dress disappear into a secret passage—why, imagine my surprise at that, which is something you should have mentioned when I had had an intruder—anyway I was following the direction of the light when it suddenly disappeared and I found"—I gulped—"a spider."

"Miss Lovell, if you would please cease chattering, I would like to escort you back upstairs before Dobbs returns, which should be any moment now."

I shut my mouth.

"It would speed things along if you would open your eyes, too."

I popped my eyes open to see him standing in front of

me. He'd put on trousers and a shirt, but hadn't taken the time to button it. He held a lantern and had pushed the panel to the secret passageway open.

"We must hurry, Miss Lovell."

"Yes." I stood on shaky knees. As mortified as I was, it would have been worse if Dobbs had witnessed this debacle.

Benedict grasped my arm and nearly pulled me into the passage. I made it up to the next landing with his support and watched him press open the panel that led us into the schoolroom.

"Next time you go exploring dark places, Miss Lovell, I suggest you carry a lamp."

"Indeed, Mr. Trevelyan, I will seriously consider your advice." I finally summoned the courage to look him in the face. Amusement still ruled his dark features and something else, something akin to the gleam of the demon door.

I gasped.

"You have managed to attract a web, Miss Lovell," he said softly, reaching up to brush something from my hair.

"Yes," I whispered.

He didn't say anything then. He set the lamp on the floor, grabbed my shoulders, and connected his lips to mine. This was no barely there thing. This was . . . everything. His entire body enveloped me as his mouth slanted over mine, parting my lips. Then, warm and shocking, his tongue thrust into my mouth and he pulled me flush against him. My breasts pressed to his chest, his thigh pushed between my legs, and my tongue instinctively swept against his as liquid fire erupted inside me. I moaned.

He kissed me until I thought I would die from the pleasure of it. His body was hard to my touch, velvet and iron, just as I thought. The grip of his hands was firm upon my back, and the huge part of him that made him male pressed against my hip, leaving a lasting impression of his arousal.

"My heavenly word," I gasped when he broke off the kiss. We were both breathing heavily. I felt as if an entire universe that I'd only heard or seen bare glimpses of had been revealed to me.

Benedict took a step back. "Fortunately neither words nor heaven have little to do with desire between a woman and man, Miss Lovell. Consider yourself kissed. And should you go exploring again, I would not only take a lamp, I would be prepared for more than a kiss. You know the way to my room."

Taking the lamp, he disappeared into the passage. I stood stunned, my body burning, my mind already imagining a study of exploration into desire. Running back to my room, I locked both doors, more to keep myself locked in until I found the place where I'd lost my mind. I not only knew the way to his room, but I most surely knew the way to my ruin.

Robert still slept upon the settee. I lay on the bed, my breasts aching and my body burning. I had no doubt that I had been well and truly kissed. In fact, I'd been so well kissed that had Benedict kissed me that way in the stables, I may have very well gone running from his employ.

As it was, I'd no one to blame but myself for the state of affairs between us, for not only had I invited him to kiss me again by my words yesterday, I'd invited a great deal more from him by my blatant fascination with his body. And to my shame, I wasn't the least bit sorry, nor was I going to leave Justin and Robert. They meant too much to me. But I did claim an illness, and had dinner in my room instead of facing Benedict over the dinner table.

11

The next morning, at the last possible moment, Benedict Trevelyan entered the music room where I waited with Justin, Robert, and the three auditioning teachers. He said a perfunctory good morning to everyone and ordered the auditioning to begin. He didn't look at me once.

As the third and last teacher auditioned, playing a moving assortment of Beethoven's masterpieces, I was tempted to step on Benedict's toes. The man acted as if nothing had happened. As if he'd not kissed me at all.

Not that I wanted him to act as if anything had changed between us, but I was hoping for some small indication that things were *different*. That I hadn't imagined the kiss, which I knew was impossible. My imagination was nowhere near that remarkable.

The audition ended, and Benedict chose the pianist who'd played Beethoven so well, then quit the room.

Last night I had opted to stay in my room, pleading an ailment because his kiss had left me so flushed. After his morning rudeness, I'd worked my outrage into a fine steamy feather by the time it came for Justin and Robert's riding lesson. How dare the man treat me as if I wasn't even there?

I marched into the stables with the boys beside me,

promptly at two, prepared for battle. Benedict Trevelyan
met us immediately with a startling half a horse. The top of
its ears only came to about the middle of my stomach. A
good amount of shaggy hair tufted between its ears, spread
in waves down its neck, almost covering its body, and
bunched at its feet and tail. It looked at us, its long-lashed,
warm brown eyes curious.

The boys were completely fascinated, and I have to
admit, I was a bit taken myself. "What is it?" I asked, the heat
of my anger evaporating a little.

"This is a Shetland pony, and the horse Justin and Robert
will begin their riding lessons on, Miss Lovell."

He handed the reins to Justin. "You can consider her an
early birthday present. You will be turning eight in a few
weeks, on the fourteenth, right?" Justin nodded, his eyes
wide, as if he hadn't expected his father to remember his
birthday. I made a mental note to do something special for
Justin on that day.

"Why don't you and Robert walk her around the stable a
bit? See if you can get her to tell you what her name is,"
Benedict said.

"Horses don't talk," Justin said grumpily, but it was clear
he was very interested in the horse, and he took control of
the reins without being asked twice.

"Sure they do," Benedict said. "You just have to know
how to listen to their language. It is like talking to Aunt
Katherine. So, I will leave it to you and Robert to tell me her
name after you have learned to listen to her."

The boys, acting stiff with the big responsibility handed
to them, began gingerly walking the pony. Benedict followed them, and I kept pace with him. I felt as if I needed to
say something, but I didn't know where to begin.

"Mr. Trevelyan, I am sorry for the awkwardness—"

Gunnlod popped her head from the stall next to me,

startling me. Benedict reached over and brushed his hand down her muzzle. "There's a good girl."

I gulped, feeling the nearness of his body, remembering the feel of him holding me against his heat, his hardness.

Still caressing Gunnlod, he spoke to me. "Miss Lovell. There is no need to apologize. We will just forget the incident ever happened. I am quite inured to the situation. My attentions made my wife frequently . . . ill, also. I am glad to see you are feeling better today. I will have the children brought to you in about an hour. Considering your aversions, I thank you for bringing them on time."

Before I could say a word, he left me for the boys, and although I was confused by his words, I had no real choice but to leave. At first I was stunned, but as I slowly walked back to the manor, I became incensed. Why, the man thought he knew everything, even what I myself felt!

I looked heavenward, searching for an answer to my exasperation, and froze in mid-step. The woman was back in the tower, standing in the window, looking out toward the bay. She lingered a moment and, I thought, even glanced my way before she disappeared into the shadows of the turret's interior. A ghost indeed! This time I wasn't going to let Dobbs say this was a figment of my imagination. I dashed into the house, determined to find the way to the tower.

A maid stood in the solarium. "Miss," I said, catching her attention. "Where are the stairs to the tallest tower?"

She looked at me as if I'd asked for the stairs to hell. "You don't want to go there, miss. It's cursed as the devil."

"I won't. I just want to know where they are located."

"At the top of the stair, miss. On the third floor. There's a door, but it's locked, miss."

"Thank you," I said, dashing off. I ran up the stairs faster than I had ever run in my life, determined to catch my ghost. Out of breath, flushed, and out of sorts, I made it to the third floor. To the left, opposite the way to my room, I found a door with an imposing padlock and no one about.

It was proving to be a most frustrating day. In the schoolroom an hour later, I awaited both the boys and Stephen Trevelyan, who'd promised to play a game of chess with Justin. I'd accomplished absolutely nothing since leaving the stables and seeing my ghost again, except perhaps a good amount of pacing. My dilemma with Benedict was uppermost in my mind.

I decided I'd been insulted. What exactly did he mean by "inured to the situation"? His attentions had made his wife ill? How so? To be sure, he'd made me swoon, but I'd quite liked the sensation. So how dare he decide I didn't? And however was I going to speak to him if he kept stomping away? I was in quite a state.

Stephen Trevelyan arrived before the children did.

"Ah, Miss Ann. You are a lovely sight for sore eyes."

I narrowed my eyes and gave him a healthy dose of my ire. "And you, sir, are a scoundrel. How can you tell someone you hope it's not too late and never enlighten them of what it may be too late for?" I set aside the book I'd been unable to read.

"Too late? When did I say that?" His brow furrowed.

"In the music room. After dinner?" I prompted, miffed that he couldn't even recall the incident. Apparently what it might be too late for wasn't all that important.

To my surprise, his expression became oddly serious. "My apologies. I had no right to say that to you. In fact Benedict has called me to the carpet for airing our personal family matters before you. And he is quite right about it. You are here to teach Justin and Robert, not save the children from the sins of their family. I merely spoke of Justin's withdrawal, hoping it was not too late for him to go back to being the happy child that he was. When he was little, Cesca, his mother, taught him a game, and he never outgrew it. She called it 'making sunshine.' If you did not have a smile on your face when he saw you, he would not go away until you smiled. He did everything an imp could do to make you smile, especially with Dobbs. Poor Dobbs never had a moment's peace when Justin was making sunshine."

I laughed. I couldn't help myself when I pictured Dobbs being hounded to smile. Stephen Trevelyan laughed, too. He sat down on the seat next to mine; both of us oversize for the tiny chairs.

"You have a beautiful laugh, Miss Ann. It is like sunshine."

"All that warmth makes things rather cozy, doesn't it, Stephen?" Benedict's tone blew a chill into the room that went right over Justin and Robert's heads as they ran to me. I stood to greet them, distancing myself from Stephen Trevelyan.

"I see you have been eating sour apples again, Benedict. I was just telling Miss Ann how Justin made Dobbs miserable while making sunshine. Do you remember that, Justin?"

Justin shook his head no, but from the shadows moving into his eyes, I wondered if he was telling the truth. I hurt for him, thinking how drastically his mother's death had changed his life.

"Miss Wovell, the horsey tolded Jus her name."

"What, a talking horse? I daresay you are pulling my leg, Robert." Stephen acted as if an unseen person was jerking his leg.

"I am not. My hands are right here," Robert said, holding up his hands and stamping his foot. "And horses do talk. My father says so. You just have to know how to wisten."

"All right, then. What did the horse say his name is?"

"Cesca," Justin said with conviction. "Her name is Cesca."

The blood drained from Stephen Trevelyan's face. His gaze shot directly at Benedict. "How could—"

"Justin picked out the name. Alone." Benedict's eyes were like daggers.

Cesca. It was the name Stephen Trevelyan had just called Francesca. The chill in the room seeped into my blood, and I shivered. Stephen made nicknames for almost everyone. That he'd called Benedict's wife Cesca wasn't unusual, but the frigid look in Benedict's eyes said differently.

"I have had some unexpected business problems. I will be out of town until next week. So I will leave things here in your hands, Stephen. I see you have a cozy handle on them already." Nodding, Benedict spun on his heel and left.

Justin took three steps to the doorway, and I watched as his shoulders drooped.

Tears stung my eyes. I'd never uttered a curse, as best as I could recall, but several sharp ones hung on the edge of my tongue. They cut my insides as I swallowed them and put my arm around Justin's shoulders. He pulled away, as I expected.

Benedict Trevelyan needed to replace his sour apples with prunes.

Thirty minutes had passed by the time I'd settled Robert with a picture of the Cheshire cat to copy at a table near where Justin and his uncle were playing chess. Stopping by my room, I checked up on my appearance, then went looking for Benedict Trevelyan with a battle in mind.

A battle that would have to wait. He'd already left. That fact made me ache inside, as if I'd been shunned.

Instinct took me to the foyer, and I stood within the dancing colors of the stained glass windows, letting their beauty soothe my nerves and ease the twinges inside my heart. Soon the many wonderful hues made me smile; they emitted such a joyous picture, one of hope. I realized it at that moment, what it was that made the insides of Trevelyan Manor so dark. Why Benedict's eyes were so grimly black, and why Justin's heart was so painfully determined to be alone. It was the lack of hope.

I also thought that just as the inhabitants of Trevelyan Manor seemed blind to the beauty of its saving grace, the stained glass, they must be blind to the one thing that could give them hope back—love.

"Is there a problem, Miss Lovell?"

I didn't welcome Dobbs's intrusion. "No. I was actually just, uh, making sunshine to the suit of armor." I nodded to the stiff metal man in the corner. "Making sunshine is a popular pastime that I am considering teaching to Justin and Robert. Have you heard of it?"

Dobbs's jaw seesawed before he snapped his mouth closed. "I have not, nor do I care to. It does not sound as if you are teaching Justin and Robert anything of worth."

"Oh, I am. Smile," I said to him as I spun in a circle through the colored light. His frown was more dour than I could ever recall it being. I left the foyer, smiling.

The grandfather clock struck the midnight hour, and I rolled out of my bed, deciding I'd rather get a new book from the Trevelyan library than spend the rest of the night tossing and turning. I couldn't sleep.

My door, the schoolroom's door, and the children's door to the hall were all locked, and I'd set an alarm of sorts in front of the secret passageway's door. A chair with a basketful of blocks would crash over should anyone attempt to use it. The only door I couldn't safeguard was that of Maria. With her in the nurse's room, it was like living with the enemy at my back door; but it couldn't be helped, and I didn't think myself to be in any real danger anyway.

I'd locked everything just so that my intruder in the

night, whoever that had been, would know I was aware of him—or her. So it wasn't fear that kept me awake. It was Benedict's kiss and the sensations that kiss's memory kept rampant in my body. I ached until I thought I'd go mad. And I wondered what I would do with my growing feelings for him, for there were too many distances between us, and not just the miles.

Now that I'd had time to reflect, I decided that it would be best to put Benedict's kiss behind me. To forget it for now and only pull it from my memories when, years from now, I could look back and reflect upon the moment that I'd known a man's passion. That's all our kiss could ever be. That's all I could let it be, no matter how I ached for more. If nothing else, I was a practical woman.

Pulling on my robe and sliding into my slippers, I gathered my lamp and locked the door to my room behind me, pocketing the key. I walked down the narrow hallway, listening to the house, which breathed like a sleeping beast with the little noises and groans that disturbed the eerie silence. I liked the house best when Justin and Robert were running through it, laughing, and when Benedict was home.

It didn't take me long to reach the foyer and its sleeping stained glass. I saw a faint glow coming from the library's doorway, only two doors down from Benedict Trevelyan's study. Anticipation seized me at the thought that he'd returned.

The light emitting from the library wasn't bright enough for someone to read by, and as I stepped inside the room, finding it empty, I decided someone had accidentally left the lamp on low. I sighed, needing to release the disappointment flooding me.

Setting down my lamp, I wandered to the shelves, perusing the books, marvelous leather-bound treasures with gold engravings along their spines. I ran my fingers across the titles, breathing deeply of the enriching musty smell that only a book can have, and smiled with pleasure.

I knew exactly how I'd tame my midnight demons. I had the world at my fingertips.

For the love of it, I pulled a book of Shakespeare's plays off the shelf. Then I spied a little used book, so small I almost missed it hidden in between the other books. Elizabeth Barrett Browning's works. I'd heard of her and her husband, but had yet the opportunity to read any of her poems. I slipped that off the shelf along with a worn volume of Edgar Allan Poe's stories.

Feeling guilty, I nervously looked to see if Dobbs were watching from the doorway. Then I grabbed one more book quickly, not even checking out the title, and hurried over to my lamp. I hoped Dobbs was having nightmares about making sunshine. He deserved to for making me feel like a thief just because I wanted to borrow a book for pleasure. Juggling the books on one arm, I dropped one. It slid beneath the couch, and I had to go to my knees to reach it.

I heard a *scrape-thump-thump, scrape-thump-thump* noise in the room with me, and my blood went cold.

Scrape-thump-thump.

The sound grew louder, coming in my direction. My stomach clenched, my palms dampened, and a lump filled my throat even as my muscles froze.

Scrape-thump-thump.

I angled up from the floor, edging my nose to the top of the chair, and gasped.

Mrs. Trevelyan, in a white nightgown and her hair flowing all the way to her knees, walked my way, using a cane. She appeared more slender and younger now that she stood upright and wore white. Hunching over in her wheelchair and covering herself in black had added twenty years to her age. She came to a stop when she saw me, her eyes widening with the same surprise as mine.

"What are you doing?" she asked, recovering first, anger spitting from her dark eyes.

I stood, hugging the books I'd collected to my chest. "Research for the boys' lessons." I prayed that God wouldn't strike me dead for my fib, but I didn't want her to know I couldn't sleep. The implications of seeing her walking and dressed as she was, like the lady ghost I'd seen, were just starting to sink in.

It would explain the tower, but the woman in the hallway had moved too quickly to be her. Unless there was another secret passage near the stairs, or she'd slipped into Maria's room. I almost smiled that I'd discovered the source of my ghost so quickly. "You can walk."

Her lips pursed to a sour point. "That is none of your business."

"Does everyone know?" I shouldn't have asked, but I couldn't help doing so. Since my arrival, she'd been tended to as an invalid, and I wondered why she'd choose to spend her life in a wheelchair. She was a striking woman.

"Are you stealing about the house looking for something to pilfer?"

I straightened my back. "I assure you, Mrs. Trevelyan, I have permission to use the library." Taking my lamp, I turned to leave.

"I will expect you for afternoon tea. We can discuss this then. Do not mention this if you value your position."

Why was she keeping her ability to walk secret? The thought of having tea in her overheated sickly sweet rooms was nauseating. I faced her and smiled. "Perhaps, if you do not mind, could we meet in the garden, or even the solarium?"

"How dare—"

I looked pointedly at her cane. "I will not mention seeing you tonight, but you will have to treat me with some decency in return. I will not be subjected to the Inquisition again."

Her eyes brightened with anger. "The solarium, then." Her voice was clipped with tension.

"Good," I said. As I turned, I noted the book she held. *The Romance of the Rose.* The author's name caught me by surprise. Benedict W. Trevelyan, Sr. I decided to wait until tomorrow to ask her about it. I knew if it were my husband who'd died, I'd want to speak of him during the bright warm hours of the day and not in the deep and cold loneliness of the night.

Once in my room, I dropped the books upon my bed and paced to the window. I didn't know exactly what to make of Mrs. Trevelyan. I couldn't dismiss her as a harmless old woman. She had too many dark emotions ruling her actions, and she had kept hidden the fact that she could walk. At least, that is what I assumed. Maybe I was the only one who wasn't aware that she could walk on occasion.

My thoughts ran in circles, trying to puzzle out the events of the past and the people involved. Could she have murdered Francesca? Had her hatred of her daughter-in-law been that virulent?

My restless seething for answers was just as frustrating as the memory of Benedict's kiss, and my growing list of grievances with the man—his aggravating assumptions, his rude behavior, and my hopeless obsession with his infuriatingly pleasurable touch.

For indeed, having been truly kissed by the man, I had every desire to be kissed again. And just exactly where was that merry road going to lead me—through the secret passage to his bed and my ruin? I couldn't let that happen, not ever.

My mother had been seduced and tricked by the promise of love and marriage. I had no such illusions or excuses. Every practical fiber in my body demanded that I put Benedict's kiss from my mind like a saint casting away the devil.

Yet, having felt the heat of desire, how could I banish myself to a cold spinsterhood without even a memory of that fire to warm me?

No. It didn't matter what I felt. I had to put any such thoughts from my mind. Anything else was unthinkable.

Sighing, I settled in my reading chair with Shakespeare, amusing myself within the bantering lines of *Much Ado about Nothing*. Beatrice and Benedick's wit and "denied" affection for each other warmed my heart, and I found myself dreaming of the impossible.

The clatter of blocks tumbling upon the floor startled me from my sleep. My alarm at the secret passage! Jumping up, dressed only in my thin nightgown, I ran to the schoolroom. Benedict stood there, looking amused at the mess. Dressed in only his breeches, he appeared as if he'd stepped from his bath and lightly dried himself. I could see errant beads of water on his chest, his back, and dampening his silky hair. He made me thirsty.

"You are back," I said, licking my dry lips. My breath, shallow with anticipation, caught in my throat as he lifted his gaze to mine. The stark hunger and desperation I'd seen before when my breasts had shown through my threadbare gown was back.

"I had to come back. I could not stop thinking of you."

"Nor I you. Benedict, please. This is not easy for me. You must understand that I cannot—"

"No, Titania, this is the only thing we need to understand." He grabbed my shoulders, pulling me against him. My gasp was timed perfectly to the lowering of his lips. His mouth covered mine, angling my head back, giving him access to my neck. He stroked me there, his touch burning a path down my body, making me greedy for more and more pleasure. My breasts ached.

"Please," I said again, meaning the exact opposite of before. He knew what I wanted, what I needed. His scorching hand covered my breast.

"I cannot think anymore. You have driven me insane with desire. Can you feel it, Titania? Can you feel my heart thunder, my blood boil? I must have you as my wife. Will you marry me?" He set me back on my feet, his dark eyes intent as he searched my face.

"Yes," I whispered.

Grabbing the hem of my gown, he pulled it over my head, leaving me naked. He looked his fill, then held out his hand. "Come, Titania, let's have our midsummer night's dream. Come be my lover."

The clatter of blocks tumbling to the floor startled me from my dream. The secret passage alarm! Jumping up, I ran to the schoolroom, heart pounding, in a replay of what I had just dreamed. No one was in the schoolroom. The chair still sat against the passage's door, but the blocks were on the floor.

My alarm had stopped an unwelcome guest. I couldn't call a household member an intruder, could I?

My dream had been nothing but the impractical imaginings of a spinster's loneliness, best buried forever. I dragged a heavy desk across the passage door and set my chair alarm in front of that.

Benedict was out of town; but given my dream, I would have blocked the door anyway. No matter how seductive his kiss was, I would not walk to my ruin.

Dawn was ebbing the darkness from the night by the time I shut my eyes and fell into a restless sleep.

12

"Not so fast," I called out to Justin and Robert as they dashed ahead of me in the formal gardens.

"I want to hurry," Justin said. "After our lessons I want to go and play with Cesca."

"I want to play with Cesca, too," Robert chimed in, jumping up and down.

"Can you do that with your father out of town?"

My question turned his slight smile to a determined frown. "I don't care. I want to, and I will. He gave her to us."

"Cesca is ours," Robert agreed. "I want to see Cesca."

"Stop!" My disapproving shout rang out through the morning air. Everything seemed to fall so quiet that I swear the birds stopped singing and the bugs quit buzzing. Robert and Justin looked at me with shock on their faces. I don't think I had ever yelled at them so sternly before.

"You were given a wonderful gift, which I thought you two were mature enough to have. But I must have been mistaken. Surely I did not hear you say you did not care about what is right and what is wrong. Surely I did not hear you say you were going to do whatever you wanted to do, because you felt like it?" I shook my head. "I am severely disappointed to hear you speak so disrespectfully and so irresponsibly. Do you know everything you need to know about a horse yet?"

Both of the boys shook their heads.

"Yet with very little experience and without even asking permission, you would take her out to play? What if something went wrong? What if you, Robert, or even Cesca got hurt? Badly hurt? Cesca is a precious gift, and as her owner, it is your responsibility to keep her safe, even if it means you can't have the fun you want to have until you're ready. Do you understand?"

Justin nodded, real repentance in his eyes. Robert, too.

"Now, let's figure out the best thing we can do. I don't know what I need to know to be safe about horses either. What if we ask your uncle Stephen to take us to play with Cesca? Or maybe he can have one of the groomsmen in the stable help us?"

Both the boys smiled.

I narrowed my gaze at Justin. "Defiance will only bring you trouble and make you lose in life. You must deal with life and its disappointments as you would a game of chess. Consider the moves available and choose the best action to help you win."

Justin's eyes widened, then he nodded his head, telling me he understood.

"Can I pway chest too?" Robert asked.

"Yes. You'll start learning how to play chess soon." I held out my hands to them, and we made our way to the herb garden.

My steps slowed. Across the tops of the cheery roses, I could see the dark patch of dirt for our herb garden. Something was very wrong. There was no ring of stones, no neat rows of sprouts, only a churned-up, jumbled mess. I had no choice but to continue with the boys and face what had been done.

Robert started to cry. "They killeded the babies, Miss Wovell," he said through his tears.

"I know." Tears filled my own eyes. It wouldn't have done any good to tell him that we could plant more seeds at that moment—that plants weren't like people and could be easily replaced. His heart grieved.

Justin fisted his hands. "Why should I care about what's right and wrong when no one else does? I don't want to play with Cesca, either. Everything dies."

Robert cried harder. I picked him up, holding him to me. I put my other arm around Justin's shoulders. He didn't pull away. "I know," I said. He was grieving. Not for the plants, but for his mother. As we stood there looking at the fresh dirt, I knew what I had to do next, even before I gave the adult inhabitants of Trevelyan Hill a piece of my mind. Disturbing my personal belongings and disrupting my peace of mind was one thing. Hurting the children in the process was completely unacceptable.

Pulling my gloves on, ready for battle, I found Dobbs in the foyer, overseeing the maids cleaning it.

"Miss Hain, this is the most important room. Everyone who comes to Trevelyan Manor sees it. I expect this floor to be spotless. There's a streak on the tile in the corner."

I found it surprising that Dobbs agreed with my feelings about the stained glass foyer. Even though his reasons were different than mine, the fact that we were in agreement about anything just wasn't acceptable. I pressed my lips to a grim line.

Moving across the room, taking care to avoid the cleaning areas, I passed though the brightly hued beams streaming from the stained glass. They were warm and felt like a heavenly blessing upon this mission I was about to embark on with the boys.

"Mr. Dobbs, I would like a word with you, please," I said, drawing his attention.

"Miss Lovell. I am sure even you can see that I am rather busy at the moment." His nose lifted, and I had the sudden urge to push smelling salts beneath it. I didn't think he'd be so highbrowed then.

"I am afraid I must insist. Masters Justin and Robert and I have little time to waste if we are going to return by afternoon tea."

"Your lack of discipline in regards to keeping a teaching regime is—"

"Not of your concern. Mr. Trevelyan is more than capable of monitoring my competency." I lowered my voice. "I need to know where Francesca Trevelyan is buried, please. The boys have some flowers they wish to put on her grave."

Dobbs jaw dropped even as his back stiffened. "Really, Miss Lovell. You go too far. Taking the boys to their mother's grave is not within the realm of your responsibilities."

"I assure you, Mr. Dobbs, if I did not deem this essential, I would not be asking. They have had a rather upsetting morning. Someone destroyed the children's herb garden last night. Most probably to strike out at me, since this is not the first untoward incident I've had to deal with. Now if you will please tell me what I need to know, you will save me the trouble of inquiring in town."

"The family has their memorial at Prynne Hill Cemetery," he replied, his words terse with disapproval. "Now would you care to inform me of what incidents you speak?"

"No," I said. "But you can tell me what the plans are for Master Justin's birthday. He will be eight in a few weeks."

"Plans?"

"Yes. What sort of celebration is planned?"

"There is none. We are not a trivial household."

"A celebration of thanksgiving is not a trivial matter. I will attend to Master Justin's birthday. The children and I will be back for tea." I left before he could delay me further.

No matter what little we had, my mother had always spent the day of my birth giving thanks and making me feel very special.

Within minutes I had gathered the children, and we sailed out the door, ignoring Dobbs's glowering expression. I led them first to Holloway Park, where I'd planned to tell the children what we were about. I decided to take them to visit my mother's resting place first, then to their mother's.

They didn't even smile or try and run down the lazy green slopes as the other children were doing. "We need to find the prettiest flowers to take with us."

"Where are we going, Miss Wovell?" Robert put his hand in mine. His tears had dried, but the hurt dealt to him this morning still lingered in his young eyes.

I knelt down to meet them eye level. "First, I would like us to visit the place where my mother is buried. I want to take her some flowers just to let her spirit know that I love her. Then, if you would like, I will take you to do the same for your mother."

Robert's eyes widened. "My mommy has a resting place I can see?"

"Yes. Would you like to go?"

"Oh, yes. And I can take her flowers, too?"

"I think that will be a very beautiful thing to do. Why don't you collect some of those purple flowers over there and let me talk to Justin."

It was good to see Robert dash off eagerly after the flowers.

"I want to take a rose," Justin said. His voice was flat, as if he didn't dare let the tiniest bit of emotion escape from him.

I met his gaze, wondering how long he'd be able to keep the dam from bursting. I prayed it would be soon, for I was beginning to understand Stephen's concerns. I'd heard of children who'd shut themselves off from the world and never opened to it again.

"We will go to the florist in town and buy one, then."

He nodded. "What will it look like? My mother's resting place."

"You have never been?"

"I don't remember if I have."

"If your mother's grave is like my mother's, then it will be not too different from the grass where we stand and a headstone with her name. But I am sure your father made her place more special."

Robert ran back, arms full of purple flowers, cheeks smudged with dirt, and grass stains on his knees. His eyes shone with triumph. My heart squeezed as it hit me. I loved them with all of their problems and moods, smiles and sadness. They'd become a part of my heart.

Helping Robert with the flowers, we made our way to town. At the florist, Justin chose a large red rose, and Robert picked a daisy to add to his collection.

We soon reached my mother's simple grave. I lovingly set the flowers at the foot of the wooden cross with her name on it. Justin stood off to the side, not getting close to the grave. "I come here and talk to her sometimes and tell her what's making me happy or sad."

"Does she hear you?" Robert asked, moving to my side.

I looked up at the sky. "I do not know, but if she can, I want her to know that I love and remember her." Leaning over, I pulled away a few weeds trying to grow among the thickening grass. "Someday I will be able to buy her a special headstone, so everyone who passes by will know how well she was loved."

"Do you think my mommy has a special headstone?"

I stood. "Let's go see. She is resting in a place closer to the town."

Leaning down, Robert set one of his flowers on my mother's grave, then put his hand in mine.

"Thank you," I whispered, squeezing his hand.

The walk to Prynne Hill Cemetery passed in silence. I'd hoped to find a gardener or caretaker to tell the exact location of the Trevelyan's memorial. As it was, we had to search through the place. Every now and then the boys would stop and ask me to read a marker, and Robert and I would talk about what that person's family or life might have been like. They were surprised to see a good number of the buried were children.

"Your father is blessed that you both are so healthy. Other parents are not nearly as lucky."

I breathed a sigh of relief when we came upon a beautiful granite statue, a replica of the angel that graced Trevelyan Manor's gardens. There were two headstones at the foot of the angel, under her protective shadow.

" 'Benedict W. Trevelyan, Sr. Born 1815. Died 1871. Loving husband and esteemed father. Though lost at sea you'll remain in our hearts forever.' This would be your grandfather." No wonder Benedict's mother looked so sadly out to sea.

"I didn't knowed he was here with my mommy. He can take care of her, can't he?"

"Yes, he can. So can the angel. She's the same angel in your garden at home."

Robert nodded solemnly. "That is good."

"Very good." I looked over to see Justin near the other headstone and nudged Robert that way with me.

" 'Francesca Ortega Trevelyan. Born 1848. Died 1872. Wife of Benedict W. Trevelyan, Jr., and beloved mother of Justin and Robert.' " It was a beautiful headstone, engraved with a fancy scroll along its edges; the grave itself was well tended. Both the boys stood silent. I knelt down and placed the few flowers I carried at the foot of the grave. She'd only been twenty-four years old. I was twenty-four years old. My stomach churned.

"Did our father putted our names there, saying we bewuved her?"

"I am sure he did," I said quietly.

"Can I touch it?"

"Yes."

Robert walked hesitantly up to the headstone. He squatted, carefully laying his bouquet against the headstone. Then he traced his mother's name with his finger.

Justin hadn't moved, though he looked as if he were barreling forward or about to do so. It was as if he stood outside an invisible barrier, unable to press himself through it. His breaths seemed ragged, and I wondered if I'd made a mistake in bringing him here.

"Justin." I kept my voice quietly soft. He didn't answer or look my way, but he did move closer to the headstone. His hands shook as he held out the rose. I winced as I saw how he held the flower. He had both his hands wrapped tightly around its thorny stem.

He dropped the flower on the grave. I could see blood staining the white paper the florist had wrapped the stem in. And I felt as if my heart bled at the sight. I moved to stand next to him, unable to leave him so alone.

"Why?" I asked softly, taking a handkerchief from my pocket and pressing it gently upon his cuts. "Why did you hold the thorns so tightly?"

He looked up at me, pain etched tightly upon his wan

face. There were tears trapped behind the shadows of his dark eyes, tears with no hope of ever being freed. The set of his shoulders was too rigid. Just like his father.

"My hands are full of thorns," he said. Then he turned from the grave and walked away, leaving me with the blood-stained handkerchief.

The tears I'd been holding back quietly streamed down my face. He remembered the story I'd told him about Cynthia Parker and her son Quanah.

"Justin? Robert? Miss Ann?"

Looking up against the bright glare of the sun, I saw Stephen hurrying our way. Justin stopped walking and shoved his hands into his pockets.

"Uncle Steph, are you here to surprise us?" Robert ran to greet his uncle.

I dashed at my tears, scrambling to gather my composure.

"I do not suppose you are here by coincidence," I commented as Stephen approached.

"No, Dobbs contacted me. I would have been here earlier, but I was in the middle of a meeting with my banker. What the devil is wrong?"

"Aside from our garden being vandalized, circumstances just led to this being an appropriate time for Masters Justin and Robert to express a remembrance to their mother. I do not believe they have ever been to do so. It is an important part of easing grief."

Stephen's eyes widened. "I was not aware they had not been here." He looked over my shoulder to the memorial, and sadness filled his eyes. "She should not be there, so alone."

"It is all right," Robert said, patting Stephen's hand. "Grandfather is there. He can take care of her. The angel, too."

Stephen blinked, surprised. "I guess you are right. You know what else you are right about?"

"What?"

"I am here to surprise you. They have a new flavor for a candy stick, and I need your expert opinion about it. In fact, I told the proprietress that she could not sell any until she had your approval. Shall we go to the confectioner's shop? Perhaps even get some gumdrops and chocolate as well?"

Justin shrugged, but began to follow his uncle.

I welcomed the distraction, thinking it would be best for the boys to have a little bit of sweet added to the bitter tastes of the day. The candy was nice, but the laughter Stephen's antics elicited when he made coins disappear, then found them behind our ears, was even better. We barely made it back before it was time for me to meet Mrs. Trevelyan for tea.

As it was, I had to rush to the solarium. Stephen stayed in the schoolroom with the boys to play chess, after which they were going to eat an early dinner and go to bed. Stephen promised to take them to play with Cesca in the morning, an activity that I'd somehow involved myself in.

I wasn't sure exactly what I would say to Benedict's mother. I couldn't very well come right out and ask her if she'd murdered her daughter-in-law. Yet I was determined to find out if she was responsible for all of the odd incidents. I feared she was not. Churning up her grandson's garden didn't seem to be in character.

"You are almost late," she said as I strode into the room.

"Good afternoon to you, too." I smiled, noting that she was alone. "Is Maria planning another visit to my room while we meet?"

"Miss Lovell, I have no idea what—"

"Mrs. Trevelyan. Neither of us have time to waste on pre-

tenses, and we are too intelligent to spend energy on frivolous inanities."

"No. Maria is out with Constance today."

"Good," I replied, sitting down before she invited me to
do so. "I have several untoward incidents that I wish to clear
up. But first, I find myself thoroughly fascinated by what I
saw last night."

"An old woman walking with a cane?" she asked, pouring two cups of tea from a server situated next to her.
"Sugar?"

"Yes, please. Actually, I was speaking of the book you
held. Did your husband write and publish a book, or was I
mistaken in the author's name?"

Setting down the sugar, she stared at me a moment.

"You were not mistaken." She handed me the tea, and I
took a sip. "Ben was an expert hybridist. He loved roses and
went around the world collecting different varieties.

"He was in the middle of writing a second book on the
subject when he died. He was returning from collecting
more specimens abroad when his ship wrecked." She sipped
her tea, seemingly staring into its depths a moment. "And
his book was never finished."

"I know that is not an easy thing to live through. The
death of a loved one."

She set her teacup down. "Miss Lovell, let me be frank
with you. I do not want you in this house."

"Your reasons would be? And please do not tell me it's
because I laundered clothes. Your dislike of me is entirely
too personal."

Her dark eyes burned with anger. "You are a threat to
my family because both Benedict and Stephen are somewhat intrigued by you. Francesca succeeded in almost
completely destroying Benedict and Stephen and nearly
Katherine as well. It will be years before my sons' wounds

will heal, if ever. Both are teetering on a precipice. And as I see it, you are the very breeze that will push them over the edge."

"How? What did Francesca do?"

"Evil has no greater face than that of an angel. While you are no beauty, Miss Lovell, I see you are like Francesca."

I placed my cup of tea on the table. "Mrs. Trevelyan. Were you standing in the tower window looking at the bay the first day I began work, and again the other day? Did you stand in the hallway behind me only to duck away when I turned?"

"And if I did? This house is my home."

"Did you enter my room in the middle of the night? Did you send me a note telling me to stay at my own peril? Did you destroy your grandsons' garden?" With every sentence, her eyes grew wider with surprise.

I had the answer I needed for now. Whatever Mrs. Trevelyan might have done to Francesca, she was not behind the most disturbing incidents. I had an even more dangerous enemy within the house on Trevelyan Hill than she. And I began to question the wisdom of confronting the situation as directly as I had planned to do this evening.

Standing, I said, "There is one thing you may have not thought of, Mrs. Trevelyan. What if I am the wind that's blowing your sons back onto solid ground? What if your withdrawal into grief and infirmity is only making the precipice on which they stand even shakier? You have grandsons that need you even more than your sons. Are you going to wait until they disappear over a precipice before you realize that? Unless they know it already, I suggest you let your family see you and up walking. They need signs of hope that the future is not condemned to the pain of the past."

"How dare you!"

"I learned today that there is nothing I would not dare when it comes to protecting Justin and Robert. I love them." I left before she recovered.

※ *13* ※

Thursday, Mr. Anthony Simons arrived early for our ten-thirty sign language lesson to find us romping around the stained glass foyer like cowboys gone mad. Justin, Robert, and I had had a very busy morning. We'd met with Stephen in the stables and spent two hours with Cesca. Even I'd been forced to pet her and give her a carrot.

Keeping up my fear in the face of a furry horse half my size that looked at me with eyes as meltingly warm as Robert's was beyond my capabilities. Cesca simply won me over. But then anything or anyone who brought the light of laughter to Robert's face and interest to Justin's won my allegiance.

As did Stephen, I'm afraid to say. The man had a knack of knowing exactly what to do and what to say to make Robert bounce with merriment, me giggle, and even Justin cough up a reluctant smile or two. But what finally grabbed my affections was Stephen giving the boys romping "horse" rides on his back in the stained glass foyer, sending Dobbs into a hullabaloo. It was a wonder he didn't grab the armored man's sword and begin chasing us.

Not even the knock at the door and or Dobbs's escalating apoplectic fit halted the fun. Mr. Simons stepped into the foyer, his manner as hesitant as a defeated soldier holding a white flag facing enemy troops. Even before he glanced our way, I saw his gaze center on the stairs and linger a moment. I wondered how many times he'd watched Katherine rush down to greet him.

With Robert still on his back, Stephen came to a stop before Mr. Simons, offering his hand. "Good to see you, Anthony. It has been too long."

Relief eased the man's grim smile, and he shook Stephen's hand. "Far too long." He swallowed as if he had too many words in his mouth. "Not since the funeral. . . ." His voice died to a whisper, and he shook his head as if to wake himself. "When did you get back from the East?" Dobbs took the man's coat.

"A few weeks ago," Stephen said, shrugging. "I see you must have decided to stay with the Institute of the Deaf and Blind rather than move back to New York."

"Yes, my work here was not done. Once I could see past my personal situation, the decision to stay was easy to make." Even as he spoke, he looked up the staircase again, as if he expected someone to appear. There was no mistaking the tightness of sorrow etched upon his face. I realized it was this that gave him the saintlike aura I'd noted.

Stephen cleared his throat and set Robert down. "She knows you are expected. I do not know if she will come down or not."

Mr. Simons stiffened his shoulders. "I did not come here to see Katherine. I am here to teach. If I have arrived too early, I can come back later."

"Nonsense, Mr. Simons," I said, straightening my dress and joining them. "We are ready for the lesson. Master Justin and Master Robert, please come meet Mr. Simons. He's here to teach us a special language."

"Miss Wovell, can I ride horsey one more time?" The

look on Robert's face pulled at my heart. It was as if he was afraid the fun would go away and never come back, and he wanted to have one more memory of it. Had I not felt the same way after Benedict's second kiss?

"Always ask permission to do something by saying, 'May I.' Now, if your uncle wants to give you a ride to the day parlor, you may. But once there, I expect you to settle down and give Mr. Simons your complete attention."

"I promise." He turned his imploring gaze to his uncle. "Pwease?"

"Do you think I'd leave you stranded, partner?"

Though he'd been speaking to Robert, Stephen's question triggered a response from Justin. "Yes," Justin said, sadly, the fuzzy warmth and beauty of the colored beams falling from his hunched shoulders as he left the foyer. I thought Dobbs would faint with relief as we followed Justin to the day parlor.

Robert got his ride, but the sparkle in Stephen's laugh had dulled. Stephen surprised me by joining our lesson, claiming he needed to brush up on his sign language skills. But the real shock of the morning was seeing Constance, artfully turned out in a lacy day dress of cream and shell pink, appear to take part in the instruction.

After I saw her bat her eyes at Mr. Simons when he touched her hand to bend her finger in a simple movement she couldn't seem to grasp, I knew why she'd come. Yet Mr. Simons didn't acknowledge her efforts to attract his attention.

I'd wondered before if Francesca had been the dividing tool between Katherine and Mr. Simons. I hadn't considered Constance.

The children were more adept at picking up the new language than Stephen or I. Constance didn't do well. I don't think she was trying for anything other than attention, though. Otherwise, I considered the class a worthwhile success.

Once we were done, I stood, explaining that the children were due in the kitchen for their lunch.

"Actually, eating is a wonderful idea," Constance said, then looked at Mr. Simons. "Mr. Simons, would you care to join us for a meal? You have the time for lunch today, do you not, Stephen?"

"Of course. Should have thought of it myself, Connie. Will you stay, Anthony? And Miss Ann, you must join us as well."

I shook my head. "I have to see to the children's lessons this afternoon."

"We will not keep you long. No reason for you to eat in the kitchens with the boys when you can eat with us. Hurry back," Stephen said, dismissing my protests.

Living in the Trevelyan household had a way of leading me down paths far from the straight and narrow. I hurried, oddly looking forward to lunch and learning more about Mr. Simons. His relationship with Katherine and its mysterious demise intrigued me. The kitchen bustled with activity; Cook Thomas was on top of the world. "Will ye be needing a basket of goodies for your outing tomorrow? I have meat pies tasty enough to tempt a saint to gluttony." He rubbed his ample girth with a jolly fist.

"Unfortunately, we will have to postpone our trip to the bank until next Friday. I hope Mr. Trevelyan will be back by then and be able to accompany us for the outing."

"I don't think that boy has had a moment's ease since his father died. Even before that, if the truth were to be told. Haven't seen him smile since he gave up his ship."

"Why did he?"

"Bad investments. Bad times. The railroad's sudden appearance nearly wiped out the Trevelyans' fortune. The captain's father had more of an eye for a rose than he did for finances." Cook Thomas shook his head and sighed. "The captain had to sell everything he'd built up to save his father, then he had to marry a lass who had no heart for him. 'Twas a sad day it were."

I wanted to know more, but I also felt if I asked any questions, I'd be invading Benedict's privacy. Besides, I was expected back in the dining room, so I bit back my curiosity. "I hope an outing with the children will help."

"Aye, that it will. A man with too many responsibilities forgets how to live."

As does a woman with too much practicality. The thought, which came at me from nowhere, shook me. "Please have Maria notify me when the children are done. I'll be in the dining room."

When I arrived, I found Mr. Simons telling Stephen about a man who'd be speaking at the institute on Saturday. "Mr. Forester is a staunch believer in oralism. I do not agree with forcing deaf students to speak and read lips to communicate, but I do believe in the movement's desire to make deaf people less isolated from the world around them. He will be speaking on ways to do just that."

"Pardon me for joining this discussion late, but did you say who could attend this lecture?"

"Anyone in the community who is interested," Mr. Simons replied.

"Then I could attend?"

He raised his brows. "Absolutely. We are striving to educate everyone that deafness is not leprosy. This is the second in a series of lectures we have planned."

Constance spoke before I could. "That's wonderful. I wish Katherine would realize . . ." She shook her head, as if she shouldn't have mentioned Katherine's name. "Would you mind if I joined you, Miss Lovell?"

"No, not at all," I said slowly, trying to fathom why Constance would attend a lecture.

"I will be expecting you two then. I can reserve special seating in the front."

"Add me to the event as well," Stephen said. "And Katherine. They will have an interpreter, correct?"

"Yes," Mr. Simons paused and ran a shaky hand through his hair, clearly more troubled than he wanted anyone to know. "Is she ready for that? She wasn't before, and I am not an advocate of force—in any matter."

Stephen shrugged. "Birds never pushed from the nest never learn to fly. I will bring her."

I know Stephen was in no way referring to Francesca's death, but in my mind, I kept seeing her pushed from the tower. She hadn't flown. She'd died.

"Cesca did not," Mr. Simons said softly. I barely heard the breathy words. They were but a fleeting whisper that I thought I imagined until I saw the sharp look Mr. Simons and Stephen exchanged. I shivered.

The decision I had made yesterday not to confront everyone about the herb garden and my threatening note had been the right one. I didn't know friend from foe and deemed hiding behind a thin veil of polite falsehoods prudent. Thankfully, all I had said about the herb garden at dinner last night was that animals had damaged it, and we would plant another one.

The rest of Thursday and Friday passed without any major difficulties. We made up for missed lessons, planted a new garden, and spent time with Cesca and Stephen in the stables. My heart didn't pound every time I entered the building, and I'd taken to speaking a word or two at Gunnlod whenever she popped her head out of the stall.

I pretended that Cesca and Gunnlod were the only two horses in existence. It helped.

• • •

Saturday morning dawned. I awoke tired, with hardly the energy to rise and meet the sun. My dreams had ruled again, casting Benedict as friend, lover, husband, it didn't matter. Whatever I dreamed, he was there, and Cook Thomas's words were, too. *He had to marry a lass who had no heart for him.*

I pinched my cheeks, looking for color to hide the dark shadows under my eyes. Benedict and sleep were like oil and water; no matter what I did, they didn't mix.

Dressing, I decided to run errands before attending the lecture at the institute later this afternoon. I hoped Stephen had made progress in convincing Katherine to come. As of last night, she was adamantly against it.

A sharp knock on my door made nerves tingle. For some reason, Benedict immediately came to mind. I suppose whenever he was away, I felt his absence and expected his return at any minute. The reaction was disturbing.

Quickly slipping the last button on my lavender pin-stripe into place, I answered the door. "Miss Ortega," I said blinking. "Is there a problem?"

"No, Miss Lovell, other than I owe you an apology, no? Stephen has quite reminded me that I have been very remiss in welcoming you to our home here."

"Thank you, but there is no need. The Trevelyan household has been more than generous. Indeed, I'd not expected my accommodations to be any different from those of the household servants. But I am afraid Mr. Trevelyan insisted, and I have to admit, being close to the children is very important."

Constance sighed, her dark eyes narrowing. "You speak the truth, no? Then I owe you another apology. You come here and are treated as one of the family, and I say to myself, Constance, this woman is trying to take advantage of a family to whom I owe many things. I did not like you for that."

I blinked. She had no problem coming right to the point of a discussion. Past conversations had led me to believe she'd avoid any confrontation of truth.

"Well," I said, making myself smile, "I must apologize to you. I did not like you very much either. At least I did not until you sang. I envy your poise."

"But I sing awfully."

"I know. I am cursed as well when it comes to singing, but you did it so beautifully, I had to admire you."

She laughed. "You are good for me, no? For you to like my singing makes you quite unusual, as am I. I am off this morning to do some shopping. Would you care to join me?"

Her offer took me aback. That we had cleared a bit of the air between us in no way made her my friend. Yet I did want the opportunity to find out more about her, possibly learn what her relationship with Mr. Henderson was, and even learn more about Francesca.

"I have several errands to do, and I will need to stop by my friend's shop, McGuire's Bookstore. Will that accommodate your plans?"

"Of course, we will have a grand time, no? I will instruct Dobbs to have the carriage ready for us in an hour. That will still give us three hours to shop. The lecture is not until four this afternoon, correct?"

"Yes," I said, stunned. Three hours to shop? How could anyone spend so much time shopping?

Constance departed, leaving me standing at the door. To be honest, I didn't think we would have a grand time. And I felt as if my day of freedom had just been caught in the noose of a lasso, wrapped tight, and snatched back from its intended goal.

Worse yet, rather than walking, I had to face the notion

of a *horse* taking me. Not a relaxing thought. At least in a carriage I'd be completely protected from the beast.

The only bright spot was that I loved the idea of telling Dobbs to ready a carriage. The order had quite a dignified ring to it, so the day wasn't going to be a total loss.

I made sure I was in the foyer extra early with my gloves on. Dobbs stood like a sentinel by the door.

"Do you have the carriage for Miss Ortega and me ready, Mr. Dobbs?"

His eyes narrowed above his stiff nose. "Mr. Trevelyan will hear of all these goings-on, Miss Lovell, I assure you. The carriage will be out front shortly."

"Thank you. I will be in the music room." I went immediately to the piano as I entered the room and slid my gloved fingers across the ivory keys. Just to be able to touch so grand an instrument filled me with awe. Until coming to Trevelyan Hill, I'd only seen grand pianos in books. That I now could touch one, even possibly learn to play, still stunned me.

I'd paid sharp attention when Justin and Robert had had their lessons. I knew the letters of notes now. Soon I'd play a song. But for now, I set my fingers silently on the keys, closed my eyes, and remembered how Benedict had played, so movingly, so deep. I pretended that I was he and playing how he played.

The air about me stirred, causing tendrils of my hair to brush at my neck, and I slowly opened my eyes.

"Why, Miss Ann, that is the most beautiful song I ever heard." Stephen leaned upon the edge of the piano, his face close to mine, his bright eyes smiling.

"Now I know you for the scoundrel you are. I did not play a note." Still, I had to smile.

"I beg to disagree, Miss Ann. I had only to look upon your face to see how beautifully you played. The heart of music is not always in the striking of a note."

"Is that similar to saying that the heart of a man is not always in the words he speaks?" I replied tartly, not about to fall to his smooth words.

Stephen leaned his head back and roared with laughter. "I do believe I have been soundly put in my place. And if I had more time, I would let you do it again. You are a delight. But for now, I have a favor to ask."

"Which is?"

"I need you to come and talk to Katherine about the lecture this afternoon. She has some questions, and I think you are the one to answer them. Will you come now?"

"Well, yes, I suppose. I am to meet Miss Ortega to go shopping, but that is not for a quarter hour yet."

"So Connie's decided to be nice. Good for you, Miss Ann. I do believe you could ease the fangs off a rattler and he would never know he had been changed. Connie's always late, so don't hurry. I will notify Dobbs that you will be in Katherine's rooms."

My interest grew as I followed Stephen. Katherine's rooms were in the wing opposite mine, above her mother's. I'd never been in that section of the house and was curious about Katherine's quarters. Rather than a lone window at the end of the hallway, there appeared to be a sunny sitting area, lending the entire hall a feeling of light and warmth instead of the chill darkness in the corridor to my room. I commented about this to Stephen and learned that this wing of the house faced south and therefore received the most light.

Stephen stopped just outside Katherine's rooms. "I must warn you, Miss Ann. Katherine paints. She used to paint beautiful scenes, happy scenes, full of light and love. Now she paints pain. Please don't let it disturb you. I'll wait for you downstairs."

Had Stephen not warned me, I might have gone running

from Katherine's rooms. The pictures hung on her wall were beautiful vignettes of life—a wedding, a christening, a sun-drenched garden as the setting for a ladies' tea. But in every picture, one person among all of the people painted stood alone, his face contorted with pain, his body wrapped in chains. It was shockingly disturbing. And in all of the pictures, not a single person painted was looking at the person tied in a living hell.

Other than the pictures, Katherine's rooms were as light and breezy as her mother's rooms were heavy and oppressive. Lots of white and sunshine dominated the touches of pastel colors and cream furniture leafed with gold. It was the room of a princess or an angel. Or maybe not, I thought, looking at another one of her pictures—a family at Christmas, wife singing, children playing, husband bound in agony.

I resisted the need to shake the vision from my mind and greeted Katherine as she stood. She invited me to sit down. I did, thankfully noting a tablet and pencil upon the table before me. I pointed to them. "May I use these?" I asked.

She gestured for me to. And I wrote.

"*Your work is beautiful and provokes deep emotions when you contrast the beauty and the pain. It is not easy to understand.*" I didn't know what else to write, but I didn't want to ignore her art. It would take a great deal to get used to. Most people would not want to see life painted so realistically.

All of my life, I'd known people who were trapped in the drudgery of being poor. Some were in pain, some had been content, but all had looked upon the rich as being free of pain. I knew, for I'd done the same. It wasn't until I'd come here that I'd realized the life of the rich wasn't necessarily any better. Sometimes they were even more trapped than the poor.

I also wondered if the person in pain in the pictures

wasn't Katherine herself—part of the world around her, yet so isolated and alone.

Katherine read my note and answered. *"You are more understanding than most. And more forgiving. Stephen tells me that you alone went to the Institute for the Deaf and Blind and engaged Anthony to come here and teach Justin and Robert."*

I smiled and nodded. *"Yes. And me too. We all wanted to know your special language. Mr. Simons is a very good teacher."*

Katherine only nodded when she read the note. She didn't smile. *"Stephen says Anthony was not upset by the suggestion I attend the lecture. That he did not appear to be troubled over the possibility of seeing me. It this true? I must know. I have caused him great pain, and I cannot add to it."*

I bit my lip as I read her note. To tell her Mr. Simons was completely unmoved by her existence or lack of appearance would be wrong. But to give her the impression that he outwardly was in agony would be wrong too.

Looking up again at one of her pictures, an idea struck me. *"Your art,"* I wrote, *"holds beauty and light, things that I see live inside Mr. Simons. Your art also holds pain. Something that lives inside Mr. Simons as well. But unlike your pictures, he is not frozen in his pain. He has moved past that. His mission in life drives him, frees him.*

"Who is in pain? Who do you paint?"

Katherine read the note. She nodded. Then she wrote a name upon the paper. She watched me as I read it.

"Benedict."

My breath caught. But she wasn't through.

"Stephen.

"Francesca.

"My mother.

"Anthony.

"Constance.

"*Myself.*

"*Justin.*

"*You, eventually.*

"*We are all cursed. You will be, too.*"

Cursed? My stomach clenching, I met her gaze, expecting to see the hostility that had dogged me since coming to Trevelyan Manor. I only saw great sadness in her silent tears. She'd been crying, and I'd been so absorbed in the names that I hadn't even realized it.

Katherine left, dashing to her bedroom and shutting the door. I went back down to await Constance, wondering if Katherine would come to the institute this afternoon.

Sometimes events and people influence you. In a moment all of life changes, as it says in the Bible, in a twinkling of an eye, and you're never the same again. I'd had moments like this since I'd come to Trevelyan Manor. Seeing the full effect of the stained glass windows. Benedict's kiss. Justin's hands, bloody from the thorns. Katherine's art, but even more than that, the pain in her golden eyes. She honestly believed the Trevelyans and all those drawn into the web of their lives were cursed.

Two hours in Constance's company, and I wondered if Katherine hadn't been right about being cursed. I wasn't sure how Constance managed it, but we'd been to two dressmakers and a milliner's. She conversed incessantly about fashion, quoting *Godey's Lady's Book* and *Frank Leslie's Illustrated Newspaper*—her definitive judges for what comprised a lady.

In each store, she inquired without fail about everything on display. She also bought two hats, three pairs of gloves, and a shawl imported from Paisley, Scotland, the cost of which nearly made me swoon. I wondered who paid for such extravagances.

All in all, I had the makings of a most unusual headache, and I knew without a shadow of a doubt that no matter how much I reveled in my new things, I would never be in danger of allowing fashion to consume my life. After we quit the last store, I couldn't contain myself a moment longer.

"Miss Ortega, however do you find the energy for this? I do not believe you have missed examining a single item in any of the shops. I am amazed." It was the most polite way I could express my overwhelmed state.

"You are not a woman who finds joy in beautiful things, no?" She ran her hand lightly over the box next to her that held her new shawl. The rest of the things she'd purchased would be delivered to Trevelyan Manor.

"Certainly I do, but I suppose my joy is found in other things as well as fashion. Books. Art. Nature. People. I have not had the occasions nor desire to make fashion a focus in my life."

"You are like Katherine, then. She contents herself and does not allow herself to hunger for new things. Someday she will wake up and wish she had lived differently, for she will have missed so much. Francesca was different. I am different, especially now that she is gone. I do not let life escape me. When I look at new things, buy new things, I do not do so for myself alone. I do so for Francesca, too. She loved them." Constance's voice thickened on her last sentence but didn't lower as if with sorrow. I almost thought she sounded angry.

"You must miss your sister," I said softly. Constance looked out the carriage window, and I did too. San Francisco life on a bustling summer Saturday passed in a lazy blur, just slow enough that you could see, but too fast to note any details.

"She was the only family I had left in the world," she finally said.

I swallowed the lump that rose in my throat. "I know how you feel. I lost my mother recently. She was my only family. When did your parents pass away?"

"Before . . . before I came to Trevelyan Hill. It was shortly after Francesca married."

"What happened?"

"There was a fire, a horrible fire. I was saved. They were not."

I gasped. "How awful. I am so sorry."

Constance remained silent. She brushed her hand repeatedly over the box. And I began to understand that there were many ways to deal with grief.

"I have learned that life goes on no matter what horrors befall one, Miss Lovell."

"Please, call me Ann."

She nodded. "And you must call me Constance. It would seem we have some things in common after all, no?"

I nodded. "Yes."

"The mood to shop more escapes me. Do you wish to attend your errands now?"

I had lost heart for anything other than seeing Mr. McGuire, and we headed directly there. I decided that asking Constance more about her sister or even mentioning the morning I'd seen her slap Mr. Henderson would break the tenuous bridge we were forming. So I kept silent.

"Poor Tom's a cold. Et tu, Brute?" Puck squawked, bringing Constance to a sudden halt as we entered the shop. She stared at the bird as if he were possessed.

Laughing, I brushed his feathers. "He is quite a Shakespeare fan." I didn't see Mr. McGuire at his desk. "Mr. McGuire, it's me, Ann." Rounding the corner, I saw him on a ladder, reaching for a volume on the top shelf.

"Ah, lass, did ye see him? He waited for you to stop by, but then had to go."

"Who?"

"Dr. Levinworth. He was just here." He lowered his voice. "He said she feared that her mortal—" Mr. McGuire's head snapped up as Constance came around the corner.

I cleared my throat. "Mr. McGuire, this is Miss Ortega, Mr. Trevelyan's sister-in-law. Miss Ortega, this is Mr. McGuire, owner of this marvelous shop of wonders. I think I love books as you do dresses."

The loud thump made me jump. I quickly saw that Mr. McGuire had dropped his book. "Are you all right?" I asked, rushing over to him. He wobbled oddly on the ladder, and my heart leapt into my throat. I thought he was about to fall.

Hands shaking, he climbed down. "Just a bit of a dizzy spell," he said as he stepped from the ladder. I took his hand and led him to his favorite reading chair.

"Sit here, and I will fetch you some water. This is not the first time you have had a spell. I am sorry I missed the doctor, but you can tell me what he said about your spells just as easily." I prayed that Mr. McGuire would take my hint to keep our inquiries into Benedict's wife's death private. Not only did Constance not need another reminder of her loss, but also I didn't want Benedict to know either.

"It's just old age," Mr. McGuire said grumpily.

"Old age or not, you should not be up on one of those ladders anymore. You need to hire yourself an assistant." Seeing a pitcher near his desk, I hurried over and poured a glass of water.

Mr. McGuire thirstily drank it down. "Thank ye, lass."

"When will the doctor return? Later today?"

Mr. McGuire shook his head. "Not until next Saturday."

As I felt his forehead, checking for a fever, he sent an assessing glance Constance's way, probably wondering if she'd connected Dr. Levinworth to her sister. She didn't appear as if she had.

"Are ye here for a book today, lass?"

"Yes, I wanted to know if you had any of John Muir or James Audubon's publishings. Master Justin is quite interested in their work." I leaned over and brushed some dust off his coat. "But we will worry about it another time. You are as pale as a ghost and need to rest."

"I'll be fine in just a moment. I may have something in the back room for ye." He tried to stand, and I gently pushed him back into the chair. The back room was like a complex maze of cartons, the last place he needed to scurry around in.

"No. You rest, and I will come back next Saturday. Then I will have a good excuse to see if you are taking proper care of yourself. And perhaps I will have a chance to question the doctor about you. Meanwhile you need to stay off the ladders. Promise me you will hire an assistant."

"I am fit as a fiddle," he said, avoiding my gaze.

Crossing my arms, I tapped my foot. "I have a lecture to attend at the institute this afternoon, which I fear I am going to be quite late for unless you can see fit to give me your promise. You are too important to me."

He sighed. "Very well, lass. But you have to promise to take care, as well."

"I am," I said, thinking of the desk I'd pulled in front of the secret passage, and wondering if I was only fooling myself. I know Mr. McGuire meant to guard my safety. Yet I feared for my virtue more. And it wasn't Benedict who I thought would deliberately compromise me. It was my own feminine urgings that had me worried. Desire was a most intriguing subject, and not one a book could exactly educate me in. However, I had no doubts about Benedict's capabilities in the matter.

✎ *14* ✎

Stephen slid into the carriage next to me, opposite Constance, and slammed the door behind him, his manner as grim as the set of his mouth. Apparently he'd failed to convince Katherine to attend the lecture.

He did not take failure well. The jovial shine of his countenance had tarnished like silver left in the rain. I'd seen occasional glimpses of the shadows that lurked behind his smiles, but this was the first time I'd seen his genteel mask stripped away completely. I found the experience disconcerting, as if I'd discovered a beast within a lamb.

"She has not left the bloody house since my arrival." He glared at Constance. "Has she gone anywhere at all in the year I have been away?"

"Once or twice, and only for a short time during the day."

"Benedict should be shot." Stephen spoke with enough force to make me jump. My mind scrambled for a connection between Stephen's anger at his brother and Katherine's isolation. "He should not have let her do this to herself."

"She is a woman grown. What can he do?" Constance said with a shrug.

"He can damn well pay more attention to the sorry state of his household than to finances and business."

Stephen's words surprised me. Not because I thought his statement untrue, but because he concisely summed up a general feeling I'd had. Especially when Benedict had left so quickly the day after kissing me. My eyes widened as the realization hit me. The master of Trevelyan Hill, a man large enough to battle any fabled Viking and win, buried himself in work to escape the unpleasant realities of his life.

Constance crossed her arms. "You are one to talk. At least business produces money. What have you done to help?"

"I had no choice. I had to do what I did." Stephen sighed, and his anger disappeared like a breath of smoke stolen by a stiff wind. "You shop as if money was like manna."

"Then maybe none of us has a choice either, for I have few joys in life. I have lost everything else." Constance sounded as if a thousand years of futility underlined her words, and I wondered if she was the same person who'd spent the morning with me frivolously shopping. She looked at me, her dark eyes burning with emotion. "Do you believe in fate, Ann? That no matter what you do you can never change who and what you are? That in the end, it is all you will ever be?"

My gaze went immediately to my hands. Hands that were now elegantly covered. But no covering could change the reddened stains of lye and labor. "No," I said quietly. "I believe you can choose." I wouldn't allow myself to believe otherwise.

The rest of the carriage ride to the institute passed in silence, each of us isolated in our thoughts. Mr. Simons met us at the door, his welcoming smile broad until he realized that Katherine wasn't among us.

"She would not come," Mr. Simons stated simply.

"No," Stephen said. "I have learned she has not left the house but twice in a year's time."

"I . . . I did not know." Mr. Simons paled and seemed to

falter. Stephen grabbed the man's shoulder. But Mr. Simons stiffened, and Stephen released him.

"She is a woman tied to her fate." Constance boldly looped her arm through Mr. Simons's. "Come, Anthony. Show us to our seats. You must tell me of your fascinating work here at the institute." She smiled at him as if she'd just entered a dress shop full of the latest fashions.

Stephen offered his arm, and we followed. His smile was forced, and not a glimmer of light flickered in his eyes.

"You are worried about Katherine?" I asked.

He frowned. "Yes. There is not a doubt in my mind that she loves Anthony and he loves her. Yet neither Anthony nor Katherine will tell us why she ended their engagement. I do know one thing for sure; if Constance sets her cap for Anthony, it will kill Katherine."

"But if he loves her, surely he wouldn't—"

"A man will only dangle for so long before he will break his own neck to be free, Miss Ann. Believe me, I know."

I had no doubt that he did know, and I suspect he had dangled at Francesca's feet. What I did not know was what he had done to break his own neck. That question cast an ominous shadow over the hallowed experience of my first official lecture within the coveted walls of a learning institution.

Constance had spoken of the inescapable fate to which we were born. I chose to think of it differently. That fate hinged on what decisions are made in critical moments, like Caesar crossing the Rubicon. Or, even on a smaller scale, when I passed through the demon-carved doors of Trevelyan Manor and found Benedict standing in the colored light of the stained glass. And more recently, when I'd stumbled upon him at his bath. At that crucial moment, I'd chosen to stare at him rather than to turn away. I touched my lips as my blood heated from the memory of his kiss.

Was it fate that drew me to Trevelyan Hill? Or was it my bid to alter my fate that brought me to the mansion?

I didn't know. I did know that with every breath I drew, I awaited the return of the master of Trevelyan Hill.

Upon returning from the lecture, I found myself dwelling on the tense emotions swirling around me, like the thickening of the air before a storm. The grief underlying Constance's obsession with fashion. Katherine's art, mirroring the pain of those surrounding her and her self-imposed imprisonment. The stark break in Stephen's carefree facade, and the antagonism with his brother. Benedict's difficulty relating to his sons, and Justin's growing isolation. Even Mrs. Trevelyan's hidden grief and anger. The myriad of conflicts and troubles encircling me kept pulling me closer and closer to the torn fabric of their lives. I wanted to take the needle of truth and the thread of wisdom and mend the gaps between them before the edges of their lives became too frayed to ever repair.

But as I lay down to sleep, it was Benedict who had me tossing and turning until I thought my sanity would flee. Finally, when I reached the screaming point well into the dark hours after midnight, I arose and checked on the sleeping boys, then returned to the windows of my room. I stared out at the mists swirling around the manor in the moonlight and imagined that I saw ghosts dancing at a grand ball until rain chased them away.

Then Benedict stole into my mind. I saw him as he stood on his doorstep that first morning, when I'd come to apply for governess. I saw him relaxed and laughing as I told him about Captain Balder's wish to add my mother to his list of wives. I saw him rising from his bath naked. But when he advanced on me and kissed me rather than covering himself, I just simply had to do something to distract myself. Upon my night table, I found Elizabeth Barrett Browning's little book of poems that I'd borrowed from the Trevelyans' library the other night and settled on the couch to read. Opening the book, my mind stumbled over what I saw. On the inside cover of the book was an inscription in faded ink:

Dearest Cesca,

I die each day I spend with you, even as I live for your every smile. My heart beats with a love I can never give. And though we are destined in this life to be apart, prisoners of circumstance, know that in the immortal words of Mrs. Browning's *Sonnets from the Portuguese,* our love will live through eternity.

" 'Guess now who holds thee?—'Death,' I said.

But there,

The silver answer rang,—'Not Death, but Love.' "

You'll forever make sunshine in my heart.

The note was unsigned. But "make sunshine" was as clear as a signature.

Stephen had told me a cherished memory of Francesca teaching Justin to play that game. The proof before me came as no surprise, but still my heart twisted painfully at what Benedict must have suffered, to be betrayed by his brother and wife.

Had jealousy and rage driven Benedict over the edge? Or even Stephen? What if it wasn't his own neck he broke to free himself? What if it had been Francesca's?

It was with dread that I turned to the sonnets and read some of the most beautiful words I'd ever read. Tears filled my eyes, and an odd yearning gripped my heart. It was as if a tide of feeling, of wanting, pressed so heavily against my practical nature that I thought I'd burst.

"Titania, how do I love thee?"

Startled over how clearly I'd heard Benedict's voice in my sleepy mind, I jumped up from my reading chair, confused.

"Damnation, what in the devil?" came a deep voice from the other room.

Blocks clattered on the floor as a heavy scraping sound snatched my attention. I ran to the schoolroom with my lamp. Benedict came barreling through the secret passage door, thunder furrowing his dark brow. I stared at him, drawn as one might be to gaze at the beauty and fury of a dangerous storm during the dark of the night.

"Miss Lovell, what in the bloody hell is going on here?" His clothes were dripping wet and plastered to his imposing body. His dark hair gleamed with moisture, and a rakish stubble shadowed the determined set of his jaw. From the look he centered on me above his Roman nose, I got the feeling I was in for a good dose his of dominating character-istics. "I will have that answer immediately. You are boxed in like a bloody rebel unit with nothing but bluecoats in sight."

I stiffened my spine. "I was merely being prudent, Mr. Trevelyan."

"Indeed, Miss Lovell?" He raked his fingers through his hair, sending droplets of water flying as he stepped over the blocks and advanced on me. "Did you fear I would steal in upon you in the middle of the night? Good God, woman, if nothing else, I am a man of honor."

He was so close I could smell the rain on him and feel the damp chill of his body. "P—Pardon? I do not see—" My eyes widened. "Mr. Trevelyan, do you think you're the only person on earth? Might you consider that there are others about who use the secret passage? That perhaps I sought to warn them that I would not tolerate being spied upon? And that I most certainly would want to warn myself if they did?"

He took hold of my shoulders, dampening my gown with the water dripping from him. I shivered, but not from the cold of his fingers. I shivered with the need to warm him.

"What are you talking about? Dobbs telegraphed me that my household had run amuck. Justin and Robert were in tears, and you had overstepped your position and taken them off to picnic at their mother's grave. I come rushing home to find you barricaded in your room. What is going on?"

"What is going on?" I blinked, quite taken by surprise that Dobbs had contacted Benedict. I considered the battle that Dobbs and I waged a private one. The man had had no right telegraphing tales. It had never occurred to me that Dobbs could be my intruder, the author of my warning note, and the destroyer of the children's garden. Maybe it should have. I then recalled that I was miffed at Benedict. "If you were not always running off, maybe you'd know what was going on in your own household."

"Running off?" He released me and took a step back as if I'd slapped him. "Running off!"

"Precisely," I said. I knew I'd more than overstepped my boundaries. In fact I most probably had obliterated them, which left me no choice but to brazen out the truth. I decided to pace, for an instinctual self-preservation told me that a moving target was harder to shoot than a standing one.

Benedict looked as if he were a loaded six-shooter in what Captain Balder would have described as a poker game gone sour.

"I have been giving a great deal of thought to the situation and can see how business decisions rather than the complexities of personal problems could have an appeal to a man of your nature," I said. Benedict crossed his arms, and his gaze targeted me. I paced faster and spoke faster, too, feeling the urgency to get everything said while I had the chance. "It is entirely logical for you to gravitate toward financial dealings. You are a man who requires instant results. You see situations as clear cut and have little time for emotional difficulties, such as Justin's fear that something dreadful will happen to you and he will have lost both his mother and his father. Then there is Robert's fear that while you are away you will find a boy who will behave perfectly and you will love that boy better. And I must say that considering birthdays as frivolous is quite—"

"Miss Lovell!" he said tersely, the muscles of his hard jaw drawn so tightly, I thought his teeth would crack. "I have ridden without stop for fourteen hours, the last two in a torrential rain, all because of a telegraph from Dobbs concerning my sons, and you have the audacity to tell me that I—good God, woman—I cannot even formulate the words to describe what sort of man you are attempting to make of me."

I bit my lip but didn't stop pacing. "Mr. Trevelyan, perhaps I am mistaken, but did you not kiss me last Monday? An event that left me so out of sorts that I was too flushed to attend dinner that night."

"You were flushed?" He looked surprised. "That was all?"

Heat stung my cheeks anew. "Quite flushed, a most embarrassing condition. Now, the next day, I attempted to discuss the situation with you, but before I had a moment to explain, you had already reached your own erroneous conclusions and promptly departed *on business.* What other conclusion can a woman draw, but that business has more appeal than—"

I paced past him. He grabbed my shoulders and swung me around to face him. "Than what, Miss Lovell?" His voice had lowered and softened, doubling its smoothness. My heart raced like a runaway stagecoach.

"Than . . . complexities," I whispered, the heat of my ire dampened by his obvious concern.

"Would that I had an aversion to . . . complexities, Miss Lovell. Unfortunately, I find myself quite attracted to them." His words seemed to be forced from him, confirming his turmoil.

He had come rushing back home, clearly worried by Dobbs's telegraph, an action that told me that not all of my suppositions were true. Maybe he didn't run away. Maybe he just didn't see the problems as I saw them. And maybe— no, more than maybe—he'd had no hand in his wife's death. But he'd suffered pain and betrayal, and my heart twisted for him.

I reached up and brushed away a droplet of water dangling on his chin, and I let my fingers linger against his rough beard. "I did not mean to imply you do not care about your sons, and I apologize for causing you worry. Justin and Robert have been grieving for their mother a long time. Part of healing from a loss is being allowed to continue to love that person. They have not been given the opportunity to love their mother since she died. When we had an upset with their herb garden, they needed to express their grief before it swallowed them. We took flowers to my mother's grave and then to their mother's grave. I cannot educate their minds and ignore the needs of their hearts. It is not within me to do so."

He didn't say anything, nor did he release his hold on me. I saw a battle wage within his intense eyes, and I wondered what he wrestled so hard with—until he moved his head. When his lips brushed my fingers still lingering on his chin, he sent a shock of fire racing though me. I knew then that he warred with his attraction for me. I could feel it now that the steam of my words had cleared. My mother hadn't kept me ignorant of the relations between a woman and a man. Though briefly, she'd spoken of it, believing foreknowledge would save me from the mistakes she'd made. Yet here I was, about to toss her wisdom aside. I had to know another of his kisses, as if my very life depended on that knowing. He was a storm I couldn't seem to keep myself from walking out into.

My lips parted, and I leaned to him, pressing my fingers into the supple heat of his lips.

"Miss Lovell," he whispered hoarsely against my fingertips, "I must warn you that—"

"No," I said, stopping his words. "I want no warning, Mr. Trevelyan. I fear all I want is for you to kiss me aga—"

Before I could finish my sentence, his mouth fell upon mine, and he pulled me into his embrace. His body was wet and hard against my warm softness, and I needed to press him closer to me more than I needed to breathe. I wrapped my arms around his neck, driving my fingers into the silky dampness of his hair. He groaned, and his large hands slid down my back, pulling me even tighter to his hardness. His tongue plunged into my mouth, searching for everything womanly within me. And I responded in kind as my hunger for him erupted into a burning need that grew with his every touch.

He ended the kiss before I was ready, and I clutched him tighter against my breasts. "Miss Lovell, we—"

"We have not investigated this kiss thoroughly enough, Mr. Trevelyan." I kissed *him* this time. Twice he'd kissed me and then stopped before I'd had the presence of mind to enjoy the experience. This time I wanted to explore all of the sensations he sparked inside me. I moaned from the pleasure filling me and delved deeper into the passion of the kiss.

My word, I thought, as my action spurred Benedict into motion. He swept me into his arms and carried me into my bedroom, kissing me again and again with a passion I'd never imagined possible. The brush of his beard, the soothing feel of his lips, and the plundering quest of his tongue held me captive. In a haze I saw the curtains of my cloudy blue bed over me, and it seemed right that he should be there, for I'd dreamed of him there. My back sunk into the softness of the bed, but I didn't want the comfort. I wanted to feel every inch of his lean hardness against my body. He stepped back as I reached for him.

I would have spoken had not the stark hunger in his gaze taken my breath away. That and the sight of him so obviously aroused. His pants clung to every nuance of maleness that seemed to grow with his every harsh breath. He stripped off his wet shirt, exposing the massive expanse of his chest, and my fingers itched to feel him. I had to grip the covers, for I knew not what to do. How could I tell him what I had no words to describe? I just knew that I needed him next to me. I needed his kiss. I needed more of the wondrous world of desire he brought to me.

In the flickering lamplight, I saw that water from his body had rendered my gown transparent. The coral tips of my breasts strained against their prison, begging to be freed. I moaned with need.

"Shh," he said softly. Lying next to me, he brushed his fingers against my cheek. "It is all right. I will not hurt you. I am a large man, but I know only gentleness with a woman. You do not have to fear me."

"I know," I whispered. "I have never feared you. I hurt with yearning . . . for you . . . for your kiss."

He gasped for air like a man drowning, then he groaned

as if he were in pain. "Miss Lovell—Ann—I do believe you have quite undone me."

His hands were no longer cold, yet I shivered when he began to unbutton my gown. For I feared that the master of Trevelyan Hill wasn't the only one undone.

❮ 15 ❯

Benedict slid the last button of my gown's bodice from its mooring and leaned over to kiss me again. My heart thundered partly with desire and partly with the fear of being seen naked.

Before he could open my gown, I turned toward him, pressing myself against his chest, to feel him and to keep myself from being exposed. He seemed to sense my shyness and kissed me again, burying his hands in my hair, taking his time, kissing my cheeks, my neck, and my lips.

Slowly my desire to know more of his touch grew to overflowing. I eased back from him and ran my fingers up his chest, across his shoulders, and down his back. I reveled in the heat of him, in the supple strength pulsating within his brawn. His lips left mine, and he kissed a trail down my chin to the sensitive skin of my neck. His beard pricked and tickled slightly, but his lips spread fire.

I was lost in the new sensations, overwhelmed by them, yet my body seemed to know what to do to respond to him. I leaned my head back, threaded my fingers into the full silkiness of his hair, and his kisses moved back to my mouth, then lower again, and again, and again. The passion of his touch stole away my shyness, making me forget about improprieties or anything to do with any sense of practicality I ever possessed. A madness filled me with such agonizing pleasure, I thought I could take no more. I arched to him, and his lips moved lower still, parting the edges of my gown until I could feel the coolness of air upon my aching breasts.

He leaned back from me to gaze at me, and I squeezed my eyes shut, feeling as if I wanted to cover myself again, but I couldn't move. I was paralyzed, frozen at a place where I could not retreat, but neither could I face going forward.

"Ann, you are so beautiful, everywhere," he said, and shifted on the bed. My eyes flew open as his heated hands cupped my breasts, lifting their aching fullness to his kisses.

I gasped. I couldn't breathe as his mouth covered the tip of one breast and he suckled as a babe might. But there was nothing motherly in the shock of pleasure so intense that my heels dug into the bed and my hips lifted.

Proving that it knew no bounds, my blood rushed wildly, and the light-headed sensation that had enveloped me in the stable returned. A fever washed over me. My skin grew damp, my lungs barely functioned, and my mind abandoned me. I wanted nothing else but to know where this sweet road of pleasure led.

He moved to my other breast and did the same. I could feel the fever in him, too. His hands shook, his breaths rasped, and his body quivered.

"Please," I cried, and he kissed me silent. The aching pleasure had grown so great that I thought I'd scream.

"Shh," he whispered. "I know." Shuddering expectation filled me as his heated hand eased down my stomach and brushed over the heart of my femininity. "Let me show you there is pleasure in my touch."

Did he not think that he was driving me insane with the pleasure?

I grabbed his broad shoulders. "Show me," I demanded. Then, over the damp gossamer cotton of my gown, he firmly pressed his hand between my legs. Though I had asked for his touch, I still gasped at the newness of it. He slid his wet leg over mine, urging my legs apart, and through the soft cotton, he caressed me where I ached the most. A whirling wind of sensation wrapped around my body, tighter and tighter.

I thought that at any moment I would die, for I couldn't possibly live through the pleasure consuming me. My body fled from my control and wavered upon every brush of his finger against me and every kiss he gave until stars burst before my eyes. Heaven reached down and captured me in a golden light. I felt more glorious, more beautiful, than the stained glass windows, and I shuddered uncontrollably in his arms. When I stilled and a warm peace covered me in a cloudy cocoon, I slowly realized the desperation in the quivering tenseness of Benedict's body still wrapped around mine.

The mists cleared from my eyes when he rolled on top of me, sliding between my legs, pressing me into the softness of the bed. The hard ridge of his maleness covered by his wet pants thrust intimately against me, and an odd, almost welcome but uncomfortable sensation of being invaded flooded through me. He levered up on his arms, his body shaking with an effort I didn't quite understand as he pressed his hard maleness against my soft femininity.

The lamplight cast the hewn lines of his face into shadows made deeper by the stubble of his beard. His hair was rakishly tousled, and his skin gleamed with underlying power. His eyes burned so darkly that he brought the demon door to my mind. I realized then that I, as a fair maiden, hadn't fled. I'd succumbed.

Leaning on one hand, he unbuttoned the top of his

trousers, and I tensed, remembering the fullness of him I'd seen at his bath. Though I'd dreamed of him, I hadn't imagined the joining of our flesh, hadn't known this sensation of being vulnerable and invaded were part of the pleasure. I gasped, tensing as I realized what would happen next. Was I ready to know a man's passion completely? Ready to fall completely to my ruin?

Benedict rolled off of me, groaning as in great pain. Covering my breasts, I sat up, unsteady from a strange dizziness. He must have sensed my tension, felt my question, my dilemma.

"Benedict?" I whispered, setting my hand upon his back.

He jerked from my touch, standing, but keeping his back toward me. His massive shoulders shook as he drew in deep breaths of air.

"Miss Lovell, life has taken many things from me. My honor, such as it is, I still call my own, although others do not. You must forgive me and forget this ever happened. You are a woman under my protection. I was wrong to ever kiss you. Wrong to ask you to come to me. And wrong to have awakened you in the mad hours after midnight. I can only claim temporary insanity to have allowed this to happen, for I have nothing but dishonor to offer a woman." He spoke harshly, his words sounding like a storm-swelled wave crashing against the dark cliffs of the bay.

He left without a backward glance. Left me aching for the man who'd just spoken with such hopelessness. The smell of rain and his scent—sandalwood and leather—clung to me from his wet clothes. I sat for a long time amid the damp covers in my rain-wet gown, feeling the chill of the early hours of dawn steal around me. What had he meant? No honor but dishonor? What had happened that had put such hopeless pain in his voice? Only then did I recall Stephen's inscription to Cesca, and anger filled me. What had they done?

And what had I done? I'd aroused the passions in a man that I could never openly love. And I was a woman who'd never accept a relationship out of wedlock. I knew what pain that brought. It was something my mother and I had had to bear every day that we lived.

I arose the next morning with the sniffles and a heaviness burdening my chest that declared Sunday wouldn't be as bright and promising as the weather indicated. Benedict was a tortured man, and my inquisitiveness, this need I had to explore the sensations of his kiss, had only added to his pain. For surely I'd provoked him into our passionate encounter.

Yes, he'd kissed me, but I'd been taunting him by pacing around in my nightgown, and I had *asked* him to kiss me. And when he tried to bring a halt to the madness, I'd kissed him. I couldn't let him bear the full responsibility. I decided to address this situation where it had all begun, in the stable. Benedict was wont to spend his early mornings there, and since the day saw fit to dispense with the nighttime rain and mete out a bit of sunshine amid the clouds, I knew I would find him there.

It was amazing what a difference a little time made, for I marched into the stable without even a thought for the horses housed inside. My mind was filled with Benedict, which had my stomach twisted in knots and my heart teetering on a precipice. For I knew what I had to say would seal my fate to forever remain a spinster, and a great part of me wasn't happy with that decision. Indeed it was most miserable at the prospect of never again experiencing the incomparable pleasure he'd given me. But there was no other choice for either of us.

I saw him the moment my eyes adjusted to the dimness. He wore breeches, boots, and a shirt that seemed to cling to him as his rain-sodden clothes had—or my imagination had them doing so. His sleeves were rolled to his elbows, leaving his strong, corded forearms bare as he worked, unaware of my arrival. The immense broadness of his shoulders moved with power and surety. He brushed Gunnlod with exquisitely long strokes and murmured softly to her.

My mouth went dry. Everything feminine within me throbbed as I recalled his strokes and whispers last night and the pleasure that followed. Never had I thought I'd envy a horse, but I did. Perhaps I was being too hasty in my decision to speak with Benedict. I'd driven him to passion once by my unseemly behavior; Surely I could do so again. One more kiss wouldn't hurt . . .

A picture of Benedict's face twisted with pain flooded my consciousness. No. I would own up to my responsibility, assure him that I understood the situation, and give him my word that I'd not entice him again. Dabbing at my nose with a handkerchief, I readied myself for the confrontation. I'd give him my solemn oath that what happened last night would never happen again.

"Benedict," I croaked meekly, instead of speaking with the firm decisiveness necessary to my new resolve. He swung around to face me. The tired lines of a sleepless night made his stern expression harsher. I stepped hesitantly his way until I stood before him. "Might I speak with you on an important matter?"

My word, where had my determination run off to?

"Very well, Miss Lovell. I expected you would have no choice but to do so." He sighed even as his body tensed, as if a heavy weight had dropped upon him.

I hesitated a second. It would seem we were back to our

customary formality, which might be a good thing. What did he mean by no choice? "It, um, concerns . . . Master Justin's upcoming birthday. I think it necessary for us to have a party for him. Making a child feel special, letting him know that he is valued, is essential to his self-worth. Also, there was a problem with their herb garden. We have replanted it, and our profits will be delayed, but a trip to a financial institution this week will give them something to look forward to while they wait for the new plants to grow. Do you have time in your schedule? Wednesday would be best, as they have music lessons on Tuesday and sign language instruction on Thursday."

Benedict blinked. He drew a breath so deep that when he exhaled, the warmth of his breath washed over me, carrying with it a scent that reminded me of the taste of his kiss. My mouth watered.

He shook his head as if he'd been asleep. "Did you say a birthday party and a trip to town, Miss Lovell?"

I forced a smile to my lips. "Yes. If possible."

"They are more than possible," he said, staring oddly. "I consider myself blessed, Miss Lovell."

Blessed? I wondered what he meant, but I couldn't seem to formulate any thoughts. I could only return his stare. My lord, I had no idea that when I looked at Benedict this morning, I'd only be able to see him as he was last night— half naked and burning with passion. Did he see the same?

The same heat that scorched my cheeks flamed in his eyes.

Thank goodness Gunnlod intervened by nudging Benedict's back. Apparently she wanted more of his caresses. I understood her completely.

"Tell me, Miss Lovell. Is it my imagination, or are you no longer terrified of this hoofed beast?" Benedict turned back to brushing his horse.

I watched his strong hands. Gunnlod seemed to quiver beneath his attention. I knew how she felt. "I must confess that I have developed a kinship with her."

Benedict's head snapped around. "Indeed? What brought about this miracle?"

Good Lord! Had I just admitted kinship to a horse? I straightened my spine; hopefully he wouldn't guess at the true meaning behind my words. This would never do. "It was a practical decision," I said, searching for an answer. "Based on her superior intelligence in her dealings with Odin, I have decided that Gunnlod isn't a horse."

My gaze settled on the broadness of Benedict's back, and I had to fist my hands in the skirts of my dark green muslin dress, for my fingers itched to touch him.

Benedict stopped brushing and faced me. "Are you well this morning, Miss Lovell?"

I dabbed at my nose again. "Fairly well, Mr. Trevelyan, just a case of the sniffles."

"I meant mentally. If Gunnlod is not a horse, then what is she?"

"Why, a-a-a kindred spirit, Mr. Trevelyan," I said, parroting the first thing that managed to penetrate the fog in my mind.

His lips twitched. "Excellent. Then you have no aversion to taking her for a ride this morning?"

"Me?" My voice barely peeped past my clogging throat.

"Yes, a quick turn about the training ring. We have just enough time before Justin and Robert are due for their lesson."

The moment he said that Justin and Robert would soon be arriving, I knew my fate was sealed. Still, I tried to avert disaster.

"Why, you have just brushed her down. I am sure she'd rather relax in her stall than cart me about a circle."

Benedict raised one eyebrow. "On the contrary. I think she would enjoy the company of your kindred spirit." He handed me the brush, his fingers lightly touching my palm. The wood of the brush was warm with his heat, which flowed right to my unmentionables. "Finish brushing her while I ready up a sidesaddle." He left, moving to the saddles.

I had two choices: throw down the brush and run as if my life depended on escaping, or stay just a little longer with Benedict. Perhaps if I were to gather my courage enough to sit a moment in the saddle, I'd find the strength to say what I'd come to say. Not that I didn't need to speak with him about Justin's birthday and the trip to the bank, but those issues weren't as imperative as addressing last night's events.

Gunnlod stood perfectly still. Slowly, I moved the brush to her side and gently stroked her. She smelled of hay, sunshine, and something more primal, something as alive and powerful as the heated muscles quivering beneath my touch. She reminded me of Benedict's restrained strength, and my desire to soothe him doubled.

Before I realized it, Benedict had returned, and I'd brushed Gunnlod with more than just a stroke or two. It shocked me to find that my fear had abated like mists beneath the rays of the sun.

Setting down the brush, I stood aside as Benedict slid a blanket and padding on Gunnlod's back, then hefted the sidesaddle in place with ease. Soon he had all the buckles adjusted and declared her ready to ride.

"Today, I will lift you into the saddle. We can work on having you mount another time. I just want you to get the feel of a horse beneath you. I think, Miss Lovell, that given your nature, once you have galloped with the wind, you will be addicted to the freedom."

Before I had a chance to ask him what in my practical nature had misled him to think such a thing, he encircled my waist with his hands and lifted me from the ground.

"Oh," I gasped, my hands settling on his shoulders for balance. I nearly sighed with the pleasure of touching him again. The sensations of being close to him, even under the pretense of a riding lesson, were too sweet to sour with a discussion of my unseemly behavior last night. I decided to enjoy Benedict's touch for now and speak with him later. Perhaps the discussion would be more suited for the oppressiveness of his study.

He set me in the saddle and showed me where to hold on, which was a good thing. For had I not had something to anchor me, I would have fallen when he adjusted the stirrups. Having his hands under my skirt, guiding my boot into the leather straps, was nearly as intimate as a kiss.

"All set," he said, stepping back. Upon the huge horse, I towered over Benedict, but the strangest thing happened. As he led me from the stable, I felt as if I were daintily small— a diminutive lady with a conquering knight. It wasn't nearly as terrible as I thought it would be. The experience lifted my heart a little, as if I'd won a major battle that I hadn't even known I was losing.

We made one trip around the training ring, and I'd just grown accustomed to the precariousness of my perch when Justin and Robert scrambled up, laughing and excited to see their governess upon a horse and asking to ride Cesca. The rest of the morning passed quickly as Benedict led Robert around on Cesca and then taught Justin how to use the reins. It was an easy time of laughter and fun, exactly what the children needed to share with their father.

We were just finishing up when Robert came and pulled on my skirt. "Miss Wovell, can we check for babies, yet?"

I took his hand. "Sprouts. I think it is too early yet, but we can go to the garden and see."

"Jus, you want to come?"

"No," Justin said, kicking the dirt in the training ring. "Somebody will just destroy it again."

"They will not," Robert cried, eyes and fists scrunching tight. I could see the thundercloud about to burst, and I rushed to stop it. I took hold of the back of Robert's loose shirt.

"Wait!" I said, but they were too angry to hear.

Justin yelled back. "Will too. You just wait. They will destroy it again."

"Will not," Robert screamed. Pulling from my grip, he went flying at Justin with fists ready.

"What is this about?" Benedict boomed, snatching Robert up by the back of the lad's pants.

Robert punched the air. "They killeded our babies, and Jus says they will do it again."

"That is enough, young man." Benedict set the boy firmly on the ground but held him captive by the steel of his authority. "Calm yourself," Benedict said, squatting to Robert's level. "The only place violent anger is acceptable is if someone is attempting to kill you. Otherwise you will learn to conduct yourself in a gentlemanly manner even in the face of difficulties. Do you understand me, son?"

Robert's face fell, and tears flooded his eyes. "What if they killeded your babies? What would you do?" he asked his father.

Benedict, in the act of standing, froze. He set his hand on Robert's shaking shoulders. "If anyone ever tried to hurt you or Justin, they would not live to see the next day."

Benedict spoke with fierce sincerity. And even though I saw how his words reassured Robert, I still shivered at the deadly menace in Benedict's voice. He was indeed capable of murder. And more frightening than that, I was, too, should I need to protect Robert or Justin. The crime of murder, it seemed, wasn't based on any deep moral conviction, whereupon one could assure oneself of never committing that crime. Instead, it hinged on a primal part of oneself that could never be driven into extinction. Stephen was right; circumstances did mitigate the crime.

"Can you tell me the meaning of this outburst, Miss Lovell?" Benedict stood and pinned his direct gaze on me.

"Last Wednesday we found our herb garden destroyed."

"Did a storm ruin it?"

"No. It had been deliberately vandalized."

"Surely you must be mistaken. Perhaps a deer or a rabbit ate the plants."

I shook my head. "And churned up all of the bordering rocks? The plants were not eaten, they had been dug up and left."

"But who would do something so senseless, and why?"

I glanced at the boys. I didn't want to say anything else in front of them. "Might we continue this discussion later, please?"

"Certainly. Be in my study an hour before dinner."

Providence smiled on my plan to speak with Benedict about last night, and for the first time in my life I frowned back at it. I thought perhaps I'd take a brisk walk to town and see Mr. McGuire. Not only would I learn what he'd wanted to tell me yesterday, but I'd most probably clear my head and rediscover my determination. For once, the thought of going to see Mr. McGuire didn't bring a smile to my lips. I'd much rather climb into my cloudy blue bed and pull the covers over my head and . . . feel Benedict's touch all over again.

I was still frowning when I returned to my room a short while later, whereupon I discovered my things out of order, as if they'd been hastily searched. My gaze immediately located the book of poetry inscribed to Francesca. It thankfully was on the settee where I'd left it last night. After some thought, I decided that Benedict didn't know of the book's existence. It had most probably been placed on the shelf after Francesca's death by a maid, and had gone undetected since. I knew I couldn't chance leaving it in my room again.

I was almost completely certain Stephen had given it to Francesca in a declaration of his love, but I wanted to know for sure. I wanted to look into Stephen's eyes when I gave him the book. I wanted to know if a murderer lurked behind his laughing blue eyes. I'd have a note delivered to him, asking him to see me in the family's sitting room on his floor.

Taking the book, I wrote a quick note and set about my mission. I passed Dobbs in the foyer, then turned around, deciding to settle a matter with him, too. He was studiously examining the furniture for dust.

"Mr. Dobbs, it is imperative that I speak to you about a certain matter."

He turned, lifting his nose a tad. "Indeed, Miss Low-well. And what would that be?"

I ignored his deliberate name goading and went directly to the problem. "It has come to my attention that you are carrying tales like a pack of coyotes."

His mouth gaped as far as his eyes popped. "Whatever are you babbling about?"

"I am speaking of telegraphed tales specifically. In the future, should you take umbrage with my conduct, I appreciate it if you would wait and discuss it with Mr. Trevelyan upon his return. To endanger his life by sending him an urgent telegraph, simply to strike out at me, is underhanded and unnecessary."

Dobbs turned purple. "Miss Lovell. I determine what is

necessary and what is not. How dare you infer that I am incompetent!"

"Not incompetent, Mr. Dobbs. Just crying wolf over a mere dog. Now, where will I find Mr. Stephen Trevelyan at this hour?"

I decided to deliver the note myself, by slipping it under Stephen's door and then waiting for him in the family sitting room. Stephen's rooms were located across the corridor from Katherine's. I knew the way, yet the impropriety of what I was about to do had my nerves jumping. I shouldn't be meddling in the Trevelyans' affairs, and I knew the sooner I began conducting myself within the stiff strictures of my practicality, the better off I would be. But every time I closed my eyes, I saw Benedict as he was last night. Torn by honor. In pain. And I couldn't seem to keep myself removed from the fabric of the Trevelyans' lives.

When I slipped the note under the door, I sneezed. My heart nearly exploded when Stephen opened the door immediately. He appeared rumpled and surprised as well. "Miss Ann?"

"F-forgive my intrusion, but it is important that I speak with you, privately." It took me a moment to find my balance. He looked more like a big sleepy boy than a murderer, and I took a deep breath, calming myself.

"Uh, certainly." He looked about as if he were lost a moment.

"I will await you in the sitting room at the end of the hall," I said.

Relief smoothed his brow. "I will be only a moment."

Unfortunately, I was too tense to enjoy the full effect of the sunny area. Taking up the entire width of the wing, with a multitude of windows on three sides, the sitting area was wonderfully cozy and warm. The scent of oil paint and linseed oil emanated from my left, and when my eyes adjusted to the brightness, I saw an easel set up to catch the full rays of the sun. Curious, I wandered over to the painting, only to find the canvas covered with a cloth. I considered peeking beneath it, but Stephen walked into the area, and I turned to face him.

"Is there something wrong, Miss Ann?" He was holding my note, frowning.

"Yes, Mr. Trevelyan." I held out Elizabeth Barrett Browning's book of poems. Stephen paled. Instead of taking the book, he sat quickly in the nearest chair as if his legs would no longer support him. My note requesting to see him fell to the floor, but neither of us picked it up. Nor did he look at me. He kept his gaze upon the book in my hand, staring as if I held a snake.

"Where did you find it?"

"Among other books in the library."

He sighed. "I have looked for it everywhere."

"Please, take it." I held the book closer to him.

His hand shook as he grasped the slim volume. "I did not mean for it to happen, you know. Cesca did not either." Fingers trembling, he opened the cover. Tears filled his eyes as he stared at the inscription. "I do not think she ever read past what I had written. I do not think she understood what I meant. Her pain was too great."

My throat tightened with emotion so heavy I thought I'd choke. "How could you?" I whispered. "How could you do this to your brother?"

Stephen lifted his gaze to mine. I knew at that moment that I looked into the tortured eyes of a man living in hell. "I do not know. But she is dead because of it. Because of me."

"How?"

"She haunts me from the grave, you know. Just as she said she would." His words broke on a sob of pain.

I ran from him, from the bright sunny room so full of darkness, my sniffles increasing tenfold as tears fought their way to my eyes. Stephen didn't stop me from leaving. I don't think he was capable of stopping anything, even his cries.

Katherine exited her room just as I dashed by, but I didn't greet her. I was too upset. Francesca's murderer lived within Trevelyan Manor's walls. I was sure of it. But who?

I have nothing but dishonor to offer a woman. Benedict's tortured words from last night loomed like a funeral pyre over my spirit. For I realized why I was so burdened with the tragic past, why I nearly swooned from his kiss, why I couldn't bring myself this morning to promise never to ask for his touch.

I loved him.

❧ *16* ❧

By the time I reached my room, I'd slowed my pace to a brisk walk, but my thoughts continued to race. How could I have been so impractical to fall in love with Benedict, a man I could never hope to have? A man whom others believed capable of murder, but I couldn't?

Stephen had said Francesca died because of him, but he hadn't actually said he'd killed her. But then why would Francesca haunt him if he hadn't?

Why did Benedict have nothing but dishonor to give? When it came to him, my heart was a jumble of agonizing knots. I was so blind with the emotions swirling inside me that I didn't even see Constance until she called to me.

"Ann. I was just at your door, looking for you."

I stopped abruptly. "Is there something you needed, Constance?"

"Company. I am having Dobbs set up tea in the garden and thought you would like to join me."

A chat over tea was the last thing I wanted at the moment, but it seemed rude not to accept her offer. After their morning riding lesson, the boys were resting under Maria's care, so I didn't need to worry about them. But I had planned to work on their lessons this afternoon, my usual routine for Sunday afternoon. After speaking to Stephen and my looming meeting with Benedict this evening, though, I seriously doubted I'd be able to comprehend a thing.

And shamefully, having Dobbs see me enjoying the fruits of his labor had an irresistible appeal. "That would be lovely. Give me a moment to freshen up, and I will be right with you."

Unexpectedly, Constance followed me to my room, giving me no choice but to invite her in. In quick order, I went to the washstand and bathed my face, feeling as if I was a bit more flushed than usual, an understandable condition considering my agitated state.

In the mirror I saw Constance wander over to the bed curtains and run her hand across the cloudy blue silk. "She slept here often, you know. My sister. Though this wasn't her room, she loved the color blue. I think she came here to dream, like a child who has a favorite spot to pretend the world was nothing but sunshine and rainbows."

A chill racked my spine. Francesca slept here? Dreamed here? Spent time here? Benedict had assigned me his wife's favorite room? Had insisted upon me using it despite my protests?

I shivered again. And what about last night's passionate encounter upon the blue bed? Was I a substitute for a wife who left him mired in scandal?

"I did not know she came here," I whispered.

Constance turned and smiled firmly. "Of course you wouldn't. It was silly of me to even say anything. I just could not help but remember."

"Your sister sounds as if she liked to smile a lot."

Constance shrugged. "To her, happiness was like stars in the heavens. She would gaze and gaze. She would dream and dream. But in the end they were never hers. I do not think happiness ever belongs to any of us here on earth. Are you ready for tea?"

My mind reeled. I blinked twice, then tried to focus on Constance. She'd already moved to the doorway, waiting for me. "Yes, tea would be good," I said, but in my mind I was thinking I needed a good dose of Benedict's brandy.

Dobbs waited in the garden. Chairs, small tables, and a silver tea service graced the ground next to the angelic fountain. Dobbs's expression drooped when he saw me with Constance.

Glad that I'd ruffled his cocky feathers, I pasted a smile on my face and took the chair he was forced to ready for me. After seating Constance, he inquired if anything else would be needed. He clearly addressed Constance, even going as far to angle his back to me. I noted that only cream and sugar accompanied the tea and biscuits.

I was not about to let him ignore me, or my own needs. "Yes, Mr. Dobbs. My throat is a tad scratchy this afternoon. Would you mind bringing me some lemon and honey to have with my tea?"

He turned my way with his long nose lifted high enough to be a bird's perch. I immediately imagined Puck sitting on it with his prickly claws digging in.

"Honey and lemon?" Dobbs's mouth puckered with disapproval. "Will there be anything else?"

"Some jam, please."

"Jam?"

"Strawberry if possible."

"Anything else?" he asked, his voice rising with annoyance.

I blinked innocently at him. "An extra napkin would be quite nice."

He opened his mouth as if he were about to ask again, but then gritted his teeth and turned on his heel. As soon as he stalked inside the house, I was surprised to hear Constance giggle.

"You are not easily daunted," she said, humor lighting her dark eyes. "We have more in common than I thought."

"I think if a woman does not stand her ground, especially in the West, she will end up like a tumbleweed being blown across the desert."

"True, but the results can sometimes be detrimental. Many who stand their own ground are buried beneath it."

I nodded, realizing there were probably more pine boxes in the ground than tumbleweeds on the desert. It was not a reassuring thought.

Sunshine, spread about in warm fingers of light, cast a golden glow throughout the garden. Roses, bursting spots of red, pink, and yellow, crowned the bellflowers and phlox. The day was as serenely bright as it had been this morning when I'd laughed with Benedict, Justin, and Robert during the riding lessons. Only instead of warm, I felt chilled.

Dobbs returned with honey, lemon, a worn napkin, and blackberry jam, then left without a word. I preferred Cook Thomas's blackberry jam, and outwitting him was sweet indeed.

Constance poured the tea, and I added a healthy dose of lemon and honey to mine, hoping to soothe myself. But the turmoil within me seemed to repel any warmth and refuse any comfort as it held my mind captive to images of Stephen, Francesca, and Benedict caught up in a tragic and deadly play. The play ended in Francesca's murder just before the curtain closed, leaving Benedict holding a smoking gun. Yet I couldn't believe that to be true.

"Speaking of standing ground to one's detriment, Stephen and I encountered the governor's sister, Mrs. Harriet Hampton, this morning. She wore an appallingly antiquated bloomer outfit and was handing out notices of a meeting for the Women's Equal Suffrage Society. The woman has no sense whatsoever."

I took another sip of my tea before commenting. Her opinion surprised me. Though my mother and I had had little opportunity to publicly discuss the unfairness of women's place in society, we'd read every article that we could find on the subject. She'd been disappointed that the suffrage movement had made no difference in her life. Twenty-five years ago, accounts of the Women's Rights Convention had promised so much more, but very little victory followed. "You do not believe women should be given equal consideration?"

Constance shook her head. Her teacup rattled, and she set it down, then folded her hands with deliberate slowness. "Experience has taught me that real power lies in not letting a man know what you want. Then he can never stand in your way. I do not waste my time with dreams of the impossible, which is exactly what women's rights in a man's world are. I thought you too smart to believe in fables."

"I believe in truth."

"What is a fable but an unobtainable truth?" She paused, smiled sadly, then picked up her tea. "Francesca believed in truth and love."

Learning about Francesca was more important than philosophical differences. I seized the opportunity. "Tell me about your sister. Perhaps I could help Justin and Robert more if I knew what she was like."

Constance set down her tea, picked a biscuit, and spread a bit of jam on it, her expression sad. "What was Francesca like? A delicate flower too fragile for this world. I loved her. Growing up she was always ill, and I always tried to help her, make her happy. But she was sad."

"Stephen said her favorite game to play with Justin was 'making sunshine.' That sounds like a woman who loved to smile."

"Stephen's a man, and men only see what they want to in a woman, whether it is true or not, no? Now, you must tell me what you know about steamships."

"You mean steamboats?" I questioned, thinking Constance had more than just a leisurely chat over tea in mind before she asked me. The conversational change was too abrupt, or her grief over losing her sister was still too painful.

"Ah, yes, steamboats. I am so used to speaking of vessels as ships, forgive me. This morning Stephen took me for a ride on one in the bay, and I find that I was quite taken with the experience. I say to myself, Constance, these steamboats Benedict is investing in may be a good thing."

I explained what I knew of how pressure from steam forced parts of an engine to move, which in turn propelled the inner workings of boats and trains. Constance shook her head and waved her arm.

"You misunderstand me. I have no interest in such things. I would like to know more about the usage of the steamships."

I shrugged. "Steamboats have been essential to travel and the shipping of goods along rivers for years. I know here in the bay, they ferry cargo and passengers from ships to docks all along the bay. More than that, I cannot tell you. Why don't you ask Stephen or Benedict?"

She waved her hand with annoyance. "Stephen will tell me anything, whether he truly knows the answer or not, just to make me happy. And Benedict is worse. He does not think I should ever concern myself with business and will not tell me anything at all. I used to be able to count on Alan, then he . . ."

Her voice trailed off, and I waited for her to continue. I recalled their encounter in Holloway Park, and once again I wondered what they had fought about. "You mean Mr. Henderson?" I prompted.

"Yes. An infuriating man at times. He seemed to be quite taken with you, once he accepted your role as a governess. He is not one to put a tremendous amount of importance on class. You would do well to encourage his interest."

I nearly dropped my teacup and had to set it quickly down. "I beg your pardon?"

Constance settled a firm expression on her face, her gaze piercing. "Though from different stations in life, we are both women without a man in a man's world, Ann. A very difficult position to be in, no? I merely mentioned that should you wish to improve your lot in life by marrying . . . well, he is a good man. I believe Alan is due to visit again soon."

I stared at her a moment, completely unsettled. "I am surprised to hear you say such a thing, considering the apparent intimacy of the argument you had with Mr. Henderson in Holloway Park." I lifted a questioning brow.

"We merely settled an old argument." She set her cup on the table and stood, brushing imaginary crumbs from her skirt. "My, I have no idea where the time went, but I am afraid I must go now. I will see you at dinner shortly. Thank you for joining me." She nodded a smile and turned to leave.

The argument hadn't looked old or settled to me. I

stood, feeling as if I had to say something. Her suggestion that I'd form any kind of an alliance just to improve my station in life disturbed me greatly. Never would I do such a thing. She had to know that. But I saw Dobbs coming our way, and I had to let the subject drop until later. Nodding curtly in Dobbs's direction, I decided to go rest in my room a short while before dressing for dinner and meeting Benedict in his study.

For the first time in my entire life, except for the morning I'd first gone to the stables, I was late, and not by mere minutes. I was over a quarter of an hour late. I'd fallen asleep while resting on the settee and had awoken just minutes ago. My cheeks were hot from embarrassment and my mind fuzzy with sleep. Indeed, I likened myself to a cart behind a runaway horse that would upend and crash at any moment.

And I knew that moment would be in Benedict's study. This time I was determined to own up to my behavior and to assure him no such lapses would occur again.

I marched right to his study and knocked firmly. He opened the door. "Mr. Trevelyan. It is of utmost importance that I speak to you immediately about a matter. Last night when you—"

"Miss Lovell," Benedict's voice boomed over mine. "You are late for our appointment, but it is just as well." He motioned to the room behind him. "Stephen and Alan needed to consult with me on a matter, and we were just finishing."

"Oh," I gasped, blinking at the shadowy images standing in Benedict's study. I am not sure if my eyes had trouble adjusting to the dimmer light, or if shock over almost revealing what happened last night had me unsettled.

Mr. Henderson came my way. "Miss Lovell. It is so lovely

to see you again." He took my hand in his. His greeting of me seemed so much different than when I'd first met him. Before he'd made me feel as if I didn't belong at the Trevelyan family dinner, but now he didn't seem to shun me at all.

"Thank you," I said, pulling my hand back before he could bow to kiss it. Constance's observation rang in my ears and made me leery. His smile stiffened, and I chastised myself for being so cautious. Surely Constance had to be mistaken. I sought to repair my slight. "Your trip to the north went well?"

"Extremely well." Mr. Henderson's gaze seemed to search my face, making me wonder again about Constance's comment. "In fact, several new opportunities have arisen, and Ben has graciously invited me to stay at the manor while I look into them. Perhaps I can tell you about them later."

"Yes," I said, feeling a little dizzy. Had his voice taken a personal tone?

"Miss Ann. Might I speak with you a moment in the foyer?" Stephen, looking as ragged and worn as a Confederate flag in Federal hands, joined Alan at my side. I'd deliberately avoided looking his way, hoping to escape having to face him yet. He seemed completely oblivious to the awkward position in which he'd placed me. Both Benedict and Mr. Henderson had raised their brows.

I cleared my scratchy throat and winced as a twinge of pain shot to my temples. "Only for a minute. I need to speak to Mr. Trevelyan about planning a party for Justin's birthday." Even more heat fired my checks.

"A party?" Stephen said with surprise. "An excellent idea, and I promise not to take more than a moment."

"Very well," I said, following him into the foyer, thankful to note that Dobbs was not standing guard at the front door.

Stephen grabbed my hands, pulling me close to him. "I beg of you. Before you speak to my brother, please, let me explain about Cesca," he whispered, so low that I could barely hear him. I could smell the whiskey on his breath, and his hands shook.

Heart pounding, I stepped away, snatching my hands from his. "You embarrass us both. I have no plans to speak of it to your brother. As I see it, his pain is already more than any man should be forced to bear. Please don't mention the matter again." When I turned to the study, I saw a dark shape slip quickly out of sight. Had Benedict stood in the doorway, watching?

"You hate me," Stephen said.

I drew a deep breath and released it slowly before facing him. "No. I am angry. Why do you act as if your brother is wrong when he is the one who has been wronged?"

Stephen's expression went from despair to anger. "He judges and condemns without mercy, and not even heaven can help you if you fail. Do not ever fail him, Ann."

He left, his words deepening the chill of doubt wrapped around my heart. *Judges and condemns without mercy?* I couldn't help but think of Francesca and her unborn child.

Exiting Benedict's study as I approached, Mr. Henderson stopped in front of me, a worried expression on his face. I forced a smile to my lips.

"Miss Lovell, forgive my forwardness, but I fear I must caution you." His gaze shifted to the doorway Stephen had disappeared through and then to Benedict's study. "Never mind—even a fool can see you are not Francesca."

"I beg your pardon?" I couldn't have been more shocked. In truth, my mind felt so fuzzy, I thought I'd mistaken his words.

He sighed, deeply, as if a heavy sadness weighed upon him. "Francesca was too delicate, too sensitive. She was not for this world. Please forget what I said. You are not any-thing like her." He caught my hand and brought it to his lips before I could react. "I will see you at dinner tonight." Dropping my hand, he hurried in the direction Stephen had taken.

"But—" My protest fell to a whisper. Why had Mr. Henderson felt it necessary to warn me? Stomach churning, I walked into the study with Francesca's murder and the reasons behind it fresh on my mind. Benedict stood at the window, his large hand fisted in the curtains as he looked outside. I couldn't see him as the man responsible for his wife's murder. As before, a stream of late-afternoon sun-shine beat a sure path into the gloom of the room and glis-tened off his rich raven-hued hair. His square jaw and Viking-broad shoulders appeared set, ready for battle.

I decided to have my say before we had any other inter-ruptions. Shutting the study door firmly, I marched into the room, feeling unsteady. Determined, I anchored myself in place by gripping the back of a wing chair.

"Mr. Trevelyan, I cannot let you accept full responsibility for last night's unfortunate incident. Indeed, I am entirely at fault for what happened. Not only did I gad about inde-cently clothed, but I provoked you with thoughtless words, then shamefully forced you to accommodate my spinster's folly of knowing your kiss. I beg of you to forgive me, and you have my solemn vow that such a thing will never hap-pen again. I have rediscovered my practicality and can assure you, I will wear it over my inappropriate tendencies like a suit of armor. I understand you are at a vulnerable point in your life, with your wife . . . no longer alive . . . and . . . I think you may have . . . mistaken me for her in your late-night passions . . ."

I thought I had more to say, but found myself completely undone. I had no idea what his reaction was, for he simply continued to stare out the window, a completely unacceptable situation.

Letting go of the chair, I marched his way. "Mr. Trevelyan. Did you hear anything that I said?"

He moved like a flash of lighting against a stormy sky as he turned and grabbed my shoulders.

"Every bloody word, Miss Lovell." I blinked at the anger pouring from him in torrents of unspoken words. His eyes spit flames, his breath rasped harshly, and his roughly hewn face was so sharp, it seemed to slash through the air as he planted it an inch before my nose.

"When did you receive a threatening note? And why in the bloody hell did you neglect to tell me about it?"

"Who told you?"

"Unlike you, my mother thankfully has some sense."

I'd just spilled my pride on the floor before him, and he wanted to talk about an inconsequential note! Spots wavered before my eyes. It didn't matter that they were red spots, they still made me dizzy. "Mr. Trevelyan. I do believe I am so angry I am going to faint if I do not sit this instant."

His grip on my shoulders loosened, then tightened again.

"That makes two of us, Miss Lovell. And if we are still standing in a moment, I do believe I am going to kiss you again, or throttle you. I cannot quite make up my mind which. But know this one thing, I have never and will never mistake you in any way for the ghost of a wife that I had. Do you understand?"

"I quite think that I do," I whispered, though I wasn't even sure what he'd said. He exhaled sharply. His head lowered, and I shut my eyes. My lips parted, anticipating his kiss, without a thought to the vow that I'd just made. Only no kiss fell upon my trembling lips. His cool forehead touched mine, and his thumbs caressed my shoulders as his grip gentled. He groaned as if in pain, as he had last night within the intimacy of my room. The sound scraped across my heart.

"I am sorry," he said softly. "I should not touch you like this."

"It is all right," I said, splaying my hand over his heart, feeling its strength and racing tempo through the cloth of his shirt. Suddenly exhausted and confused, I let my head rest on his broad chest.

"Miss Lovell, you are quite warm, rather burning."

"I have no doubt, Mr. Trevelyan. You have this effect on me." Where was my practicality? I didn't have the strength to summon even a small measure of it.

Still holding my shoulders, he eased back, concern creasing his brow. "Are you feeling ill?"

"Surely not." I straightened my shoulders. "Just a little fatigued and unsettled and flushed."

He lifted a hand to my cheek. "I think you have a fever."

"I assure you. I have a very strong constitution. I am never ill."

"I do believe, Miss Lovell, that I have told you before there most certainly is a first time for everything." His gaze searched mine intently, and he brushed my bottom lip with his finger. "You have taught me that quite thoroughly." He shifted, and before I had a clue what he meant to do, he swept me off my feet, into his arms, then marched to the door. "You are going to bed. Dobbs is sending for the doctor. And while we wait for him, you are going to tell me every bloody thing you have neglected to mention, starting with the threatening note."

"I insist you put me down this instant, Mr. Trevelyan. I am perfectly capable of managing on my own two feet. And I do not need a doctor. Perhaps a spot of tea and a good night's rest will restore my constitution."

"Miss Lovell, as perverse as this may sound, you must desist from arguing with me. In fact, it is currently imperative that you do so, for now at least."

"I fear I cannot accept your high-handedness without protest, Mr. Trevelyan. I would be nothing but a dandelion seed in the wind if I did. Now put me down."

Releasing my legs, he let me slide down his body. I wavered when my feet reached the ground. Whether his nearness was at fault, or I truly was ill, I don't know, but I was unsteady, and he knew it. Then he stepped toward me, pressing me against the study door. The full length of him intimately connected to my every curve. He shifted, and I immediately felt his hard, insistent arousal. His gaze bored into mine.

"The reason you need to cease arguing, Miss Lovell," he said softly, his deep voice rasping against my every feminine nerve, "is because you provoke my passions to a fever pitch when you argue with me."

"Goodness gracious," I gasped as my mind and the room whirled.

He shook his head, stepped back, and caught me before I fell. "Unfortunately, I do not see anything good or gracious about the situation, Miss Lovell. It is completely insane, which is exactly what you are if you keep insisting you are not ill. You have a fever. You are going to bed, and you are seeing a doctor. That's final."

Whether he'd rendered me speechless or my practical nature decided prudence was the better part of valor, I don't know. I do know I did not utter another peep of protest.

As luck would have it, Dobbs stood in the foyer. His eyebrows climbed to the ceiling at the sight of me in Benedict's arms. But he only nodded at Benedict's order to send for a doctor. I was torn between embarrassment, relief, desire, and outrage. But it wasn't long before the warmth and safety of being in Benedict's arms washed over me, and desire and relief won the upper hand. When I relaxed in his arms, I realized just how sick I felt. He climbed the three flights to my room as if he carried no greater burden than a porcelain doll. He wasn't even winded when he set me on the bed. "Now, before the maid arrives to settle you into your nightclothes, I want the note. Where is it?" He towered over me, a huge chunk of granite determination wearing the same expression that Alexander the Great must have leveled on the vanquished Persian Empire.

I looked at him, considered arguing, but then my gaze drifted lower. Noting his unmistakable condition, I decided to pick another battle, another day. For I had to be honest. I didn't mind him seeing the note. "It is in the desk drawer."

Rather than watch his pantherlike grace as he moved across my room, I stared at the cloudy bed curtains. Now that Benedict had insisted on calling a doctor, I had to be honest with myself about another matter, too. I truly felt more miserable than I ever had, and my discomfort seemed to be growing by the minute.

"What in the bloody hell is this nonsense? 'Remain at your own peril.' And signed as if Francesca had written it. What else has happened?" he demanded.

Wincing at his anger and at the increasing discomfort in my throat, I explained the other things that had happened, ending with the destruction of the boys' garden. "I am sure these incidents are tactics designed to get me to leave Trevelyan Manor. Please, do not be so angry. There has been no real harm done. The children and I have replanted the garden, and I expect new sprouts will be popping up soon."

It was amazing how in a blink of my eye he seemed to

rope in all of his emotions like a cowboy tossing a lariat about the neck of a wild horse and bringing it to a halt. I could still see his power seething beneath his taut muscles, but it was a completely leashed power. "I am not worried about a bloody garden, Miss Lovell, but about your welfare. I will find the culprit behind these incidents."

"I was afraid of that."

"Do you not want to know who is behind this?"

"Yes, but I want to fight my own battle. I do not want you stepping in and eradicating the conflict. It is a matter of principle and respect."

"Need I remind you, Miss Lovell, that this is my household. It is a matter of my honor."

"This is a huge house, Mr. Trevelyan, and if you consider every one in it a reflection on your honor, then I fear you are doomed to be dishonored. Might I suggest you rethink your stand?"

Whatever Benedict was going to say was lost in a cry from the schoolroom. Before I managed to sit up, Benedict rushed through the door and came back into my room with little Robert in his arms.

"I want Miss Wovell," he cried. His eyes were squeezed shut, his voice sounded scratchier than mine, and his chubby cheeks were flushed a bright red. The child was clearly ill.

"Please, let me hold him," I said, reaching my arms out for him.

"You are ill yourself," Benedict said, cradling Robert. I could clearly see Benedict's turmoil, wanting to comfort his son himself, but then wanting to give his son what he was crying for.

"Please. I think both Robert and I will feel better if I do."

Benedict hesitated a moment more, then brought Robert

to me. The child leaned his head against my bosom and sighed. "Miss Wovell, I feel awful."

I brushed his unruly hair back from his face. "I know, sugarplum. I feel the same way." Even through my own fever I could tell the child was so hot he felt like he was on fire. "It is a good thing the doctor is already on his way."

"Yes." Benedict's voice was tight and full of frustration.

I realized he desperately needed to do something to help. "Can you bring me a damp cloth from my washstand? When my mother was fevered, a cool cloth always soothed her. And then maybe you should check on Justin to make sure he is not ill as well."

Benedict spun into action. For a man so large, it never ceased to amaze me how quickly and quietly he could move. By the time the doctor arrived, Robert had settled into a fitful sleep beside me, and I almost couldn't keep myself awake. My body was demanding that I rest.

I'm not sure what happened after I drifted into a restless sleep. I think I saw the doctor, the maid, I felt the light cloth of my nightgown soothe my burning skin, and I know that I heard Benedict's deep voice reassuring me that all would be well. I tried to ask him for Robert because I couldn't find the little boy next to me, and I didn't want him crying for me.

"Rest, all is well," I heard Benedict say, his strong hand holding mine. Then I must have dreamed, for I felt the coolness of a damp cloth upon my cheeks and about my neck, and time became a blur, as if I dreamed but could see nothing and feel only fire and pain. The only thing that assured me that I yet lived was the comfort of Benedict's scent. I felt as if he'd enveloped me with it, and I continued to breathe, for I knew he was there. And I prayed that little Robert knew that I was with him in my heart.

17

I awoke suddenly, with a sense of impending doom lurking within the midnight shadows of my chamber. A lamp, turned low, sat across the room on the side table next to the winged reading chair. My throat, a desert past the point of parched, hurt and my body ached all over. I had to sit up, had to find out what was wrong, for I felt a terrible knot squeezing my heart.

Moaning, I turned to my side and pulled off the light coverlet, noting the musky scent of sweat mingled with the far from fresh aroma of roses. It took a major effort, but I managed to slide my feet over the edge of the bed and push myself into a sitting position. The room wavered like a ship riding ocean swells, and I had to shut my eyes to quell the nausea.

"Miss, you shouldn't be gettin' up now. Mr. Trevelyan will be sorely displeased."

Popping my eyes open, I saw one of the young cleaning maids jump up from the reading chair and rush my way. She wore a white cap on a head of bouncy red curls, and her freckled brow was crinkled with worry.

"Where is . . ." I spoke, but the words mired in my throat and only sounded like a crackle. "Water," I rasped again.

"Yes, miss." She fetched a glass of water from the ewer on

my desk and brought it back to me. I could drink but a little; the soreness in my throat was like a raw scrape being rubbed with salt. "Mr. Trevelyan will be glad to see that you'll recover. If only Master Robert would show some improvement. But I fear he only worsens."

My heart bounded with fear, and the sickening feeling that awoke me landed heavily in my stomach. "Robert? Where is he?"

"Why, the nursery, miss."

I stood, wobbling unsteadily, as I clutched the coverlet and pulled it from the bed.

"Miss, you need to be back abed. You've been very sick indeed. The doctor said scarlet fever. There's nothin' you can do for Master Robert. I should know, me mum did everything she could, and the fever still took my brother and sister. They were wee ones like Master Robert."

"No," I cried, tears stinging my eyes. Pulling the coverlet with me, I moved as quickly as I could to the nursery with the cleaning maid fussing a trail behind me. The closer I drew, the tighter my stomach cramped, for the shadowing doom seemed to thicken the air with my every step.

I stumbled through the door into the nursery. Benedict, on his knees beside the bed where little Robert lay, looked up at me. Tears streamed down his face, his expression bleak.

"No," I said, shaking my head in disbelief.

Benedict stood. He was a man completely undone, unshaven, soiled and rumpled, and without hope.

"No. He cannot have died!" I cried, my heart breaking. God couldn't have been so cruel. I forced my legs forward, determined to reach Robert, determined to wrap my arms around him and never let anything harm him.

Benedict caught me. "There is nothing else to be done.

The doctor just left. He does not think Robert will make it through the—"

I could see Benedict's throat spasm and knew he couldn't force any more words out. All he could do was shake his head.

"He's still alive!" As long as there was but one beat of the child's heart left, there was hope. I pulled away from Benedict's grasp and staggered to the bed. My arms ached as I scooped Robert up, but it didn't matter. I needed to hold him. My heart broke as his body lay limp. Tears filled my eyes.

I pulled him close against me and cried out to him. "Robert! Please, sugarplum, you have to wake up and get well. It's Miss Wovell." I kissed his fevered cheek and brought him as close as I could to my heart. I paced as I held him, rocking him in my arms as I spoke. "I need you to get well and help me. Why, we have so many things left to do this summer. The baby plants are sprouting in the garden. We have Justin's birthday to plan, and it is going to be so much fun." More tears fell from my eyes, and although a fire raged in my throat, I couldn't stop talking to him. "Why, I even heard that a noted inventor will test his first streetcar right here in San Francisco. Just think, we could travel about without the need of a horse. And Cesca, she misses you terribly. So do you understand, sugarplum? There are just too many things that need to be done that I desperately need your help with. You must work very hard to get yourself better."

Benedict laid a hand on my shoulder. "You are only going to make yourself worse. You need to be resting."

"No! He needs me. He needs to know deep in his spirit that he is loved. If I have to cry to him with my last breath, so be it, but I will not stop until he hears me."

"My God, woman. You shame me." Benedict moved like

lightning, scooping Robert from my arms into his strong embrace. "Robert!" his deep voice boomed. "Wake up, son. I-I-I need you, son."

Robert moaned, shifting in his father's arms a little. It was the first he'd moved since I'd picked him up. Benedict came to an abrupt stop. He stared at me, and I could see hope cut through the worn grief in his haggard face. I moved over and took Robert's hand in mine, listening to the strength in voice. "Speak to him, sing to him, let him feel your love through the vibrations of your voice."

Already, exhaustion caused my arms to tremble, but I tightened my hold on Robert's hand and whispered in his ear as Benedict talked. He spoke of the first time he'd seen Robert and how lovable he'd looked cradled in a blanket. He told Robert how happy he'd been and how much his mother had loved him. And he told Robert how he had named him after his great-grandfather. They had the same smile. Sentences began to run together in my mind, but the reassurance of Benedict's voice was a steady resonance of hope in the dark hours before dawn. At some time, exhaustion claimed me, and I sank into a chair.

I must have fallen asleep, for I woke to streaming sunlight and the sensation that I was wrapped in wet cloths, adrift on a lazy sea. In actuality, Benedict had somehow managed to gather both Robert and me in his arms. Robert, wedged between his father and me, was warm, not hot, and his breathing was easy. Benedict was asleep, his head angled awkwardly back, telling me that he was going to be in a lot of pain when moved.

Moving a hand that was almost numb, I brushed Robert's cheek, feeling the natural temperature of his skin. His eyes fluttered open, and a tiny smile curved his cherub lips. A deep sigh of relief escaped me. I knew he would recover, and I would, too. Already the soreness in my throat had eased, and I didn't feel feverish. Benedict's arms tightened. Glancing up, I saw he'd awakened.

"Your mother named you well, Titania. You fight like a queen, and your touch is full of magic," he said softly. "You saved my son."

"No. It was your voice that reached him."

"But it was your love that would not let him go."

Our gazes met. The heat of attraction that always flared was there, but something warmer and deeper lay beneath that fire. And I knew my life had met another moment that would change me forever. I also knew without a doubt that this man was innocent.

"Today is the day!" Robert declared. It was Friday morning, nearly two weeks after we'd fallen ill, and he came bouncing into my room with no end to his smiles.

"Yes, today we will go to the bank and even get a candy treat, if your father thinks it is all right." The trip to town was the very first thing Robert had asked to do when he'd awoken from his fever, and Benedict promised we'd go as soon as he was well. Robert immediately began declaring himself well and continued to do so every day until Benedict promised that Friday would be the day.

Though Robert was still pale and his clothes hung a little loosely, he'd recovered all of his radiant exuberance. I, on the other hand, struggled to keep up with a day wherein I did nothing more than read with Robert and Justin in the schoolroom and confer with Cook Thomas about Justin's birthday party. I'd taken my meals in my room, and in spite of retiring to bed early, I was still tired. It was a battle to gain back my strength, but it was a very sweet battle indeed. Most especially because Robert was here, pulling on my skirt. Heaven didn't know a sweeter touch.

"Can we go yet, Miss Wovell?" he asked.

"In a minute," I said gently, kissing him on his head, then checking my wan reflection in the mirror of my washstand. I chose to wear the lavender pinstripe today, remembering how Mrs. Talbot thought it perfect with my brown hair and gray eyes. In two week's time I'd become thin to the point of being frail, and it had changed my appearance. My cheekbones were more prominent, my eyes bigger, and my lips looked fuller. Around my neck, hidden beneath my gown, I wore a key on a ribbon. Benedict had had a lock placed on the secret passage's panel in the schoolroom after Robert and I had begun our recovery. He didn't want me worrying that anyone could come into our room. I now held the key, and I chose to wear that key close to my heart. There'd be only one reason I'd unlock the door, and my mind still wavered on the precipice of knowing the pleasure of a man's love or clinging to a cold practicality. To choose between purity and ruin was easy enough. But to elevate that choice between love and emptiness made the decision much harder.

My world had changed in two weeks, in a way I'd never forget.

One morning Robert had ridden Cesca with joy, and in the dark hours a few days later, he'd almost died. I would never forget how fragile the precious gift of life was.

I'd seen Benedict several times since awakening in his arms with Robert cradled between us. Each time had been in the afternoon in the schoolroom, with Robert and Justin present. His every word and movement were filled with a polite, gentle warmth. Anything else we'd shared, the passion, our tempers, the tenderness, were all banked into a bed of coals that secretly simmered. I'd no strength for more, but I think even if I had, it wouldn't have changed anything.

There was a reserved air about Benedict that echoed his

words, *I have nothing but dishonor to give a woman.* I promised myself that soon, I'd delve deeper into what he'd meant. For now he'd left the issue of dealing with the threatening note in my hands. Eventually we'd probably disagree, and considering the results of our last argument, I wondered what would happen. Would he kiss me? How would I react? But for now everything seemed stagnantly content as we healed. For I had no doubt that Benedict had lived every moment of Robert's illness as if it were himself who'd been sick and near death.

"Are you ready yet, Miss Wovell?"

"I'm ready. Where is Justin?" The boy's withdrawal seemed to be more pronounced since my recovery.

"He is in his bed. He does not want to go."

Fear gripping me, I rushed to the nursery. All I could think of was that Justin had now fallen ill with the fever. "Justin!"

He wasn't in his bed. I searched the room and almost missed him sitting on the window seat, his knees drawn to his chin, his arms wrapped tightly about his legs. He didn't look up at my call, just continued to stare out the window. But from what I could see, he didn't appear ill, only sad.

I drew a deep breath to settle my heart back into its proper place and walked over to him. Through the window I could see that he watched the carriage awaiting us. Did he think we'd leave without him?

"Justin," I said softly. "Let's go down and find your father."

He took a shuddering breath and turned to let me see his tears. "I want us all to stay here. I do not want anything bad to happen ever again. But even here's not safe. My mommy died. You got sick, and even Robert almost . . . he almost died, too. I don't want anybody. Please go away."

I sat down next to him and placed my hand over his

fisted one. "You think the pain will go away if everyone goes away. You are tired of worrying. Tired of hurting." He didn't say anything, but his fist tightened, and more tears fell down his cheeks.

"Why don't we pretend for a minute? Let's say that your father, Robert, and I go to town and leave you here. Will you feel any better alone in your room?"

Justin remained silent.

"Let's pretend you are lots older, and you could leave here and go anywhere you wanted. You would never have your brother around to take your toys or to laugh with. You would never have your father around to show you how to ride Cesca. You would never have your grandma, or Uncle Stephen, or anybody else you know. Do you think you would be happy then? All alone?"

Justin slowly shook his head, his answer only making him more miserable.

I sighed. "I wish I could promise you that nothing bad will ever happen again. But I cannot. As I said before, life is like roses with thorns. There are a great many wonderful, joyous things to share, and then there are the painful, hurtful things, too. All I can tell you is that sharing life with those you love makes the good parts better and the bad parts easier to bear. Maybe you would not hurt so much if you did not keep your heart so all alone."

Justin choked back his tears. He looked so old, so solemn for a boy of almost eight. Anger nearly squeezed the breath from my lungs. It was so unfair. He needed to be running through the grass, climbing trees, and jumping with excitement at the prospect of going to town for fun.

"Are you scared, Miss Lovell? Of the bad things? Are you afraid that they will happen and you cannot stop them? That all you can do is watch?"

"Yes," I said softly, wondering myself if I was expecting

too much to want Justin to heal and to be happy again. For I had to be honest with myself. If Robert had died, his death would have been a thorn in my heart that I don't know if I could have released. "Yes, I am scared. Being brave does not mean you are not afraid bad things will happen. Being brave is having fears, but still having the courage to live."

I held my hand out to him. "Come share today with us, and we will be secretly brave together."

Justin looked at my hand for a long moment, and just when I thought he'd say no, he unclenched his fist and put his hand in mine. When we stood, I saw Robert standing in the doorway, looking very serious.

"I always thoughted that you were the bravest and I was stupid for being scared," he said.

Justin's eyes widened.

I smiled and held my other hand out to Robert. "Maybe you two can share what makes you scared, and then maybe it will not be so scary."

Robert nodded as he took my hand. Justin shrugged nonchalantly, but I could tell the idea interested him.

"Can we check our babies before we go?" Robert asked.

"If we hurry." The trip to the back of the garden didn't take long, and both boys were satisfied that their "babies" were doing quite well.

"I watered them and took care of them while you were sick," Justin told Robert. "I made sure they were well for you."

Robert reached over and hugged his brother. "Thank you, Jus. You're the bestest big brother."

Justin looked surprised. Then he hugged Robert back. It was the first real affection Justin had let himself express since my arrival at Trevelyan Hill.

Tears were still stinging my eyes as we rushed into the foyer. Benedict was waiting for us, hustling us to the carriage, but I still took a moment to glance at the glorious stained glass windows and whisper a prayer of thanks for that little sign of hope from Justin. I even gave the suit of armor a loving pat for guarding over the stained glass so diligently.

Once in the carriage, I found it most difficult to keep my mind on what Robert was saying to me as the carriage moved down the drive. My attention kept wandering to Benedict and how disturbing it was to be in the close confines of a carriage with him. I almost thought that riding Odin would be less intimidating. Almost.

Benedict was so broad that he nearly took up the whole seat. His long legs lay stretched across the floor of the carriage, close enough to mine that our calves brushed slightly with every bump in the road. He wore dark brown again, pants and jacket. His white ruffled shirt, crisply fresh, struck me as being at odds with the tiredness creasing his face. Robert's illness had taken a toll.

"Look, Miss Wovell, there's some pretty purple flowers. Can we pick them like last time and take them to our mommies?"

"Uh—" I hesitated, wondering what Benedict's reaction would be about going to Francesca's grave.

Benedict frowned, and a twinge of disappointment touched my heart. Didn't he realize how much Justin and Robert needed to express their feelings for their mother?

"Why don't we get a bouquet from the florist after we go to the bank? Picking wildflowers like a poor man is not what a Trevelyan would . . . do."

My cheeks flushed hotly. I hadn't considered that I'd taught Justin and Robert an action not in keeping with their position in life. In fact, in all of my teachings, I never once remembered taking their financial standing into consideration. Was I doing them a disservice?

Benedict's gaze shot to mine, surprising me as he winced, having realized he'd labeled me a "poor man." I smiled tightly back, suddenly too aware of the class difference between us. Seeing him only within the setting of Trevelyan Manor in many ways had masked that difference, which was odd. I would have expected the richness of his home to make it more pronounced. Instead, I could see that exposed to the dictates of society, the distance between us would become more glaringly apparent, like revealing my work-worn hands to the bright light of day instead of hiding them beneath kid gloves as I did now.

I told myself it was a good thing to be exposed for what I was, even by something so simple as picking wildflowers for graves. I was a woman of extremely modest means, who'd been born out of wedlock. A man of Benedict's breeding and money was a man that I could never hope to openly love.

The brightness of the sun dimmed a little, and a slight weariness threaded through my body. Constance had asked me if I believed in choosing one's fate, or if one could never change the fate to which one was born. I believed one could choose, but I now saw that change could only go so far.

"Roses," Justin said into the uncomfortable silence filling the air in the carriage. "I want to give both Miss Lovell's mother and my mother lots of roses."

Benedict cleared his voice, as if he had words caught in his throat and couldn't speak. "Roses it is, then. But why roses?"

"Because they have thorns," Justin said. "That makes them real."

Benedict lifted a brow my way, but didn't comment further. I bit my lip. This outing of fun and sunshine I'd been picturing to bring Benedict and his sons closer together wasn't off to a good start.

Thankfully, the next few hours progressed on a lighter note. At the bank, Benedict gave each of the boys twenty dollars and opened an account for them. And the bank clerk swore Justin and Robert to secrecy, claiming accounts for children weren't something they did for every customer. This impressed them immensely. The candy store and the florist followed. Benedict, Justin, and Robert each bought two bouquets of flowers, and at Benedict's insistence, I chose an arrangement of white and yellow daisies. We were on our way out when little Robert gasped. "I forgotted. Grandfather is watching over Mommy." He looked at his father. "Would he like flowers, too?"

I saw Benedict take a deep breath, as if the death of his father was still a fresh wound. "I had forgotten, too, son." Benedict took a whiff of the fragrant blooms cradled in his arms. I couldn't help but remember the night he held Robert and me, cradling us both with his warm strength. I blinked, refocusing on Benedict's words. "Your grandfather loved roses. They were his favorite. He even wrote a book about them."

"A real book?" Justin, who thus far today had only spoken when asked a question, drew closer to his father. "He liked roses, too, like me?"

"He loved roses." Benedict jostled the bouquets to one arm and set his hand on Justin's shoulder. "He went to Europe and chose the different roses in our garden at home."

"May I see the book and read it? Miss Lovell is teaching me to read."

"Yes. I also hear Miss Lovell has taught you how to play chess."

Justin nodded.

"How about this afternoon we play a game and then read a little of what your grandfather wrote together?"

Justin nodded, but not even his reticence could hide the pleased gleam in his gaze.

Benedict squeezed Justin's shoulder affectionately. "Why don't you and Robert each pick out a rose to give to your grandfather."

"What color did he like?" Robert asked.

Benedict smiled. "All of them. So you will just have to pick out the two prettiest."

The boys ran back to the florist, asking to see all of the roses he had, and I rolled my eyes. "You know this may take them a while?" I spoke with a smile curving my lips that said I had all the time in the world. When it came to moments that brought Justin further from his isolated shell, I did have all the time in the world.

"You looked as if you needed a moment to rest anyway. Is this excursion too taxing?" Benedict motioned me to a chair at the front of the shop, and I sat, more tired than I'd realized.

"Heavens no. My constitution is—"

"In need of rest. Maria informed me that you kept Justin and Robert with you all afternoon yesterday doing lessons." His heated gaze examined me from head to toe, leaving a trail of fire behind. "I thought we agreed that you were going to spend this week recuperating."

"We only read, nothing strenuous." I'd only been able to tolerate lying in bed for so long before thoughts of Benedict in my bed sent me scurrying for something with which to occupy myself. Remembering what condition arguing with me induced in him, I thought it best to change the subject. "Writing a book is quite an accomplishment. I, too, am interested in reading your father's book. *The Romance of the Rose* is an interesting title."

Benedict's eyes widened. "You have seen the book then?"

"Yes. I encountered your mother in the library late one night. She had it with her."

"My mother had my father's book out?" More than surprise settled in his expression. He looked shocked. "She has not touched a rose since he died, much less his beloved book. It has been too painful for her. Are you sure?"

"Quite sure." I frowned. "Though she had given me quite a fright. The scrape of her cane had me imagining that a—"

I pressed my hand to my mouth, too late to stop or undo what I'd accidentally revealed. I forced myself to meet Benedict's gaze, thinking there might be a slight chance he hadn't heard. He had.

He stared at me over the top of the roses. "I beg your pardon?"

"I believe I said I was sure she had the book."

"Miss Lovell, I think you had better tell me what in damnation is going on." His voice, though lowered to a barely audible whisper, was sharp enough to slice through stone.

Wincing, I took a deep breath. How did I always seem to end up in the middle of things? In some ways, I felt as if I'd betrayed Mrs. Trevelyan's confidence, though I knew she held no loyalty to me. "Um, I think perhaps you misunderstood me, Mr. Trevelyan. I meant to say—"

"Miss Lovell, please do not argue with me further. We are in public." His voice sounded strained, reminiscent of his confession in his study.

"Here?" Shocked, I dropped my gaze, but didn't see anything out of the ordinary. Still, I thought it best to be prudent. "Very well, in light of your condition, I will concede. Your mother was walking with the aid of a cane, but it is her secret to tell when she's ready and not mine. So could we not mention this and put this with the other thing that never happened?"

"Miss Lovell, I fear we are both doomed. You are as big a fool as I."

I blinked. What had he meant by that cryptic remark? And why did he appear to be laughing at me?

"We've the two bestest roses ever." Robert held his prize, a large, deep pink rose. Justin followed. I noticed he carried a big red bloom, but this time he didn't have his hands fisted around the thorns.

Benedict and I both exchanged a look that mutually ended our conversation for now; but it was far from over. I marched out to the carriage, wondering why he thought he was the only one who could do something and then pretend it didn't happen. Didn't I have the same prerogative?

By the time we approached the Trevelyan family monument, I'd put the conversation from my mind. It warmed my heart to see that being here this time was easier for both Robert and Justin. Robert chatted about the angel watching over his grandfather and mother. Justin, still quiet, kneeled near his mother's grave, his hands loosely clasped—a marked difference from before.

Benedict, on the other hand, stood between his father and his wife's graves, looking like an overdried hide stretched between two sticks, so taut it might crack at any moment.

I left Robert and Justin and moved to where he stood. Unsure of what I could say, I stayed silent, but I couldn't seem to stop myself from touching him. I set my hand upon his shoulder, feeling his heat through his coat and my gloves.

He didn't turn to look at me, and I was thankful. For even this small impropriety in a public, though empty place had my cheeks burning. The dark of night hid barriers that were too glaring to overcome during the day. Perhaps that explained our fall into passion during the midnight mists surrounding Trevelyan Manor.

"I have never read his book. Before he died, I resented his interest in roses. He lived and breathed them, ignoring all else to the point that the Trevelyan fortune was nearly gone. We never understood each other. He and Stephen were a lot alike." He spoke reluctantly, as if the words were being pulled from him by an outside force.

"What happened to him?"

"There was a storm at sea. The ship went down. There were no survivors."

I shivered, and Benedict shook his head, as if to awaken himself. I hesitated only a moment before I leapt to where I knew I should never tread, but I had to hear it from him. I had to hear him tell me of his wife. "Tell me about Francesca," I said softly.

"There's nothing to say." Benedict jerked away from my touch as if wounded, his expression guarded, his mouth grim. "Justin, Robert, let's go. We have still to visit Miss Lovell's mother's grave."

Tears stung my eyes, and I blinked them back as I curled my hand into a fist. I felt as if I'd had the wind knocked from me. I followed them from the cemetery, thinking that I'd lost something within its shadows. Or maybe all that I felt existing between Benedict and me was merely the illusions of a spinster's heart. I would never know unless he decided to tell me what lay beneath the fire in his dark eyes. But even then, if all that I thought he felt turned out to be false, what I felt for him would never change.

And as I left the cemetery behind, a thought scraped over my heart. If Robert and Justin's mother were still alive, and I was their governess, I'd have loved them the same. And Benedict, too. If he'd been married, I would have loved him still. For love didn't come upon command, but grew where it chose.

It was not a reassuring realization. I'd like to think that

if he'd been married, this fire between us would have been nothing more than a fleeting gleam of light destined never to shine. Surely I had that much fortitude. At least I prayed that to be so. Had Stephen thought the same and failed?

As we got into the carriage, I glanced Benedict's way. Even as I wondered if I'd ever have the courage to ask about Francesca again, I knew I didn't have the right to do so.

The ride to my mother's memorial park passed quickly, and as I approached her grave, my steps slowed. In the time since her death, I'd changed from the woman I'd been, and I wondered if she would recognize me today. I liked to think so. She'd always looked upon people's hearts to see the potential within. Robert and Justin rushed ahead, setting their rich flowers at the foot of the grave. Benedict slowed his gait to match mine.

"You miss her?" he said, surprising me with the intimacy of his tone. Apparently I hadn't stepped too far past the bounds of forgiveness by asking about Francesca.

I studied his eyes a moment, searching for what feelings lay within the darkness, wondering about the change in his manner. "Yes."

I brushed my fingers over the bright daisies I held. "Her special kind of love still lives in my heart. It is like a benevolent sun that never sets, always showering me with warmth."

"Miss Lovell, you have been richly blessed in life."

A slow smile curved my lips as truth dawned. "Yes, Mr. Trevelyan, you might say I have a rich inheritance. As soon as I have saved enough funds to do so, I am going to have a headstone engraved for her. I want it to read that her life was as finite as the earth, but her love reaches beyond the stars. Maybe those who happen upon her grave will know what a loving woman she was."

He caught my hand in his and brought my gloved fingers

to his lips. "The moment anyone meets you, Miss Lovell, they cannot help but know," he said softly.

My eyes clung to the warmth in his, and my heart raced ahead, plunging headlong into my ever-deepening well of love for this man.

≪ *18* ≫

The dinner hour approached, and I was in an unacceptable state. I stood in front of the armoire in my undergarments. For the very life of me I couldn't decide what to wear, and I had begun to think my fever had returned. In truth, it was thoughts of Benedict that plagued me. My mind had never been in such a muddle.

I'd vowed to wear my practicality like armor and had yet to don a bit of it. Completely frustrated with myself, I shut my eyes and reached blindly for a dress. I'd let Chance decree what I should wear. Decision made, I opened my eyes, beheld my old gray serge dress, and frowned. If anything, it was a full armor of practicality, and I had vowed ...

I stared at its worn, dull lines. Then I glanced at the array of fancy dresses still hanging in my closet.

I decided Providence had shoved Chance out of the way and interfered with what I was destined to wear. Putting back the gray serge, I snatched out the cornflower blue with its white lace trim and dressed quickly before Providence could make another move. Pinching my cheeks after I tightened the pins confining my hair in a neat bun, I hurried to the nursery. Justin and Robert were ready for bed and playing with wooden horses on the floor, spinning around in circles. Maria was with them, sitting in the rocking chair, frowning at their antics. I knelt down next to them. "Are you two having a race?"

"No, we're not letting the bad witch catch us," Robert whispered. "It's Jus's secret that I promised never to tell, right?" Robert looked proudly at Justin.

Justin scowled, and I could see a fight brewing. "Then you're doing a good job, keeping his secret." I smiled at Justin. "Today was fun, and I wanted to thank you both for being such exemplary gentlemen. I am sure we will be able to plan another outing soon. Would you like that?"

Justin shrugged, but Robert shouted a loud "Yes!" and gave me a big hug. I hugged him back, then stood and kissed the top of Justin's head. "Who won your chess match with your father this afternoon?"

"My father, of course," he said, as if any other answer was inconceivable. "But I did capture three of his men." A slight smile curved his lips and lit his eyes. "He does not make it easy like Uncle Stephen does."

"Yes, I imagine your uncle Stephen wants everyone to feel good, whereas your father wants everyone to be good. Everybody needs a little of both, so you are lucky."

I said good night and nodded to Maria as I left, noticing that her frown had deepened. I needed to have a discussion with Benedict about her. It didn't matter that the elderly woman had been Francesca's nurse; her dour nature wasn't good for Robert and Justin.

Everyone was awaiting me in the parlor, even Constance. I was an unbearable half an hour late, which only added to the knots tightening in my stomach. I hadn't seen Stephen, Constance, Benedict's mother, or Mr. Henderson since the Sunday I had fallen ill. That was two weeks ago, and according to my hazy recollections, it had been a disturbing day. The weight of everyone's regard nearly knocked me off my feet, but Benedict's was the heaviest. He stood near the window, his dark gaze raking over me. I should have worn the gray serge. "Forgive my tardiness," I murmured.

Stephen, who stood closest to the door, approached to take my hand. "Nothing to forgive," he said. From the look of him, I expected to hear he'd been ill, too. His eyes were bloodshot, his skin pale, and his hand trembled. The mask of humor he used to face the world had become tattered.

"I doubt Cook Thomas would concur, Stephen," Mrs. Trevelyan said from the confines of her wheelchair, next to Benedict. "Well, Benedict, do not just stand there. Wheel me over to Miss Lovell." Had Benedict confronted his mother about her ability to walk?

I winced and glanced her way as he pushed her toward me. Expecting to be on the sharp end of her axlike disposition, I stiffened my spine, determined I wouldn't let her behead me with her wit, but she surprised me. "I hear you were instrumental in my grandson's recovery."

"Not necessarily," I hedged, shooting Benedict a wary look, only to encounter his own surprised expression. If he hadn't told his mother about holding Robert and me all night, then who had? I blushed at what the household staff must be gossiping about.

"Nonsense," she said. "From the look of you, a light breeze would finish you off, so I offer my thanks before it does. Have they fed you nothing but broth? I suggest we eat dinner without any further delay, Benedict."

"For once we are in agreement, Mother," Benedict said. He shrugged at my questioning glance, telling me he'd been no more a part of his mother's confidences than I had.

Standing back to let Benedict wheel his mother into the dining room, I felt a light touch upon my arm. Katherine stood at my side, smiling as she signed something to me.

"She says that it is good to see you recovered," Stephen

said, stepping up and putting his arm around his sister's shoulders. "I must agree with her. We would have visited, but the doctor ordered everyone to keep away while you and Robert were ill. Only two maids who had scarlet fever before stayed, and Benedict of course."

"I had not realized." So Benedict's presence when I'd been sick wasn't a figment of my imagination. Smiling at Katherine, I signed "Thank you" to her.

Mr. Henderson, with Constance at his side, joined us. "It is indeed good to see you, Miss Lovell. May I have the pleasure of sitting next to you at dinner?" Mr. Henderson held out his arm to me.

"Of course." Doing anything else would have been rude. Still, an uncomfortable knot tightened in my stomach, which worsened with the knowing look Constance sent me over her shoulder. From the moment Benedict stepped through the threshold of the demon-carved door, he'd captured some part of me. In truth, even before then. I could still remember the deep timbre of his voice, reaching inside of me, sparking a fire that grew hotter with our every encounter. Yet even if Benedict's presence hadn't already filled me, I'd find it difficult to entertain a romantic notion for a man of Mr. Henderson's stature. Being next to a man who stood half a head shorter than me magnified my ungainly proportions to a painful point. It was almost as bad as being compared to Constance's petiteness.

I wondered if Providence was punishing my dress rebellion when I ended up being seated between Mr. Henderson and Constance, with Benedict at one end, Mrs. Trevelyan at the other, and Stephen and Katherine across.

Constance was the first to speak after the oyster stew was served. "Miss Chapman stopped by today. You remember her, don't you, Stephen?"

For some reason Stephen paled. "Yes."

"I believe her brother was a regular acquaintance of yours before you went East. I even thought you had called on Miss Chapman for a while, too."

Stephen cleared his throat. "I haven't seen Henry or Miss Chapman since my return."

"Well, Miss Chapman was beside herself with glee. Apparently Henry has written a play that's become a major success. All the critics are raving about it."

"That is interesting. I may have to look him up."

"She invited me to attend a performance tomorrow, but I declined. I just do not think I would be able to watch it. He's set the play during the war, about which everyone is extremely sensitive. But that is not as disturbing as the plot. Two brothers fall in love with the same woman, and in the end she kills herself over it."

Dropped spoons clattered into bowls, and a dead silence followed.

Stephen stood, tossing his napkin onto the table. "If you will excuse me. I am feeling rather unwell."

He left quickly. Katherine, ignorant of Constance's revelation, watched Stephen a moment. She signed something to Benedict. He replied in the same manner, and she left the table too.

"I have never known you to show such lack of decorum," Benedict said, his voice tight with anger.

"Well," Constance said, "perhaps I should not have mentioned the play, but I thought it best. You see, since Henry and Stephen were known to each other, there are now more rumors about . . . my sister, and she would have—" She tossed her napkin on the table and stood. A welling of tears sat in her eyes. "I for one am finding it most difficult to never be able to speak of the sister I loved. It is as if every memory of her has to be killed so that the rest of you can live." Constance left the room in a rush.

My lungs were shouting for air before I gathered myself enough to breathe. What could one possibly say in the wake of Constance's storm? I had to view it as such. She could have spoken to Stephen and Benedict in private, but she had chosen to air her grievances in public, and I couldn't help but wonder why. I also wondered what Benedict would do now.

He picked up his spoon. "I suggest we continue with our meal. Not only does Miss Lovell need sustenance, but Cook Thomas will have a fit if we don't. Alan, what came of your meeting today?"

As they launched into a business discussion, I glanced at Mrs. Trevelyan. She'd remained strangely silent during the emotional uproar, and I wondered why.

"I do not suppose we ever escape from the dead, do we, Miss Lovell?" She spoke low, so only I could hear. "It would seem that they live on, no matter what. As do we."

I blinked and scrambled for a reply. "True," I said haltingly. "Anyone who touches your life is never really gone."

"Unfortunately, the evil ones that pass have more presence than the good."

I shook my head, ignoring the shiver running down my spine. "No. I think the truly good in people leaves a deeper impression than evil. But given the frailties of the human heart, very few truly good are known."

"Very well said, Miss Lovell," Benedict said, startling me. I hadn't realized he'd finished his conversation. The moment our gazes connected, I lowered mine, not trusting in my ability to hide what I felt. "Do you agree, Alan?"

"No, I find that I do not agree. You spoke eloquently enough, Miss Lovell. But the truth of it is that evil has had the upper hand since Cain slew Abel. A man cannot help but become what he despises. Not deliberately so, but slowly, through a series of choices he has no idea are going to lead to that end. It is fate."

I swallowed my automatic denial. The truth of Mr. Henderson's words could be seen in Benedict's stark expression. Was it possible to become what you despised? How could one make choices and not know where they'd lead? I blinked suddenly and looked down at the cornflower blue dress I'd chosen to wear instead of the gray serge and the reasons behind my choice. Vanity? A wish to attract Benedict's attention? To what end? I didn't want to face the questions my actions proposed.

Thankfully, Mr. Henderson changed the subject, and the rest of the dinner conversation passed in relative frivolity after the heaviness with which the meal had begun. When we'd finished, the men excused themselves to Benedict's study, and Mrs. Trevelyan and I went to our rooms.

Halfway to my room, I decided that I needed a breath of fresh air before retiring and directed my steps to the gardens. The moment I was out of the house, a gentle breeze from the bay wrapped around me like a lover's hand, teasing my senses, enticing me farther into the shadows of the night. Moonlight, beacons of magic in the dark, kissed the blooming roses and cast the streaming waters of the angel fountain in silver. I wandered over to her, mentally tossing all of my worries upon her winged shoulders, and shut my eyes to breathe deeply of the scents filling the air—roses and honeysuckle laced with a dash of salt.

The tension knotting my neck and shoulders eased. Opening my eyes, I stretched my hands out to the stars, wishing they weren't so far away.

The scrape of a boot startled me, and I swung around. Stephen sat on the ground, his back resting against the base of the fountain.

"Now hast thou but one bare hour to live,
And then thou must be damn'd perpetually,
Stand still, you ever-moving spheres of heaven,
That time may cease, and midnight never come.

"Ever wonder what Marlowe's own sins were that enabled him to write *Dr. Faustus*?" Stephen asked. His words were slightly slurred, letting me know that the flash of silver in his hand was a flask.

A bit surprised, I didn't know what to say, but he didn't really expect an answer.

"I think about those lines often. Having but an hour to live, facing eternal damnation, wanting to stop time so that midnight might never come."

"Is that what you want to do? Stop time?"

He saluted with the flask. "And be perpetually drunk? I think not. Death would be preferable to this."

"Then why do you drink?"

"It is the only way to forget. They say she jumped at the midnight hour. Cesca. And all of her frail beauty lay ruined until she was found at dawn."

"Dear God," I whispered. It was all I could do to keep from turning and running away just to escape the images of death he painted. It was also very clear that Stephen believed wholeheartedly that Francesca really did kill herself. Then why was he wallowing in guilt? Why was he so condemning of his brother? *He judges without mercy. Don't ever fail him, Ann.*

"That's the moment I would stop time. Before that fateful midnight hour, before she damned us both. Damned us all. Cursed us to hell."

Anger streaked through me. I marched over, grabbed the flask from his hand, and tossed it into the fountain. "You do not drink to forget. You drink to dwell, so that you can wallow in self-pity instead of standing up like a man and facing your sins. Is it your wish for Robert or Justin to dash into the garden tomorrow, only to discover their beloved uncle lying on the ground, drunk?" The more I thought about it, the angrier I became. I stamped my foot. "Get up this minute. You are going to your room. I will not leave you here for that to happen. Those boys have enough problems as it is."

To give Stephen credit, he did try to rise. He just wasn't very successful at it. I took hold of his arm, and we managed to get him on his feet and walking toward the house.

"Miss Ann," he slurred. "You truly have no idea just how beautiful you are."

"What I am is an inch away from pushing you into the fountain to sober up. If I did not fear you would drown, I would do it anyway."

"The avenging angel. Drink to dwell. Too cowardly to face my sins. By damn, Miss Ann, I think you are on to something. Perhaps I will put it to verse. 'Ode to Miss Ann,' or something such as that."

"You would better serve us both if you took the words to heart rather than to pen."

He stumbled, and I had to wrap my other arm around him to keep him upright. This was a most unseemly mess. If I'd thought about it, I should have found Dobbs to see to Stephen. In fact, I decided to do just that. "Stephen, do you think you could—"

The door opened, and Benedict and Mr. Henderson stepped from the house. Over Stephen's shoulders I could see their horrified expressions as they saw Stephen and me in each other's arms.

"Forgive our interruption," Benedict said, his words puncturing the night like slashing daggers.

I saw him turn, and I panicked, letting go of Stephen.

"Mr. Trevelyan! Don't you dare run away! This, uh, er, complexity is not what you think."

Stephen wavered, wobbled, and pitched to his side. Unfortunately, I happened to be standing in his way, and I went flying. I heard him hit the ground as I tried to catch my balance. I couldn't. My nose was headed right for the cobblestones faster than I could get my hands out in front of me.

I'm not sure how he managed it, but Benedict caught me around my waist, twisted, and broke the impact of my fall with his own body. I landed on top of him with a whoosh, and there I lay, unable to breathe. Not because I'd been harmed or had the air knocked from me, but because having my body all over his was, quite frankly, supremely pleasurable. I must have wiggled a little to fit closer, because I heard him gasp softly and tighten his grip on me. The passageway's key nestling between my breasts made a deep impression.

"I assume that you are unharmed, Miss Lovell."

"Quite so, Mr. Trevelyan," I whispered. "I feel rather good at the moment." I breathed enough to inhale the aroma of sandalwood and spice.

"Indeed."

"Most certainly."

"Is she unharmed, Ben?" Mr. Henderson called out. "Stephen's bloodied his nose."

"Miss Lovell is fine. We will be right there, Alan."

I felt the brush of Benedict's lips against my temple as he untangled his legs from my skirts and helped me rise. His thumb rubbed across my palm, and he held on to my hand, supposedly to help me walk safely in the dark. Every unmentionable part of my feminine body sprang to life, demanding to be mentioned. My breasts ached, my feminine flesh grew damp, my lips parted in unreasoning expectation, and my toes even curled. And all of this happened in the space of three steps. Not even my gray serge dress would have been armor enough. I had the presence of mind to wonder what good a whole suit of real metal armor like the one in the foyer would do, if all I did was itch to get out of it.

Mr. Henderson held Stephen, who had a dark-spotted handkerchief clutched to his nose.

"He's in his cups again," Mr. Henderson said.

"I am not surprised," Benedict replied, sounding suddenly weary. "He's been heading for it all week. For a while I really thought he was pulling himself together."

Stephen wavered and spoke, his voice muffled. "Not into my cups, just my flask, which the avenging angel threw into the fountain. She quite read me the riot act, you know. It was magnificent."

"I am sure." Benedict lifted a questioning brow, and I shrugged.

"Let's get him to his room," Mr. Henderson said. "Perhaps you can come back to Kansas City with me, Stephen. I could use some help on the ranch."

Benedict and Mr. Henderson hefted Stephen to his feet. Just before they entered the manor, Stephen looked up at the upper floors and quoted Dante: "Abandon hope, all ye who enter here."

Both Benedict and Mr. Henderson's expressions were grim. I shivered. Surely Trevelyan Manor and hell weren't one and the same. Once inside, I excused myself and hurried up to my room, exhaustion suddenly dogging my every step. *Abandon all hope?* I would not. I could not.

The next morning I hurried into Mr. McGuire's Bookstore with the gates of hell still heavy on my mind. I hoped to have the opportunity to speak to Dr. Levinworth.

There were several customers in the shop when I

entered, which thankfully gave me a few minutes to gather myself. The walk to town had fatigued me. After waving hello to Mr. McGuire, I went over to Puck. It was time that the bird and I had a talk.

"This is Titania, your queen, speaking here," I whispered. "If you are indeed a fairy trapped within a parrot's body, then you need to give me some other indication of it than quoting Shakespeare. Perhaps you can bob your head or something such as that."

Puck did nothing, only stared at me with his beady bald eye. "What, a head-bobbing too much? Then why not prune your raggedy feathers? They are truly in sad shape."

Puck yawned and stretched a scaly foot.

"Hmm. Do you think I owe you something more? As I am your queen, it is you who are to entertain me."

"He that dies pays all debts," Puck squawked.

I blinked and stared at him a bit fearfully. Surely Puck had to be a fairy trapped in feathers. I decided to spend my time looking through books until Mr. McGuire was free. Books didn't talk back.

Not more than a quarter hour later, the shop cleared out. Mr. McGuire motioned me over to his desk, which impossibly held a dozen more books than last time. Now that I'd a moment to look at him, my heart winced. He looked older than ever before, his skin more pale, his wispy hair sparser and disordered, and his watery blue eyes bloodshot. "Come, lass. Let me have a look at ye. I've been so very worried ever since I heard ye were ill. If you hadna come this morning, I was going to close shop and go see ye for myself."

I situated myself in a chair as he perched on his high stool. "How did you know I was ill? And if you say a little bird told you, I fear I'll go mad. I already think Puck is the fabled fairy trapped in a parrot's body like a genie in a lamp." Mr. McGuire didn't even smile at my jest.

"Miss Ortega came by the shop last week and said you'd been very ill, but were recovering. Now tell me the truth of it."

"Constance was here?"

"Aye, for a book on steamboats, I think. She's a chatty lass, for sure. And a strange one. Now, were you truly ill? I couldna help but wonder if ye had been poisoned."

"Good Lord! No. Both Robert and I contracted scarlet fever. I was told the rash was quite evident." I knew without a doubt that Robert and I had been truly sick. But Mr. McGuire's question alarmed me. I'd never considered that anyone would or could poison me. I shivered as I realized how very vulnerable I was. I didn't think someone wished me physical harm, but they could.

"Lass?"

I shook my head. "No, we weren't poisoned. We were both sick, but Robert was worse." Emotion clogged my throat. "I consider it a miracle that he recovered."

"So that's the way of it, lass. You've already given your heart to the wee lads." Mr. McGuire let out a deep sigh. "I was afraid this would happen. And now, if I were to ask ye to leave there for your own safety, ye wouldna hear of it, would you?"

I picked a spot of lint from my dress. I saw the remain-at-your-own-peril-note as not life-threatening, but I didn't think Mr. McGuire would consider it so. "Why would you think I am in danger? I am just a governess." My heart winced at my bald-faced lie. But I couldn't tell Mr. McGuire the intimacies that had sprung up between Benedict and me.

"There's a murderer among those upon Trevelyan Hill. You mark my words. Dr. Levinworth told me last week that Francesca Trevelyan intimated to him that she feared for her mortal soul."

I recalled what Stephen had said last night, but before I could speak, Mr. McGuire continued.

"As Dr. Levinworth tells it, she feared eternal damnation to the point of desperation," he whispered low. "Now I ask ye, lass. Would a Catholic woman with such fears commit suicide?"

"No." But Stephen, a man who claimed to love her, thought that she had. Was he lying?

The shop door opened, bells clanged, and Puck bristled his feathers. "Blow, blow thou winter wind," Puck squawked.

The spectacled and studious looking man who walked in the door smiled sadly. " 'Thou are not so unkind as man's ingratitude.' Shame on you, Puck. Half a quote is no quote at all." The man's features matched the somberness of his gray suit, which was a shade darker than his hair.

"At last ye both shall meet. Dr. Levinworth, Miss Ann Lovell. Perhaps you can convince her of the danger at Trevelyan Manor."

Dr. Levinworth held out his hand, and I stood to greet him. "Forgive the forwardness of this, Miss Lovell, but I must add my concerns to Mr. McGuire's. He speaks of you often. It is nice to finally meet you. I am just sorry that it is over such a tragic affair."

I nodded. "Mr. McGuire informed me that you treated Francesca for several years."

Dr. Levinworth sighed. "I have always held my patient's confidences, but the circumstances of Francesca's death, as well as Mr. McGuire's real concern for you, force me to speak. Francesca was often ill, usually from nervous afflictions more than anything else, but never more troubled than during the months before her death. She was in a rather—" He paused and glanced toward Mr. McGuire.

"I told the lass," Mr. McGuire said.

Dr. Levinworth nodded. "She was in a difficult situation, being with child and her husband having been gone for some time."

I cleared my throat. "Did she, um, fear Mr. Trevelyan?"

"She lived in terror of the man."

Shocked, I stepped away from the doctor and paced to the bookshelf. "You speak as if Mr. Trevelyan is a violent, horrible man. I find that hard to believe."

"A poor choice of words on my part, Miss Lovell. There is no delicate way to put this. Francesca was a very petite woman, even smaller than her sister. Mr. Trevelyan is a very large man. The first time I was called to treat her was just days after their wedding. She'd fainted the moment the priest pronounced them man and wife and took to her bed for a week. Laudanum was the only thing that calmed her nervous state."

Francesca truly had to have been unreasonably high-strung. I'd witnessed Benedict's gentleness and care, had even been on the receiving end of it, though I was nothing but a governess not even of his class. I couldn't imagine he'd be any less thoughtful to his bride.

"Why ever did she marry him if she feared his size so greatly?" I asked.

"An arranged marriage to save both families' shipping businesses. Francesca had vowed to her father that she would bear an heir."

I wondered how many lives had been ruined for money's sake. "Who do you think killed her, Doctor?"

Dr. Levinworth drew a deep breath. Though I could tell he found it difficult to speak, his gaze never wavered. He clearly believed in what he said. "Her husband, Miss Lovell. He does not strike me as a man who would tolerate being cuckolded."

Sunday evening brought a thickening fog upon Trevelyan Hill that only seemed to worsen every night during the next week. It was as if during the midnight hours, the fog mirrored the growing tension within the manor, and within me, too. My ever-growing awareness of the key that would lead me to Benedict's arms seemed to cast a fog over my vision of practicality. The key dangled between my breasts, and with every beat of my heart I ached to use it, especially during the echoing hours of the night.

It was Thursday morning. Last night we had celebrated Justin's birthday, and I had spent yet another sleepless night in worry. The sun had finally beaten back last night's fog, but it wasn't helping clear the fog in my mind at all. The boys were getting a riding lesson on Cesca, and since I'd be having one later in the afternoon, I chose to avoid the stables. The less I thought about my first ride on a horse outside of the training ring, the better.

Mr. Simons was expected shortly for our sign language lesson, and I decided to spend the spare moments I had in the garden with my drawing pad. But instead of bright blooms and the angelic fountain, my pencil raced across the page, drawing the worried lines of Justin's face, as I thought about his birthday.

My hopes for his party had come to fruition, but Justin's response left me aching for him. Justin had smiled, thanked everyone politely, and appreciated his gifts—a saddle from his father, a chess set from Stephen, toy trains from his grandmother, an easel and paints from Katherine, a nice cap from Constance, a cowboy rope and hat from Mr. Henderson, and a James Audubon book and sketch pad from me and Robert. Cook Thomas had prepared a chocolate and cream cake, and the decorations Robert and I had spent the day making had given the parlor a festive air. Even Dobbs seemed to get into the mood of the party. After peeking into the parlor several times as Robert and I decorated, he finally marched in and declared we didn't know how to properly outfit the room, and then set about rearranging our efforts. Unfortunately, I had to admit to myself he had a better eye for decorating than I did, but I swore on my life never to tell him that. Not even in my deathbed confessions.

Yet I had the distinct impression that through it all, Justin was on the outside of the room looking in, as if none of us could really reach him or touch him. And I realized with a sickening dread that if Justin had fallen ill with the scarlet fever, neither I nor Benedict would have been able to reach his inner heart to will him to live. I sincerely believed he would have given himself over to the cold hands of death just to escape the pain he felt.

I was also worried about my conversation with Dr. Levinworth. He had no doubt that Benedict was guilty, but I had every doubt, and I wondered how I could prove him innocent.

A hand on my shoulder startled me. I looked up to see Katherine. It was unusual to see her in the garden this early, for she painted until late into the night and slept during the morning hours. Her ethereal beauty was even more breathtaking in the harsh glare of the sun. Blue-black highlights gleamed in her hair. Her amber eyes were made more golden by the rays of the sun, her skin more ivory, her lips more red, her delicateness more frail.

"Good morning," I signed, greeting her.

She took out a notepad and wrote, "*I saw you sitting here from my window. You looked sad, and I thought I would come see you. May I see what you are drawing?*"

I hesitated a moment, then handed her Justin's picture. She studied it intensely. I took the pad and wrote, "*I am worried about him.*"

She nodded and wrote, "*He, like those in my pictures, is a prisoner of pain.*"

I wrote back, "*I must find a way to help him heal.*"

She sighed, then wrote, "*For some there is no hope.*"

"*I refuse to believe that,*" I wrote her. "*Why do you imprison yourself?*" Then I paused, wondering if I was trespassing too far, then plunged ahead. "*Why did you not marry Mr. Simons?*"

Tears filled her eyes as she read my questions. "*It is a matter of honor,*" she wrote back.

"*How can a matter of honor forbid your and Mr. Simons's happiness?*" I wrote quickly.

"*How can I seek my own happiness when all those I love are trapped in pain? Besides, you have seen how little I can help Justin. What kind of mother would I make? I cannot even hear the cries of a baby.*"

"*But there are ways to overcome those problems. You can hire someone to be your ears. Are you not causing more pain by not giving your love and Simon's love a chance? Love brings hope to all. Your happiness could bring happiness to others.*"

She shook her head, telling me she didn't believe me. She went to hand me my sketchbook and accidentally dropped it. We both reached for it, but she picked it up first. The picture it fell open to was the one I'd drawn of Benedict after he'd kissed me in the stables. The one of him steering a ship through a storm, with the miniature of him kissing me in the upper corner.

Katherine's eyes widened. She ran a loving finger over her brother's image, then handed the pad back to me. "*You love him,*" she wrote in the pad.

I couldn't deny it. I nodded.

She shook her head sadly, then wrote again. "*You are cursed.*"

She dashed into the house, and I ran after her. "Katherine, wait," I shouted, forgetting in my need to stop her that she couldn't hear me. We bounded through the solarium and into the foyer, where Katherine came to an abrupt halt. I nearly ran into her. Mr. Simons stood in the foyer.

"Katherine." With her name on his lips, he sounded as if he'd been granted his greatest wish in life.

Katherine shook her head and stepped back, bumping into me.

She turned to look at me, her eyes wide and tragic. She looked back at Mr. Simons, then doubled over as if in pain.

Mr. Simons caught her shoulders, keeping her upright, making her face him.

The moment was so emotionally intense, I had to turn away from them, give them whatever privacy they needed. I went directly to the library and shut the door.

But I found I wasn't alone. I smelled his scent first.

Benedict, dressed in tan riding breeches and a loose white shirt, lay impossibly wedged on a small sofa, one leg bent at the knee and planted on the floor, the other sticking off the end. A book rested on his chest. One arm was thrown over his eyes; the other hung off the side, his hand lax upon the floor. The deep, even rhythm of his breathing told me he was asleep.

I didn't move. I barely breathed. I didn't want to do anything that might wake him. Since Robert's illness, he'd been looking more and more tired every day, as if his nights were as restless as mine. My gaze ran down his form, committing every nuance of his male contours to my memory. His broad chest and shoulders seemed capable of carrying the weight of the world, but I'd seen them bent in worry and grief. I knew a mortal man lay beneath his heroic stance. And that human vulnerability made him that much more dear to my heart. His hands, more than ample enough to cause harm, had tendered only gentleness. His legs, the long sinewy length of them, made me ache to feel them against mine, to be once again trapped against his study door with the hardness of his male arousal insistently pressing against me, making me want what no proper spinster should ever consider. The key to the secret passage hung in the balance between my breasts.

I longed to go to him in the restless mists of the midnight hours. It was as if no armor of practicality could protect me, nor threat of ruin dissuade me. I yearned to hold him within my arms as a woman holds a man more than anything else, and I felt I'd go mad for the want of him. I should leave Trevelyan Manor, but I couldn't bring myself to do so. So I stayed trapped, yearning, and yet knowing I could never have him.

Some women in the West were known to reach out and take what they wanted from life, whether what they wanted was in the bounds of propriety or not. I wished I were such a woman, at least just long enough to hold the man I'd grown to love.

Suddenly I tensed and tingled. My gaze darted up his body and met his. Heat and fire slammed into me with the force of a train at full speed. We stared at each other. Neither of us spoke. Neither of us had to. We both well knew the hot iron of desire branding us. He'd moved his arm up, just enough to watch me look at him. No heated blushes stung my cheeks. No oh-my gasps escaped my lips. I'd moved beyond that. I stood before him as a woman ready for a man, but the gap between us was too great a distance ever to cross. I turned my back to him and quit the room.

The moment I shut the door, I ran, my courage fading as I wondered if he'd pursue me, since I'd so boldly gazed upon him. I headed blindly for the day parlor, where our sign language lessons were usually held. Dobbs appeared out of nowhere. One moment my path was clear; next I had barreled into him, and we both went sprawling right into the suit of armor, which promptly toppled over. I'd never heard such a clattering din in all my life as the armor bounced over the marble.

Dobbs sat up, so utterly flabbergasted that he just looked about his wrecked foyer, speechless. Benedict came barreling out of the library. Justin, Robert, and Mr. Simons dashed into the room from the parlor. Stephen came flying down the stairs, and Mr. Henderson came in the front door with Constance at his side. I kept my composure, determined not to give in to the hysteria of laughter boiling in my stomach. But when Cook Thomas came to a skidding stop, his hat askew and a spoon dripping gravy clutched in his hand, I couldn't hold my mirth back any longer. "Mr. Dobbs . . . you . . . really need to . . . watch where . . . I am going."

"Watch where *you* are going!" Dobbs sputtered, his hair sticking straight out in undignified tufts.

Stephen started laughing, and everyone there succumbed to the hilarity one by one. Robert, Cook Thomas, Mr. Henderson, Mr. Simons, Benedict, Constance, and then, God bless my soul, Justin too. Whatever my dignity suffered, it was worth the price, though I'm not sure Dobbs would ever forgive me. I looked up at the stained glass, feeling the warm dots of color dance over me. Hope for a happy future filled my breast.

It took quite a while to settle down to our sign language lesson, but we eventually did so. Stephen and Constance joined us again. This time Constance didn't seem as determined to attract Mr. Simons's attention; she appeared distracted. I know I was. I kept wondering what the outcome of Katherine and Mr. Simons's encounter had been. Although it would be highly forward and completely improper, I decided that, if after the lesson, opportunity shone my way, I'd ask Mr. Simons about Katherine.

Timing handed me a golden opportunity. The boys went to Cook Thomas for lunch. Constance received a summons from Benedict's mother, and Stephen had something to give Mr. Simons and ran back to his room to get it.

I delved right in before I could change my mind. "Forgive this intrusion, Mr. Simons, but about you and Katherine . . . I care a great deal for her and can't help but see her pain. Nor can I find the strength to ignore yours. Is there more that stands between you than her fears of not being a good mother and her concern for her family?"

"No." He fisted his hands, his anger catching me by surprise. "If there were any way to change her mind, I would move heaven or hell to make her my wife."

"Does she know you love her that much?" I asked softly, wondering how Katherine could deny herself so great a love.

"She knows," he said tightly.

"I am sorry. I know she loves you."

"Not enough," he said, his anger spilling into an almost hopeless tone. "She does not love me enough to come to me no matter what." He sounded as Benedict had, saying that little Robert would die, that the doctor said there was nothing left to do.

"No," I said firmly, standing up and pacing across the room. "Maybe she does not know. Maybe you have not shouted it loud enough from the treetops. Maybe you have not lain siege to her self-imposed prison. Maybe you have not shown her the depth of your love. Maybe you have accepted the fate that she believes, so she sees no other future."

I quite lost myself in my supposing and came to a startled stop in the middle of the room. My speech must have been rather impassioned, because Mr. Simons was looking at me, completely surprised.

"Bravo, Miss Ann." Stephen stood in the doorway, clapping. "You wield a sharp sword. The Trevelyans' very own avenging angel. May nothing stand in your way until you slay all the beasts lurking within our lives." He turned to Mr. Simons. "Anthony, I think we need to do some strategy planning. Since Katherine will not let down her hair, there must be another way up to her tower."

"Then, gentlemen, I leave you to it." I quit the room, wondering if I weren't already going mad. I didn't quite know what to make of myself. I didn't seem to be the same woman who'd torn the employment notice from the window of Mr. McGuire's Bookstore. Or maybe I was.

The time for my riding lesson approached, and I promptly made my way to the stables. It was late afternoon. I'd finished with the boys' lessons, and left them with Stephen for horsey rides and a chess game. A lively wind whipped up from the bay with enough gusto to steal away the scent of the roses from the garden, leaving behind a briny smell that spoke of seaweed and salt and sailors. As I neared the stables, I could hear the waves crashing against the cliffs in the distance and the neighs of horses romping in the pasture behind the stables. Excitement pranced in the air and in my breast, and it wasn't the prospect of riding on the horse that had my heart dancing. Other than that brief moment in the library when I'd come upon Benedict sleeping, we hadn't been alone together since before I fell ill. We weren't going to be exactly alone today, but last I heard, the only tales horses carried were those firmly attached to their rears.

There were a number of things Benedict and I needed to talk about, and I had already made up my mind that if we argued about them and this led to his becoming aroused—well, so be it. I rather enjoyed his study door at my back—among other things.

Benedict, holding Gunnlod's reins, walked from the stable as I approached.

"Right on time, Miss Lovell," he said, his voice as cool as the breeze. If it weren't for the way his heated gaze took its sweet time rising up my body, I might have thought I'd imagined his heated look from the library sofa. "I have Gunnlod ready, so we can start immediately. Now, do you remember how to mount?"

I blinked. This rushed, businesslike interaction wasn't exactly how I'd pictured our lesson. I furrowed my brow, wondering with no small amount of irritation what had him on edge.

"Of course, I remember," I said. At his motion, I set my boot in the stirrup, grabbed the saddle horn, and slid gracefully into the sidesaddle. He adjusted the stirrups quickly and handed me the reins.

"The next step is up to you. The best way to ride is to feel. Tune your body to the movements of the horse. I am going to walk beside you and guide Gunnlod. I want you to shut your eyes and tell me what you feel as you ride."

He led Gunnlod to the copse of woods away from the manor, his strong hand clasping the leather strap of Gunnlod's bridle just below her ear. He was close enough that my skirts brushed his arm and his side. My gaze drifted across his broad shoulders, seeing the play of muscle beneath the thin cotton of his shirt, and my hands itched to feel the fabric. To feel him.

"Miss Lovell, I believe I asked you to shut your eyes."

I snapped my eyes closed. "They are, Mr. Trevelyan."

"Now what do you feel?"

Seeing as he was determined on this lesson, I concentrated on what he asked, surprised by the senses that seemed to take over now that I couldn't see. "She walks with a steady motion."

"Good. Relax into the rhythm. Do not fight it. Let yourself become part of it. What else do you feel?"

"Power."

"How can you guide that power the way you want to go?"

I opened my eyes. "I am not sure what you mean."

"The reins, Miss Lovell. You hold them. You are in control."

We were out of sight of the house, upon a path shaded with trees that shielded us from the bay breezes. Late-afternoon sunshine dappled through the leaves with penetrating warmth.

"Would you like me to show you how, Miss Lovell?"

I nodded, and he brought Gunnlod to a stop.

"Then shut your eyes again."

I shut them. "I am ready."

I felt his arm across my leg one moment, and the next he'd swung up behind me on the horse. His chest pressed to my back, and his arms came around mine as he slid his hands over my hands. I kept my eyes shut, not daring to open them, lest I break the spell that had him so very close to me.

"Ride with me," he said softly. His voice was deep and smooth against my ear and rumbled along my back through his chest. His thigh brushed mine as he urged Gunnlod into motion, and I opened my eyes, feeling a new world unfold before me. Minutes later we cleared the trees to a hilly stretch of grass that slowly sloped to the deep blue of the bay. He pushed Gunnlod into a canter, and we went racing across the turf. I could feel it all. The power. The freedom. The excitement. Experiencing the exhilaration within the safety of his arms made me feel as if heaven had reached down and carried me to the stars. He stopped on a knoll, and one of his hands left mine to curl around my stomach and press me tighter against him. His lips brushed over my ear.

"God help me, Titania. I can do naught else but fall beneath the spell you cast."

I leaned into him, turning my head to his questing lips. His mouth covered mine, his kiss demanding as his tongue sought to ease his burning need. Fire flared between us, insistent, desperate to feed its licking flames with my very soul. He leaned me back against his arm, urging me around on the sidesaddle's seat until I was completely sideways and could twist to press my breasts to him. I wrapped my arms around his neck, eager to touch him, feel him, know every curve, every silken hair, every ripple of muscle, every difference that made him a man.

One of his hands supported my back, and the other cupped my breast, spreading sweet fire to my loins. I moaned, arching to him, needing so much more than this embrace could give me. I slid my hand down his chest, pressing and kneading the contours of his chest and abdomen, moving down until I brushed his hard arousal. He groaned harshly, jerking as if he'd been shot.

"Every night I long for you," he said.

I placed my hand over his heart, absorbing its thundering beat. "And I you. It is most disconcerting to know that I care for naught else but your kiss, your arms, your love." My body froze. Love? I'd not meant to reveal my heart to him. Not ever.

He pulled away from me, groaning as if I'd stuck a dagger into him. I had to grab the saddle horn to stay upright.

"I am sorry," he said, moving back and sliding from the horse. As before, he kept his back to me, breathing deep, ragged breaths.

This couldn't be happening again. He couldn't be shutting me out as he had before. I refused to go back to being Miss Lovell in private.

"What is it?" I demanded. "What is it that drives you away from me?"

"Honor. What little I have left of it."

"But why? Is there not honor in love?"

He turned to me. "Do you understand that I cannot offer you love? The shadow of my wife's death hovers over my life. The world sees me as a murderer, and it is a burden I cannot allow any other to bear." His eyes were stark, burning coals that were turning to hopeless ashes.

"But the inquest ruled your wife's death a suicide." Though I knew that Francesca had been murdered, I found myself searching for ways to prove him innocent and to prove it to the world. Why wasn't he trying to prove to the world his innocence?

"The court ruled what I paid them to decree. Did you know that the rich can buy justice, Titania?" His voice rang bitterly. "The only thing I cannot buy is innocence."

Buy innocence? The blood drained from my head, rushing to my heart to keep it beating. Only one who was guilty would need to purchase that. Had he truly had a hand in his wife's murder? No. I knew that he hadn't. So who needed innocence? Then it hit me. Benedict wasn't trying to prove his innocence because he was protecting someone else. Someone he loved and felt responsible for. Who? Stephen? His mother? Katherine?

Cursing, Benedict turned from me. Then he took up Gunnlod's reins and walked back the way we'd come. We traveled in silence. I gripped the saddle horn with one hand. In the other, I pressed the secret passage's key against my heart. I wanted to prove him innocent.

For a man who claimed he didn't run away from complexities, Benedict was very good at avoiding me. At least, avoiding being alone in my company. By Saturday morning, I deduced from the servants' activities that Benedict was planning on leaving for a long business trip the next day.

Part of me thought that his departure would be best. We both needed time to reclaim our sanity. But another, more truthful part of me dreaded his leaving.

Longing for Benedict when he was gone was more difficult than longing for him when he was near, for when he was near, I had hope, and the ever-growing choice of going to him. When he was gone, I had nothing. Rather than brood in my room all day, I made my way to town—more for the need to clear my head than for any errands I had to attend. It didn't take me long to purchase the few items I needed; then I went to Mr. McGuire's. As always, he was relieved and glad to see me. Neither of us had any new information about Francesca's death, and I was reluctant to discuss the Trevelyan family too much. I feared my feelings for and involvement with Benedict would become too apparent.

I didn't want Mr. McGuire to learn that I'd been foolish enough to fall in love with the master of Trevelyan Hill. Nor did I want to hear another person claim him guilty. But Mr.

McGuire noticed my distraction, my evasiveness about his inquiries, and several times I caught him looking at me with concern and a question heavier than he wanted to ask in his watery blue eyes. I decided not to linger for the tea he offered. I was glad to see he'd kept his promise and hired an assistant, though. Manuelo was a boy of no more than twelve, but eager to help and more than capable of moving Mr. McGuire's cartons of books and climbing ladders.

Upon leaving Mr. McGuire's shop, I felt oddly strange, as if I'd lost my hold on something precious, but I refused to examine myself too closely. I didn't want to see anything that would sway me from the path I'd chosen. I went to the florist, deciding the single bloom that I could afford to buy more decorous than a handful of wildflowers. I bought two blooms at the last minute, deciding to place one on Francesca's grave for Robert and Justin.

At the cemetery, I stopped suddenly and ducked back into the shadows when I saw Constance at her sister's grave. Her voice drifted my way. She was talking to her sister as if her sister sat beside her, discussing a day of shopping. She held up a scarf, modeled it, then drew a hat from a box and put it on, asking Francesca what she thought of the combination. Constance had said that when she shopped, she shopped for her sister, too. Grief had many faces, and I was learning that some of them were very strange indeed. I left without her seeing me; some moments weren't meant to be disturbed.

Taking both of the blooms, I went to my mother's resting place, looking for the white wooden cross marking her grave. Only it wasn't there. I swung around, thinking I'd mistaken my way, but I hadn't. I was exactly where I should be, but . . .

Moving closer to the beautifully carved granite headstone, I looked with disbelieving eyes. There, etched in stone, was my mother's name. I read the words he must have remembered by heart: *Her life was as finite as the earth, but her love reaches beyond the stars.* He'd added another line. *Beloved and missed by her loving daughter Titania Lovell.* Tears filled my eyes and ran unchecked down my cheeks as I knelt near the headstone. Just as Robert had, I took my finger and lovingly traced every letter engraved upon the stone. Then I cried, not from sadness, but from the love bursting inside of me. Only one person on this whole earth had known of my precious wish, and his caring struck me deeply.

Taking lavender-scented water, I washed myself, scrubbing every part of me to a rosy, tingling awareness. Then, leaving off any undergarments, I put on a soft nightgown, one that I'd yet to wear from my treasured collection of clothes from Mrs. Talbot's Fashion Emporium. I followed that with my robe and slippers and brushed my long hair to a silky shine. Finally, I was ready. I could no longer deny my love, deny myself the memory of his passion. The grandfather clock struck the eleventh hour. I gathered my lamp and entered the schoolroom.

My hand trembled as I placed the key in the lock and turned it. The soft click seemed to echo in my mind. After tonight, there would be no going back. I'd chosen, and that choice would forever be etched upon my heart.

It took only a moment to descend and press open the panel to Benedict's room. He stood looking out the window of his room, wearing only his trousers, a drink in his hand. He didn't turn my way, though I knew he heard me. He could see me reflected in the glass. I set down the lamp, slid off my slippers, and slowly untied my robe, letting it fall from my shoulders into a puddle at my feet.

I watched him watch me. He took a drink, downing what was left in his glass in a single gulp.

"You should not be here, Titania. I am not strong enough for this, and I do not think you realize what you are asking for. I cannot marry you."

"I never thought that you would. I want to be here," I said. "And I do not want you strong. I want to feel and know your weakness for me, for I have a weakness for you that knows no boundaries, no shame." Stepping closer, I undid the top button of my gown.

"I cannot marry *any* woman," he said harshly.

With each step, I let loose another button, until I reached his back. "I am not asking for marriage," I said softly. "Only to know you." Then I pressed myself to him, wrapping my arms around him, laying my cheek against his warm, supple skin. He smelled of fresh sandalwood, and his skin was slightly damp, as if he too had just washed. I shut my eyes and breathed deeply several times.

I knew without a doubt that this was what I wanted, to know this man that my heart ached for, that my body longed for, that my mind fought for, that my spirit sang for.

"Please," I whispered softly. "Please do not turn away from me. Do not deny the passion that I never thought would be mine. Give me the gift and pleasure of being in your arms."

"Your gift is infinitely more worthy than mine." He groaned deeply, and his shoulders slumped as if he could no longer bear the weight resting upon him. When he turned to me, there were unshed tears in his eyes.

"Titania, my midsummer night's dream," he whispered. Laying his hands upon my cheeks, he directed my gaze to meet his. Then, holding my gaze captive, he kissed me slowly, with an exquisite gentleness that melted my soul. He spread kisses over my face, and with each brush of his lips, desire fanned hotter. I kissed him back, kissed the indentation in his chin, his bottom lip, and his corded neck. He threaded his fingers into my hair and kissed me harder, his tongue thrusting and seeking mine. I met him eagerly, my hands questing for every treasured nuance of his male body, the supple strength and power of his shoulders and back, the rugged ridges of his chest, the pleasurable intrusion of his hard thigh between my legs.

Instinct had me clamp my thighs around his, forcing his leg tighter against my femininity, so that when I arched to him, pleasure coursed through the damp flesh that ached to know his touch more intimately than before.

He pushed my gown down my shoulders, raking the soft cotton over my breasts before they sprang free, more than ready to feed his hunger for me. I stood naked before him as my gown slipped to the floor, but he gave me no time for shyness. Cupping my breasts, he pressed their peaks upward and laved them with his tongue, nipped gently with his teeth, then suckled my sensitive nipples to excruciating points of need.

"Benedict, please," I cried out to him, feeling as if I were fevered, on fire, and knew no source to bring me ease.

He swung me up in his arms and carried me to his bed, where he tossed me in his haste. I bounced once, then my eyes widened with surprise. He didn't unbutton his trousers; he ripped them open and shucked them down, snatching at the material covering his body until he stood naked, teeming with desire. Every movement, every ripple of his muscles, screamed that his passions were on the brink of exploding out of his control.

I ran my gaze along the full length of his male arousal, then up the full length of his body to meet his burning gaze. He stood there, both powerful and vulnerable at the same time, for there was a deep question in his eyes.

"I have not done this since Robert was conceived. I do not know how gentle I can be."

I opened my arms to him. "I welcome your passion, Benedict. I do not fear you."

He shut his eyes and exhaled as if he'd been holding his breath. He joined me on the bed, his hands trembling as he began exploring my body anew, setting me afire for more of his touch, for another of his kisses. This time he didn't stop his caresses at my breast; he moved lower, delving gently into my feminine flesh with his fingers. As before, he caressed me there until my hips undulated with the rhythm of his stroke.

"Titania, forgive me if this hurts, but the pleasure will come twofold if you relax, feel the movement, and move with me rather than fight the magic."

"I am ready," I whispered, but then had to question myself when he slid a finger into me.

I must have tensed, because he eased his finger out and stroked my most sensitive parts again.

"Believe me. God made a man and a woman to be together, and everything works beautifully."

"Show me," I said, drawing a deep breath. He urged my legs apart and slid between them. I felt the hard, insistent heat of his arousal press softly against my damp femininity. He angled up on his arms and looked down at me. Trembling with restraint, he slowly pressed into me. Just a little, then he stopped. I held my breath, waiting for something to happen, be it pleasure or pain. He moved a little more, then stopped again. My frustration over the matter built until I could no longer stay silent.

"Benedict, you are killing me—"

Groaning in pain, he froze, then tried to move back from me.

"No," I moaned, wrapping my arms around him. "You are making me insane with this infernal waiting." I pressed my hips to his. "Can you not make this happen any faster? I feel as if I am burning alive, and you've no water to douse my fire."

He blinked, groaned as if his agony knew no end, and then kissed me more deeply than before. I'd broken through his restraining wall, and his passion flowed over me. He pushed himself all the way within me in one thrust. I felt a burst of pain, then a burning that, when he thrust again, began to tingle with pleasure.

I opened my legs wider, wanting to feel more of him against me as his thrusts grew more and more insistent, until my body arched to meet his every move. My heart thundered, my blood rushed, and an ever-tightening need coiled in my loins.

"Ride with me," he demanded. "Feel me. Let yourself go with me."

I remembered our ride, the racing excitement, the freedom, and I shut my eyes, giving myself over completely to him and the frenzy consuming our passions. His body tightened, shuddered, and he pressed deeper. The force of his thrust lifted my hips high, and he slid his hand between our bodies, brushing over me just where I ached the most. Pleasure burst within me and went flooding through my body. I shuddered uncontrollably, totally at his mercy. But he was unmerciful. He thrust hard again, lifting my hips higher, pressing my head and shoulders deeper into the bed. Again his hand brushed insistently against my flesh as if he knew some magical place to touch me. Then an even greater pleasure tore through me, ripping apart my world with unimaginable sweet, agonizing pleasure. Stars exploded before my eyes, and his name exploded from my lips. I groaned softly as wave after wave of exquisite heaven washed over me. I was a mere grain of sand upon the shore of an ocean of pleasure, and Benedict was the tide of that new world.

❧ *20* ❧

"Titania," Benedict breathed as he lowered his lips to mine. He kissed me so softly that tears sprang to my eyes. His tenderness in the wake of the passion we'd just shared touched my heart with a sweetness I had never known. I wrapped my arms around him, pulling him closer to me, wanting to feel his heart as intimately against mine as I felt his arousal within me, but he held himself back.

"Let me hold you closer," I said.

"I will hurt you." His arms trembled with the strain of holding his full weight from me.

"I assure you, my constitution is not so fragile." I wrapped my arms tight about his neck and pulled hard. His arms gave away, and his full weight pressed me deeper into the bed. My breath flew from my lungs, and the immediate sensation of being close to him changed to one of being buried beneath the largest pile of laundry I'd ever known. I squirmed a little, trying to adjust, but couldn't seem to draw enough air into my lungs to function.

"Perhaps I was . . . a bit hasty in my estimation of my . . . constitution."

His chest shook with laughter before, in a lightning-quick movement, he was on his back, with me on top of him, and him still inside me. I placed my palms on his chest, lifting myself enough to see his smile.

"I find your constitution extremely pleasing," he said. His hands slid down my back, and when he reached my bottom, he quite shockingly cupped my rear end and firmly pressed me against him. Then he continued to caress my bottom and the top of my thighs, evoking a rather disturbing response. The need that I thought he'd satisfied well enough to last me to eternity heated again. "Do you know why?" he asked.

I shook my head, staring at him, not trusting my voice to work. He paused, and his eyes darkened as he seemed to realize how important his response was to me.

"Let me show you." Hooking his hands around my thighs, he urged me to bend my knees to his hips. Then he eased my shoulders back from him until I sat upright upon him. Without his body pressed to me, hiding my nakedness, a sense of vulnerability stole through me. I felt unsure until I saw the hungry look in his dark eyes. He arched a little, seating himself deeper inside me, and an increasing pressure told me he was more aroused as well.

"Besides the fact that you're are woman to my man, an irreplaceable and infinitely gratifying fact"—he threaded his fingers through my hair, arranging the long tresses over my breasts and shoulders—"your hair is like silk between my fingers, soft and minklike in color, especially in the sun. Many times since that first day when I checked you for an injury, I have closed my eyes and imagined threading my fingers through your hair again.

"Your eyes are the color of the early-morning mists upon the bay that I see from my window, and the sailor in me cannot help but want to explore deeper."

He brushed my hair aside and cupped my breasts, making me gasp with pleasure. "You have a fullness to your body that adds grace and stature to your height, which is a more perfect fit to me than any woman I have ever met. I can touch you without fearing that you will break." Urging me forward, he leaned up and suckled one breast, bringing it to an aching peak as his fingers did the same with my other breast. "You respond to my desire with the heat of a blazing fire. In fact, I have lived so long in the cold, I had forgotten how good a fire can be."

I sighed, arching to him as his thumbs relentlessly brushed over the peaks of my breasts until my hips responded to his every touch. He pressed upward to the rhythm of his strokes. Not deep and thrusting like before, just a slight rock that left me aching for more.

Understanding his words was becoming fearfully difficult. Inside me, the tension felt like a gathering storm.

He placed his hand over my heart. "You have a giving heart that knows no end to what it will battle for another.

"You have a mind that captured my interest with your first words and continues to pull me ever deeper into its complexities. And you have a mouth that inflames me not only when you are lecturing, but when you are silent as well." He lifted his finger to my lips and slid it inside my mouth, searching until my tongue brushed against his fingertip. A stab of pleasure darted all the way to my toes then back to my femininity, which he filled so completely.

"But it is your passion, Titania, that enslaves me and fires my imagination with the thousands of ways to bring pleasure to us both." He drew a wet line down the center of my body with his damp finger, and he didn't stop until he found that very sensitive flesh so near where our bodies joined.

Thousands? I wondered for a moment, but my body wanted nothing more than to lose myself within his. I vibrated with his every stroke, rocking gently, hearing the music of our lovemaking in the rushing of my blood. And he was a master caught within his own tune, because he arched off the bed like a string wound too tight, plucked too hard. This time the heaven and the stars slammed into me with the force of a runaway train, knocking the very breath from me. I fell against him, too weak to move, and he wrapped his arms around me, pulling me close.

"Whatever are we going to do?" he whispered.

Guilt tried to reach out and pull me from his arms, but I turned my back on it, refusing to let this moment of happiness escape me. "Thousands?" I asked, not capable of saying more. I fell asleep, listening to his soft sigh.

It was still dark outside when I awoke to Benedict's kiss upon my neck and his hands cupping my breasts. I lay on my side with him pressed against my back. Moaning softly, I arched my back and felt the heated hardness of his arousal against my bottom.

He slid his hand down my stomach and cupped my feminine flesh. I was surprised to feel a slight soreness there, but the brush of his finger upon that place he seemed to find so easily overrode my senses with pleasure. "Titania," he whispered in my ear, his voice deep and rough with sleep and desire. "We should not be here. We should not be together, but I cannot let you go. Will you come to me again? Tonight?"

I knew he spoke true. I never should have crossed the threshold of his bedroom door, but I had to know him, just as I had to love him. Just as I loved Robert and Justin. Just as my heart thirsted for more of life than I had. I wasn't ready to let go of him. I wanted more than one night to remember.

"Tonight will you let me show you more pleasure?"

"Now," I urged, wiggling against him.

He sighed, then chuckled. "I fear you're going to be the

death of me, woman. Or I of you. You need to rest some, or you will be too sore. But I want you to think about me pleasuring you. I want you to think about my kiss, my touch. I want you to think about me being inside you, filling your every desire. I want you to think about that all day."

Shifting my hip, I pressed against his hand, wanting more of his touch, feeling a little out of sorts. "Why ever did you get me so ... so ... expectant if I have to wait?"

"It is part of the fun," he said. Rolling from me, he patted my bottom lightly. "Now let's get you back to your room before we become fodder for the servants' gossip."

"More like torture than fun," I muttered, frowning at him as I sat up, clutching the sheet over my breasts. I stared at him with irritation as I watched him dress. His every muscle rippled with power as he moved. I couldn't help but notice how he filled everything. His trousers stretched taut across his buttocks and thighs, and his arousal made its own impression against the buttons. His shirt covered the breadth of his chest and shoulders like another skin; its tailored cut conformed to his every contour. His presence within a room seemed to take up any empty space, so that no matter which way I turned, I was aware of him there. Yes, the man filled everything to completion, but nothing more so than me. Tonight was an interminable time away. "Does that mean you are not running away on your business trip today?"

He turned to look at me, raising an eyebrow that said I'd best tread carefully. Then he sauntered to the bed and, with a devilish gleam in his eye, took hold of the sheet, snatching it away. His bold gaze roaming over my nakedness had me tingling everywhere. "No, I am not leaving. I am of the mind to delay that trip for a while and deal with the complexities here." He took another look at my "complexities." "And you, my dear, are seconds away from being completely ravaged this morning. But if you do not mind Dobbs walking in on that tableau, then . . ." He started unbuttoning his shirt.

"Dobbs?" I squeaked, scrambling from the bed. "Where's my nightgown?"

"Here," Benedict said, chuckling. Instead of handing me the gown, he put it on over my head, holding the sleeves out as I dressed, and then buttoned it up. He did the same with my robe and slippers, showing a gentle care in his every move. Taking up my lamp, he opened the door to the secret passage and led me to my room. Once there, he set the lamp down and pulled me into his arms, hugging me close to him. After a moment he stepped back, and with one hand on each of my cheeks, he gazed into my eyes. I saw so many things within the dark depth of his eyes that I wondered why I ever thought a woman would never be able to see his soul, because at that moment I did. I saw the soul of a man so needy that my heart ached for him, a man who'd stood alone so long that he no longer knew how to share the burdens he carried. I felt as if those burdens were going to suddenly descend and rip him away from me, for I could see the guilt lingering in his gaze, just as it lingered in my heart. But I refused to give it purchase on this moment of my life.

"Tonight," I said softly.

"Tonight." He sighed and placed a kiss upon my forehead, then left.

I stood there alone, seeing my reflection in the glass of the windows, wondering who the woman there was. She wasn't the same woman who'd come to Trevelyan Manor with determined practicality, but I liked her. I liked her warmth and passion and hope. The promise of dawn had yet to break through the mists surrounding Trevelyan Hill, yet I felt as warm as if I stood but inches away from the sun, and I turned my eyes away from any dark clouds looming ahead.

Come what may, last night would be forever mine. And tonight, too.

"Well, Robert," I said, looking down at the herbs we'd grown. "The plants will soon be big enough to pick and sell to Cook Thomas." Though it would be several weeks until we picked them, I thought it best to prepare Robert for what lay ahead.

Robert glared at the plants, looking upset. This wasn't going to be easy. The month since we planted them had passed in a blur of changes, all of which seemed to have hinged on the bond Benedict and I forged when Robert had been so ill. If that had not happened, I wondered if I would have gone to Benedict last night. Yes, I admitted, refusing to lie to myself. It might have taken me longer, but I would have eventually gone to Benedict, for I loved him.

Half a day had passed since he had seen me to my room, and I still felt all warm and wonderful inside, but troubled too. I wondered if I should question him about preventative measures against childbearing, but then I decided to educate myself about the matter first. I spent the morning in town scouring through the only other bookstore besides Mr. McGuire's. My search for material addressing the subject of how to avoid bearing children proved to be frustrating. I had but one medical book to show for my efforts, and I'd yet the time to read it.

Benedict's passion was more than I ever hoped to have, and I prayed with my whole heart that history wouldn't repeat itself, and have me bearing a child out of wedlock. That thought cast a dark shadow over the inner glow of Benedict's lovemaking.

How could I go to him a thousand times for pleasure and

not care that I would bear a child? I couldn't. Soon I would have to lock the door to the secret passage and throw away the key. But not yet. I would chance fate just a little longer before I denied myself my heart's desire. And I would thoroughly investigate methods to prevent childbearing, but I'd do so with a heavy heart, for I could think of no greater joy than to hold my very own baby within my arms.

As I looked at Robert and Justin, I longed to bear Benedict's child, to carry his seed within me and nurture it to life. But I well knew the difficulties of that kind of life, and I prayed that I wasn't already with child. I also knew I had to settle for what blessings I had. Being Justin and Robert's governess had brought a fullness to my life that was irreplaceable. My time with them today seemed to take on an even deeper meaning in my heart. Not only did I love them for their own sake, but they were also a part of the man I loved, and that seemed to make the bond I felt stronger. Justin sat on the blanket, drawing in his science notebook, ever distant from what was happening around him. And Robert was about to be Robert.

"They are not big plants yet," Robert said, stamping his foot. "They are still babies. How can they be all growed up when I'm not?"

Smiling, I brushed a lock of hair from his forehead. "Plants grow much faster than people do. They have to."

He scrunched his brow. "Why?" he asked, not liking this situation one bit.

"Because God made them that way. Every drop of dew and rain along with every beam of sunshine is sent to make plants grow fast so that people will have food to eat. It is His way of taking care of you. And you have to be wise about how you treat His gifts. Some plants are meant to live a long time, like trees, and other plants, like these herbs, are meant to die when winter comes."

"Does it hurt them to die like it hurts us?"

"No. Plants do not have feelings."

He took a deep breath. "So even if I keep these plants and take good care of them, they will die when winter comes."

"Yes."

Robert squatted down and brushed his fingers over the green leaves. "I do not want it to be that way."

"I know," I said, putting my arm around him. "Life rarely is exactly the way we want it to be. Part of growing up is learning to accept that and doing the best we can anyway."

"When I get as big as my father, can I make life the way I want it?"

"Not even then." I didn't have the heart to tell Robert that it was even worse when you were older. "But for now you are going to have to decide to do the best you can."

"You are sure I can't make the plants live forever?"

"I'm sure. It will be best to pick them in a few weeks, then plant more."

He sighed. "I will pick them, but only because it is the best thing to do. Can we plant a tree next time? One that I can keep for my very own always?"

"Yes," I said softly, wanting to make him my own and watch him grow into a man. But as with the sweet rose of Benedict's touch, I knew that someday I'd have to hold the bitter thorn of saying good-bye. I was not born to his world nor he to mine. I knew before I ever went to him that marriage was not something he could give to me, and hearing him say so last night came as no surprise.

I shook off my sadness, determined to let go of the thorns of my situation, and looked at Justin. He was alone; much as I sensed his father was alone. They were very much alike.

"Justin, why don't you come help Robert and me water the garden, and then we will have some special drawing time later for your science book."

Justin looked up and frowned, clearly not wanting to be a part of the project. It seemed to me that the step forward he had made by hugging Robert and going with us on the outing to town had resulted in him taking two steps back. Perhaps he was uncomfortable with revealing his fears, or with the affection he'd expressed to Robert.

He walked over to where we stood, but he didn't look at the plants. He looked at me, and he was angry. "When are you going to leave?"

I blinked, squatting down to meet his eyes. Robert grabbed my skirt, as if my departure was within the next moment. "I have no plans to leave here. I will stay and teach as long as your father allows me to do so. Why do you ask such a question?"

"Nurse Maria told Grandmama that you had to leave before it was too late."

"When did you hear her say that?" I wouldn't have been surprised if Justin had said that it was his grandmother who'd made the comment. That Maria had been the speaker seemed far past the boundaries of propriety. Why would she tell Benedict's mother that? *But what you were going to say to Benedict about Maria wasn't so different,* an inner voice taunted. Had Maria instinctively known that I thought she was unfit to care for Justin and Robert, given the tender state of their situation? I shook off the thought to focus on Justin's reply.

"When I went back inside to get my science book just a little while ago. If you are going to leave ever, I want you to leave now. I don't want you here anymore." Tears filled Justin's eyes, but his chin was set to a stony angle. He was so much like his father that my heart ached.

"Miss Wovellllll," Robert wailed, burying his face into my skirts.

Heedless of the dirt, I sat on the ground and pulled Robert into my arms. Then I held my hand out to Justin. "Come sit with me, and we will talk about this."

He took my hand. I could feel him trembling, and my insides twisted painfully. I had to blink back tears just so I could see. I pulled Justin down onto my lap, too. He didn't jerk away, so I drew a deep breath and wrapped my arm around him, too. "I swear to the both of you with every bit of my heart that as long as I can, I will stay here and teach you. But I have to be honest with you. I cannot be here forever. Nothing in life is forever, because it is always changing, always growing, sometimes in a good way and sometimes in not so good a way. Do you understand?" They both nodded, their brown eyes so darkly solemn that I wanted to cry, but I knew I couldn't. Instead I gave them the biggest smile I could muster. "There is one thing that I can promise you that my mother promised me."

"What?" Robert asked, sniffling.

"I can promise you that no matter what happens, no matter where you go in your lives, or I go in mine, that even if I should go all the way up to heaven, I'll love you forever. And you can take that love inside your hearts and keep it there no matter what. That's the promise my mother made to me, and even though she is in heaven, her love is in my heart, hugging me tight, and helping me whenever I need her."

"Do you wuv us, Miss Wovell?" Robert asked.

"Yes. I do. I love you both with all of my heart."

"Even if we are not always good?" Robert questioned.

"Even if you are not always good."

"Even if I hold on to thorns?" Justin whispered, so low I almost didn't hear him.

"Even then," I told him. Especially then, because that's when he needed love the most.

I dressed for dinner with a heaviness weighing in my heart over what Justin had heard. My mother couldn't promise me a forever, and I couldn't promise them a forever. But I could pledge my love to them, and I hoped that love would steal into their hearts and chase away the shadows hovering there.

Thinking about love brought my thoughts to Benedict. My love for him had grown even more after knowing the pleasure of his arms, and each minute that passed made me ache to be with him. That ache also brought apprehension, for I'd yet to read about preventative measures for child-bearing.

I hurried down to dinner, thinking that the sooner I got there, the quicker the evening would pass, and the more time I would have to find an answer to my dilemma. As it turned out, I was a quarter hour early, and no one else had arrived yet. Moving over to the window, I almost had to press my nose to the glass to see through the room's reflection in the glass to the gathering night outside. The sun, a big orange ball in the sky, seemed to be bouncing on the horizon, and with each slight drop, a little less of it could be seen. The sky was bathed in a purple-red glow, so vibrant I had to squint my eyes to watch it.

Even if I hadn't seen his approach reflected in the glass, I would have known he was there.

He didn't touch me. He didn't have to, for me to know he stood but an inch away from me. I could feel the heat of his body, smell the scent of sandalwood and spice, and sense my every feminine nerve spring to attention.

"It is almost nighttime, Titania," Benedict whispered in

my ear. "Have you given thought of what that means today?"

"Yes," I said softly as pleasure shot to my toes.

"I have thought about you all day, too. I know just where I am going to kiss you. I know just where I am going to touch you. I know just how I am going to come in—" He stepped to the side and pointed out the window. "It is indeed a beautiful sunset, Miss Lovell. Come tell us what you think, Alan."

I looked around to see Mr. Henderson step into the room. Benedict had to have the instincts of a mountain lion, for I swear, not only could he hear the impossible, he was a deadly predator to a woman's sensibilities as well. My heart pounded, and my underclothes became damp. My blush felt as if it blazed as red as the sunset. I could only hope Mr. Henderson would somehow think the hue of my cheeks was due to the reddish cast of the sun through the window.

I took a step back and nodded toward Mr. Henderson. "How are you today, sir?"

"Excellent," he said, walking our way. He glanced out the window. "It is a noteworthy sunset, but it in no way compares to you, Miss Lovell. I must say I have never seen you looking lovelier." He leaned closer to me, peering at me intently.

My word! Were last night's activities engraved on my forehead? "Thank you," I said lowering my lashes. "It must be the dress."

"I think we are just seeing Miss Lovell regain her health after being so sick. Did your meeting with the Bryson Company go well today?" Benedict thankfully diverted Mr. Henderson's attention, and I hurried over to the sofa to sit and hopefully escape anyone else's notice. It was most unfair of Benedict to fire my thoughts and senses while I had yet hours of propriety imprisoning me.

Perhaps there was more of the devilish gleam of the demon door in Benedict than I thought. The man was a master at creating expectations—and fulfilling them, too.

Stephen entered the room, escorting Constance and Katherine. Everyone seemed to be ignoring the emotional outbursts that had occurred at dinner the other night. And I wondered if that was the way things were always dealt with in polite society: never directly confront and resolve issues, but skirt around them and ignore the moments when an ugly face chooses to reveal itself. It didn't seem to be a healthy way to live, like never laundering your clothes, and I could see the effects showing upon everyone. Constance's smile was overbright, her chatter about fashion more effusive and less coherent. Stephen's smile wasn't anywhere in sight. He'd taken on a brooding air that made his once laughing blue eyes haunted. Katherine, who always looked so serene, seemed almost fearful, as if she didn't dare take another step for fear that she'd fall. Even Mr. Henderson's presence within the home had taken on a hovering sense. I couldn't decide if he played the role of a bird of prey waiting to strike or a mother hen looking to save, and I wondered if he, too, had played a role in the events surrounding Francesca's death.

"Where is Mother?" Stephen asked as he glanced about the room. "I thought we would be the last to arrive, since Katherine and I waited for Constance."

Constance rolled her eyes. "Everyone thinks that it is easy for a woman to be beautiful, no? I tell you, it takes a lot of time and a tremendous amount of effort. Maria spent two hours on my hair alone."

I never thought I'd pity Maria, but perhaps I judged her morose attitude too harshly. I wouldn't be cheerful if I'd the task of arranging Constance's hair for two hours. Then I wondered exactly what Constance and Maria talked about during that time. Did Maria also tell Constance that I had to leave before it was too late?

I had considered confronting Maria when I saw her next, but perhaps I could speak to Constance about the matter. Maria would be a prime candidate for being the author of the threatening note and the destruction to the boys' garden. I'd eliminated her before because I believed Benedict's mother innocent of the deeds, but what if Maria was acting on her own?

"True beauty does not need hours to prepare, Constance; only vanity does," Mrs. Trevelyan said.

Everyone turned to look at the doorway, and gasps of surprise followed. Mrs. Trevelyan, dressed in her customary black gown and dour expression, stood upright with the aid of a cane instead of being ensconced in a wheelchair.

"Well, do not gawk. Stephen, help me to the dining room. Benedict, I have realized in my grief that I have been extremely remiss in performing the duties of mistress of this household. Rest assured that will no longer be the case." She looked directly at me, and my stomach clenched.

I stood to join the group for dinner, though my knees were even shakier than before. It seemed to me that Mrs. Trevelyan could have been induced to leave the safety of her chair only by a monumental event. And as far as I could tell, the only thing of significance that had happened recently was last night when I went to Benedict's bedroom. The butterflies in my stomach turned to rocks for a few minutes before I decided I was reading too much into Mrs. Trevelyan's seemingly miraculous recovery. Surely there was no way anyone else could know what had happened last night between Benedict and myself.

≈ *21* ≈

It was half past the eleventh hour before I finished reading the medical information about contraception. I'd readied myself to go to Benedict's room the moment I'd returned from dinner, which turned out to be uneventful despite Mrs. Trevelyan's dramatic appearance. Everyone seemed to be in a hurry to dispense with the formalities and attend to other things, all except Constance. As the meal progressed she seemed to become unusually quiet; then, during the last course, she pleaded a headache and left. I wondered why. Could Mrs. Trevelyan's recovery and intent to take up her responsibilities bother Constance? I pushed aside the question to face tomorrow. I had other things on my mind tonight, and it was necessary to discuss my findings of preventives with Benedict. The situation looked dismal.

Gathering my lamp and key, I hurried through the passage to his room. He swung around the moment I stepped through the panel's threshold. His hair was a hand-raked mess, his features harsh, and his dress rumpled.

"I thought you were not coming."

I drew a bolstering breath and decided to tackle the issue immediately before I lost my nerve. I held up the medical book. "I have been doing a bit of research, and we have several . . . complexities to address before we . . . undress."

Benedict, in the process of advancing toward me, came to a halt. He crossed his arms over his chest and frowned. His feet were planted in a stance of a ship's captain steering his vessel through a storm. "Exactly what *complexities* did you have in mind to discuss, Titania?"

I cleared my throat, and found that I needed to pace to proceed. I turned away from him and strode across the room. "The complexities we need to address deal with preventative methods in regards to contraception. I realize it's somewhat improper of me to bring up this discussion, but we aren't necessarily being proper, um, together. And considering my circumstances, I have no one else to confer with about the matter. And since you seem extremely well versed in these acts of passion, I thought perhaps you would have more information concerning these various methods."

I paced back toward him, daring a glance at his face, knowing my own had to be scorching red. He had both his brows raised. "Acts of passion? Well versed?" he repeated dryly.

Humph. Not a very helpful response. "You know," I said, waving my hand toward the bed, "those things that you did last night. Now, according to this medical book, there are several female preventatives available."

"Really," he said. "Do tell."

My mouth went dry. "You mean you want me to describe them?"

"That would be a start," he commented. His expression didn't reveal anything he might be thinking.

"Well, according to this book, a female syringe and chemicals can be purchased for contraceptive purposes, but I haven't exactly figured out when one is supposed to use such a device. The book doesn't really say."

"How remiss of it. Is there more?"

"Very little, I'm afraid. In their discussion of contraceptive instruments they refer to a female preventative known rather oddly as a pisser, but I have not quite decided what good cotton or a silk-wrapped sponge with a thread attached would do other than be rather uncomfortable. That only leaves us with coitus interruptus, I am afraid."

Benedict's chest heaved, and I realized the incorrigible man was holding back laughter. "Coitus interruptus, did you say?"

"Most certainly, though it reportedly has ill effects upon a man's constitution." I stopped pacing and crossed my arms to tap my foot in irritation. "This is not a laughing matter. I find it rather dismal that science can make a telescope to see planets in the heavens, but has very little knowledge when it comes to female parts."

"Coitus interruptus," Benedict said, then gasped for air, only to howl again with laughter.

I wanted to hit him with the medical book I held. Instead I marched over to him and shoved the book into his chest. "When you recover from your mirth and can address the discussion with maturity, perhaps we will have something to talk about."

Then I turned on my heel and marched determinedly in my slippers—not an easy task, for they weren't meant for marching—back to the secret passage.

"Titania, wait," Benedict said, catching me and wrapping his arms around me to pull me back against his chest. "I am sorry. Your rather direct manner caught me off guard, though I should not have been surprised."

"This is important, Benedict," I said, feeling a sting of tears in my eyes, which he must have sensed because he immediately swung me around to face him.

He looked deep into my eyes and brushed hair from my damp cheek with a gentle finger. "I am sorry," he said softly.

"Please understand. I cannot negligently let a child bear

the stigma that my mother accidentally placed upon me."

"As far as I can see, there is only love upon you. But I understand what you are saying. The truth of the matter is that I spent the whole of the day addressing this very issue."

I blinked. "The whole of the day? How?" I was amazed to see him wince.

"Well, you might say I too went on a fact-finding mission. The results of which we will employ at the proper moment during our, how did you phrase it? Acts of passion?"

"You have a contraceptive instrument? Where did you purchase it? Which one?"

"Well, I conferred with several women known for their female services to men and received advice at a few parlor houses that cater to such services. The result is that I determined the best contraceptive isn't a female device. There's something out for men to use, though I had a difficult time finding a supply of them here in San Francisco. Few men are choosing to use them, and I must admit that I'm not even sure I will find it all that comfortable, but I'm hoping that the pleasure of our 'acts of passion' will override any problems."

"A male device? What are they made of?" I asked, for I'd read about the use of certain things that I would never consider getting near.

Benedict laughed. "You read too much, my dear. These contraceptives are made of a harmless, somewhat elastic substance." He slid his hands down my back and pulled my hips against his. "Now I think it's time we practiced a little coitus noninterruptus."

I pushed him away and turned my back. "You are making fun of me."

"No. I am not. I am amazed and delighted with you." Once again, he slid his arms around me and pressed himself intimately against my back. His hands delved into the opening of my robe and cupped my breasts. "Let's make that very amazed and delighted." He brushed my hair away from my neck with his chin and kissed the tender skin just behind my ear.

My breath caught, and I shivered with the need to touch him. Raising my arms, I threaded my fingers through his hair, pressing his kiss deeper against my neck.

"Did you think about me today, Titania? Did you think about where I would kiss you? Did you think about where I would touch you?"

"Yes," I said, arching my breasts against his questing hands.

"I thought about you, too." Moving like a master, he opened my robe, and urging my hands down, slid it off my shoulders. Then he pulled off my nightgown, leaving me unclothed. I had but a moment to shiver before the warmth of him covered my back. His kisses began at the top of my spine, his caresses began at the tips of my breasts, and the magic fire he spread ignited my senses as he moved down my body. His kissed every inch of my back, making me tingle in new places. His hands molded my breasts, soothed their way over my stomach, then explored their way down my legs. He touched me everywhere but the very place I needed him most.

"Benedict," I said urgently, wanting him to abandon his leisurely pace.

"Shh, Titania. Let me know you the way I need to." He turned me around to face him. He was on his knees before me, looking up at me with such a naked hunger burning in his dark eyes that I nearly took a step back from the force of it. Instead, I set my hands upon his shoulders and urged him to remove his shirt. He shrugged it off, leaving the broad expanse of his shoulders, back, and chest open to my touch. I eased my hands over his head, down his neck, and across his shoulders, slowly, gently, committing every indentation, every sinewy ripple, to memory.

He shuddered beneath my touch and bowed his head, letting his forehead rest upon my stomach as he drew in ragged breaths. My heart tripped over itself at his vulnerability. How could I, so spinsterish a maid as I was, bring such a man to his knees? I never thought it possible, never believed that I would be a magical queen with a knight at my feet. But perhaps he was a man who looked upon the beauty of the heart.

Humbled, I eased myself to my knees, letting Benedict's head brush up my stomach, between my breasts, and finally to my lips. I kissed him tenderly on his forehead; then, looking deeply into his eyes, I pressed my lips to his. Silently, with everything in me, I told him I loved him in the kiss.

The tenderness disappeared beneath a wave of passion as he kissed me back, holding me in place by cupping my neck. His tongue delved into my mouth, searching and questing to mate with such fervor I thought there'd be no end to his hunger.

I felt his other hand unbutton his trousers and then the heat of his insistent arousal against my stomach. I started to reach for him to touch him there, where he must ache for me as I ached for him, but he raked his hands to my bottom and jerked me against him. My hands went to his shoulders to balance myself, and my thighs spread to the outside of his.

"Wrap your legs around me, Titania, and hold on tight," he urged, pressing my femininity closer to him.

I hooked my legs around his hips. He locked his arms around my back and stood, holding me against himself. Then he carried me across the room to the bed and set me upon the soft mattress.

"We have things to explore."

"Things?" I said, turning to look at what he meant. Neatly set on a table beside the bed were a number of vials of different colored liquid and a couple of other "things" I didn't quite know what to make of. It would seem his penchant for the unusual applied to something besides naming horses. I was rather intrigued with the "things."

Keeping one arm around me, Benedict picked up a vial of amber liquid that had already been opened. I gave the vial a wary look. "Uh, Benedict, shouldn't we discuss these things?"

He swirled the liquid in the glass, then waved it beneath my nose. "Fragrant oil, my dear. Smell."

I breathed in. The scent eased like warm butter over my sensitive nose, bringing to mind a rather exotic scent, something that I may have possibly smelled once when my mother and I visited a woman of Asian descent for a healing herb. The smell made me tingle inside, similar to the way Benedict's sandalwood and spice did. "Oh," I said, leaning forward to take another whiff.

"Not too much," he said, slipping the vial away. "The lady called it Ambrosia and said to use but a little in very special places." He set the vial down, picked up a glass tube, and dipped it into the oil. "Let me have your hand, Titania."

He spread the oil across my fingertips. They tingled. He guided my hand to his arousal. "Touch me."

My breath caught, but I didn't hesitate to feel him. Iron hardness, velvety smoothness, and throbbing heat were the words that first came to my mind as I spread the oil over his maleness. He groaned and shuddered.

"My turn now," he said gruffly. Putting oil on his hands, he eased my legs apart and smoothed the oil over my damp femininity. I gasped and shuddered as an arousing tingle flowed over my flesh.

"Benedict," I breathed, grasping for his shoulders. My need to have him within me became suddenly urgent.

"I know," he said, sounding desperate. He quickly sheathed his arousal and pressed himself inside me. I scooted closer to him, needing more. Frantic to have more.

Sliding his hands beneath me, he drove himself deep inside me. I gazed up at him, meeting his hungry gaze with mine. He stared into my eyes, and he thrust himself into me. My hips arched to him, caught up in the heated storm overtaking us both. His hands covered my breasts, and the residual Ambrosia on them set me even more on fire. I met his hips with thrusts of my own, caught up in the fervor of reaching that heavenly satisfaction before I went up in flames.

But satisfaction kept slipping from my grasp. Perspiration beaded my skin and dripped from his burgeoning muscles. Our bodies crashed together like waves upon the cliffs, moving so fast that all movement became a blur.

"I am going to die," Benedict said, his every syllable like a shattering glass.

"Take me with you," I cried, moaning.

Benedict grunted as if he knew no greater pain, no greater pleasure. And just when I thought we were about to truly expire from a frenzy of unquenchable passion, the pinnacle came in a bright burst of light and a soul-dousing wash of exquisite pleasure.

He shouted, and went taut. Then he crashed on the bed beside me. Neither of us could breathe, and both of our hearts were pounding so hard and so fast that our chests were quivering.

"Perhaps . . . it would be . . . best to . . . read about . . . certain things . . . before we use them."

He rolled over and put his arm around me, seemingly recovering faster than me. "If anyone ever wrote that down and passed it around, humanity would be doomed. They would all be in the bedroom, and the world would come to an end."

"Surely . . . not everyone . . ."

He lifted a questioning brow, amazing me that he had the stamina to lift anything. "Where would you be?"

"Perhaps you have a point."

"Perhaps?" he asked, pulling me against him.

He definitely had a point, but I thought it best to let him wonder about it. So I shut my eyes and snuggled up to him, hoping I'd be able to move before Dobbs made his morning appearance. I didn't have to worry. Benedict made sure my reputation didn't suffer.

My desire to be with Benedict seemed to know no limits. It grew from each minute to each hour, and from each hour to each day as the week passed. I spent my days with his sons and my nights in his arms. Thoughts of him consumed me, and today seemed to be worse than ever. I just had to see him, even just to hear his voice.

Stephen had sent word that he'd come to the schoolroom after tea to play chess with Justin and Robert. I decided that I would seek out Benedict then, for just a moment. Justin and Robert, having finished their lessons, were once again playing with the wooden horses. This time they'd built a fort out of the blocks and were hiding from the bad witch in the fort. Stephen walked in just as Justin shouted, "All is lost, but we're going to fight to the end, Sir Robert."

Stephen smiled at the boys' play. It was the first I'd seen him smile in a while. "We used to play like that, Benedict and me, and Katherine, too. We were knights pledging to uphold all things honorable and true, and Katherine was the queen we protected with our dying breaths. But I could never quite match Benedict's strength. He always prevailed, and I'd fail. Odd, how childhood games can often mirror our lives."

My heart clenched for Stephen; growing up in Benedict's shadow must not have been easy. "I suppose life does mirror our childhood sometimes," I said, thinking back upon the days in Holloway Park that I'd dreamed of those here in Trevelyan Manor. Perhaps just by dreaming, I'd placed myself within it.

"I have given a lot of thought to what you said to me the other night in the garden. I was in my cups, but your words still hit home. Standing like a man to face my sins is going to be a tall order to fill."

I took a deep breath and ventured a guess. "Isn't that why you came back?"

His eyes widened in surprise. "Yes, but the doing of it turned out to be a great deal more difficult than I expected."

"When I was younger, I would arise in the morning and look at the huge task of washing mountains of clothes with dread. My mother always seemed to know what troubled my heart, and she said, 'Just as a babe learns to walk one step at a time, a man climbs a mountain, or a woman raises a child alone.' Any of life's tasks, no matter how great, can be achieved by so simple a way as one step at a time. And when the heart is willing, the job is easier. I sense your heart is willing."

"So you think I can redeem myself one step at a time?"

"I believe so."

"You do not hate me for what I did, do you?"

I sighed, since loving Benedict as I did, I found I could not condemn another for loving. "I do not condone what you did, and I believe that you are truly repentant. I see a great many worthy things within you, and I believe the greatest sin of all would be to let those things die by drowning yourself in drink and self-pity."

"The avenging angel bestows mercy. It is a gift that I will cherish and not waste."

"I am but a governess who prides herself on being practical as much as you thrive on drama. Perhaps once you have taken truths to heart, you should put them to pen after all, and try your hand at poetry. It may be that you will write the words that will keep others from your folly."

"I think I just may do that."

"Uncle Stephen, I drew a picture of Cesca in my notebook. Do you want to see her?" Justin came up, holding the drawing pad I had given him for his birthday. My heart swelled a little. Justin was returning to the circle of his family, one small step at a time.

Stephen paled, and I realized that though Justin referred to his pony, Stephen would always think of Francesca when he heard the name. I left, asking Stephen if he wouldn't mind taking the boys down to Cook Thomas for dinner after their chess game. I wondered if one small step at a time was going to work for Stephen.

And what about myself? I'd made very little progress in figuring out what had really happened to Francesca. This whole week I'd thought of nothing but being in Benedict's arms. He had a way of making everything else become unimportant.

Walking down the hall, I realized that it had been quite some time since I'd had the sensation of being watched. In fact, I think the last time I'd felt it was when I'd gone through and opened all of the doors. Tackling things in a direct manner worked.

Thankfully, Dobbs wasn't standing guard in the foyer, and I took my time, turning circles through the dancing colors of light, lifting my face to their warmth. A soft laugh escaped from me as I realized I was so full of love that my heart was bubbling over with it.

"May I?" Benedict asked.

Swinging around, I came to an abrupt stop. He stood, leaning against the frame of his study door, his arms crossed, the length of his legs molding buckskin-colored breeches to an almost indecent degree. But it was the sensual question in his dark eyes that made my senses tingle and my insides turn all buttery.

"May you? I'm sorry, I must have missed what you said."

"You have not missed anything yet, Miss Lovell, I assure you. Come, I will show you." He held out his hand. Crossing the few feet separating us, I placed my hand in his. The warm strength I always associated with his touch eased into me. He led me into his study and shut the door, then pulled me into his arms.

"May I have this dance?"

I blinked up at him, my heart melting even more at the curve of his smile. Little things about him, a look, a touch, the timbre of his voice both in passion and in pain, kept redefining my world, kept picking me up, swirling me around, and when everything settled, nothing was the same again.

"Would that I knew how to dance," I said softly. "For dancing in your arms would indeed be a treasured memory."

I saw his eyes darken, as if he knew what we shared couldn't go on forever, just as I knew it.

"Then let me have the pleasure of showing you." He caught up my hand, firmed his hold on my back, and swung me around. I found myself stepping with him, not unlike swirling within the dancing lights of the stained glass windows. When he stopped minutes later, I was quite breathless.

"May I have this kiss?" he asked, but didn't wait for an answer. He bent to me, his lips capturing mine with a quest-

320 JENNIFER ST. GILES

ing fervor that matched our midnight adventures. Pressing against him, I moaned, my body instantly awakening to the call of his passion.

His arms wrapped around me, his leg found purchase between mine, and his palm cupped my breast through the thin muslin of my dress. I slid my hands over the hard contours of his shoulders and back, feeling the remarkable breadth of him and wondering how he could be so gentle and yet so strong. Then I ventured lower, remembering how his breeches had clung to him, and knowing that I'd feel the hard length of his arousal, straining against soft cotton. I pressed my hand over his need, wanting to give him as much pleasure as he gave me. He shuddered and responded with an even greater, insistent need.

"May I have you?" he asked, his voice strained and as intense as the hammering of his heart.

"Yes," I said, arching to his touch, wanting him as much as I wanted to breathe. "But what about—"

"Interruptus, thy name is heaven," Benedict said, kissing me harder.

"But . . . what about . . . the detriment to your . . . constitution?" I asked between kisses.

"As you are wont to say, my constitution is remarkably strong."

"Strong constitutions are a very good thing to have, Benedict. Especially right now." Minutes later I was half sitting, half reclining in his massive wing chair, my skirts hiked up and my drawers snatched down. Benedict kneeled between my legs, his arousal freed from its cotton prison and sliding inside me, driving me heavenward. At some point, the light-heartedness fell away like a mask being torn from us, and the desperation of our passion, made even starker by the light of the day, revealed itself. I knew this time we were stealing together wouldn't last, but I couldn't let him go. I couldn't find the strength to deny myself his touch.

I was still shuddering with the force of our passion when a knock sounded on the study door.

Dear God, not only had I lost any sense of practicality I'd ever possessed, but I had to have lost my mind with it. The look on Benedict's face seemed to mirror my own horror.

"The window seat, behind the curtains. Hide there quickly." He stood, scrambling to fix his breeches. "Go," he urged.

Standing up, and trying to hold on to my drawers as my skirts fell down, I rushed to the window and dove behind the curtains onto the cushioned seat. It took me but seconds to gather my skirts and curl myself into the space. I was slightly cramped, but not terribly so.

It wasn't until another sharp knock resounded that I heard Benedict open the door.

"Benedict, I need to speak to you about a troublesome situation." Mrs. Trevelyan's voice cut straight to my stomach, making it flip-flop with nausea.

"Mother, this is not a good time. Might we discuss this before dinner? You are walking well enough that I will take you on a stroll through the garden."

I thought I was about to expire with embarrassment. The position I'd placed both of us in was completely intolerable. I should have stayed in the schoolroom or my quarters.

"The matter is rather private, and I do not wish to be overheard. I will take but a moment. Are you feeling well?" Mrs. Trevelyan asked.

"Yes. Very well," Benedict said, sounding harried. "But this discussion really needs to wait."

"You look flushed," Mrs. Trevelyan said.

Could this situation become any more horrendous?

"Just returned from riding Odin to a business matter that needed my immediate attention," he said.

Yes, I answered my own question. Much more horrendous. Riding Odin indeed.

"Then I'll get right to the point. I realize that Miss Lovell is doing a fine job with Justin and Robert, but I have some serious reservations about her continued presence here."

"Mother, we discussed this once, and I said the subject was closed. Miss Lovell has proved herself to be an exemplary governess."

"But at what cost, Benedict? I hesitate to say this, but I must. Have you seen the way Stephen looks at her? The boy has found another angel to worship. And I have seen you watch her, too. It is happening again. The whole sordid situation that happened with Francesca, only this time over the reddened hand of a washerwoman. I will not have it. She does not belong here. She's another charity project you have allowed yourself to become responsible for. Just like that lad you hired, who then ran off with the silver. Just like that woman you—"

"And I will not have this," Benedict's voice lashed out. I flinched, shoving my hands beneath my skirt, for not even I could look at my reddened skin.

The room vibrated with the force of Benedict's anger. "Stephen ceased to be a boy at least ten years ago. It is time you stopped pandering to his sensitivity just because he's like Father. Perhaps then he will find the strength to stand without a drink in his hand. And washerwoman or not, Miss Lovell shows more strength of character and intelligence than any simpering lady of social standing dillydallying through life."

"That does not change the facts, Benedict. So it would behoove you to stop pandering to the fantasy of—"

"Of what, Mother? That a man's worth should be measured by his word rather than his ancestry? The world is changing."

"Not that much. This is not the deck of your ship. This is a city with a social structure that must be adhered to. And you had best remember it before you damage this family and your sons. Find Miss Lovell a post somewhere else. Preferably East. And find a male tutor for Robert and Justin, as you had planned to do. Do it before it is too late."

Benedict didn't say anything, and I heard the study door shut. I closed my eyes and fought for the breath that the truth of his mother's words had stolen. Though I sat in the basking warmth of the sun shining through the glass, I grew cold inside.

Benedict pulled open the curtain, and I turned from him, too shamed to face him.

"Titania," he said, reaching for me, pulling me against him even through I fought him. "I am sorry. You must not take her words to heart. She's of a different era and does not understand."

I shook my head, not believing him.

"Please, do not turn away." His voice deepened with emotion. "Robert needs you. Justin needs you. And God help me, so do I."

I could not keep from him. I turned to him, burying my face against the surety of his chest, and I wrapped my arms around him. I wouldn't let myself cry. I wouldn't let him know, for he'd surely try and argue, but I knew his mother had spoken true. It cut me deeper than any pain I'd ever known to realize that the more I stayed within the circle of his arms, the more I'd rather die than leave him. To stay here long enough to help Robert and Justin, I could no longer be with Benedict. But I couldn't force the words from my mouth. I needed time to think, to figure out the best way to say all that was in my heart. Tonight, I would have to tell him.

22

The rest of the evening passed in a blur. I dressed for dinner, spoke to the children, went to the parlor. I smiled when I was supposed to, spoke when appropriate, and managed to push my food around on my plate so that no one noticed that I barely ate a thing. I couldn't. I was crying inside, hurting as much as I hurt when my mother had passed away. Maybe even more so, for I'd a long time to prepare for her passing. With Benedict, I felt as if I had to rip him from my heart while I still had strength enough to keep it beating when I did. But I thought it was too late already.

Benedict looked my way several times, a worried frown marring his chiseled features. But I could tell by the pointed effort he made to keep his distance from me that he was as much aware of the eagle eye of his mother as I was.

Tonight of all nights, it was decided to return again to the music room. It wasn't until we all entered the room that I realized I'd paid little attention to the others. I hadn't even looked at Stephen, and I wondered if he was as enamored with me as his mother seemed to think. When I sent a nervous glance his way, I found him looking at me with an odd expression, almost as if he was worried about me.

"I have a recitation that I would like to do for everyone

tonight," Stephen said. "And I would like to dedicate this especially to Miss Ann."

My breath froze in my lungs. No, Stephen, I thought. Your timing couldn't be worse. I shot my gaze to Benedict, only to see his jaw clench.

Mr. Henderson, who stood near Benedict, seemed to catch the sudden tension and set a hand on Benedict's shoulder. "It has been quite a long time since you've done a recitation, Stephen. I have missed your flair for such things. What did you have in mind?"

"Words from the master of witty prose, Shakespeare. And tonight I would like to share with you the wisdom of Portia, the rich heiress of Belmont, from *The Merchant of Venice*, as she speaks of mercy as a 'gentle rain from heaven.' " Stephen stood, cleared his throat and began his speech.

> *"The quality of mercy is not strained;*
> *It droppeth as the gentle rain from heaven*
> *Upon the place beneath: it is twice Blest,—*
> *It blesseth him that gives and him that takes:*
> *'Tis mightiest in the mightiest; it becomes*
> *The thronèd monarch better than his crown;*
> *His sceptre shows the force of temporal power,*
> *The attribute to awe and majesty,*
> *Wherein doth sit the dread and fear of kings;*
> *But mercy is above this sceptred sway,—*
> *It is enthroned in the hearts of kings,*
> *It is an attribute to God himself;*
> *And earthly power doth then show likest God's,*
> *When mercy seasons justice."*

My fears eased as he spoke. Stephen's recitation was beyond compare to any performance I'd seen, which I had to admit was extremely limited. Still, I could see he had a great talent. I stole a glance at Benedict and was glad to see that his attention was riveted on his brother. Though Stephen had dedicated the recitation to me, the words were clearly meant for his brother, and I think Benedict realized that.

When he finished, the room was silent. Mr. Henderson clapped first, and everyone followed suit. Stephen took a bow. "Now, dear brother, would you grace us with your expertise upon the piano?"

"Anything else would prove to be anticlimactic, I am afraid. That was extremely well done," Benedict said.

"I did not waste my time back East, but sought to make myself a better man. I had no place to go but up, you know." Stephen spoke as if he'd made a joke and laughed, but I caught the look he exchanged with Benedict, and I thought that just maybe one small step had been taken.

Constance slipped between the brothers and pouted at Benedict. "But you just have to play a song, Benedict. I would love to hear Alan sing for us before he leaves for home. Play the one he used to sing all the time with my—" She hesitated, swung around, and looked at everyone. "Please, just once can we sing the song she loved?"

A long silence followed Constance's plea, and though I thought her request ill timed, I felt for her. She truly seemed to be grieving for her sister and wanted to have good memories to cling to. It wasn't much different from Robert and Justin's need to express love for their mother with flowers on her grave.

Mr. Henderson cleared his voice. "Well, Ben, I think I am up to it. I hope your playing is not as rusty as my singing, or we are really going to need a brandy before we sleep."

"We will need that anyhow," Benedict said, but he moved over to the piano and settled himself to play. Katherine, as she had before, went and sat on the floor next to the piano and placed her head against it, a woman reaching for something she could never have. As I sat and watched Benedict play, absorbing his every movement, feeling every note he struck as if he played upon my soul with the gentle strength of his hands, I too knew that I had tried to reach for something I could never have.

When the clock struck the midnight hour, I made my way to Benedict's bedchamber. My plan to tell him of my decision to stop this fever between us before it destroyed us both fell silent as I opened the passage's door into his room. I stood there stunned. Candles lit the quarters, and an exotic scent hung enticingly in the air. A trail of roses lay upon the floor, leading a path to the bed, where Benedict, dressed in his robe, reclined with a rose in his hand.

He held it out to me, and tears stung my eyes. No man had given me flowers before. I was awed by how this man, this busy man, had taken the time to reach all the way into my romantic soul. Had he known what I'd planned to tell him?

I looked into his eyes, and could do nothing else but go to him. Morning would be soon enough to face the harsh truth. Just one more time, during the mists of midnight I'd pretend that what I wanted most in life was truly mine. Just one more time.

Reaching the bed, I took the rose from him, noticing that this rose, so perfect and beautiful, had no thorns. He'd sheared them away. Would that pain in life could be so easily dispatched.

"Thank you," I said softly.

Benedict rose to his knees and gazed directly into my eyes. There was a deep well of unspoken things between us, a well that now swirled with turmoil, for there was no denying that his mother's words had affected us both.

"No," he said, taking hold of my hand, urging me to kneel upon the bed before him. "Thank you. Come let me love you tonight, Titania. I need you."

Easing the rose from my fingers, he set it aside, then slipped my robe from my shoulders. With a slow gentleness, he unbuttoned my gown and lifted it over my head. He wore only a robe, which he untied and shook off, then pulled me into his embrace. He kissed me tenderly, barely brushing his lips over mine before he kissed my cheeks, my eyes, and my forehead.

Tonight I felt a difference in his manner, in his touch. He moved as if he had all the time in the world, as if he'd brought time to a halt, and we were the only two people in the universe unfrozen. Then he kissed me deeply, with a longing and a reverence that wrapped a bittersweet chain about my heart. This man had captured my every dream, my love, and my soul and freed them to soar. I kissed him back, equally meeting his every touch.

Leaning, he softly brought us both to the mattress, I upon my back with him over me. I thought he would kiss me then, love me then, but he didn't. He sat back, picked up the rose, and brought it to my lips, brushing the fragrant velvety petals gently across my mouth. I inhaled, taking in the scent of rose, of sandalwood, of him, and felt as if a different kind of ambrosia fed my senses.

He bathed me then, bathed all of me with the petals of the rose, from the tip of my nose to the tender flesh of my instep, from the peaks of my breasts to the valley of my femininity. And finally he took each of my hands, my reddened, work-worn hands, and bathed them with the softness of the rose. He made me feel beautiful, made me feel cherished. I thought I could know no greater tenderness, but I was wrong. He followed the brush of the rose with the brush of his lips. Every place the rose had delved, his lips kissed until he again reached my hands. He kissed my fingertips and threaded his fingers through mine so that we were palm to palm. It wasn't until he gazed into my eyes at that moment that I saw the ferocity of the passion he held in check. And I knew even before I arched to him that I would be unleashing a fire that might consume us both.

"Yes," I said to him with conviction. "Love me tonight. I need you, too." The fire erupted, instant, blazing, scorching. His lips claimed mine, our tongues mated in a primal dance that fired our need as air fueled the heat of a fire. I locked my legs about him, urging him to join with me. No words were said as he thrust into me and I arched to him. We needed nothing but each other's touch and the perfect mating of our bodies and hearts.

I awoke several hours later, surprised to find myself alone in Benedict's bed. Where was he? The expanse of his room, its richness, the luxury of his jumbled covers, didn't belong to me. I didn't belong with him. I'd hoped to spend the night in his arms before I told him of my decision.

It was probably better this way, I thought as I rose and dressed. I'd leave his bed with the memory of a perfect night, and in the morning I'd go to his study and say the words that we both had to face.

After I dressed, I picked up each rose he had left for me and gathered them against my heart, feeling tears fall in my soul. He'd removed the thorns from them all. And I knew I would have to hold on to that forever. I'd have to hold on to the passion we'd shared, keep the roses next to my heart, and remember that thorns didn't have any place in the beauty he'd shown me, no matter how painful our parting would be.

Taking my lantern and my roses, I left Benedict's room. My stomach knotted, as if what I was doing wasn't right.

No, I told myself, taking a deep breath. This is what I had to do, for Benedict, for Justin, for Robert, and for myself. I shut the panel to his room behind me and started up the stairs. Now that I was completely in the dark, I realized the oil in my lamp was low, and only a sputtering flame was left to guide my way. But I knew there was enough of the wick to last for a while yet, so I continued up. Three steps from the landing, I thought I heard a noise behind me. I swung around, expecting to see Benedict there. Yet only darkness met the glow of my lamp.

My heart sped up even as I chastised myself for being overly imaginative.

"Hello. Is anyone there?" Only my own voice echoed back at me. I never felt more alone than I did at that moment. Not even when my mother died had I felt so completely vulnerable and alone.

Turning, I hurried up to my room, my feet moving as quickly as I could safely go in my slippers. I rounded the stairway to my floor, and suddenly something black and hard hit me, knocking me backward.

I screamed as I fell back. The lamp and my roses went flying. I tried to twist my body to put my hands before me, to do anything to break my fall. My hand caught the rail, and I clutched it desperately. The impetus of my body plunging downward ripped the rail from my hand, and my knee and hip hit the wooden stairs hard, sending pain shattering through my body. I rolled. My back scraped across the stairs, and my head slammed hard, making my stomach clench with nausea. I came to a stop as my side rammed into stone.

I groaned, too stunned, too hurt, to move. I could only lie there, alone, in complete darkness.

23

"Titania!"

I heard Benedict's call from somewhere above me. A rumble of heavy footsteps came down the stairs, and the ever-brightening glow of approaching light made me shut my eyes in pain.

"Here," I said, but my voice came out as nothing more than a groan. I ached everywhere as I moved first my fingers and toes, then my feet and hands. I still wasn't sure how badly I was hurt. I was still stunned. I thought I must have fallen only moments ago, but I felt disoriented and wasn't sure how long I'd lain in the darkness.

"Titania! What in God's name happened? Bloody hell!" Benedict's cry was one of horror. The volume of it set my head to throbbing. I felt his hands upon my face.

"Shh," I whispered. "Hurt. Head hurts."

"Thank God, you are alive. Where else are you hurt? "

"Not sure. My constitution—"

"If you say one bloody word about your constitution, I am going to thrash you. Can I pick you up?"

I hurt all over, but other than the throbbing in my head, no one place seemed worst. "Just a bump on my head."

"I am going to pick you up. Tell me if I hurt you."

His strong arms slid around me and pulled me close to

him. His warmth eased into me, and I sighed. I was no longer alone in the dark.

"We will go to my room. It is closer," he said, swinging around.

Cracking my eye open, I realized I had only fallen one level down. "No. My room. Do not want anyone to know about us. But they must. Pushed me."

"What did you say?" Benedict's arms tightened about me.

"Pushed. Someone pushed me."

"Someone's a dead man. Pushed you from where?"

"From the landing by the schoolroom."

"Titania, I was in the schoolroom, coming back down to you. I heard you scream. Within seconds I was in the passage. No one else was there."

"No. I was pushed. I am sure of it."

He pulled me closer. "Shh. We will worry about this later. You need a doctor."

There was no dissuading him. So a mortifying hour later I found myself ensconced in my bed, suffering the poking and prodding of a doctor's examination while a wide-eyed maid looked on and the sounds of Benedict pacing outside the door reverberated throughout the room. I'd yet to face Dobbs, but I did hear Benedict speaking to the man, telling him that my curious nature had me discovering the secret passage in the middle of the night. And my penchant for accidents had me falling on my head. I wasn't sure if I was more miffed at Benedict for concocting such a story or for Dobbs's ready belief of it.

Yet I had to admit that it was better than telling the truth. As dizzy as I felt, I wasn't sure if it was better to be a falling woman than a fallen one.

"Well, Miss Lovell, you are a lucky woman. That is all I can say." The white-haired, bushy-browed doctor, whose frown was bigger than his girth, pulled the sheet back up, covering my hips. "Bruised and slightly concussed seems to be the worst of your troubles. I will leave you something for pain, and after a couple of days of rest you should be able to be back on your feet. But I warn you now, you are going to have a mighty big headache, and the rest of you is going to feel twice as bad."

"Nothing is broken then?"

"No. I think your elbow and hip came close, but something must have broken your fall just enough to keep that from happening. I do not have to warn you that this could have been much worse, do I? No more strange stairs in the middle of the night, do you understand?"

I nodded, not trusting my voice. The fear that I had felt was still too fresh in my throat.

The doctor left, and Benedict burst in. He looked as if he was about to say something that was going to let everyone within hearing distance know we were on much more intimate terms than governess and employer.

"Mr. Trevelyan," I said sharply, stopping him in his tracks. "It is kind of you to be so concerned for me." Speaking forcefully cost me. My head began to throb, and the room around me wobbled.

Benedict visibly sucked in air, then his gaze raked down me, not with desire, but with assessing concern. "Miss Lovell. I am just thankful your injuries are not life-threatening." He turned to the maid. "Will you need to collect anything from your quarters in order to spend the night looking after Miss Lovell?"

"Yes, sir. I'll be but a minute, sir," the maid said, curtsying before she left the room.

Alone with me now, Benedict came over and sat on the edge of the bed. I winced as my body shifted toward his weight. He took my hand and brought it to his lips.

"Titania, this charade of distance is going to kill me. I swear to you, I am going to get to the bottom of all this. I refuse to believe in a bloody curse."

Curse? I wondered, but my head hurt too much to ask. I groaned with pain.

"Here," Benedict said. Reaching to the bedside table, he picked up a small cup and pressed it to my lips. "The doctor left this for pain."

The sickly sweet smell of laudanum syrup, which I remembered giving my mother during her last days, assaulted my nose. All I could think of through the haziness in my mind was Francesca, drugged and falling from the tower. I didn't want to die like Francesca. I turned my head quickly, suddenly nauseated, and closed my eyes.

"Titania!" Benedict said my name sharply. I opened my eyes and looked at him. He'd become as white as a ghost. The hand he held the medicine in was shaking like a leaf. "Why did you say that? Why did you say that you don't want to die like Francesca did? Dear God. You think I would do that? You think I did do that?" He threw the medicine across the room.

"No, I did not say that," I said, but there was no conviction in my voice. The presence of the drug and my vulnerable and confused state had me completely unnerved. A woman had died once in this house, and it had never felt more real to me than it did right then that I could, too. I didn't doubt Benedict, but there were others, and I'd be helpless drugged.

"You did." His dark eyes were filled with pain, his voice more hopeless than I'd ever heard. The distance between us was suddenly greater than any class difference. Tears stung my eyes, but I couldn't cry. I let false doubt fill the void, thinking it was better this way.

We had to part. To my fuzzy mind, letting him think I

distrusted him made that parting easier. It was for the best, for I was fast losing myself so deep inside of him that I'd rather die than leave him.

The next day passed in a blur of pain and maids. I was never alone, and I had never been more alone. I hadn't realized just how bleak my heart would be without the warmth of his presence. I didn't even have the comfort of his scent about me.

It wasn't until that night, when the mists that I saw from my bedroom window surrounded Trevelyan Manor like a shroud, that I let myself cry. I hugged my pillow close to my breasts, my breasts that ached for his touch, and tears fell. My body ached all over from the fall, but I hurt more deeply for the feel of Benedict's touch, for the heat of his gaze, for the strength of his presence. I prayed that my tears would wash away some of the pain from my heart, but they didn't. The pain seemed to grow. The room was dark except for the glow of a dim lamp. The maid who'd been watching over me had fallen asleep, sitting up in the reading chair. So I shut my eyes and gave in to the quiet sobs wrenching through me. I wondered what would happen once I recovered. Would Benedict send me away? I couldn't leave Justin and Robert yet. Their hearts were just beginning to heal.

I heard a slight noise, just the rustling of the bed curtains. Startled, I sat up quickly, sending a fresh wave of pain stabbing through my head. My breath clogged in my throat as I searched to see who had come to my room in the dark hours of the night.

"Miss Lovell?" came Justin's whisper. Relief swept through me.

"Yes?" There was no way to hide the fact that I was crying. Still, I dabbed at my cheeks with the corner of the bedsheet. Justin hesitantly stepped from the shadows beyond the bed curtains and stood there, looking lost. He had something bundled up in his hands.

"What is it?"

"This . . . this is for you." Tissue paper crackled as he set the bundle down next to me. "Don't cry," he said.

"Tears can sometimes help the roses grow," I told him, but I didn't think there were going to be any more roses in my garden of love for Benedict. Winter had come too soon.

"You . . . you are going to get better, aren't you?"

"Yes. I have just a few bruises and a bump on my head, but I will be up and about before you know it."

"Good," he said, sighing as if the weight of the world had been lifted from his shoulders. "This is for you," he said again and pushed the package closer. "But be careful when you open it."

"Do you want me to open it now?"

"Yes . . . please."

Tearing back the paper, it took me but a second to realize what he'd brought me. "They are beautiful," I said, as more tears began to fall.

"I do not need them anymore." Justin placed his hand over mine, which rested upon the bouquet of thorns he'd brought to me. "I am not going to live like Cynthia Parker's son Quanah—holding on to thorns at the death of his parents. I want to be like you."

"Justin, thank you. Thank you. This is the best gift ever."

"Miss Lovell, can I have a big hug? Like the ones you give Robert?"

I opened my arms and wrapped them around Justin and pulled him close to my heart. More tears fell. "You can have all the hugs you can stand," I whispered softly, praying that I'd be around long enough to fulfill that promise. I feared that rather than helping repair the fabric of the Trevelyans' lives, I'd done more to tear it apart.

• • •

Turning over in bed the next morning, trying to ignore the pain screaming at me as glaringly as the sun beat through my window, I pulled the sheets over my head.

"That will not make me go away."

My eyes popped open. Surely I hadn't just heard Mrs. Trevelyan's acid voice. Not even fate could be that cruel on a morning like this.

"I do believe, Miss Lovell, that you were hired to tend the children, not contract fevers, fall down stairs, and hide beneath bedsheets. I have sent the maid Benedict left here back to her household duties."

Good Fortune had most assuredly washed her hands of me. I pulled down the covers. Mrs. Trevelyan stood, dressed shockingly in something besides black—a dark blue dress enhanced with a beautiful cameo pinned at the gown's cream lace neckline. For the first time since meeting her, I saw remnants of the beauty that graced Katherine and could pair them as mother and daughter. Too bad her disposition hadn't changed with her appearance.

"We both know where I would rather be at the moment, Mrs. Trevelyan. Is there a purpose to your visit this morning besides tormenting me?" I asked, folding my hands calmly. I wasn't about to let her unnerve me.

"Perhaps not." Dashing my fervent hopes that she'd depart, she pulled a chair close to the bed and stiffly situated herself in it. "You have proven yourself a liar, so I wonder myself why I am even bothering to speak to you."

"I beg your pardon?"

"If you recall, Miss Lovell, I said just after you came here that you were sowing the seeds that would destroy my sons, and you replied that your purpose here was to teach my grandsons. I have seen my prediction come to fruition. You are obviously more involved with my sons than my grandsons. Whatever grasp Stephen had gained on his life when he went back East, he has now lost. And when he is sober, he looks at you as if you are his saving angel. Benedict has never been this on edge, not even when Francesca died. You have managed to ensnare them both. What is it you hoped to accomplish? Do you think that Stephen or Benedict will marry a laundress?"

She continued before I could speak.

"Benedict is accusing everyone from scullery maid to me of harming you. It was very clever of you to arrange such a dramatic fall in the middle of the night so near my son's private quarters. No man can resist the appeal of rescuing a woman in distress. Neither can he resist the role of protector. So claiming you were deliberately harmed was a master touch. And waiting to do it until after I had forsaken my wheelchair allows me to be suspect, too."

"Did it occur to you that I might actually be telling the truth, Mrs. Trevelyan?" Anger gave me the strength I needed.

"Who else but me wants you to leave?"

"Maybe you can answer that question better than me. Maybe it is not me affecting Stephen and Benedict, but the past." That wasn't anywhere near the whole truth, and I hoped lightning wouldn't strike me dead, but Benedict's mother had painted such a twisted picture. "Perhaps whoever murdered Francesca wants me gone because I make them uncomfortable."

"Murdered!" Benedict's mother stood so abruptly that she knocked the chair over backward. "How dare you bring the filth of gossip into my home! Believe me, that evil woman killed herself and left a curse damning my entire family. She lived on laudanum, could not make it a day without it. And when she could not have what she wanted, she devised a plan to destroy everyone."

"How?" I asked, wondering if Mrs. Trevelyan had as inaccurate a view of Francesca as she had of me. Yet, even distorted, I had the feeling that I was about to learn more than I ever had about Francesca.

"By pretending to be the innocent, a tragic victim. By making everyone feel responsible for her unhappiness, then leaving a note telling everyone they drove her to her death and that she would haunt their lives, destroying anything and everything that they loved."

"Surely no one believes that possible."

"You would think that. But I ask you, what are the results? Look at Stephen, Benedict, and Katherine, and you tell me." She paused. "I warn you, Miss Lovell, I will do whatever it takes to protect my family this time. I have learned the hard way not to trust an innocent face, and I will not make that mistake again." She left the room then, and thousands of questions filled the void of her abrupt wake, questions I had to get out of bed to answer.

It took me most of the morning to bathe and dress myself. Though clothed, I wasn't quite ready to face walking down the stairs until I'd rested, but a little knock sounded at my door before I could sit down. Robert ran inside. "Miss Wovell, I'm scared. I'm scared."

Constance came through the door on his heels. "Dear Robert, it is nothing more than a clever poem."

"I don't wike spiders!" Robert ran right to me and wrapped his arms about my legs. I wasn't quite steady on my feet yet, and I thought for a moment we'd both topple. Thankfully, we didn't. I set my hand on top of his head and looked at Constance.

"Whatever has him so upset?"

Constance held up a book. "I found this clever little poem by Mary Howitt, and I thought the boys would love it. 'The

Spider and the Fly.' Have you had the opportunity to read it?"

"No, I do not think I have heard of it."

"You would know if you had, it's rather amusing. The spider invites the fly into his parlor. The fly, thinking itself wise, declines, only to succumb to the spider's flattery and become a meal."

"I don't want to be eaten," Robert cried.

I patted his back. "No one is going to gobble you up. I'm sure that Aunt Constance wouldn't let that happen. Would you?" I asked, tossing the question to Constance so that she herself could reassure the little boy.

"Indeed not. Now come along. We need to find something for you two boys to do until Cook Thomas is ready with your lunch."

Now that I had Robert with me, I was reluctant to let him go just yet. I had missed the boys yesterday. Now that I thought about it, I wasn't quite sure what day it was. "How about we all go sit in the garden for a little while?" I smiled at Constance. "I could use some fresh air and company."

"Very well, then, to the garden. Perhaps the boys can run off some of their energy. They have the hardest time sitting still. I will bring this poetry book, and perhaps we will have the opportunity to read them another poem."

Robert looked as if he was about to wail in complete rebellion over hearing more of Constance's brand of poetry. I set my finger upon his lips, warning him of his gentlemanly duties. "Thank your aunt Constance and run get Justin. Tell him we are going to the garden and to bring his sketchbook."

"I fear Benedict is going to be displeased if he sees you about, especially with the boys," Constance said, and my heart squeezed painfully hard.

"Oh." I feigned surprise. "Why is that?"

"Because you are suppose to be resting. I assured him

Maria and I could handle the boys. We got along well enough before."

"I will have to thank him for his consideration, but I think I have rested long enough. I am not even sure I know what day it is."

She narrowed her eyes. "My, you are in a state. I had not realized you had hit your head that hard. It is Sunday."

"Yes, I suppose it is. I missed seeing Mr. McGuire yesterday. He must be worried about me. I will have to send him a post."

"Did you get your post this morning? I believe it was from him."

"No. I have yet to receive anything. I'll have to ask Dobbs," I said, shaking my head. I had to be more addled by my fall than I thought, for I had completely forgotten that I was to see Mr. McGuire yesterday.

Constance frowned, then shrugged. "I could have been mistaken about the letter. But I will be going into town in the morning. If you need, I will gladly deliver a message to Mr. McGuire. He is a dear old man. In fact, I purchased this book of poems from him just last week."

"Thank you. I will write a note tonight for you to take to him. He means a great deal to me." I gathered my sketchbook and called to the boys, telling them we were ready to go to the garden. My progress down the stairs was slow, for Justin and Robert spent their energy "helping me." Being up and about made me feel a great deal better, and I was glad to have Constance and the boys for company. If nothing else, they kept my mind off Benedict and my pain.

I should have checked the weather outside before I made the suggestion. Today the garden wasn't a nice bright spot. Dark, angry clouds hung thickly on the horizon, and a sticky, humid breeze held the promise of a hot thunderstorm. The malevolent portent of the black mass made me shiver despite the heat. Constance must have felt it, too, for she stared at the horizon with a look of intense worry on her face.

The boys didn't even seem to notice. Justin settled himself at the far end of the garden and began sketching in his notebook. Robert stared into the pool of water at the fountain and then dribbled his fingers through it. "Come look, Miss Wovell. I can make my face look funny."

Setting my sketchbook on the bench, I went over to him. We stared at our wavering reflections in the water together until Robert laughingly splashed and made them disappear. My heart squeezed as I realized how fleeting the precious moments of our lives really were. I knew I would treasure forever my memories of Benedict, Justin, and Robert, and I prayed that years from now they would be just as real as I saw them now, not a watery reflection faded by time.

"Can I go collect rocks, Miss Wovell?" Robert asked with enthusiasm.

"Only if you stay where we can see you. No wandering off, you hear?"

"Yes, Miss Wovell, I promise," he said scrambling off to where a number of rocks were, not far from Justin.

"These are quite good," Constance said.

I turned to find her studying her way through my sketchbook and had to fight back the flash of anger I felt over her not asking permission first. Some of my penciled musings were private.

She set the book aside and didn't comment further, but looked at the sky again. "Sometimes that's what the future looks like to me, a jumbled mass of angry clouds waiting to devour me. Do you ever feel that way?"

I took a deep breath. I would never know more about what happened to Francesca if I didn't risk a few more questions. My experience in the stairwell seemed to have turned my curiosity about Francesca's death into an imperative quest. "As I see it, it aptly describes the past here at Trevelyan Manor."

Constance turned to study me. "The past? How so?"

I hesitated.

"Ann, surely you know me well enough to be frank. What are you thinking?"

"I'm thinking about all of this tension hovering over the Trevelyans. What exactly happened a year ago between Benedict, Stephen, and your sister?"

Constance narrowed her eyes, and I wondered if I had pushed too far. Then she shrugged. "Like most of us, Francesca wanted what she could not have, but she could not accept that. It is not something I like to talk about. Her death and why. She chose to die, but I want to remember the good things and let her live in those." Constance shivered. "I think I will see if Dobbs can serve tea in the solarium. Will you join me shortly?"

"Yes. Thank you." She left then, leaving the past still hidden in shadows. But maybe not. It would seem that Constance and Mrs. Trevelyan, women who had known Francesca, and Stephen, a man in love with her, believed that she'd killed herself. Dr. Levinworth was sure she'd been murdered. And Benedict? If he didn't have his doubts, if he wasn't protecting someone or hiding something, he wouldn't be so tortured over his honor, or so shadowed by Francesca's death. What was the truth?

I collected my sketchbook, finding the pages open to my picture of Benedict. I'd done my best to ignore my heart all morning, having decided my tears during the night were all the sorrow I could allow myself. I let my gaze drift to the stables in the distance, wondering if he was there, wondering if he was out riding, facing the rising wind of the threatening storm.

It was all I could do to keep my feet planted in the garden, for my heart wandered its way to the stable, to the very first time his arms wrapped around me, to the first time his lips touched mine. Robert called me, and I turned to him, smiling back my tears, reminding myself that I'd hold no thorns.

"Miss Wovell. Miss Wovell. You have to come look. There is a mommy and a baby, and I found them all by myself."

I hurried his way. As I passed Justin, I saw him set down his sketchbook and rise. He too wanted to see what Robert had found.

"You have to be very quiet," Robert said, oblivious to the fact that he'd been shouting. I took his hand and Justin's too, and we tiptoed around the rosebushes. There, feeding along the edge of the garden, were two brown, white-tailed rabbits, one large, one little. Their long ears twitched in the breeze as they hopped from tuft to tuft of grass and clover.

"You most certainly did find a mommy and a baby," I whispered, squeezing Robert's hand. We stood watching them for a long moment.

"Miss Lovell, could Robert and I have another mommy?" Justin said, holding my hand tightly.

The soft question centered a heavy weight upon my chest. "That's not an easy question to answer, and one that you should ask your father."

"Can we choose you, Miss Wovell?" Robert leaned his little body next to mine.

Letting go of their hands, I wrapped my arms around both Robert and Justin, knelt painfully down, and pulled them close to me. "No," I said, my voice so thick with emotion I almost choked over the simple word. "But I will tell you two a secret that you must always keep close to your hearts. In my heart and in my dreams that reach out to your dreams every night, I could not love you any more even if I was your mommy. I love you that much. Do you understand?"

Justin nodded. Robert frowned. "But I want you to be."

I wanted to be, too. My heart squeezed so painfully that tears threatened. I ruffled Robert's hair, loving every wild curl. "Sometimes everything we want doesn't happen. Now, I bet Cook Thomas has something delicious cooked up for your lunch. Let's go see."

Cook Thomas informed me that Mrs. Trevelyan had requested that Justin and Robert visit her after lunch. He rolled his eyes as he told me of her elaborate plans to teach Justin and Robert the proper etiquette for an afternoon tea. Then he showed me the platter of treats that he'd prepared—scones with strawberry jam and clotted cream, delicate chocolate-lace cookies, and tiny lemon cakes that made my mouth water. I smiled, knowing that no matter how torturous their tea lesson would be, the boys were going to love it. I went to join Constance for tea in the solarium.

Either I was more restless than I had ever been in my life, or I was desperate to keep my mind from thinking, for I couldn't seem to sit for more than just a few minutes at a time. After half a cup of tea and one lemon cake, I left Constance immersed in an illustrated fashion newspaper and checked with Dobbs about the letter Constance had mentioned earlier. In the middle of instructing the maids on how to clean the parlor, he was quite put out to see me. His "I assure you that no post came for you, Miss Lovell" clearly stated that I was taking on airs to even think I was important enough to receive a letter. That I didn't argue with him, insist on seeing the mail myself, or return his insult spoke volumes about my state of mind. It was as if everything in life had lost its importance compared to facing life without Benedict, Justin, and Robert.

I didn't know where I was going until I ended up in the entry hall. The colored lights of the stained glass were dim because of the gray skies, barely painting the room. Still, I went and stood beneath the faint hues, looking for some small glimmer of the joy and hope I'd always found there. All I could see was the closed door of Benedict's study. I'd not seen him since the night I'd fallen, and the ache in my heart grew with every lonely moment. I went to the door and raised my hand to knock, but turned away before I could. Tears filled my eyes as I relived my last visit to his study and the joy and despair that I'd experienced. I'd never forget him asking for a dance, for my kiss, or for my love. Nor would I ever forget the truths his mother had forced me to see.

We'd both changed. Benedict hadn't left to tend some business situation to avoid the complexities between us. It was I who was hiding now. And coward that I was, I would continue to let the misunderstanding lie between us. It was easier than the truth. Blinking back my tears, I looked up to see Katherine. Crying, she looked at me with a despair that seemed to mirror my own heart.

"What is it?" I asked, forgetting that she couldn't hear. She seemed to understand me anyway. She held up a letter that she'd obviously read and placed a fist over her heart.

"Anthony," I said, mouthing the word, knowing instinctively that must be what had her upset. She nodded, and motioning for me to follow her, led me to the library and pressed the letter into my hand. Her actions told me that she wanted me to read the letter.

My Dearest Katherine,

After speaking with Miss Lovell, I have come to realize that I can no longer live the life that I have been living this past year. When you broke our engagement, I told myself that you did not love me enough to be with me. That I did not mean as much to you as the others you cared for, and that their problems were more important to you than our life together was. I have lived with this sadness, and yes, resentment, in my heart, believing these things to be true.

I am writing to you now to tell you that I was wrong. Wrong to have left your side when you set me free, because I have learned that my love for you is greater than all else and greater than any shortcomings that I or even you have. I should have loved you enough to stand by your side when you needed the heart and hand of a friend rather than the demands of a lover. I should have stayed and understood rather than insist that there is only one way for our love to be.

I am humbly asking you, Katherine, to let me be a part of your life again in any way. That I may see the joy of your smile as you walk in the garden, share the glory of a sunset on a quiet evening, and write the verse that lights your eyes with laughter. For having lost these small things, I have learned what makes life richer than anything else for me. You.

Forever Yours,
no matter what your decision,
Anthony

Tears filled my eyes as I realized how great Anthony's love for Katherine truly was. I looked at Katherine. She stood by the window, gazing out at the gray skies as her tears fell. When I gave her the letter back, she pulled out a pen and paper and wrote, *"What am I going to do? What of the curse? Even you have almost died."*

I shook my head and took the pen and paper. *"There is no curse, and I don't even think that is what you really fear. I think you fear the future, and that since you cannot hear, you*

*will not be the perfect wife and mother, but it looks as if
Anthony loves you no matter what. You have to decide what is
greater in your heart—fear or love."*

Katherine shook her head, but I could see in her eyes
that my words had reached her. I left her in the library
and went to my room, wishing that the gulf between
Benedict and me was as bridgeable as Katherine and
Anthony's appeared to be. But I didn't see any way to
overcome the fact that I was a laundress born out of wedlock, and he was the master of Trevelyan Hill, with a family to protect.

Entering my room, I found a note beneath my door.

> Come to the family sitting room near my quarters
> as soon as you can. I urgently need your help. It is
> about Katherine.
>
> Yours,
> Stephen

Thinking that Stephen wanted to speak to me about
Anthony's letter to Katherine, I quickly freshened myself
and hurried to the opposite wing of the house, but I found
the sitting room empty.

I was deliberating on whether or not it would be too
unseemly for me to knock on Stephen's door when I
noticed a note on the sheet covering an easel set in the middle of the room.

> Look at your own peril.
>
> F.

I froze, realizing that someone had deliberately lured me
here.

"Who are you?" I demanded, swinging around in a circle.

No one answered, but I once again felt as if someone watched me. I wasn't alone in the room. I knew it. "You are a coward," I said. "Do you think you can frighten me?"

I marched over to the picture and snatched the sheet away. I'm not sure what I expected, but as I looked at the canvas, a cry of surprise erupted from me. It was a picture of me, and clearly Katherine's artwork. She'd painted me as a magical queen of the fairies in a scene that seemed to be from Shakespeare's *A Midsummer Night's Dream*. Only this dream had been turned into a nightmare by the knife plunged into the canvas right through my heart and the blood-red words written over the masterpiece: *Leave or die.*

❦ 24 ❧

"No. Never!" I shouted even as I backed away from the picture, my heart thudding with fear. The sensation that someone was about to attack me crawled up my spine, and prudence outweighed my bravado. I turned and ran blindly, my lungs burning for air that I could not give them, my bruised body screaming with pain, and my mind grappling with my fear. I ran right into Stephen.

"Dear God, Miss Ann. I heard you yell. What's wrong?" He caught hold of my shoulders.

I tried to speak, but my throat seemed paralyzed. "Th-th-the—"

"It is all right. Whatever it is, just tell me, and we will fix it," he said, pulling me into his arms.

Feeling safe, I leaned my head upon him and fought for air, fought the dizziness and the pain in my sore body, fought to think. I'm not sure if only a moment passed, or if it was longer. "There's a painting in the sitting room. It is horrible."

Stephen expelled a long breath, clearly relieved. "Is that all? Remember? I spoke to you about Katherine's paintings—"

"No, you don't understand. It is Katherine's, but someone—"

"I suggest a bedroom is better suited to your depravity." I heard Benedict's voice as if coming from afar, for my blood still roared through my ears. I wondered if I'd imagined Benedict's voice until Stephen turned. Looking up, I saw Benedict standing in the hall, his face twisted in anger, his hands fisted at his sides.

"I suggest you look for a new post, Miss Lovell." His gaze raked down my body. "I no longer require any of the services you render." He threw something down, turned on his heel, and left.

"Bloody hell. You merciless bastard," Stephen shouted at Benedict's disappearing back. "I'm going to kill you for that."

"No." I grabbed Stephen's arm. "Dear God, no." It was at this point that I had the presence of mind to notice that Stephen wore his breeches only. His torso was completely bare and as damp as his hair. I'd apparently disturbed him at his bath. Shocked, I stepped away.

Stephen turned to me. He blinked, shook his head, and gulped in air. "Poor choice of words, Miss Ann. I'm going to beat him into a bloody pulp, though. You love him, don't you?"

I bit my lip, tears flooding my eyes. I didn't answer, but I didn't have to. Stephen was already cursing.

"He's compromised you, hasn't he?"

"No," I said, but he just looked at me sadly.

"We have too much truth between us, Miss Ann, for either of us to start lying now."

"Please, it was of my own doing. I went to him. I had to. I loved him, and I had to know him." Tears filled my eyes.

Stephen looked down at himself. "It would seem I had rather forgot my appearance myself. Let me grab a shirt, and then I am going to go bloody Benedict's face."

"No, I have to speak to him. I have let a misunderstanding hurt him because I was too much of a coward to tell him the truth. All of my fuss about him running away, and it was I who did so. I should not have run from the picture, either. I should not have let the knife upset me so."

"Knife?" Stephen said sharply. "What knife?"

"The one someone stabbed though Katherine's picture of me. In the sitting room. That's what frightened me so."

"My God, Ann." With a horrified look, Stephen turned and marched to the sitting room. Deciding I didn't want to be left standing alone, I hurried after him. The easel sat in the middle of the room, just as I'd left it. Only now, a different painting sat serenely in place of the butchered one of me. It was a beautiful picture of horses running in a pasture.

"Ann?" Stephen turned to look at me.

I shook my head. "It was here, just minutes ago. A picture of me as a fairy queen. Someone had put a knife through the queen and wrote 'Leave or die' in red on it." I looked at Stephen, feeling an uneasy sensation of unreality steal into my heart. "You do believe me, don't you?"

Stephen blinked. He looked back at the painting, then at me. "Yes, Ann, I do believe you, and I think we need to go discuss this with Benedict, though I doubt he will be able to hear us. He's deafer than Katherine when he's hurt or angry."

In my mind's eye, I saw Benedict questioning and accusing everyone, just as his mother claimed he did after I was pushed down the stairs. And considering that the picture had already disappeared, his mother would no doubt say that I had once again concocted a story to force Benedict to protect me. "No, Stephen. I do not want Benedict to know about this yet. I need to speak with him first and set a few things straight."

"The avenging angel is back? Good for you, Miss Ann. In fact, tell my brother he cannot fire you because you have already quit. I have a post for you to fill. Since I will be putting my pen to paper, I need a practical person to organize my prose. Will you be my assistant, Miss Ann? This is a completely respectable position that I am offering, I assure you." Stephen smiled softly. "You might say that you know me too well for me to ever sweep you off your feet, which, given the romantic nature of my heart, is an absolute must for me."

His offer touched my soul. I smiled back at him, feeling as if I had truly gained a friend, though I knew I could never accept his offer. "Thank you, but—"

"No, don't answer now. Just know that you have a respectable place to go should you need to. It is rather ironic that my mother was right after all." Stephen said.

"How?" I asked, surprised at his remark.

"About Titania falling in love with an ass."

Despite the situation, a small laugh escaped through my turmoil.

"I have a few words for Benedict myself, so I won't be too far behind you."

"I fear this is going to take some time to straighten out. I've made a terrible muddle of everything."

"He's a fool if he does not listen to you. You know, Miss Ann, something strange happened the other night when I was drunk in the garden. I stumbled into the house shouting, 'Abandon Hope all ye who enter here.' And guess what happened?"

"What?"

"I found hope."

"I'm glad for you, for at least one thing will come aright from all of this. It's more than I could have hoped for." I was thankful in some part of my heart that someone had found the hope that I had lost. At least it would live on, just not in my heart. Turning from Stephen so he wouldn't see the unshed tears in my eyes, I left to go find Benedict. I stopped and picked up the paper Benedict had thrown down. It was the note I'd written to Stephen, what seemed like ages ago now, asking him to join me in the sitting room. How had Benedict gotten this? I closed my eyes and remembered that Stephen had dropped it on the floor when I'd returned Elizabeth Barrett Browning's book to him. I had to go to Benedict. I couldn't let this much hurt lie between us. I couldn't run away any longer.

At first I headed to the study, but then I instinctively knew he wouldn't be brooding in the darkness. I started to run to the stables, my hip and side hurting, my heart and head pounding. I passed by Dobbs when I entered the solarium in a blur, and unfortunately I left him standing. He called after me with no small amount of asperity, but I ignored him, running out the door.

As I dashed across the stones of the garden, past the angel, I saw Benedict, astride Odin, come thundering out of the stables. I knew if I ran hard enough, I'd make it to the narrow opening through the copse of trees where he was headed. Then he'd have to either stop or trample me. I didn't hesitate. No matter how angry he was, I knew with my whole heart he wouldn't hurt me with anything but words.

I'd just made it to the opening in time to look up and see him heading right for me. I don't know if he'd been looking the other way, or if he'd been too blinded by his own emotions, but I saw the moment of shock when he realized I was there.

And maybe that moment was a bit too late for him to bring Odin to a stop. I saw him jerk the reins. Odin veered, and I tried to dodge to the side. I felt the rush of Odin's body skimming behind my back, then suddenly an arm slammed into my side. I was snatched off my feet and brought up against Benedict's body, then pulled across his lap, imprisoned in his arms with the saddle horn digging into my side.

I thought Benedict would stop immediately. He didn't. He raced through the trees at a terrifying pace. Any moment I expected for all of us to miss a turn and go slamming into an unyielding oak. But we didn't; we flew from beneath the cover of the trees to the open field we'd ridden to before. Only this time the sky was a dark gray, and the wind seemed to be lashing the land as forcefully as the waves crashing against the distant shore.

The saddle horn dug painfully against my bruised hip, and I wiggled, searching for relief. My situation must have broken through Benedict's haze, because he brought Odin to a stop. Benedict's breathing was just as labored as Odin's. Torrid anger poured from his every muscle. He looked as fierce and as terrible as the hot storm blowing in from the ocean.

He grabbed my shoulders, turning me to face him, and I was about to set him straight on his jealous rage, when he spoke and ripped my own words right from my mouth.

"Are you trying to get yourself killed? You were almost trampled beneath Odin's hooves. How could you do something so foolhardy?" His voice was as hard as the distant cliffs. Then without waiting for me to answer, he kissed me, his passion ruthless in his quest of my response. I knew I should pull back. I knew I should deny him, but I couldn't. I needed him too much.

I returned his desperate passion with one of my own, matching his kiss, pressing my body against his. His tongue delved deeply into my mouth, questing, as if he were searching for my soul. I pressed my breasts hard against his chest, wanting with my whole being to go straight though to his heart. The embrace consumed me, consumed him, stealing away reason, leaving our need for each other stripped naked, vulnerable. In one quick motion, he slid me down his leg to the ground and swung off Odin. Then he swept me into his arms, kissing me again and again as he walked. I cared not where he went. I cared only that he took me with him, that his passion would brand my soul one last time. It wasn't until he set me down that I knew he'd brought me down to the sandy shore, behind a private outcropping of rocks, where the roar of the waves lashed the land wildly, impassioned by the approaching storm.

His dark gaze held mine as he stripped off everything. He gave me time to run from the fury of his emotions, but I didn't. My hands went to the buttons of my dress, slipping them from their moorings as easily as my sensibilities had loosed themselves from my mind, for I wanted him amid the building wildness of the hot summer storm. He came to me, adding his efforts to mine until we both stood as Adam and Eve had. I brushed my hand along his rough, clenched jaw, running my finger along the slight cleft of his chin, then over the sensual curve of his lips. "I knew you would not harm me. No matter how angry you were."

He didn't speak; his eyes only darkened, and he pulled me into his arms, renewing the onslaught of his kisses until we were both breathless, our bodies throbbing to fulfill the promise of our embraces. The pile of our clothes made a soft bed in the sand. He lay back upon them. "Come to me, Titania. Bring me your magic."

I went to him, and he pulled me to him, kissing me

deeply. Every place he touched, I burned with need until nothing could satisfy me but having him within me. "Benedict, please," I cried out to him.

"Love me, Titania," he said softly, pressing me upward until I sat upon him. Then, anchoring me with his hands on my hips, he arched up, filling me completely. I shuddered with pleasure. The wind of the storm whipped at my back and hair, but its power couldn't even come close to matching the passion of the man who drove himself into me until we both crashed like a helpless wave driven relentlessly upon a shore of pleasure. I fell against his chest, pressing my ear to the thunder of his beating heart, and he wrapped his arms around me.

"Why," he asked softly. "Why did you say what you did about Francesca after you fell in the stairwell?"

My eyes popped open, and the sensual haze blew away with the wind. Of all the times he could have chosen to speak of his dead wife, was it quite necessary to do so when he was so thoroughly buried within me? I started to lift from him, but he held me against him, only allowing me to angle up enough to meet his gaze.

He must have read my mind. "We will talk while we are together like this so there is no room for misunderstandings. We have nothing to hide behind, except for these rocks to keep us from the prying eyes of the world. We're both naked and vulnerable."

"This is completely impractical, Benedict, and impossible. My mind is always in a muddle whenever you're inside me."

"I like your mind in a muddle." He brought his hands up to my cheeks, framed my face, and kissed me lightly, then sighed. "We will dress, but we aren't leaving here until everything between us that needs to be said is spoken."

Dressing did indeed put a barrier between us. I felt it the moment I looked at him after I anchored my last button in place. With him inside me, I'd lost sight of the reasons why we couldn't be together, and I regretted not bearing the awkwardness of staying wrapped in his arms as we spoke just so that I could be in his arms for a few last moments.

Benedict sat in the sand, leaning his back against the rocks, and patted the ground next to him for me to sit. He went right to the heart of the matter with his first question. "Do you believe I killed Francesca?"

Settling myself, I angled enough so that I could meet his gaze. "No. But I believe she was killed, and I believe you are protecting someone from the authorities. I have a dear friend in town, Mr. McGuire, the bookstore owner, whom I think of as my grandfather. He's always been so kind to me, and he was very worried over my employment here. He's also an acquaintance of Dr. Levinworth. His concern drove him to ask questions. He . . . he had Dr. Levinworth speak very frankly to me about Francesca's death. I know she was with child. I know you had been away quite some time. I know there are strong arguments that Francesca would not have taken her own life in so painful a way by jumping from the tower. She would have taken laudanum."

He gave me a sad smile. "Why am I not surprised you have learned so much?"

"You said you paid the authorities to have her death declared a suicide. Who are you protecting, Benedict?"

He sighed heavily. "That is not a question I can answer. Ever. Don't ask me again."

"I thought you just said that there would be nothing but honesty between us."

"I am sorry, Titania. I told you I had nothing but dishonor to give to a woman."

I wanted to be angry with him. I wanted to shake him, but instead I knew too well the honor that kept him silent. It was the same honor that would keep me from his arms. The honor of protecting those whom I loved. "Is it your mother?"

"I cannot answer that," he said harshly.

I turned from him, tears filling my eyes. He set his hands on my shoulders and pulled me back.

"Can you still love me?" he said softly against my ear. "I apologize for what I said when I saw you with Stephen. I know in my heart you would never become another man's lover, not now, maybe never. But when I saw the note on my desk and then saw you in his arms when I went to speak to him about it, I . . ."

I turned in his arms, facing him. "I wrote the note last month. I had put the pieces together about him and Francesca. I was angry at him, hurt for you, and I had to speak to him. I don't know who put that note on your desk, though. You lashed out at me when you saw me with Stephen because part of you is still wrapped up in what happened with Francesca and Stephen."

He stepped back, his fists clenched, and closed his eyes. "My own brother and my wife were lovers. I cannot forgive what they did."

I placed one hand over his fist and the other over his heart. "I am sorry."

He slit his eyes open, his gaze burning with emotion. "I did not kill her, and I am not sure she did not kill herself. She left a note."

"Your mother told me about the curse, vowing to haunt and destroy all whom the Trevelyans love."

That brought his eyebrows up. "And what else did my mother have to say?"

"She's worried about things she has every right to worry about. What she had to say in your study is true. I was going to tell you as much when I came to you that last night, then leave you. But you had the candles and the roses, and I could not turn away from you. Yet I had to. When you misunderstood what my pain-hazed mind was saying about the laudanum, it was easier to let you believe that I feared you than to tell you we could no longer be lovers. Your mother is right, Benedict. This passion we share has no future, and it can only bring harm to everyone."

His fist tightened beneath my hand. "I refuse to believe that. I have let society determine what I can and cannot do with my life for too long. I thought I could not marry without bringing dishonor to my bride because of the rumors. I will never send any member of my family to the gallows, so I will never press to answer the questions behind Francesca's death." He unclenched his fist and caught my fingers with his, pulling me toward him. "But I want you in my life, Titania. The circumstances of your birth and your station in life do not matter to me."

Tears of love filled my eyes even as my heart broke. I pulled my hand from his and turned to gaze out at the turbulent waters of the bay. "You do not understand. They matter to me. I am not willing to burden your sons with the scandal. Their hearts are just now starting to heal. I will remain here long enough to see them healed, but then I must go. To be able to do that, I can no longer share your bed."

He grabbed my shoulders and turned me to face him. His eyes were as stormy as the clouds. "No. That isn't how things are going to be. This isn't a choice between you and my sons' well-being, or my family's honor."

"Yes, it is, and you cannot change it. Can you guarantee me Justin and Robert will not suffer ill from the scandal? They already have too much to face. I will not be responsible for adding to their burden." Fresh tears stung my eyes. "Just as you can never answer the question of whom you protect, I can never cross the lines that would bring harm to you, to Justin, and to Robert. Don't ask me again." I pulled from his grasp and ran from him, up to the field, past Odin grazing, through the trees, and back to the dark brooding shadows surrounding Trevelyan Manor and my room. No sun would shine through the stained glass this day, for only the lashing of the coming storm lay ahead—a storm that was no match for the sorrow churning in my heart. I loved him, could never have him, and would have to leave him. I loved Robert and Justin, too. And when I left Trevelyan Manor, I'd leave my heart behind, buried in the cold mist, far from the light and the warmth of the sun. I went over and picked up a thorny stem Justin had given me last night. I wrapped my hands around it, heedless of the pain cutting my hands; then I cried, for all that I'd been given and for all that I would leave behind.

The storm came with the night, hitting Trevelyan Manor with a ferocious malevolence that had my nerves completely on edge. I couldn't stay alone in my room, and I stole out to check on the boys, only to find their beds empty. Their favorite wooden horses lay mangled on the floor.

Panicked, I pounded on Nurse Maria's door, but only the echoes of my knocks answered me between the roar of thunder. Her door was unlocked, and when I opened it, I found the room empty.

Where were Robert and Justin? If they'd awakened afraid, surely they would have come to me. I hurried out into the hall but found it dark and empty. All I could think about was getting to Benedict. I gathered an oil lamp from my room and rushed down the stairs, going directly to Benedict's door, and knocked hard. "Benedict! Benedict!"

I got no answer. As I opened the door to his room, a heavy hand fell upon my shoulder. Crying out in fright, I turned around. Dobbs stood there, his disgust leaping out at me.

"Whatever do you think you are about, Miss Lovell? I will not allow you to sully Mr. Trevelyan's reputation with your scandalous manipu—"

I grabbed his stiffly knotted ascot and shook him silent. "Robert and Justin are not in their beds. Where are they?"

"What do you mean, not in their beds?"

"Just exactly what I said! They are not in their room, not in the schoolroom, they are not upstairs, and Nurse Maria isn't either. Where are they?" I shouted. "Where is Mr. Trevelyan?"

"He and Master Stephen left here about an hour ago. I expect the storm will delay their return."

"Wake everyone, even Mr. Henderson. We need to find Robert and Justin. I will go back and check the schoolroom again, just in case." I didn't wait to see what Dobbs would do. I turned and ran back upstairs and searched every nook and cranny between my room and Nurse Maria's. Nothing. I heard voices downstairs and went back to the landing. But before I could call out, Constance came running from the opposite hall. She wore her robe and bed slippers, and her hair was mussed as if she'd been pulled from her bed. But her eyes were wild with terror. She grabbed my hand.

"Good, you have a lamp. Come with me. The lock on the tower door is broken. I think Justin and Robert have gone up there."

"Surely not," I said, even as my heart raced and my feet ran to the door that had been bolted shut. Just as Constance claimed, the wood around the lock had been splintered, and the door hung ajar. A sick feeling knotted my stomach. Why would Justin and Robert go up there alone?

"Justin? Robert?" I called, pushing the door open. I thought I heard something at the top of the steep spiral steps, but it might have been the sounds of the storm. At any rate, I detected the glow of a lamp from above.

"Where's Nurse Maria?" I asked Constance.

"Isn't she looking for the children? We must hurry, Ann. I have this awful feeling inside. My sister died on a night like this, during a storm. What if . . . what if . . . she's come back for her children . . . to take them with her?"

I wanted to slap Constance. "That's utter asinine nonsense." I held up the lamp and started up the stairs, determined to show an unruffled, practical face in response to her ludicrous words. But a sense of dread filled me. The sounds of the storm seemed to be amplified in the tower, and it wasn't until a wild breeze whipped down through the tower, followed by what seemed to be a misting of rain upon my face, that I realized the tower's windows must be open.

"Robert! Justin!" I quickened my steps, nearly tripping on the steep stairs.

Reaching the top floor, I opened the door and came to a halt. Maria sat in a rocking chair, swaying back and forth, back and forth, as she stared out at the storm. Wind and rain blew into the room through the open windows. Justin and Robert were nowhere in sight.

Constance pushed me into the room and slammed the door behind her.

I heard the scrape of a key in the lock as I grabbed her shoulder and forced her to face me. "What are you doing?"

She smiled slowly, and her eyes darkened with satisfaction. "Come into my parlor, said the spider to the fly."

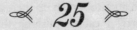

25

Constance set her hand on my shoulder. "I am sorry, Ann, for I really like you. You are so much more like me than Francesca. If you and I had been sisters . . ." She shrugged. "Who knows, maybe the past might have never happened the way it did. But it did, and this is the way it has to be, no?"

I backed away from her, my skin crawling with disbelief and fear. "Where are Robert and Justin?"

"Maria has them locked away."

"They ran from the bad witch," Maria said tonelessly, staring at the night. "I couldn't catch them."

Constance laughed. "Silly Justin. He's been talking about the bad witch since his mother died. You and Francesca are so predictable. Francesca came to the tower, too, worried that Justin and Robert had come up here when they were not in their beds. She checked them every night just like you do, Ann. All it took was an extra dose of laudanum to confuse Francesca, and she followed me right up here." Constance frowned then.

Nausea and horror churned in my stomach as she continued to talk. "You know, I heard Stephen and Benedict fighting over you tonight. It was rather violent and moving. When they left, I knew you would have to die tonight. You should have heeded the knife I stabbed through your picture and left here. I would have let you go. But now it is too late. My sister's ghost has come to destroy what Benedict and Stephen have grown to love, just like she promised in her curse. A good story, no? The curse I wrote seemed to be working well until you came."

She stepped closer, peering at me intently, and continued to talk. "I have been here for years, and no one has paid the slightest attention to me, other than to humor my shopping desires. You are here two months, and both Benedict and Stephen are so enamored of you they are at each others' throats." She cocked her head. "I do not understand it. You are not beautiful. You do little to make yourself appealing. So why do they love you?"

"They do not," I told her, backing to the center of the room. There were windows all around the top of the turret.

I could see the lightning flash across the midnight sky, lighting the angry waters of the black bay. Rain blasted in with the wind, dampening my robe and gown.

"They do. But that isn't the main reason you need to die, Ann. You need to die because you are not going to stop searching. You are not going to stop asking questions until you get the answer to Francesca's death, are you? I know that is what you and Mr. McGuire are doing. It is a shame that he will have to die tomorrow. Perhaps he will break his neck falling from a ladder. Or maybe he will be robbed and then shot." She held up my mother's pistol and stroked the barrel.

With her every word, my horror grew. I knew I had to keep her talking, keep her distracted until I discovered a way to escape. "Mr. McGuire does not know anything."

"Yes, he does, Ann. Do not lie to me. I know many things about everyone. I even read your mother's journal. She was weak, Ann, not strong like I am. If she had killed her father rather than run away, she would have had all his money, and would never have been taken advantage of."

"You are the person who kept going through my things." Forcing myself to stay calm, I took another step back and shot my gaze to Maria, assuring myself that she was still seated.

"Yes. It is time for you to die, Ann." She pointed the gun at me and looked at me sadly. "Do not be afraid. Francesca assures me that all is peaceful after death. No more pain."

I shuddered. "Why did you do it? My God, she was your sister!"

I thought thunder boomed, and it wasn't until the tower's door flew open, splintering on its hinges, that I realized it was the sound of the door being broken down. Benedict, Stephen, Mr. Henderson, and shockingly, Mr. McGuire barreled into the room.

Maria did nothing but rock back and forth in the chair.

Constance backed up to the edge of the room. She laughed and pointed the gun at them, making everyone stop in their tracks. "Come into my parlor, said the spider to the fly." She looked at me. "I thought I was the spider, Ann. I really did. But you must be."

"Why?" I shouted at her again. "Why did you kill your sister?"

Shock covered the men's faces. "Constance?" Stephen gasped, his disbelief evident.

"Look at you men!" Constance said, shaking her head. "Why are you so stunned that a woman would do what she could to shape her own destiny?

"I ask you, what choices does a woman have in this world of injustices? We are prisoners, slaves to our parents and then to men. The fire. My parents. Do you think that was an accident?" She laughed. "They made my life hell. I had no choice but to kill, just as Francesca had no choice but to marry you. See, they couldn't marry me to you to save the business, Benedict, for I had been sullied by the touch of a man my father killed rather than see me married to. He murdered first, made me watch the man I loved die. What is love compared to money and social position?"

Constance smiled at me, waving the gun as she continued to speak. "You know class is more important than love, do you not, Ann? I heard Benedict tell Stephen that you wouldn't marry him. You are smarter than I was. It took me a long time to realize that. Day after day I lived, atoning for my sin of having loved beneath my class, knowing that I killed the man I loved. I served my parents, and I prayed hour upon hour every day for forgiveness, but none came. And poor delicate Francesca, a woman who knew nothing but the fears of a child, had to marry."

She looked at Benedict with hatred. "You knew that before you married her. You knew that she feared you, your size. But you married her anyway. You did it for greed. Our ships, our trade routes, are what your father's company needed. And my father sold his daughter to have a male heir born to run his empire. Women were worthless to him except to give birth to what he wanted. Francesca kept herself drugged with laudanum. It was the only way she could face her marital obligation to produce an heir to a man she feared and did not love. So who killed Francesca? Him for selling her? You for taking her?"

She shot her gaze to Stephen. "Or was it you, Stephen? A boy fool enough to fall in love with his brother's wife, but not man enough to touch her when she came to you for the love her heart craved. How do you think she felt when you denied her, then went calling on your friend's sister just to show her you meant never to be with her? Don't you think that drove her to desolation? To more laudanum for her pain? Does it bother you that your supposed friends have written your pain in a play for all the world to see, only giving it the sordid twist of actual betrayal?"

Benedict looked at Stephen, shocked. "You did not touch Francesca?"

"I loved her. How could I dishonor her? I love you. How could I betray you?" The deep sadness in Stephen's voice resonated within the tower. "My love killed her anyway."

"No, Stephen, I thought you had, but I was wrong." Benedict looked to Constance. "She was three months pregnant when she died. Who fathered that child?"

"Pregnant? Impossible. We never—" Stephen's anguish sliced to my heart.

Constance looked to Mr. Henderson and smiled sweetly at him. "Do you not think it is time you cleared your conscience, Alan?"

Benedict and Stephen both swung around to face their friend, horrified. Alan closed his eyes, pain slashing across his face. "I'm sorry. She was so beautiful. So heartbroken. I held her as she cried. I loved her, too. I tried to give her hope. Instead I destroyed her."

"Yes," Constance said, bringing everyone's attention back to her. "You all destroyed her. And I gave her the peace she sought. We would have both been miserable at the convent where she was determined to go. Determined to spend the rest of her life in penance for her sins. I had already spent years atoning for mine, and I was not going to do that again. Not for her. Not for anybody. I was not going to let Francesca put me back into the hell I had escaped. She calls to me all the time now and tells me about her peace. I envy her, and now I've no choice. The spider and the fly."

Something in her voice alerted me. Something told me what she was going to do. I ran toward her. "Don't," I yelled, grabbing for her. I caught her wrist, and the gun fell to the floor.

"No! Let me fly!" Constance screamed and kicked me.

The blow hit me in the stomach, and I doubled forward, coming precariously close to the window ledge. Then, as if she knew I would fall, too, Constance pulled hard, jerking me toward her. I let go of her wrist and fought for balance, trying to save myself, all too aware of the smile on Constance's face as she disappeared from view. Strong hands gripped my shoulders, anchoring me in the room.

"Titania. Dear God," Benedict breathed, pulling me into his arms. I turned to him, burying my face against his chest, trying to shut out the image of Constance's fall.

"Watch out!" Stephen shouted. Benedict turned. Looking up, I saw Maria pointing a gun toward Benedict and me. She fired at the same time that Mr. Henderson grabbed her arms and Stephen barreled into Benedict and me, knocking us to the floor. The shot went wild, shattering the window over our head.

Disarmed now, Maria sat on the floor, rocking back and forth, reciting repeatedly "The Spider and the Fly."

"She will not be needing this where she is going to go," Mr. Henderson said, handing Benedict my mother's gun after everyone stood but Maria.

"The sooner she's institutionalized, the better," Benedict said with disgust.

"I will take Maria downstairs and call the authorities. They will need to see Constance's body before we move her," Mr. Henderson said. He was a man burdened by death and regret as he looked sadly at Benedict. "We will need to talk, but it can wait. And when I leave, I will not return." He looked at me. "You have a new life now—don't lose it." We all stood silent as Mr. Henderson pulled a now docile Maria up from the floor and took her out of the room. Maria never stopped mumbling about the spider and the fly. I shivered.

"Christ," Stephen said, looking at Benedict. "I don't believe this. I thought you had killed Francesca . . . or that she had been driven to kill herself by your disgust. I never dreamed Constance killed her sister."

"She was a troubled lass," Mr. McGuire said, speaking for the first time as he shook his head. I had almost forgotten his presence. He moved over to me, peering at me through his spectacles, his watery blue eyes filled with worry. "Ye have had a time of it, haven't ye, lass."

"I am all right," I said, and patted his arm. Though I had to admit my mind was still reeling.

"This wouldna have happened if I hadn't been taken in by her sweet smile at first. The lass kept returning to the shop for this book or that. She heard us speak of Dr. Levinworth, that day she came with you. That's what made her suspicious. Ye remember, Ann, lass?"

I nodded, swallowing the lump of emotion in my throat. It would have been so easy for Constance to have killed

Mr. McGuire, and it was I who had placed him in danger.

Mr. McGuire sighed softly. "The lass kept coming to the shop and asking questions, and talking about her life in a strange way. Then there was Puck. Every time she entered he quoted, 'Et tu, Brute?' Caesar's last words to his betrayer. Puck has never consistently quoted the same thing to the same person every time. I grew more suspicious and telegraphed the lass's hometown, making inquiries. My answers came Saturday, telling all about the troubled lass's past and the questions about whether the fire that killed her parents was indeed an accident. When you didna come on Saturday, I had Manuelo go ask about you. He found out from a maid that you'd been injured, but were going to be all right. I dinna like it one bit. So I sent ye a note with the story about her past and the fire, but it was apparently delivered to Mr. Trevelyan instead."

Benedict sighed. "Stephen and I were arguing, and I opened the note on my desk without reading to whom it was addressed. After seeing the information, I realized it was addressed to you. We went to Mr. McGuire's to ask a few questions, not quite believing that Constance had lived with us for years and yet had never spoken of her past hurt, and the disturbing things about the fire. Mr. McGuire didn't believe you were unharmed, and I insisted on his returning here to see for himself. I nearly died when we came up the drive and I saw the tower lit and the windows opened."

I shook myself as a shiver ran down my spine. If Mr. McGuire hadn't sent his letter, if Benedict hadn't returned when he did, I wasn't sure if I would have escaped Constance's trick.

"The children," I gasped.

"What?" Benedict cried, grabbing my arm.

"They were not in their beds. We were searching for

them. That's how Constance lured me to the tower. She said she thought they were up here."

Dobbs barreled into the room, his hair in tufts and his ascot askew. "We have searched the whole house. The children are not here."

"Cesca," I cried. "The stables! Maria said Robert and Justin had run from the bad witch, and she could not catch them. It's a game Robert and Justin played with their wooden horses."

Benedict grabbed a lamp. "God help us if they've ridden off on Cesca. They could ride right over the cliffs in this rain," he shouted as he ran out the door, Stephen right behind him, and I followed them in my bare feet. I had no idea when and where I lost my slippers. We burst out of the house into the soaking rain, heedless of the lashing wind. Entering the stables, Benedict ran to the end and came to a halt at the last stall. Cesca's stall.

He didn't say anything, but I saw his shoulders slump, and my heart dropped. The boys mustn't be there. I ran to him. He turned and opened his arms, embracing me, and I didn't care that Stephen and Dobbs were there to see.

"They are here," he said softly. Looking into the stall, I saw Robert and Justin and Cesca, lying in the hay, snuggled up against Cesca's side. They were all asleep. They'd put a saddle on her—at least, they had tried to. The saddle hung off to one side.

Justin opened his eyes and saw us. "Miss Lovell, we were responsible. We did not take her out into the dark where she might get hurt. We stayed with her, and she kept us safe from the bad witch."

Leaving Benedict, I went to Justin, knelt by him, and kissed him on the top of his head, tears filling my eyes. "Oh, Justin, I am very proud of you. You did the right thing, and now the bad witch is gone."

"Promise?" Robert said, opening his eyes.

"Promise," Benedict said, kneeling next to me, and pulling Robert to him.

Benedict wrapped his other arm around me, his body shaking with emotion. "Miss Lovell, I've come to the conclusion that marrying for social or financial conditions has brought nothing but pain to the Trevelyan name. The only practical thing I can do at this point is to marry for love. Will you marry me, Titania?"

I shook my head, trying to force a no to my lips.

"Yes, she will," Stephen broke in. "And if she says no, you will shout your love from the treetops. You will lay siege to her self-imposed prison. You will do whatever it takes to show her the depth of your love. You won't accept the fate that she believes, you will show her there's a future for you both."

I smiled tearfully as Stephen repeated back to me what I had told Mr. Simons to do to make Katherine realize his love. To make her know that nothing else mattered. I had asked Katherine if love or fear was greater in her heart, and now I had to answer the question myself.

"Well, Titania? Will you marry me?"

Robert and Justin were looking at me with their hearts in their eyes. My mouth went dry, and my heart hammered with hope as I met Benedict's gaze. Given the heartache I'd learned of tonight, how so many lives had been wasted or damaged by what I thought to be more important than love, how could I turn from love myself? "Benedict, it is a good thing that I'm a practical woman. And it is even more important that I love you. Nothing else matters. Yes, I will marry you."

I never imagined that I'd be asked to be the mistress of Trevelyan Hill, and I most assuredly never dreamed it would be when I was on my knees in a stable before a horse. It was a good thing I had such a strong constitution.

❦ Epilogue ❧

Four weeks later . . .

"Miss Wovell, can I call you Mommy yet?" Robert asked, running into my room where Katherine was helping me dress in my wedding finery. Today she would be my maid of honor, and next week I would return the favor by being her matron of honor. But after the nausea I had been suffering from every morning this past week, I might have to ask them to have a evening wedding rather than a morning one.

He skidded to a stop, his eyes widening as he saw me. "Miss Wovell, you are so beautiful," he said; then he frowned. "What's that funny thing on your head?"

"A veil," I said, ruffling his hair. "And to answer your question, yes, you can call me Mommy, or Mommy Ann, or Miss Ann, whatever your heart tells you to do." He'd asked the question no less than a hundred times in the past weeks, and I always gave him the same answer, but he wanted to wait until the "official" moment that his father and I became Mr. and Mrs. Benedict Trevelyan.

A quiet knock on the door brought my gaze up to see Justin enter the room. He had a proud smile on his face. "Miss Lovell, I picked this one just for you. Grandmother let me. It was one of my grandfather's favorites. He brought it back from Beluze, France. It is called 'Souvenir de La

Malmaison.' It is named after a famous lady's house, but I forgot her name."

"Thank you, Justin. This is so beautiful," I said, taking the huge, pale pink bloom from him. Justin's "science book" now included drawings of a number of the different kinds of roses in the Trevelyan gardens, and he and his father were reading Benedict's father's book together. That Benedict's mother let one of the garden's blooms be picked in my honor would probably be the only gesture of approval that she'd give to the wedding, but it was enough.

"I took all the thorns away. This time I wanted to give you the rose."

Wrapping my arms around Justin and Robert, I gave them a big hug. "Both of you have already given me so many roses in my heart that my garden will bloom forever."

I pushed aside the fancy bouquet I was going to carry down. "This is all the flowers I need," I said, holding up the rose Justin gave me.

Katherine tapped me on the shoulder, indicating that it was time to go down, and I sent the boys ahead. Then she handed me a handkerchief, and I dabbed at the tears in my eyes and took a sip of water to ease my queasiness. Having only dry toast for breakfast this morning helped.

"Thank you," Katherine signed to me.

"You are welcome," I signed back. "But what are you thanking me for?"

"For coming into our lives and bringing love back to us."

I shook my head. "You all already had the love in your hearts."

"But you set us free."

"I just opened the doors your grief had closed."

"And showed us the way to our hearts. Now hurry, my brother is waiting for you."

I laughed. "You just want to see Anthony."

Katherine smiled and signed back, "Yes."

Sunshine cleared the morning mists from Trevelyan Hill and burst through the stained glass windows, bathing Benedict and all those gathered to witness our wedding with dancing hues of color. Mr. McGuire escorted me to Benedict's side.

It seemed like an eternity ago that I'd climbed the steps to Trevelyan Manor and first met the master of Trevelyan Hill. His voice was just as deep and thrilling to me as it had been on the very first day. His scent of sandalwood and leather was just as intoxicating, and the man himself was infinitely more distracting because I now knew some of the pleasures hidden beneath the elegant cut of his suit, and looked forward to "thousands" more. How I had ever thought his eyes were too dark for a woman to see through to his to soul was beyond me. For as I looked into his eyes now, I saw the heart of an honorable man with a wealth of love for me. And as I took his hand to face the minister, I considered myself a rich woman, one who had always been rich, blessed with love. I was also a woman with a secret I was eager to share with Benedict.

Katherine held Robert's hand and stood beside me. But her gaze wasn't on the minister; she was looking at Anthony, her heart shining in her eyes.

Stephen and Justin stood next to Benedict. Mrs. Trevelyan looked on; her expression had progressed to reserved instead of dour. I knew only time would show her that love would heal all. Well, perhaps not all. I didn't think anything would help Dobbs's sour disposition, but I quite looked forward to keeping him on his toes with lots of little ones to run rambunctiously through the house making sunshine.

Benedict brought my hand to his lips as we waited for

the minister to finish speaking, and whispered under his breath to me, "Titania, my queen. Why is it that you are more ravishing than ever?"

I think an imp from my fairy queen heritage got hold of me, for I decided to ruffle Benedict's calm. "They did not work," I whispered.

He furrowed his brow, confused by my reply.

"Our contraceptive instruments."

His dark eyes widened as his gaze connected with mine. A gleam not unlike that of the sun glinting off the demon door filled his eyes with light, letting me see the joy in his soul. "Indeed?"

"I expect there will be more and more of me to ravish in the weeks ahead."

"That's like Ambrosia upon my soul," he said.

"Ambrosia? Truly?" My body tingled as I remembered his penchant for the unusual, which had taken us both by surprise.

"I suggest we get this wedding underway before I am overcome with passion, and sweep you away to the bedroom."

"That would be the most practical thing to do, Mr. Trevelyan."

He lifted a questioning eyebrow that melted my insides. "The wedding or the bedroom, Miss Lovell?"

"Both," I said breathlessly as he swept me up in his arms.

Benedict glanced at the stairs, then at the minister.

The minister, seeing Benedict changing everything we'd rehearsed, stopped his "We are gathered here" speech. I think that after taking one look, the man knew he was about to lose the bride and groom. Being a practical man, he quickly performed an abbreviated version of the marriage ceremony, before Benedict scandalously swept me away.

Love had carried us all beyond the mists of midnight to the bright dawn of a new day.